The End of Atlantis

The End of Atlantis

by
Jean Carrère

Translated, annotated and introduced by
Brian Stableford

A Black Coat Press Book

Visit our website at www.blackcoatpress.com

ISBN 978-1-61227-618-2. First Printing. May 2017. Published by Black Coat Press, an imprint of Hollywood Comics.com, LLC, P.O. Box 17270, Encino, CA 91416. All rights reserved. Except for review purposes, no part of this book may be reproduced or transmitted in any form or by any means, electronic or mechanical, including photocopying, recording, or by any information storage and retrieval system, without permission in writing from the publisher. The stories and characters depicted in this novel are entirely fictional. Printed in the United States of America.

Introduction

La Fin d'Atlantis ou Le Grand soir by Jean Carrère, here translated as *The End of Atlantis*, was first published in Paris by Librairie Plon in 1926.

Antoine-Jean-Louis Carrère (1865-1932) was a journalist and translator who was a foreign correspondent for *Le Temps* for many years, based for most of his career in Italy. His literary career began with the publication of a collection of poems, *Ce qui renait toujours* [That which is always renewed] (1894) and his first novel, published as a feuilleton in *Le Figaro* in 1899, was *La Dame du Nord* [The Northern Lady], although it was not reprinted as a book until 1909. The first of numerous non-fiction books based on his experiences as a reporter was *La Guerre du Transvaal* [The War in the Transvaal] (1902), based on his coverage of the Boer War; his first about Italy was *La Terre tremblante* [The Quaking Earth] (1909), based on his reportage of a series of devastating earthquakes in 1906-1908 and their aftermath—an experience on which his account of *La Fin d'Atlantis* clearly draws. The novel's most important precursor, however, in terms of the ideas it develops, was the author's most famous and most successful book, *Les Mauvais Maîtres* [The Bad Masters] (1922; tr. as *Degeneration in the Great French Masters*).

The title of the English translation of *Les Mauvais Maîtres* deliberately links it to the English title of Max Nordau's notorious study of *Entartung* (1892; tr. as *Degeneration*), which had been written in Paris and drew the vast majority of its examples from French society and literature, although it claimed to be identifying a social problem manifest throughout Europe: a literal social disease, whose alleged symptoms included a contempt for traditional custom and morality, and a narcissistic quest for nervous stimulation. Nordau makes extensive use of writers, artists and philosophers as "case-studies" reflecting the supposed degeneration of individuals and society, especially those self-identified or identified by critics as "decadent": a term with a complex history and significance, but founded on the notion that the kind of cultural decadence allegedly associated with the decline and fall of the Roman Empire, tacitly assumed to be a phase in the life-cycle of all Empires, was now manifest in modern European society and reflected in its literature.

Les Mauvais maîtres itself links ten famous French writers—Rousseau, Chateaubriand, Balzac, Stendhal, Sand, Musset, Baudelaire, Flaubert, Verlaine and Zola—by means of the assertion that although they were all great writers in terms of their literary elegance, all of them employed their enormous talent, deliberately or accidentally, in the service of a rhetoric that was essentially "demoralizing," whose effect was to oppose and weaken a virile attitude to life that is supposedly necessary to the maintenance and strength of a society. Carrère admits to loving and admiring the work of several of the writers included in his critical account, and goes to considerable lengths to avoid attaching any personal blame to them, usually regarding them as victims rather than villains; nevertheless, he argues forcefully that the effects of their work, especially when seen collectively, is psychologically and socially harmful, symptomatic of and contributing to a kind of rot that eats away moral fiber from within.

Numerous French historians, most importantly Montesquieu, had tried to account for the fall of the Roman Empire in terms of a cultural "decadence" that had previously rotted such empires as the Egyptian and the Babylonian: a typical and perhaps inevitable consequence of their acquisition of the kind of absolute power that proverbially leads to absolute corruption. The thesis evidently lent itself naturally to modern developments of the Platonic myth of Atlantis, to which numerous French historians and mystics had been attempting to attach a hypothetical historical basis for centuries, and Carrère was by no means the first novelist to use the thesis in a flamboyant literary account, but none of his predecessors had done so with the same earnest intensity.

The story told in *La Fin d'Atlantis* is, in consequence, multilayered in a more sophisticated sense than most Atlantean fantasies. Its account of Atlantis echoes theories of the fall of the Roman Empire, particularly significant to the author because of his abiding love for Italy—the novel was written in Frascati—but it also contains an elaborate tacit criticism of contemporary European society, whose own crisis of degeneration is supposedly reflected therein. One of the most interesting features of the novel, however, is that it is by no means a simple repetition of the argument of *Les Mauvais maîtres*—which was itself no mere echo of Nordau's argument—but a work written in a spirit of inquiry and investigation befitting a conscious and accomplished journalist. Clearly written as the author went along rather than planned elaborately in advance, although the outcome of its climax was inevitable, the account of the lessons to be drawn from that denouement—and hence the relevance of the novel's rhetoric to the reader's contemporary situation—remained in suspense, an ultimate conclusion for which the author still seems to have been groping uncertainly even when he actually arrived there.

There is also another factor that might warrant consideration in the evaluation of the novel's elegiac quality. The book carries a fulsome dedication, dated August 1925, to the author's wife Nelly, to whose "radiant and tender" influence he credits the strength to write and publish the novel. "Nelly Carrère," who was similarly a writer, translator and great lover of Italy, is listed by that name in the Bibliothèque Nationale catalogue, whose compilers evidently had no further information regarding her former names, or even her date of birth. (She had also published several translations in 1898-01 as "Madame Charles Laurent," so she might, however, have been married to a Charles Laurent prior to marrying Carrère.) The catalogue does record, however, that Nelly married Carrère in 1900 and that she died in August 1925—either immediately before or immediately after the dedication was penned, implying that the novel was written, or at least completed, while she was dying. That circumstance might well have a bearing on the fact that a funeral plays a central role in the novel's conclusion, while the budding amorous relationships carefully brought into focus earlier in the plot are virtually forgotten.

La Fin d'Atlantis extended a rich tradition of French literary fantasies redeploying the myth, of which the most important include Hippolyte Mettais' *Paris avant le Déluge* (1866; tr. as *Paris Before the Deluge*),[1] Charles Lomon and Pierre-Barthélemy Gheusi's *Les Atlantes* (feuilleton 1904; book 1905; tr. as *The Last Days of Atlantis*),[2] Gaston Danville's *Le Parfum de volupté* (1905; tr. as *The Perfume of Lust*),[3] Han Ryner's *Les Pacifiques* (1914; tr. as "Les Pacifiques"),[4] Pierre Billaume and Pierre Hégine's *Voyage aux îles Atlantides* [Journey to the Isles of Atlantis] (1914) and Pierre Benoît's *L'Atlantide* (1919; tr. as *The Queen of Atlantis*), but it owes no conspicuous literary debt to any of them. Although its plot echoes some of the key motifs of the pioneering epic fantasy by Lomon and Gheusi, those features are mostly natural concomitants of the myth and stock characters of remote historical melodrama, and although Carrère's novel is, to some extent, an adventure story and a heroic fantasy, it operates in a rhetorical context quite distinct from the one in which Lomon and Gheusi had formulated their narrative. Even so, *La Fin d'Atlantis* does form an element in a spectrum, and the existence of that spectrum adds a measure of further interest to its contemplation.

The novel appears to have been reasonably successful—WorldCat lists ten printings between 1926 and 1932—but it has faded from view somewhat since, as has the author, whose long residence outside his homeland apparently weakened its

---

[1] Black Coat Press, ISBN 978-1-61227-328-0.

[2] Black Coat Press, ISBN 978-1-61227-456-0.

[3] Black Coat Press, ISBN 978-1-61227-580-2.

[4] Included in *The Human Ant*, Black Coat Press, ISBN 978-1-61227-323-5.

affection for him somewhat. The critical attention paid to his work was compromised by the fact that *Les Mauvais maîtres* was widely seen as an assault on the great tradition of French literature, and hence as a somewhat treasonous action; the Bibliothèque Nationale has refrained thus far from making it available on *gallica*. Insofar as the Atlantis of *La Fin d'Atlantis* represents modern Paris as well as ancient Rome, however—and, indeed, civilization in general—it demonstrates great affection and admiration as well as anxiety, and the central argument of the narrative, whether or not one agrees with it, certainly has not lost its relevance to the world of the twenty-first century: quite the contrary, in fact.

This translation was made from a copy of the 1926 Plon edition.

Brian Stableford

THE END OF ATLANTIS

Atlantis! Atlantis! I see again the depths of the ages...
(*La Terre tremblante*)

THE FIRST DAY:
THE FESTIVAL OF THE SPHINX

A great people can only die by its own hand.

Scene I
The Herald of Glory

The Palace of the Empire, adjacent to the terrace of the Sphinx, has lost the majesty of its grandiose lines; for, following the custom adopted for the day of the festival. Several rows of scaffolding have been erected between the tall pillars of somber marble, the wooden framework of which is dissimulated beneath red curtains with golden fringes. And this time, the ladies of the Apostles' Quarter, those of the Egyptian peninsula where the soldiers' leaders are accommodated, and even those of the great mercantile port, have come in such great numbers that the architect Barkas, the steward of the festival, has been obliged to erect in the intervals of the columns, a day in advance, as many as five tiers of superimposed balconies. Crowded together, the assembled aristocratic ladies are spread out joyfully in the pleasure of gazing and appearing.

The immense Esplanade seems small today. And yet, from one minute to the next, the avenues opening into the square from all points of the city are projecting new human waves, and the people who arrived first have already slid along the vast parapet from which the view overlooks the city and the harbor, wondering anxiously whether the incessantly increasing swell of people is not going to break against the bronze balustrades.

"Fortunately," grumbles a fat man recognizable by this embroidered tunic as a merchant from the low quarters, "care was taken last night to close the public elevators and forbid people the use of all rapid transport machines. Otherwise, I think the entire plebeian population would be crammed into the square!"

"And why shouldn't we be here too?" replies a tall, thin sailor from the port. "Are we not molded of the same material?"

"So much so, my friend, that if the pressure continues to build we'll be molded for a second time."

A loud burst of laughter greets the jovial shopkeeper's quip.

"And all this," a young woman puts in, "to see the pale-hued Barbarians from a savage land where there are houses made of compressed earth."

"And you, Beauty? Have you come for something else?"

"Pooh! White men! They no longer even have the charm of novelty for us. A quarter of Atlantis will soon be populated by those moonfaces!"

"These, it appears, have invented ineffable melodies."

"And it's said that they're very handsome."

"Aha! Atlantean sirs, that will change our views somewhat."

"Since you need handsome men, slut, you're well-served. Here comes the herald of glory with a cortege of giants.

Indeed, on the perron of the Palace, dominating the entire Esplanade from the top of its red marble steps, the traditional herald of glory advances, borne on a pavis garnished with crimson, maintained on the shoulders of Nubians of colossal form. Around the pavis, Egyptian cavaliers with gilded lances allow their breastplates to glisten in the sun.

The herald speaks into a loudhailer with a copper funnel. Every grand Esplanade will hear a herald today, but the first of them speaks to the Square of the Empire.

"People of Atlantis," he proclaims, "our brothers from the red Occident, and our young allies from the Oriental lands, greetings in the name of the Empire of the Waters. Now commence the great days of celebration in which, every five years, Atlantis celebrates its wealth and the immortality of its immortal prestige. But this year, Atlanteans, in accordance with the will of the Apostles of the Sun, two further days of public rejoicing will be added to the three ancient festivals of the Sphinx, the Waters and Gold. The Apostles of the Sun, your lords and protectors..."

"The Atlanteans aren't protectors!"

"Nor lords!"

"Silence! Silence!"

"Let the herald speak!"

Impassively, the herald resumes: "So, the Apostles of the Sun have decided that two new celebrations will complete the three consecrated feasts; on the fourth day there will be the festival of the Occident, and on the fifth, the festival of the Orient..."

A stir of surprise.

"Atlanteans, know in what these two new festivals will consist. That of the Occident will be consecrated to the venerated people of the Toltec continent, from which almost all of us originated; we shall exalt the primitive hearth of our glorious red race, from which the founders of the Queen of the Waters departed thousands and thousands of years ago."

"Very good! Very just!" the crowd applaud.

"The festival of Mellena!" barks the voice of a student.

"Silence! Enough!"

"I shall conclude. We shall go in a body on the fourth day to the great Occidental port, to receive and greet the delegates of Palanque the Holy, Uxmal the Magnificent and Panuco the Rich, and those who come from Tiahuanaco, those from Idaho and those from the Great Cascades. And we shall show them by means of our urgency that Atlantis has not forgotten its ancestors."

"Atlantis is still beautiful!"

"And it will be even more beautiful, citizens, when, on the fifth day, we shall go to the great Gaelic port to the east of the city, to salute our young white colonists of the Oriental lands, who all owe it to the Queen of Waters that they no longer resemble the errant savages that our ancestors once discovered."

"Welcome to the Gaels and the Ligurians!"

"Greetings to the Etruscans!"

"And the Cantabrians and the Iberians!"

"And the men of Biscay and Basconia!"

"And those of Ys and those of Thule!"

"And the bards of Armor that we are about to applaud!"

"For," the herald adds, "if the gods have placed us in the middle of the Atlantic Ocean, it is because they wanted our beneficent and necessary Empire..."

"Yes, yes, necessary!"

"...to expand similarly over all the terrestrial continents and that the Sphinx of our Holy Terrace should become, for all peoples, the symbolic image of the Sun."

"Glory to the Sphinx!"

"And more than ever, my friends, let us repeat and meditate, in accordance with custom, the sacred words of Manou, the meaning of which appears to us henceforth unveiled: *Atlantis can only die by its own hand*. And as we know now that no people will ever desire or be able to make Atlantis die, one might as well proclaim its eternity!"

"Atlantis, eternal!"

"Eternal! Eternal!"

And the cry reverberates over the entire Esplanade, while the herald, borne on his pavis and surrounded by his Egyptian cavaliers, slowly descends the red marble steps in order to go away and recommence elsewhere.

Scene II
Hermos

But now cries ring out in the vicinity of the merchant of the low city who was deploring the access of the plebeians to the Empire Square a little while ago. The tumult of a brawl agitates the crowd; a formidable pressure, departing from the Palace of the Empire, has just thrown the last rank of frightened spectators against the balustrade.

"Clear the square!" the merchant shouts. "Have all the soldiers perished in the land of the Pelasges then?"

"Hellas, bring back Hellas!" howls a sailor. "There's nothing but disorder and riots at all festivals nowadays!"

"Or for want of Hellas, bring back Hermos!" declares a student

"Truly, I admire you," says the merchant. "It's you who are demanding Hellas, then? You who once forced him to quit the city?"

"It wasn't us! It was the rich..."

"You aided them!"

At that moment, a new pressure causes the crowd to undulate.

"A man carried in triumph!" brays a student. "He's being taken toward the Golden Gate!"

"An Apostle of the Sun. He's wearing the crimson mantle...

"...and the crown of foliage."

"An Apostle? Impossible! They all climbed up to the Sacred Terrace a long time ago for the election of the new Prince, and the Golden Gate is no longer open."

"Who, then? Hellas and Hermos are absent, and Oreus as if dead."

"Hermos! Hermos!" cries a student, who has just climbed on to his comrade's shoulders.

At the same moment, in fact, the man borne in triumph appears facing the people, and everyone recognizes the poet Hermos, the son of Hermes, the idol of the young.

"Hermos! Glory to Hermos!"

Meanwhile, the young people edge toward the enthusiastic group by whom Hermos is lifted up. They advance thus, after many undulations, all the way to the Golden Gate, before and behind which the cavaliers of the Egyptian column are on watch. Motionless on their immobile mounts, they have orders that no one profane should go through the Gate. So, when Hermos arrives borne on the shoulders of the crowd, the Egyptian cavaliers do not flinch any more than they have blinked all day long at the supplications of women, the joyful sarcasms of young men or invectives launched from a distance by the marine populace.

"Open the Gate, then!" people cry, from all parts. "You can see that he's one of the Apostles!"

"The great Hermos! Our poet!"

At those words, a few cavaliers cannot suppress a quiver of surprise and embarrassment. Without quitting their position, they consult with a sign of the head a giant in a laminated gold helmet and armor sparkling with gems, who is standing alone a few paces in front of them. He is their chief, Knephao, nicknamed "the Handsome Black" by the people, although born in High Egypt, a colony of the pure Atlantean race, at the very place where the Nile was once diverted from its former course in order to direct it toward the northern plain. But the rude soldier's face, baked by the Sun of distant battles and dried by the wind of deserts, has lost the beautiful red gleam of which the pure Atlanteans and their Egyptian colonists are so proud.

The chief of the cohorts is reputed to be invincible and a halo of heroic legends floats above his name in the imagination of the crowd: the mountains of Libya cleaved by the blows of his ax; barbaric peoples traversed on horseback, to the sound of trumpets, with an escort of only a few men, amid the amazement of the subjugated populations...

The men who are pressing against the Gate, therefore, almost under the hooves of the horses, experience some anxiety.

"Don't push! It's futile! You can see that they're not going to open up!"

Indeed, the impassive Knephao sends the order to his troops by means of an imperceptible signal, not to budge.

The members of the crowd know full well that the Golden Gate will remain closed; but a breath passes over them

"The Gate! The Gate! Open it, then!"

"Glory to Hermos!"

And now, in the crowd, Hermos, carried by an eddy of the people, finds himself face to face with the Egyptian warrior.

"Knephao," asks Hermos, "reply to me without rudeness or anger. I have just arrived from the kingdom of Saba; I have traversed lands and seas in order not to miss the arch-holy festival of the Sphinx. Are you going to leave me on the threshold for the sake of a few lost minutes?"

At that enveloping voice, the colossus lifts his head and gazes curiously at his unexpected interlocutor. Then, resuming his air of indifference: "You know full well that I cannot infringe the orders of your brothers."

"It's impossible, then, even for me?"

"Impossible, indeed."

"As impossible as opening a passage for the river Nile, which was spreading disorder in the plain?"

This time, Knephao's curiosity changes into a contained emotion.

"What are you saying? Where have you come from? Who told you about the adventures of yore? It seems to me, also, that your voice reminds me..."

"Of the song that I modulated in the evening, when you were on watch on the bank of the river..."

"And when the lions were prowling around our paltry huts! Oh, by thrice holy Horus! So it's you that they call today the famous Hermos?"

Around the two men a circle of silence begins enlarging. In the distance, uncomprehending and believing it to be an altercation, the crowd is agitating, dividing into contrary parties.

"Well, Knephao, can you open the Gate for me now? You know what place I occupied out there, alongside the great Oreus, our Master, and why I am so ardent to go and celebrate the rites of the Sun."

"May the spirits protecting the river Nile and the Sun, father of Atlantis, attest here how much I admire the great Oreus and wish him long life, and what joy I have in seeing you again, my former companion; but by the redoubtable powers that I invoke, I swear that I cannot, even for you, open the Gate to the Sacred Hill..."

A murmur of astonishment runs through the surrounding crowd. Without paying any attention to it, Knephao says: "I will be killed here, I promise you, rather than break my word, and you know..."

"Yes, I know that you're not afraid of death."

"Nor you either, Hermos! But listen. Time is pressing. Would you like to follow me to the Palace? Perhaps there are still other hopes."

And Knephao, pushing his horse, passes through the mob. The admirers of Hermos follow him, carrying the Apostle with the red cloak, and as the Golden Gate is placed at the extreme right of the square, the unexpected cortege has to traverse half the Esplanade.

Scene III
Mellena

"Look," observes the fat merchant, "look: they're going toward the central platform, where Mellena is enthroned. What does that new movement signify?"

"It's Mellena, undoubtedly, who has given him the order to go to her!" replies a woman, bitterly.

"An Apostle has no order to receive from Mellena!"

"A plea, then,"

"Or an invitation, my dear. A new lover is doubtless required by that former seller of pleasure, who once danced for barbaric sailors."

"Silence then, octopus-heads!" objects the fat man "You insult her today, but you acclaimed her three years ago, when she promised Atlantis a perpetual fête.

"Let's talk about her promises!"

Meanwhile, Knephao, followed by Hermos, arrives before the door of the Palace, beneath the balcony where Mellena, the wife of Guitche, the master of gold, is seated on an ivory throne.

In front of the wide open door between the two great pillars that sustain two bronze giants, a granite perron of seven steps remains empty, rigorously guarded by infantrymen. But Knephao, whom no soldier dares disobey, appears on horseback on the perron, dominating the crowd.

"Mellena, Mistress of Gold, Glory of the Sea, Protectress of the City, greetings! Here is Hermos, Apostle of the Sun, who has returned from the land of Saba. Come too late for the festival of the Sphinx, he cannot remain in the public square wearing the crimson mantle and the Initiates' crown. Although the Palace is left exclusively to women today, will you allow him to seek a retreat there, sheltered from popular curiosity?"

In the square, everyone remains attentive. What is Mellena going to say? The best-informed know, in fact, that she fears the presence of Hermos, and some say that she has raised various obstacles to the return of the poet, who is a friend of Hellas.

She stands up, and advances to the edge of the balcony, svelte and supple, glittering with gems, an incarnation of red beauty. Molded in a robe of assertive hues, her bare arms circled by heavy rings, her breasts swelling beneath necklaces of translucent enamel, Mellena raises her head with vermilion skin, heightened by moist crimson lips and illuminated by stormy eyes beneath eyebrows opening in deployed wings.

"Hermos," she articulates, in a slow and tender voice, "you who are returning from distant lands to which you bore the enlightenment of the Red People, I salute you."

Then, looking at the colossus, she insinuates in a tone that seems full of solicitude: "Is it true, Knephao, that you cannot open the excessively severe Golden Gate to our illustrious Apostle?"

"As you know full well, Mellena."

"And if I begged you to do so myself?"

"Even to you, I would be obliged to refuse."

"You hear him, then, Hermos; my efforts would remain as vain as yours. Come, then, since any revolt against fate is futile, and savor the repast merited by your courage, and let the Palace, today reserved for women, shelter momentarily, by glorious favor, the great poet who has so often charmed them."

Hermos bows. Knephao dismounts, and both of them go into the Palace.

Mellena's words circulate through the turbulent crowd, travestied from circle to circle.

"The hypocrite! She's feigning regret! Did you see the joy shining in her eyes?"

"She's finally triumphant. Neither Hermos nor Hellas will be the Prince of Apostles."

"Guitche will be acclaimed."

"And she will act for him."

And gradually, dull complaints and threats burst forth. In the distance, near the parapet, in spite of the fearful prudence of merchants, women are uttering strident jeers:

"Down with Mellena!"

"Go dance in the harbor for the enjoyment of Barbarians!"

"To death! To death!"

Impassive, Mellena has resumed her place on her ivory throne; however, the rumor of the people is magnified and becomes stormy. Already, Egyptian foot-soldiers are getting ready to point their spears; the tempest rumbles, the Palace is under threat...

But immediately, Mellena makes a sign, and a slow pace, majestic in their long white robes, the bards from Armor are seen to emerge on to the perron.

By a miraculous reversal, the tempest of hatred is transformed into clamors of joy; those in the first rank who were striving to invade the Palace wave their hats in a sign of delight.

"Finally, the bards!"

"Long live the white men!"

"Armor! Glory to Armor!"

And such is the exultant ardor of the crowd that the bards with the white faces and long hair, crowned with ivy, ignorant of the language of Atlantis, remain, astonished, on the threshold of the Palace.

"Armor! Armor!" the multitude continue to cry.

Seeing the crowd turned around, Mellena then leans forward and addresses herself to the men of Armor, speaking a few words to them in an unknown language with rough syllables. Suddenly, the bards, reassured, advance to the edge of the highest step, and while some sound ivory horns or bronze buccinas, the majority pick out crystalline notes on their harps, in the warm air.

The ineffable empire of rhythm! The benefit of harmony springing forth in sonorous cascades! Now, throughout that swarming and noisy crowd, through which all the passions have blown in their turn, order and calm descend in soothing waves; and everyone, instantly, finds himself in his place, silent, glad and attentive...

Music, in fact, constitutes the supreme sensuality of Atlanteans. It speaks to them in an untranslatable language that they all understand, although they are nevertheless impotent to explain it. On wings of dream, their hypersensitive souls fly away, very high, far from monotonous life, toward the only possessions that they have not yet conquered, toward the glory of the Sun or the mystery of the stars...

Scene IV
In the Palace

Hermos and Knephao, meanwhile, have penetrated via a bronze door into an immense hall, which serves as a vestibule and which, ordinarily, remains open to the people.

"Above all," murmurs Knephao, "don't manifest any haste. Any apparent impatience might betray us."

The guards salute their chief with an affectionate respect, and consider Hermos with surprise. The latter pauses momentarily, attracted by an irresistible curiosity to the magnificence of the newly edified hall.

"You're not familiar with this vestibule, then, Hermos?"

"How could I be? It's already five years since I embarked for Libya."

"That's true; and this new hall, which immortalizes the glory of Young Egypt, has only been visible for four years. Oreus himself traced the broad outlines of it, and Hellas completed it in haste. Would you believe, Hermos, that they made it a crime, accusing him of exalting Egypt in order to transport the capital of the world there? But I'll show you the reliefs of the great panels."

So saying, Knephao draws Hermos under the immense vault, the harmonious proportions of which strike the Apostle with astonishment. The hall is so vast that a hundred columns of yellow marble rise up toward the ceiling, each having for a point of support four bronze giants kneeling back-to-back, whose muscles seem to be bursting under the effort. They symbolize the Nubian warriors vanquished in Upper Egypt. Between the columns, in great vases of varnished earthenware, broad-leaved palm trees spring forth, while red granite sphinxes extend themselves, devoid of wings, with the heads of women, claws forward. A jasper basin illuminates the center of that immobile forest with bright reflections, and around the basin, green bronze crocodiles spread the water that sings in regular jets.

As Hermos pauses at every discovery, Knephao says: "Come on, come on. Here's something that will awaken other memories."

And against the large back wall, he shows the Apostle a burnished silver panel, extending over the full height of the wall, on which, in life-sized figures, the artists of the Crimson Isle have caused the great feats of the Atlanteans on Egyptian soil to live again proudly.

"Admirable sculptures!" cries Hermos. "But that's us, Knephao, do you remember?" And he touches with his finger, in the metal, the face in relief of a youth playing the lyre. "Look, here I am, preceding my father, singing a hymn to the glory of the Sphinx, which can be seen looming up on the horizon."

"What a fine voyage, Hermos! In evoking it, my heart capsizes in my breast! If only I could return to that time of youth, when all of life was radiant with hope."

"What's the matter, then, friend? What sadness there is in your words!"

But Knephao, addressing himself to the infantrymen of the guard in a loud voice, in order to be heard everywhere, says: "Hey, man over there, do you know where to find, in the depths of the palace, some solitary room where no sound can arrive from the city? Hermos has need of absolute repose."

"Great leader, go to that door of black wood facing us. In any case, I'll stand watch."

"Perfect, friend. I'll come back myself soon. Don't let anyone enter here."

Then, drawing Hermos along, the giant murmurs; "That's where I wanted to go. Follow me."

And having, closed and bolted the door, Knephao draws Hermos through subterranean corridors.

"Can I talk now, finally?" says Hermos. "Where are you taking me? What do you want with me? What does this mysterious conduct signify?"

25

"Let's sit down, Hermos, on the edge of that stone. We still have a few moments before acting."

"Speak; I'm in hate to know."

"I have no need to tell you how much the Egyptians love Atlantis. All the other nations of the world you have vanquished; to ours you have given birth. Our forefathers departed the Great Isle, bathed by the Atlantic Ocean, in order to colonize our young land. Of the Phrygians, Scythians, Gaels, Iberians, Tyrrhenians or Guitchos and all your tributaries in the vast world, nothing is expected but obedience. From us, hope for all love. That is for the people. For myself, Hermos, I have devoted my entire life to the Queen City. As a child, near the cataracts of Aboo, I helped my father and his brothers to defend the Nile against the rage of the black men. And in the evening, as recompense, my great-grandfather, who had left Atlantis when very young, told me about the splendors of the Unique City. Finally, it was given to me to see the City of my amour. Five years ago, when Abydos died, Hellas, the hero Hellas, your friend and my master..."

"My master too!"

"Hellas, therefore, having become Prince of Apostles, summoned me to him, and I arrived one morning in spring, at the very moment when the rising sun made the golden wings of the Sphinx resplendent. What emotion! First I saw on the horizon the Mount of Manou rising up, with its great artificial lake, from which the water, incessantly renewed, spreads out into the city in streams of light. And it seemed to me that the seven immense arms of the peninsulas were launching forth into the sea to embrace me, to such an extent that I fell to my knees—yes, to my knees—like a young lover. And I had, in fact, all the stainless illusions of first love. If only I had retained them!"

"But what has happened, Knephao? How emotional you seem! One might think that you, who do not tremble at the fury of men or the tempests of the sea, were afraid."

"Afraid? Yes, Hermos, I'm afraid."

26

And Knephao leans toward Hermos' ear, and weakly, as if he dreaded being overheard by the very stones: "Yes, I'm afraid for the Atlantean Empire!"

But Hermos snatches his hand from Knephao's hands and says, in a dry tone: "What are you saying? Are you mad? Immortal Atlantis! Atlantis, daughter of the Sphinx! Atlantis, messenger of the Unknown God! Atlantis, which can only die by its own hand!"

"Oh, don't pronounce those words! Know that Atlantis is no longer anything but a sick body sumptuously ornamented. Did you see them, just now, those thousands and thousands of fools on the Esplanade of the Empire, undulating and crying out to all the winds that blew? And a few sounds of the harp sufficed to appease all those frenetic people! Oh, Hermos, what a great misfortune it is for a people to have too much uninterrupted wellbeing!"

"That present wellbeing was once conquered by the virtues of our ancestors."

"And will doubtless be lost by the vices of their descendants."

"Oh, fine soldier, what a severe judge you are!"

"I'm not judging, Hermos, I'm simply observing. While you, a poet and a son of Hermes, float at sublime heights, I live in daily contact with the swarming crowd, and I know it. Now, while the vanquished people of the vast world bring you their tribute of labor and wealth, the people of Atlantis, believing themselves invincible, laugh at the Sun and sing to the Moon; they are content to celebrate their glory; they get drunk on music and pleasure; they scorn those they call tributaries; they scorn them to the point that they abandon to them, without mistrusting them, all the turmoil of active life, the fleet, the mines, the buildings and the earthworks..."

"But of what have they to complain? They participate in our civilization, which they enjoy."

"Until the moment when they want to become masters in their turn."

"Them, the masters? Those Barbarians?"

"Yes, Barbarians, as you say. Although, in reality, those most to be feared are not the new colonies of the white race but the old peoples of the Toltec continent, whom you have vanquished and replaced in the empire of the world."

"What! Do we not have a formal pact with them?"

"Oh, a fine trifle! The best pact, Hermos, is our own strength—and that strength is diminishing every day."

"What about the secrets of the Holy Terrace?"

"Undoubtedly, undoubtedly, our enemies still fear the mysterious Holy Terrace. They know that the Temple of the Sphinx and the Palace of the Initiates contain secrets by means of which the Atlanteans can cause waters to rise and displace mountains. The last rampart of the Atlantean Empire is contained in those few square yards of the Holy Terrace, under the wings of the Sphinx. Well, Hermos, that rampart will soon escape us!"

Scene V
The Secret Door

At those words, Hermos interrupts the Egyptian's harsh voice abruptly:

"In truth, Knephao, I can't allow you to go on any further. Are you not becoming alarmed, because of some weakness of the multitude and the unconscious intrigues of women, which distract the idleness of the public square?"

"Tell me, Hermos, what would you think if, perchance, the Apostles elected an unworthy Prince?"

"But until today the Apostles have never failed. Ossur, father of Oreus, Hermes, my own father, Abydos, father of Hellas, Oreus himself, the greatest of them all, and finally our dear Hellas—where could one find, Knephao, a more magnificent chain of science and virtue? And I'm only speaking of recent years..."

"And what if, this time, the college of the Sphinx were about to exalt an enemy of Atlantis?"

"I would say...I would say...but what's the point of talking about these mad hypotheses? That will never happen."

"Never? Well, Hermos, in a few hours, that great misfortune will fall upon us."

"What are you daring to say?"

"The truth. Yes, when the setting sun sets the sea ablaze, the College of the Sphinx, on the Holy Terrace, in accordance with the rite, will acclaim the new Prince..."

"What about Hellas? Has he disgraced Atlantis, then? Has he abdicated, like Oreus?"

"You don't know, then, that we have had no news of Hellas since last winter? Some say that he has vanquished, others that he is dead; others even affirm that he had founded, in the archipelago of the Pelasges, a new Queen of the Seas, from the depths of which he will one day rise up against Atlantis."

"Well, Knephao, rejoice; Hellas is alive, Hellas is victorious, and Hellas is returning to Atlantis!"

"I rejoice, Hermos, in knowing that our Hellas is alive and strong; but if his enemies have had the skill to deflect all the news received, it is because they are getting ready to fight him when he reappears before Atlantis."

"But who will take the crown this evening?"

"You have to ask? The man to whom, for three years. Atlantis owes all its disorder and all its folly: Guitche, the master of Gold."

"Guitche? That slave of a slave?"

"Yes, my dear Hermos, and you know, therefore, that when Guitche is Prince of Apostles, Mellena will become, unchecked, our veritable Queen. And Mellena, Queen of Atlantis, is the reaction of the entire ancient Occidental race, from which she comes, and which hates the Orient, of which I am a son. Everything possible has been done to contrive the death of Hellas among the Pelasges. And everything possible has been done to prevent your return, Hermos. Do you know what Mellena wants? To take possession of the Holy Terrace, the last refuge of scholars and initiates. Now, the day when the secrets of the Sphinx are violated..."

This time, Hermos, completely turned around, takes Knephao's hands emotionally. "You're right," he says. "It's necessary to act. Atlantis die? That cannot be. The gods need it, to animate the world. They've brought me to you to help you. What do you want of me?"

"It's necessary that Atlantis, this evening, escapes Mellena's party. It's necessary to save the Holy Terrace. I can't do it. You can."

"Do you want us to run to the public square? Do you want us to arouse the people? They acclaimed me just now, and I heard complaints against Mellena."

"Have you not seen the inconsistency of the crowd? It can only cry out to all winds. Listen to me. In a moment, you'll be in the Temple of the Initiates. They have to go in there, according to custom, before sunset. You'll hide there.

Then, immediately after the common prayer, you'll go out with them, and you'll appear on the perron of the Sphinx. You'll tell the truth about Hellas, and if they want to designate a new Prince anyway, you'll solicit that dignity."

"But what if they refuse?"

"It's necessary that you carry off the victory. That's not my affair; that's the secret of your genius."

"And how do I get into the Temple?"

"Look..."

And the Egyptian, approaching the thick wall, presses forcefully with his hand on a stone that suddenly rotates on invisible hinges and displays a gaping opening, in the depths of which, in the gloom, the first steps of a spiral staircase can be glimpsed.

"From whom, then, Knephao, did you obtain the secret of this door? What god or demon can open the Holy Hill?"

"Neither a god nor a demon, but the wary prudence of men. It was Ossur, the father of Oreus, who, foreseeing the possible uprising of human passions, had this hidden entrance hollowed out, personally. Ossur indicated it to Oreus, his son, and when Oreus, indignant against Atlantis, withdrew to the Green Isle, he transmitted the secret to Hellas. And that secret, Hellas, before setting out for the Pelasgian Sea, did not want to confide to anyone but me. I swore never to divulge it, except for the very salvation of Atlantis. I estimate, in fact, that the salvation in question is at stake. Up there, you'll find another door; press three times on a round stone in relief, which your hand will easily discover. The stone will open silently. You'll find yourself in the darkest corner of the Temple. Wait there. Everything will happen as I've said. The rest is up to you. May the gods help you!"

"And if I fail?"

"In that case, I'll act alone. Adieu, Hermos!"

And, curbing his elevated stature, Knephao tranquilly inserts his broad chest between the stones.

"Come back, Knephao. You're surely marching to death. I might perhaps be marching to glory. I'll be the one to go up to the Temple."

"In sum, someone has to save us!"

The two men embrace.

"Adieu, Knephao," Hermos sways, pulling away. "Whatever happens, see Oreus, and tell him that no base ambition led me to seek Hellas' place."

"Farewell, Hermos—may the gods protect you."

And abruptly, the stone, rotating on its invisible hinges, resumes its place in the flank of the Holy Hill.

Knephao, left alone, falls to his knees and, with his hands extended toward the obscure crypt where the sarcophagi lie dormant, he invokes the souls of the dead Apostles.

Scene VI
The Storm in the Crowd

The giant now retraces his steps through the dark corridors and arrives, eventually, at the door of black wood where he posted an Egyptian foot-soldier a little while before, with orders not to let anyone enter. He hears urgent blows resounding on that door, while women's voices hurl supplications and insults at the soldier on guard.

"Answer us, then stupid soldier!"

"Assassin! Slave! Son of a slave!"

"Soldier, for mercy's sake, yield; we'll give you the most beautiful gold pieces."

"What's the matter, then?" cries a powerful voice behind the door, known to all.

"Saved! Saved! Here's Knephao! Open up, Knephao. Come and save us."

The door opens wide and the tall form of the Egyptian appears.

Frightened women cluster around Knephao.

"Great chief, brave warrior, our hero, they want to kill us!"

"They're agitated by a wind of madness! The crowd isn't afraid of anyone but you. Quickly, quickly, run to the square.

Knephao detaches himself from all the imploring arms; then he addresses Mellena, their mistress, who is coming forward. "Speak, you, their mistress. Whence comes this tumult?"

"Knephao, I've never done you any harm, have I? Prove to me now that I was right to grant you my confidence. Save us."

"Whatever you have done or thought, Mellena, it's sufficient that you're appealing to me for help. What do you want?"

At the same time, thrown stones begin to resound against the high bronze portals.

"Can you hear the crowd in revolt Knephao? They're demanding my death. They want to invade the Palace."

Through the high windows, the scattered cries of the popular rumor come into the vestibule.

"To death, Mellena!"

"Let Guitche be hanged!"

"Long live Hellas!"

"Throw the women into the water!"

Mellena loses her self-assurance and presses against the hero.

"For pity's sake, calm them down. I'll give you all the treasures you want for your Egypt, Knephao."

"I'm not asking for anything, Mellena. But tell me first, why these clamors?"

"They think that Hellas is going to come back! Some imbecile sailors, arrived from Iberia, have announced that the victorious Apostle is returning to Atlantis with his fleet. They're accusing Guitche of having suppressed the news coming from the Pelasgian archipelago, and they want to prevent the election of the Prince, saying that Hellas hasn't abdicated. What can we do? What answer can we give them? They're going to kill me. They're going to kill Guitche. Oh, whatever you want, Knephao, whatever you want—but save us!"

And she presses herself against the colossus, ardently.

"Handsome hero, go and talk to them!" moan the women. "They'll listen to you."

"Yes, yes, go and talk to them," says Mellena.

"And what shall I say to them?"

"Soothe them with promises. Tell them that Hellas is, indeed, going to come back. It isn't true, but it's sometimes necessary to be able to lie. Later, we'll take our measures. The important thing is to gain time. You'll see, Knephao, how we'll reward you!"

"So be it, Mellena—but I only demand from you one promise."

"With all my heart, with all my heart, I make it in advance.

"In that case, whatever I say, whatever affirmation I take to the people, I shall make in your name, and you will approve it."

"I won't belie it, even if you proclaim the impossible."

"And it's the impossible that I'll announce."

And immediately, Knephao, pushing away the tearful troop of women, goes directly to the bronze portal, solidly closed. He opens the high doors wide, and his gigantic stature appears on the perron.

In the distance, in the direction of the Gate, the melee is commencing when cries ring out on all sides:

"There's Knephao!"

"Tell your soldiers to open the Gate for us!"

"Hellas, your friend Hellas, is coming back!"

"We're going to hang Guitche."

"We're going to send Mellena back to the Barbarians!"

"Silence, all of you!" shouts the voice of the giant. Knephao advances on to the perron. With his extended right hand he calms the rumors.

"Atlanteans, my red brothers, what do you want?"

"We want Hellas!"

"You shall have him!"

A prolonged rumor rises up. Knephao, spotting in the front rank a man with a weak face, asks him in a loud voice: "You, who seem to be reasonable and just, speak for all: what's the matter?"

"It is, great chief, that they've hidden Hellas' return from us, and they want, instead of that hero, to impose an unworthy Prince upon us!"

"You desire Hellas now? Isn't it you and your people who forced him to quit the Queen City?"

"What does it matter," cries a neighbor, "what we did three years ago? Let Hellas be master of the Empire again, since he's bringing us glory and gold!"

35

"Very well," says Knephao. "And who has given you this good news?"

"Iberian sailors."

"Well then, listen to me."

Suddenly, all noise ceases. People draw closer. They wait.

"Atlanteans, and you, Egyptians, you know that I have never lied?"

"Never! Never!"

"Well, Atlanteans, you've been told the truth. Hellas is on his way, getting nearer to Atlantis. That is what Hermos has just told me. In three days, two, or perhaps tomorrow, the Prince of Apostles, the conqueror of the Pelasgians, will return to the City. The entire Orient is resounding with his glory. He has just enlarged with unknown lands the Empire of the Queen of the Waters."

Cries of joy, agitated arms, hats thrown in the air.

"Perfect," protests the man with the placid face, "but in the meantime, they're going to elect another Prince."

"We don't want Guitche!"

"Don't worry, then" Knephao went on. "Guitche will not be elected. One more worthy than him will collect the crown, and when Hellas comes into the harbor, he will return his title and his power to him."

"Who, then?" demanded a thousand voices.

"Hermos."

"Hermos? Impossible! You wouldn't open the Golden Gate for him."

"Let me finish. Hermos has just gone up to the Holy Terrace by a route known to him alone. He will reveal the return of Hellas. Mellena, the first to learn of the return of Hellas, has just announced to me that the crown will be returned to him."

A swell of surprise, admiration and joy lifts up the crowd.

"So," Knephao continues, "resume the interrupted festival quickly."

"Long live Knephao! Long live Hellas! Long live Hermos!"

"Long live Atlantis the Eternal!"

Knephao returns to the vestibule where the bards of Armor have taken refuge, where the reassured women are jumping with delight, and where Mellena, her eyes shining and her lips smiling, is waiting for him, holding out her hands.

"Hurry," says the warrior, as he comes in. "For the moment, you're out of danger."

"Glory, glory to Knephao!"

"Knephao," says Mellena, "I thought you were simply a fearless soldier. Here you are now, a great politician. How well you can lie!"

A shiver runs through the veins of the colossus. He is about to reply...but his will dominates his nerves, and he is content to pronounce, in a low voice: "You're mistaken. I lie very badly."

"Let's say that you don't have the habit of it. What is it necessary to do, Knephao, to reward you?"

"Oh, the fortunate Egyptian!"

"Get away!" cries Knephao, impatiently. "This is no time for stupidities."

Abruptly heading for the other extremity of the vestibule, he opens a door giving access to a courtyard, where chariots are waiting, always ready to take the guests of the Palace to the various quarters of the Queen City.

"Don't lose any time," he advises. "No one knows what the crowd will do this evening."

But Mellena lingers behind, to one side, with a few friends.

"Knephao, now that all these follies are out of the way, you can tell us why you just toyed like that with Hellas."

"Me, toy with Hellas?" He feels bubble of anger bursting within him, but once again, he masters himself. "In fact," he adds, "that doesn't concern you."

"So be it. I won't ask you anything. But I can guess. It's because of Orea, isn't it, that you hate him? You're right. She made you suffer, that pedantic woman."

This time, Knephao's anger bursts forth in irresistible spurts. "Shut up, Mellena, shut up! I forbid you to talk about Orea. I've done here what I needed to do. You don't owe me anything."

"Oh, the sublime lover! Certainly, it's not good to excite your rage. But I don't hold it against you. Adieu, grim savior. We'll meet again."

And, darting a glance at the giant, charged with both mockery and caresses, she and her friends head for the stairway that leads to the balconies.

"Where are you going?" the Egyptian asks. "You're not leaving, like the others"

"You believe that I'm going to flee like those little women? I'm staying here, at home, in the Palace that will become mine this very evening."

"The Palace doesn't belong to anyone. It belongs to the Empire."

"And the Empire belongs to the Prince of Apostles."

"To Hellas, then?"

"Oh, the fine liar! He's taken in by his own stories! Adieu, adieu, Knephao. And don't think any more about the cruel Orea. There are more beautiful women!"

So saying, she disappears, her gait undulating and her head high.

The giant murmurs: "So much the worse for her. If someone tries to kill her this evening, it isn't me who'll save her."

And he departs at a pace so rapid that he collides with the men of Armor...

"What are you doing here?" he asks.

The men do not reply. Then recalling all that he knows of the language of Ys, the giant says: "You've come from the land of Armor?"

"Yes, great chief."

38

"Who summoned you here?"

"Mellena."

"And when did you land?"

"Three days ago."

"But your vessels aren't in the harbor!"

"They disembarked us on one of the islands and continued their route toward the strait of Gades. They're waiting for ships that are coming from the land of the Pelasges."

"What ships? And with what purpose?"

"We don't know. That's secret that the master of the vessels kept from us."

"Wretch!" murmurs Knephao, and turns round to see whether Mellena is still present. Then, in a different tone: "And what are you waiting for now?"

"We're supposed to go to the dinner on the Crimson Isle."

"I'll have you taken there."

Calling one of his soldiers who once served with him in Armorica, he says: "Anklios, take these bards of Armor to the Crimson Isle. Make sure that they don't see anyone else in the Palace."

The bards, visibly glad to the leaving the stormy place, follow the soldier through the high columns

Knephao remains indecisive for a brief moment. Then, stamping his foot in a gesture of anger: "The demons! I understand why they hope that Hellas won't return. Perhaps we can still save him!"

And he heads toward the square. The crowd is exultant. Groups are singing. Others are dancing. In the distance, the sun is sinking toward the sea. An immense fête envelops the city.

Full of scorn for the crowd henceforth, he resumes his place before the Golden Gate, without deigning to respond to the popular acclamations; and he waits impassively for impending events, for which he prepares with a resolute heart.

Scene VII
The Temple

Meanwhile, having taken the stairway that rises in a spiral to the Temple, Hermos stops, gropes, finds the round stone indicated, presses on it three times with his hand, and suddenly sees a door open.

All the windows of the Temple remain closed. Some light filters through the high ventilation shafts. The place where Hermos finds himself is situated in the east of the Temple, near the altar of the Unknown God. Doubts regarding himself and the City stop him, hesitantly, in his projects.

So, he thinks, *I haven't able to see any of the evil that is corroding the Empire?*

And he advances toward the altar.

Now he can make out the lines of the colonnades and the profiles of statues. The rectangular Temple extends from south to north, and the vault is supported on twenty-one rows of seven equal pillars. Between the columns, on ivory seats, the images in bronze of defunct Princes and heroes repose rigidly. A golden triangle encrusted with gems is resplendent against the wall. At the foot of the altar, three large sphinxes stand guard, whose flanks are marble, their claws bronze, their wings golden and their eyes diamonds. Between the forepaws, each sphinx holds a silver streamer on which sacred formulas can be read through the deliberate tangle of characters. The first Sphinx, the one of the right, says:

> *You will no longer be human*
> *You will not be divine....*

The second proclaims:

> *You turn yourself*
> *The wheel of destiny...*

And the third bears the troubling inscription:

A great dusk is coming
Without a new dawn.

On raising his eyes, however, between the three sides of the brilliant triangle that dominates the altar, Hermos sees shining, in luminous stones, the following inscription, which popular and traditional opinion attributes solely to the glory of Atlantis:

A great people can only die by its own hand.

On those words, many thousands of times over, the Apostles have exhausted the sagacity of their minds at every festival. Even Ossur and Hermes, and the great Oreus, have never given those strange words any but symbolic interpretations, with a triple meaning. Hermos experiences a kind of vertigo. His forehead in his hands, he bows and prays:

"Invisible Fire, Source of Life, Father of the Stars, Unknown God, Master of the Earth, Prince of the Azure, King of the Heavens, you who see simultaneously into the tremors of nebulae and the quivering of blades of grass, Lord, grant me the strength to comprehend your eternal order, to spread over the Queen City and the world which surrounds it, the heart of love with which you have burned me..."

Getting up again then, and turning toward the mages of the defunct Princes he continues: "Intercede for me, intercede for us, souls whose glare is able to illuminate the earth; souls who now rise in an infinite ladder from our obscure earth to the hearth of the living Splendor. Ensure that Atlantis never dies, either at other hands or her own, that the mysterious great dusk that no dawn will follow never extends over it!"

Now, Hermos feels replete with an unexpected strength. The exaltation of the prayer has lifted his heart toward the desire for heroism. He is no longer afraid. He feels that Atlantis lives within him, and that he lives for her.

But in the distance, in the direction of the door, noises are audible. The trumpet sounds. The Apostles are about to enter the Temple, and Hermos only just has time to take refuge in a dark corner.

One by one, preceded by Thebao, the high priest, the Apostles disperse behind the columns.

First come the Brothers of Silence, the priests of the Sphinx, bound by vows never to take part in the disputes or the ambitions of the active Apostles. They are both their servants and their masters: their servants because they execute the orders of the College; their master also because they hold keys to the hidden place in which the accumulated secrets of Atlantean science are hidden, and no one can penetrate it with them except for the Prince of Apostles, the supreme master.

Then come the Apostles, in various groups, whose number grows incessantly from year to year. In spite of the efforts of Oreus and Hellas to prevent the invasion of the Temple, the College has wanted to welcome new adepts furnished by all the classes of the City.

At the head march the architects, to whom the greatest honors revert. Behind them, the professions are mingled in disorder, and gold-changers, dye-merchants and tavern-keepers are confounded with judges, scholars, artists and the sons of heroes.

Hermos opens fearful eyes on seeing certain vulgar heads file past him.

What will happen? Hermos shivers. Has he been seen? Has he been divined? Now, slowly, a group is heading toward the shadowy covert where he is lurking. The group plunges into the corner, and if the nearest to the wall reached out with their arms, they would reach the son of Hermes in his retreat. But no one is thinking about him. The group, evidently, is seeking mystery, and Hermos, whose eyes are becoming accustomed to the gloom, recognizes Guitche among the newcomers.

"Speak in low voices" says Guitche, "no one here can overhear us. Is Barkas here?"

"Yes."

"And Belkis, tribune of matelots?"

"Here I am."

"And Moussor, master of merchants?"

"Here."

And thus are listed for Hermos' ears the chiefs of Mellena's party, the enemies of Oreus and Hellas, and his own now. Few of the names evoke anything in his memory, save one: that of Barkas, the architect of the Empire, a murky, embittered, envious genius, who hates Oreus and Hellas because any glory other than his own is a personal torture to him.

"We're all here, then," said Guitche. "Are you sure of all your partisans?"

"Absolutely sure," declares Belkis. "I hold them by interest."

"I've made a count," added Barkas. "We're two hundred against scarcely a hundred."

"However," Guitche remarked, "let's take care. Hellas might return. And if someone surges forth, and places himself before the door of the Temple, risking death on the threshold..."

"Needless anxiety," remarks Barkas. Only one man would have dared to defend Hellas, but we've made sure that he didn't arrive in time."

"Oh yes," sniggers Belkis. "That poor simpleton Hermos, who thinks himself a great poet!"

"He ought at this moment to be languishing at the Golden Gate. The Aztecs had orders not to let him disembark before midday."

"It's agreed, then? As soon as the exit from the Temple, we prolong the discussions on the nonsense of the Sphinx, in such a way that when the sun touches the sea, there'll only be time to proclaim the new Prince, and Guitche will be holding himself ready."

"It's agreed," replies Barkas. "It's necessary that the master of Gold also become the master of the World."

"And that all the gold in the Temple reverts to us."

"Shh! Let's retire. The prayer is fished..."

The Brothers of Silence are, in fact, marching slowly between the columns. Having reached the door, their chief, Thebao, in a loud voice, articulates slowly:

"Sons of the Sun, have you prayed well?"

"Yes, yes," reply hundreds of voices.

"No impure heart remains among you?"

"Our hearts are united in the Unknown God."

Then Thebao, raising his right hand in a sign of benediction, traces the sacred triangle in the air, and, turning toward the door, opens both its battens.

The sun is sinking toward the horizon and the sacred moment is approaching. The Apostles hasten toward the exit, and Hermos sees the Temple deserted. Still very troubled by the conspiracy that he has overheard by chance, he has not had the presence of mind to mingle boldly with the groups. But an ardent resolution animates him; he insinuates himself behind the portal that, according to the ritual, must remain open during the acclamation. And, ready to bound forth at the chosen moment, he listens, watches and waits.

Scene VIII
The Terrace of the Sphinx

Overlooking the sea, the Terrace of the Sphinx is the highest of the seven holy terraces built but the Atlantean architects. Several generations of men labored to accumulate the enormous blocks, regularly carved, on top of one another, whose compact and bold mass narrows from the base to the summit. A perfect unity of design has presided over the harmonious splendor of that marvel. And from the rectangular terrace, the immense city is seen extending toward the occident, enveloped by and penetrating the shining waters, extending its giant arms into the open sea like an immeasurable octopus.

The Terrace of the Sphinx, accessible only to Initiates, is a hundred fathoms above the Palace of the Empire, two hundred fathoms above the Palace of Gold and three hundred fathoms above the Palace of the Waters. To the orient it leans against Mount Manou, at the summit of which extends the beautiful artificial lake alimented by prodigious invisible machines that transport the water of several nearby rivers.

The giant Sphinx with the flanks of bronze and golden wings is enthroned on a pedestal of basalt, to which one accedes by a monumental stairway. The crouching idol, its head high and its claws extended forwards, is turned toward the occident, and the setting sun blazes in its eyes, formed by two enormous gems. Its head, as beautiful as a woman's, appears as robust as a man's, and its torso, devoid of breasts, allows powerful muscles to stand forth. It is a male Sphinx, by means of which the Atlantean Empire symbolizes its genius and order of creation, with a rump like a bull, claws like a lion, and wings like an eagle. Its gaze, turned toward the vast horizon, watches over and commands the red Empire that Atlantis has conquered.

Behind the rump of the Sphinx, a porphyry obelisk extents its pointed tip toward the sky.

Thebao, the chief of the hierophants, goes to take up his position, alone, standing on the highest step of the stairway of the Sphinx. On the pedestal, the sacred formula stands out:

A great people can only die by its own hand.

Immobile, Thebao holds in one hand a translucent enamel globe and in the other a golden crown. To his left is the Palace of the Hierophants; to his right the Temple of the Initiates.

On the steps of their palace the Hierophants, or Brothers of Silence, are arranged in tiers. They are holding in their hands the keys of the mysterious chambers placed under the crypts of their palace, where the secrets of Atlantean science are kept. On the first steps of the Temple, the chiefs of the corporations are arranged.

The rest of the Apostles and the young neophytes spread out, without any order, across the square. When the rumor caused by the exit from the Temples seems almost calmed, Thebao holds the crown and the globe toward the Sun, and then deposits one on the left claw, the other on the right claw of the Sphinx. Having done that, he traces in the air the triangular sign, and then, holding out his hands in a gesture of benediction, says:

"Go!"

It is the moment when the chiefs of the groups have the right to ask the Initiates a few questions concerning the formulas of the Sphinx. Barkas, chief of the Architects, the foremost in order of seniority, speaks first.

"Priest of the Sphinx, and you, sons of the Sun, Apostles of Light, and you, Thebao, Guardian of Guardians of the Holy Terrace, salutations!" Then, addressing the Sphinx, he adds in a solemn tone: "You say, O Sphinx, that a great people can only die of its own hand, which evidently signifies that no other people will be able to defeat it. And on the other hand, you say that a great dusk will come with no new dawn. What do you mean by those enigmatic words? Is it necessary to see, for Atlantis, the implausible eventuality of an end?"

Turning to the Apostles, he continues: "If there is one among you, O sons of the Sun, who can respond with assurance to my question, let him take my place, and let him deign afterwards, in accordance with his right, to indicate to our suffrage the one who should become our new Prince...for you all know that Hellas has left us for almost a year without news."

An ill-contained rumor greets those words. No one dares, immediately, to scale the steps of the Temple, but from the group of neophytes, silent until then, a clear voice resounds: "Your question is impious, Barkas, and your proposal criminal. And besides, why do you speak about a new Prince, since Hellas has not failed..."

"Who is the runt who permits himself to insult the great Barkas?" shouted Belkis.

"My name is Amonou, descendant of Onoube. My race was glorious in Atlantis."

"What does the glory of your race matter? All our ancestors are worthy, since they are dead. Do you dare to speak, then, while your elders are silent?"

"If the elders are afraid..."

At those words a clamor rises up. Guitche's partisans precipitate around the young man. The friends of Hellas hesitate, and Hermos is thinking that the moment has come to emerge from the Temple when Belkis appears abruptly on the highest step. Short, thin and nervous, his face wrinkled, his beard unkempt, his cloak floating, he makes jerky gestures frantically.

"People of Atlantis, you who are called the Sons of the Sun although your true father was a brave man like you or me; Apostles of a light that I do not know, for the only light that we know burns with the same glare for all of us; servants of an idol that has never budged, this is the truth, and in a few words I will resolve all the enigmas of the Sphinx. Your pretended gods only represent basalt and bronze..."

A dull murmur welcomes those words. Amonou, although maintained by the friends of Barkas, protests by means of cries. Even a few of Guitche's friends think that Belkis is

47

letting himself get carried away by too much hatred, and compromising their cause.

"Be careful, Belkis," counsels Barkas. "You're losing measure. Don't speak so of the gods. That's not your affair. Speak about Hellas. That's the important thing."

"And what do you want me to say?" Belkis went on, his shrill voice dominating the tumult. "Well, until now, you've played the role of dupes. Yes, all the religious terror in which your Hierophants maintain you has no other purpose but to impose on you the domination of a few families whose despotism still weighs upon us. What were your Princes, in fact? Pretended scholars, hypothetical heroes. The likes of Ossur, Oreus, Hermes, Abydos and Hellas, in sum! What has he done, the infallible conqueror? He's gone off to be beaten by white barbarians, and, doubtless a captive, he doesn't even know any longer that today is the day of his Sphinx. Has not the moment come, truly, to give the Empire of the Waters to those who, having become rich by intelligence, are able to enable all the people to share in the fruits of their intelligence and their labor? Apostles, I propose to you to exalt Guitche, the master of Gold!"

"Long live Guitche!" cry a few voices, without much enthusiasm.

"No, no, down with Guitche!" riposte a few young men with ardent voices.

"Liar, insulter of the gods, calumniator of the absent," shouts Amonou, "it's not the secrets of the Sphinx you want to possess, it's the gold of the Temple!"

"Impious as we know you to be," shouts a friend of Amonou, "dare then to go into the Temple and swear that Hellas has betrayed us or succumbed. For, in spite of his silence, we believe in him!"

"Ha ha! In your Temple! You think I'm afraid of that?"

And, advancing a few steps, Belkis enters beneath the door of the Temple, and proclaims solemnly: "Not by these divinities that I defy and deny, but by my honor and my will, my only gods, I swear here that Hellas…"

But the words catch in his throat. He has no sooner pronounced that name than a robust hand falls upon the nape of his neck and the assembly of Apostles, stupefied, sees Belkis emerge from the Temple, bewildered and choking, pushed by blows of the fists and feet by a handsome young man in a crimson mantle.

Fear, at first, takes possession of a few Apostles. The friends of Guitche are the first to flee in terror. Even the Brothers of Silence climb up, by an instinctive movement to the peristyle of their Palace. Belkis, precipitated from the height of the perron, has rolled on to the parvis, and, moaning, goes to seek refuge in the remotest corner of the Terrace, imploring men and even the gods.

But from an astonished group of neophytes a voice cries: "Hermos!"

And the young men precipitate themselves toward their poet.

Scene IX
Outside the Temple

It is, indeed, Hermos, who, no longer able to contain himself, has bounded upon Belkis when the matelots' orator pronounced the name of Hellas.

"Ah! You weren't expecting me," thunders the Apostle, "any more than you were expecting Hellas? Well, know that he will return, as I have returned."

"Glory! Glory! Long live Hellas!" cry the young men, comforted, who have been joined by a few new partisans, previously indecisive.

"Yes, Hellas will return, and will bring you a new empire. Hellas has vanquished, and the entire Orient is resounding with his victory. You, Atlanteans, would have been be the first to exalt the hero if his enemies, yours and those of the Empire had not dissimulated his return from you, suppressing by sacrilegious maneuvers the news arriving from the land of the Pelasges.

"You're lying!" Guitche interrupts. "We've never suppressed any news."

"Aha!" ripostes Hermos. "There is the guilty man revealing himself. Well, Guitche, it's you, I know, who has suppressed Hellas' messages, or if not you, one of your associates. And if your conscience is pure, swear that you have never caused the death of any of the sacred pigeons returning from the Orient."

Guitche, disconcerted, does not reply for a moment, and Belkis, who has recovered his confidence, says: "Are we forced to respect the birds that fly in the sky? Tell us rather how, having arrived too late at the Golden Gate, you now find yourself on the perron of the Temple. Yes, tell us where you've come from and why you've come?"

"What does it matter where I've come from? It is of Hellas alone that it's neccssary to speak here. I am the bearer of the good news, and because an invisible force directs every-thing, the protective gods of Atlantis have brought me to you mysteriously, when you were about to falter."

And Hermos, taking advantage of the general surprise, gives an account in a firm voice the story of Hellas' success, and the messages intercepted and the news known throughout Libya, and the maneuvers accomplished on the part of Mellena, and the obstacles that he had encountered himself in returning to the City.

"You're nothing but a slanderer!" howls Belkis. "How can you know the pretended intrigues of the honest men you're accusing, since, by your own admission, you've only just disembarked in Atlantis?"

"I know your intrigues from your own mouths. Blas-phemers who choose the Temple as the place for your criminal projects, don't you know that an ear was listening to your words?"

When Hermos, to general surprise, repeats the confi-dences exchanged by Guitche's party, especially by Barkas and Belkis, a great agitation is manifest on the terrace. The indecisive, whose votes have been trafficked, exchange glanc-es, draw away from Guitche and move closer to the friends of Hellas.

Barkas, sensing that the party is greatly compromised, insinuates himself on to the steps of the Temple and says, in a cajoling voice:

"Brothers of Silence, and you, Sons of the Sun, the mo-ment is grave; let us dissipate the fumes of anger. What the glorious Hermos reports merits our attention, but the scruples of Belkis appear equally reasonable. We do not cast doubt on the sincerity of the son of Hermes, but might he not be mistak-en? Remember that news often spreads through the world that has no other origin than the stories of a shepherd and inventor of fables. This, therefore is what I propose: we acclaim a new Prince, and in the event that Hellas might return, for which I wish as much as anyone, today's elect will promise solemnly to return the keys of the Temple, the crown and the globe to him as soon as he appears within sight of the City."

That honeyed speech produces an immediate effect. The old Apostles, friends of moderation, nod their heads sententiously. Guitche's friends recover their courage. Those of Hellas seem hesitant.

"Very just and very wise," approve the old men. "Let us acclaim a Prince who will consent to an intermediate role. If Hellas returns, everything will return to the anterior order."

"Guitche! Guitche!" cry voices,

"No, not Guitche," reply the young men. "Hermos! Hermos, the friend of Hellas! We have confidence that he will not betray him."

"Guitche!"

"Hermos!"

And the two parties, almost equal, are filling the air with their clamors, when Belkis, returning to the perron, says:

"Hermos, when you were only acting on behalf of others, we could not ask you to account for your actions. But now it's you that the young fools want to acclaim. We understand, now, why all these intrigues. Tell us, then, if you can, how you come to be here? By what criminal maneuvers have you reached the Temple? I accuse you of them, and, in the name of the laws that you claim to respect, I demand that you be put to death!"

"Wretch!" proclaims Hermos. "You dare to invoke divine laws, you who, just now, with your ignoble voice, insulted the purest idea of the Unknown God? So be it, condemn me! What does death or life matter, for, if our enemies win the day, it is Atlantis itself that will perish!"

"Horror! Sacrilege! He dares to blaspheme the immortality of Atlantis!"

But Hermos feels himself carried away by a superhuman ardor: "Yes, yes, Atlantis will perish if your souls are not cleansed of their soiling. The most sordid passions are agitating the people, and those debasing passions are now fermenting all the way to the Holy Terrace where once, all hearts ex alted, were ennobled and purified. So, therefore, if you desire the ruination of the Atlantean Empire, nominate Guitche; but I, who was conducted to you by mysterious forces, swear to you that I will not allow that crime to be accomplished. I will place myself on the threshold of the Temple, and when the new Prince comes to receive the sacrament, it is over my bloody body that your cortege will have to pass. Now, the Temple soiled will render the acclamation null, and our great Hellas will return in spite of you."

A silence of almost sacred terror follows those words. Never, since the Temple has existed, has the blood of an Apostle flowed over its flagstones, and a millenarian legend recounts that great misfortunes would follow such a sacrilege. Guitche's friends stop, anxiously; those of Hermos and Hellas tremble for the poet.

"Guitche! Guitche!" cry Belkis' neighbors.

And, rushing toward the Temple, they try to drive Hermos away. But he places himself resolutely on the threshold. The young Apostles, led by Amonou, throw themselves against their adversaries in their turn.

A conflict is becoming inevitable when suddenly, from the back of the square, Guitche, who has remained in the rear, cries fearfully:

"The God! The God! Bow down!" And he falls to his knees, raising his hands.

Scene X
The Living Sphinx

The nearby Apostles hasten around him,

"Pity! Pity! Here comes the Sphinx with the great wings, the one that ought to come, in accordance with the prophecies!"

Guitche's friends descend in haste from the perron, and examine the horizon. Barkas is speechless. Belkis, crawling, goes to huddle against the flank of the Sphinx. Hermos, his garments torn but uninjured, finally descends from the Temple and stands immobile, filled with astonishment.

High above, in a southern direction, in the sky, behind Mount Manou, coming toward Atlantis, is an immense bird, larger that the Sphinx of the Terrace, with a vast wingspan. Its wings are rising, lowering and extending, sometimes gliding horizontally through space and sometimes beating the azure with majestic strokes, and one might think that the entire azure is agitated by them.

Is it a monster, an enemy of humankind? Is it a protective or vengeful god? Is it the Sphinx of the Air, the one that ought to be born to punish perverse cities, whose coming is predicted by old legends?

Down below, in the city, where the altitude of Mount Manou prevents the crowd from seeing the monster, the trumpets consecrated to the Sun are sounding the death of the Star, for the moment has come to acclaim the Prince.

"Sons of the Sun," Thebao articulates, in a firm voice, still holding the globe and the crown in his hands, "Apostles and neophytes, to whom should I give the keys to the Temple?"

Everyone is silent. No one on the square dared to breathe a word.

"To me!" says Hermos, then, impassively.

"Yes, to Hermos," shouts Amonou. "The gods pronounce for him."

"To Hermos! To Hermos!"

"Atlanteans," Hermos adds, "it isn't me you're crowning but Hellas himself. I shall render to him that which belongs to him, faithfully."

Meanwhile, the great bird is approaching, and one might think that it is going to alight on the Holy Hill.

"Pity! Pity!" howl the Apostles. "Whatever you wish, we shall obey!"

And, with one unanimous voice, the assembly cries: "Long live Hermos! Long live Hermos!"

Immediately, in the air, the menacing monster is seen to turn aside in its course. It seemed previously to be coming straight toward the terrace, but now it is veering southwards. Its flight, as if suddenly lightened, rises upwards into the sky. One might think that the Sphinx of the Air is going to lose itself in some distant star.

The Apostles, relieved, utter cries of joy, get up and return to life. Then Thebao, profiting from the rumor, traverses the square and comes to place the crown of Hermos' head.

Meanwhile, the cortege forms to return to the city, and Hermos is stripped of his red mantle and clad in a long blue robe embroidered with gold. Behind him, the Apostles arrange themselves by corporations, and one by one, descend the narrow path that leads to the Golden Gate.

Soon, Hermos appears before the crowd, the globe in his hand. Then there is clamor, delirium, a storm of jubilation. Knephao, forgetting his habitual impassivity, leaps from his horse, opens the Sacred Gate himself and falls into Hermos' arms.

"Finally, Atlantis will live!"

"Perhaps," Hermos replies.

But the crowd snatches the Prince away from the giant's questions. Lifted on to the shoulders of the people, Hermos enters the Palace in triumph.

Now, scarcely has the elected Prince penetrated under the high vaults of the peristyle than a strident cry rinds out through the columns. It is Mellena, who is being dragged away by her companions and who, her lips white with foam, is struggling in the arms of women who can hardly retain her. A few young men want Guitche's wife to be imprisoned.

"Let delirious hatred pass," Knephao responds to them. "She is impotent against the will of the gods."

"Impotent!" roars Mellena, reanimated by anger, and who, upright and disheveled, stiffens herself against the disaster. "Impotent, you say? Naïve warrior, who believe yourself strong for one poor hour of victory! Oh, my masters, you believe in the return of the hero? Soon the green straits of Gades will be red with the blood of Hellas, as the port of Atlantis will subsequently be red with yours! Sing and laugh this evening, for your hour is approaching. This evening, the fête acclaims you, tomorrow...tomorrow it will acclaim us!"

And, shaken by a new crisis of nerves, Mellena falls backwards.

"Poor woman!" murmurs Hermos. "Her husband's failure has rendered her mad."

"Not mad, Hermos," Knephao replies, "but by chance, sincere. Let us watch over the city, and ourselves."

However, as the exasperation of the people is to be feared, the Egyptian takes the quivering body of his enemy in his robust arms, personally. Then, carrying it into the interior courtyard, he commands the guardians of the carriages to take Mellena to Guitche's house.

Hermos silently moves away from his friends and goes up to the balcony, where floral perfumes are still floating. In the distance, the immense sea is smiling under the oars of illuminated boats. From the resplendent city the sounds of lyres and the echoes of dances rise.

Hermos does not perceive either the radiant city or the sea florid with undulating reflections. He is gazing far into the distance, at the horizon, and expecting unknown things.

56

Then, as a humid veil passes before his eyes, the poet Hermos, Prince of Apostles, believes he can see, rising up from the heart of the Empire toward an invisible sky, the heavy clouds of accumulated passions...

THE SECOND DAY:
THE FEAST OF THE WATERS

You will no longer be human
You will not be divine...

Scene I
The Crimson Isle

The midnight hour chimes in the cupolas of the Palaces, and, responding from peninsula to peninsula, throughout the breadth of the immense city, the crystalline peals fill the air with reverberating vibrations.

On the terrace of the Crimson Isle, which overlooks the sea, the Atlantean artists and their guests exult and sing in the common delight of the repast that is reaching its end.

Sumptuously maintained at the expense of the Empire, the artists of Atlantis live apart from the popular tumult, on the most splendid of the islands, called Crimson because of its bright flowers with bloody hues. The island is one of the last left intact by the devouring genius of the architects, whose bold science conquers from the obedient sea, every few years, a terrace propitious to new buildings. Every generation sees the immense city elongating over the waves, for the pride of the Atlantean constructors has wanted to establish broad jetties between all the islands once scattered around Atlantis, and thus give the enormous metropolis the aspect of a giant hydra extending seven sinuous peninsulas over the waves like seven long and twisted necks. Seven monumental lighthouses loom up by day like the seven lofty heads of the monstrous beast, resplendent by night like fulgurant eyes.

Thamoussi, the doyen of the isle, has decided that the meal, ordinarily prepared in the sumptuous banqueting hall, should be held in the open air this evening, facing the illuminated city.

"How right you were, Thamoussi," exclaims Palmoussos the musician, "and what enchantment there is in lingering among the flowers, simultaneously near and distanced from the noisy crowd."

"There's a fête in the skies and a fête on the earth," says Asmonia, the young poetess. "Xanthes, you who know how to speak to the distant stars, to evoke vanished suns and cause the invisible spirits of the air to quiver, tell us what you are looking at out there, toward the horizon where the Sphinx is floating."

Without even turning his haughty head, as if he were speaking to the infinite universe, the handsome Xanthes, the poet in vogue, his elbow leaning on the parapet of the terrace, says:

"Caresses of the night, complicit scintillations of the stars; fortunate sea where one sees the reflections of the dazzling city snaking in undulations of blood and gold; soothing songs that float in the warm air to the rhythmic cadences of citharas; music, liberating music in which is combined the murmur of things and the secret language of our dreams; and you, perfume of amour, unique and multiple embrace of millions of confounded souls, immense breath of the immortal city, pour upon me, pour upon us, at this propitious hour, all the joy scattered beneath the sky in fête; and determine, irresistible goddess, universal sensuality, you, truly unique reason of life, determine that we always bring to your floral altar our bodies exhausted by delights and our hearts exalted by intoxication, and enable us, O goddess, in our turn, purified by the impulse and idealized by the ecstasy, to become the rivals of the gods."

"Admirable! Sublime!"

"Xanthes, here are flowers!"

"Xanthes, here are our hearts!"

And the smiling young women and the delighted young men gather around Xanthes, while Thamoussi, the president of the banquet, rises from his seat and comes to the edge of the terrace to bring the poet a cup of Etruscan wine.

"Xanthes! Xanthes! More! More!"

"Begin again?" says Xanthes, turning his head disdainfully toward the assembly. "Do I even know what I said just now? It wasn't me who was speaking; it isn't me that it's necessary to applaud; it's the voluptuous wind of Atlantis that has just blown through my sonorous breast; it's the splendor of all those lights multiplied through the surge of my golden words."

"Xanthes, you magnify the voice of Nature."

"Get away! Nature!" snaps the beautiful Asmonia. "Gross and monotonous Nature is something too vile for a genius like Xanthes. What he exalts, our poet, is the sublimity of our elite souls, and the art of living beautifully: the supreme art that Atlanteans have invented."

"Asmonia is right," Xanthes replies, finally deigning to quit the edge of the terrace. "What does it do for us, that stupid nature, which only knows how to recommence the same flourishings every year? The gods created the world in order that humankind might appear; they created humankind in order that the Atlantean race might become its sublime flower; they gave the Atlantean race the scepter of the world in order that, in an elected center of the empire, sensuality might expand in a few superior souls. Truly, we incarnate the sole excuse for the planet."

"Oh, this time, Xanthes, you'll permit me to kiss you!" Asmonia applauds.

"Us too! All of us! All of us!"

Xanthes, jostled, pulled this way and that, turned around by small feverish hands, is allowing himself, indolently, to be acclaimed and pampered when Thamoussi, intervening, yields to a triumphant impulse and pronounces in a sententious voice:

"My sisters and my brothers, I propose to you that we crown Xanthes Prince of Poets—an honor far more enviable than being Prince of Apostles."

"Oh, Prince of Apostles!" sniggers Olbios, the celebrated rhetor. "A truly fine affair, good for miserable blowers of the buccina like the popular Hermos."

"Shut up, Olbios," orders Xanthes. "You're never able to bring into our joy anything but the fumes of your hateful soul. I love Hermos, our friend and our brother, a poet like us, Doubtless he could be reproached for having deserted the purified cult of the lyre in order to throw himself, like a simple Atlantean, into the tumultuous disorders of the City. Doubtless his hymns, weighed down by ephemeral preoccupations, will fall into the depths of forgetfulness, while my songs, loved only by the highest aspirations of the immaterialized soul, will resound until the consummation of centuries—but what does it matter? Far from disdaining his success, I ask on behalf of all of us that you permit me to send him the salutations of the Crimson Isle."

"Marvelous, Xanthes!" exclaims Thamoussi, always favorable to conciliations. "I'll even ask that we invite Hermos to receive a fraternal crown among us."

"Hermos has to need of consecration!" cries a young and striking voice from the back of the terrace. "Hermos surpasses you all in head and heart!"

"Good, now there's another!" yelps Thamoussi, alarmed. "There's going to be an argument now! Is it you, Amonou, who are provoking trouble here? You'd do well to remain in your peninsula, my friend."

"Pardon me!" ripostes Amonou, advancing on to the terrace in the midst of a feverish agitation of all the artists present. "Is it me who commenced launching stupid insults against the absent? Without betraying the secrets of the Sanctuary, I have the right to say and proclaim loudly that Hermos appeared to us today, on the Holy Terrace, the purest and most splendid of heroes."

And the young man, tall, slim and broad-shouldered, enveloped in his black cloak, bare-headed, his gaze firm, advances toward the rhetor Olbios, who, plump and short, trembles on his short legs and backs up against a column.

Amonou continues, with vivacity: "Sing as much as you please about the delights of your souls and the lusts of your bodies; become, entirely at your ease, like the birds or the flowers, but don't touch those who are men, living among humans, strong enough to save humans—and save you, as well."

Tranquilly, Amonou traverses the terrace, where the artists remain silent, and comes to lean on the parapet, near the garden that descends in florid slopes all the way to the sea.

Olbios has disappeared. Xanthes is smiling and says in a serene voice: "He pleases me, this young Amonou. I like the way his youth shows itself to be combative. At his age, I too insulted the glorious elders!"

But the women, fearing a brawl, have fled into the arbors. Thamoussi, bewildered and tearful, losing his head, calls: "The bards! The bards! Why don't he bards come to make themselves heard?"

"They're asleep, Master," replies a servant.

"Wake them up! Have you ever seen Barbarians who permit themselves to sleep when they're summoned?" Then, turning to the assembly: "Come on, Brothers, come on! Let's drink! Let's laugh! Long live life! Are we not, as Xanthes says, the supreme flower of the universe?"

Meanwhile, led by a servant of the white race, the not-quite-awake bards, yawning, slightly dazed to find themselves dragged thus from one fête to another, slowly arrange themselves at the back of the terrace, where the remains of the banquet are scattered.

Scene II
Harps and Citharas

Amonou has not budged from his position. Surprised himself by his unexpected temerity, he is still wondering what gust of anger could have passed through him in order to push him to stand up against an entire assembly.

The night is already brightening toward the Orient, with nascent gleams at the level of the waves, and the neophyte is already setting forth to descend into the garden when, at a corner of a path, he feels his hand gripped by a frail hand and soft lips pose on his fingers. He turns round. A woman is standing silently in the shadows, light and slender, dressed in white.

"Who are you?" he asks.

"Shh! Come back to the terrace. You'll recognize me."

But the accent is familiar.

"Glania! The Ligurian."

"Silence. Someone might hear us. I'm going to sing with the bards of Armor. Stay on the terrace. I want to talk to you."

Intrigued and moved, although very weary, Amonou returns to the terrace, where the bright lights make a contrast with the dawn that is about to break.

Sprawling in seats or lying on couches, the Atlantean artists are drinking the last cups of wine. Women lying on carpets are plucking the petals from the last roses. But now the bards are intoning their first songs, and everyone is reanimated.

"Admirable! Divine!" exults Asmonia. "Decidedly, Hellas has done well to conquer the lands of Armor, since it has brought us these new joys."

"Come forth now, Ligurian!" commands Thamoussi.

Cithara in hand, her forehead crowned with verbena, the Ligurian woman advances, and everyone gradually draws nearer. Her complexion does not seem as white as that of the

Armorican bards, but her skin is pale in hue, her golden hair undulates, and her eyes are the color of a bright morning sky.

The Ligurian sings, and her voice multiplies her strange beauty; she speaks a sonorous and soft language, very similar to that of the bards, although in a tone that is more rhythmic and more lively. Her song bounds like the footfalls of a goat in hills with stony paths.

When she has finished, the artists get up, and want to give flowers to the triumphant performer.

"How," asks the musician Palmoussos, "have you not forgotten your language in the four years that you have been living in our midst?"

"Do you believe that one can ever forget one's mother tongue?"

Leaping as lightly as her song, she slips away from the compliments of the men and goes away, seemingly indifferent, to hide behind a pillar, while the bards intone a religious hymn.

Slowly, with muffled steps, going around the terrace, Glania slips into the garden and goes to lean on her elbows next to Amonou.

"Don't turn around," she says. "No one must hear us. Make a semblance of listening to the harps. You've just appeared to me as a savior, and I wept with joy when you surged forth alone to defend Hellas and Hermos. Anyway, this is the truth: I admire Hellas. I admire him from afar, because he's too great to cast his eyes upon a poor errant singer. Now, I'm going to tell you terrible things. And it's necessary that Hermos and Knephao know them immediately. Both are threatened, and doubtless Hellas will be attacked within three days."

And as Amonou, gripped, makes a movement, she explains: "Hear me out. I couldn't help talking about Hellas to the bards of Armor. They haven't forgotten his passage through their country. So they told me everything that the fleet that deposited them on the Great Mole is continuing on its way toward the strait of Gades; it has orders to attack Hellas, The rancor of a few old Armorican chiefs against Hellas has been exploited."

"By whom?"

"You can easily guess: Mellena. So, if Hellas is captured or killed, the Armorican fleet will return to Atlantis, and Hermos will be killed too. Oh, I implore you, take no matter what route, go and find Hermos, or, for want of him, Knephao or one of Hermos' friends; tell them to be on their guard. As for me, when the sun has risen, I'll try to procure a boat and go to the Green Isle to implore Oreus."

"But don't you know," replies Amonou, in a low voice, "that Orea loves Hellas as much as you do?"

"What does that matter? On the contrary, so much the better! A woman in love knows no obstacle, and the two of us will save him!"

"You're divine, little Glania!"

Undulating like a snake, the supple Ligurian slides through the clumps of laurier-roses and reappears at the extremity of the terrace behind the bards just as, the hymn having concluded, acclamations rose up on all sides.

"Oh, that music! The true language of the gods! What hero, Amonou, is worth as much as a good musician?"

And Palmoussos, eager to confound the young man, searches for him in all directions.

"Eh! What? Gone already!"

"Look," sniggers Olbios, reassured. "There he is on the water, alone, in a boat."

"Good," says Xanthes. "Let's forget these quarrels. And you, Glania, another song!"

"Impossible! I feel too weary."

"Please, another song, a rapid song. Dawn is about to break, it's you who'll salute it..."

"Well, so be it, but on one condition: you prepare me a boat in order to go away over the limpid sea."

"A singular caprice" objected Xanthes, "but granted, little Barbarian. And if you wish, we'll even accompany you and watch over you."

"No! All alone! Solitude is restful."

"So be it, wild beauty. We'll prepare you a light vessel."

Radiant then, transfigured, her beautiful blue eyes bathed by suppressed tears, Glania gets up; her voice rises, increasing in amorous strophes, and seems to be appealing, very distantly in the direction of the rising sun, to a hero toward whom her arms are extended...

"A true goddess," exults Asmonia, so enthused that she forgets to be jealous. "If one didn't know that the Ligurian girl is wilder than a seabird, one might believe that she were truly in love!"

But Glania no longer hears the admiring clamors. She has thrown a somber mantle over her dress, and now she runs to the shore and leaps into a boat—and the cadenced sound of oars in the waves can already be heard.

Scene III
The Ligurian Woman

The Ligurian's arms soon fall, harassed by fatigue; and the Green Isle trembles in the distance on the horizon where the vacillating light of the stars is still struggling. The light of the rising sun, which gradually fills the sea, envelops the distant rocks with a vaporous nimbus. In the orient, over Atlantis, the dawn appears. The great Sphinx, with its extended wings, seems to be launching radiance into space, and the thousand palaces, the thousand cupolas and the white porticos of the temples all light up, all quivering, all sparkling with millions of reflections.

Confused ideas are churning in the head of the young Barbarian, and whether it is the lassitude of her young body or the vertigo of her mind, she gradually senses her infinite smallness. What folly has led her to want to get mixed up in the quarrels of the immense Empire? And what is she going to attempt now? To go to the Green Isle, to the home of the mysterious Oreus, who, it is said, speaks by night to the stars and knows how to read, in the depths of invisible things, the secrets of the frightening future? Then too, is it not said that the Green Isle is inaccessible and that it is necessary, in order to land there, to know the creeks hidden in the depths of redoubtable rocks? Oh, poor little Ligurian, here come fear and shame to stop you, and bright blood to redden your pale cheeks!

But what about Hellas? Is she no longer going to do anything, then, for the salvation of the threatened hero? What does she want, after all? To carry an item of news that she knows. Are important messages not confided to domesticated seagulls or migratory pigeons?

And Glania sees then, reviving in her memory, a scene that struck her adolescent imagination, on the day when the magnificent hero entered triumphantly into Glano, near the Ligurian Sea.

Hellas, mounted on a great black horse, passed along the dusty road before the marveling crowd. Glania looked at him, and felt her heart ready to fail. A handsome giant who seemed, after Hellas, to be the great chief of the Atlantean cohorts, came before the superb conqueror and showed him a cage in which there were three doves. Hellas, descending from the horse, considered each of the birds and strove to attach thin silver tubes beneath the carrier-pigeons' wings, which doubtless bore news of the triumph. The giant was holding the cage in his left hand, but the other hand could not succeed in maintaining the struggling bird. Then Hellas, seeing the frail little girl beside him, whose delighted eyes were open wide, made her a sign to come and help him; and when he had attached the three silver tubes securely, he thanked her with a long smile. Then, taking the three birds, one after another, he kissed them gently on the head, and threw them into the air, following their flight with his eyes for a long time as they sped like arrows toward the horizon...

That memory reanimates Glania and renders her courage. Is she, too, not a voluntary dove, between the design of Hellas and the power of Oreus? Yes, yes, like the carrier-pigeons of Glano, she will go straight to the Green Isle, a little bird thrown into the tempest of the Empire, perhaps bearing over her heart the salvation of the hero.

But cruel gods, have you sworn my doom, then? she thinks, her arms aching, as she arrives under the rocks of the inaccessible island.

One might think it a fabulous tower looming up toward the sky. Not one bay, not one approachable inlet. Already, in fact, the boat is spinning in unexpected eddies.

God of Oreus! God of Hellas! Don't let me die without having delivered my news!

In her vertigo, it seems to her that she can hear living beings up above, on the shore of the island. Then, putting all her strength into her voice, seeking to dominate the tumult of the waves, she calls: "Oreus! Oreus! It's your Hellas who is going to die!"

But she collapses immediately, exhausted. It seems that the waves are about to open up, when something suddenly falls in front of her, an object both supple and solid. It is a rope that someone has thrown down to her. She clings on to it, wraps it round her body, and feels herself hoisted up slowly to the summit of the cliff.

"Thank you, god of Hellas!" she murmurs.

And at the moment when, disengaged from the rope, she places her bruised feet on a grassy border, all her strength abandons her, and, her heart failing, she falls backwards into the arms of her savior, in whom, by virtue of a strange hallucination, she believes she sees Hellas himself, peering down at her...

Scene IV
On the Green Isle

"Is she still asleep, Orea?"

"Yes, Father. Her breathing is calm. The delirium has been brief. It will pass."

"Where can the charming creature have come from? Do you know her, my daughter?"

"I believe I've seen her in the Square of the Waters, once, on the evening of a festival. She was singing sonorous strophes to the rhythm of a cithara, in a language as harmonious as waves on golden sands."

"Doubtless a Ligurian, one of those who came with Hellas' sailors."

"Perhaps, for in her brief delirium, she repeated the name of Hellas incessantly."

"Really? And what did she say?" the father asks, somewhat surprised.

"Nothing precise, except what she repeated continually: 'Save Hellas! He's going to die!'"

"Oh! Good!" says the old man, breathing deeply.

"Father," Orea murmurs, "this pale child moves me deeply. There's a mystery in her coming. Hasn't she come to inform us of some misfortune?"

"No, my child, don't worry."

"How was she able to get up all the way to the cliff? At this early hour, who can have been wandering along the cliff-top to save her?"

"The sun had already risen, and some servant from my laboratory...but let's be quiet. She's agitating. Remain alone with her. If she opens her eyes, call me."

And gently, moving backwards, contemplating with his gaze the group formed by Orea and the young Ligurian, the tall old man goes to the door, sends a smile to his daughter, and silently disappears, lifting the crimson curtains.

Glania is lying on her right side. Her wet hair, unkempt, is covering her forehead and falling over her slender neck. Slowly, with the light gestures of a young mother, Orea passes a damp cloth over the temples of the unconscious Ligurian.

A striking contrast! As much as Glania is frail and slender, Orea is majestic in her bearing. Her complexion has the warm reflections of golden red. Her bulbous forehead, high and broad, poorly hidden by black hair separated into undulating bangs, surmounts a face whose every feature is resplendent with durable beauty. The fine, curved nose terminates in quivering nostrils; the sinuous lips, with turned-up corners, are smiling; in her large dark eyes, and infinite kindness is reflected.

Now Glania sighs more deeply, and stirs. Her mouth stammers inconsequential words, and suddenly, she sits up and cries: "Hellas! Where's Hellas! He's no longer here, then?"

Involuntarily, with an instinctive gesture, Orea's dark eyebrows frown, and her haze becomes clouded. Immediately, however, the cloud passes and the beautiful Atlantean places a long, narrow hand on Glania's forehead, the attachment of which soothes the child, awakened with a start.

"Hellas isn't here? Who saved me, hen?"

"Hellas is far away, my poor child, and I don't know, unfortunately, when he will return."

Then Glania, recovering her reason, looks at Orea, recognizes her, and suddenly falls back on the bed, dissolving in tears.

"Orea, noble Orea, forgive me; I'll make myself your slave, but save him…save him…"

Meanwhile, hearing the sound of voices, the old man has lifted the curtain again and he comes toward the bed, holding a cup in his hand.

"Here, little seabird, here's a beverage that will reanimate your weary wings. Drink, and recover your strength."

The Ligurian looks at the old man with dazzled eyes.

"Oreus? It's you, the great Oreus?"

71

"Yes, yes, my dear child. You can be astonished in a minute—drink first."

And, by means of gentle constraint, he forces her to absorb the beverage, the immediate effect of which brings some color back to the young woman's pale cheeks.

"There, that's better, isn't it? Now, little conqueror," he says, patting Glania on the cheeks, "you can tell us what adventurous wind enabled you to reach our abandoned isle."

"Oh, Master, greatest of Masters, you of whom people speak throughout the world, and even the gods, as a confidant, forgive me for having dared to come to your home...I had things to say...grave things...and now...I no longer dare...."

And, so saying, Glania looks at Oreus with fearful eyes.

Oreus divines the Ligurian's embarrassment, and gives his daughter a scarcely perceptible sign, that is immediately understood.

"I'll leave you alone for a moment, Father."

"Go, my daughter. I'll call you."

Glania, her throat suffocated, her eyes still blurred by shed tears, gazes at Oreus timidly.

The former Prince of Apostles, the son of Ossur, the tamer of the waves, the builder of the Holy Mountains, the master of Hellas and Hermos, the most illustrious scholar in the entire world, the man in whom the people see a supernatural mage and his enemies a baleful demon, Oreus has already entered into his sixty-second year, but his vigor would be the envy of many a young man.

His forehead, very broad at the temples, is crowned by thick white hair maintained by a black band. A long beard, bright silver, carefully separated into two points, completes the equipment of his face with an imposing majesty, but his keen, smiling eyes, sometimes even mildly ironic, and the lips whose creased corners give evidence of an indulgent mockery, make Oreus, in the intimacy of quotidian life, spread around him the irresistible attraction of a powerful benevolence. But those same eyes, when enthusiasm or anger sets them ablaze, and those same lips, when ardent words burst forth from them, transform that physiognomy into a mask as terrible as a lion, with a gaze as fulgurant as an eagle's.

Scene V
Glania's Confidences

Now, in the brightly-lit room that the sunlight has just penetrated, the master has the tenderness of a grandfather; the mildness of his smile, and the benevolence of his eyes with the wrinkled corners, reassure Glania completely.

"Master," she begins, making an effort to sit up, "Master, you're going to think me mad. I'm only a little Barbarian, and you're as great as a god, but the gods, it's said, listen to our prayers. Will you listen to mine? In any case, someone's life is at stake."

"Dear child," Oreus replies, with a smile of ineffable commiseration, "I count for as little before the gods as the humblest sailor in the harbor."

"On, Master, don't reject me! I know that you govern invisible forces. For pity's sake, raise them up, for it's necessary that you save..."

"Who, my child?"

"Hellas, Master," she pronounces, in a stifled voice.

"Hell..."

"Don't shout that word. I don't want Orea to hear. I know that she loves him, and she's so beautiful, so good, that I'd die rather than cause her any chagrin. But it's necessary to tell you terrible things."

In a single surge, Glania recounts to Oreus the events of her own life, recalls the scenes of the previous day and the confidences of the bards.

"Exquisite soul," said Oreus, placing his thumb on Glania's forehead, "noble and truly divine heart, rest, have no fear..."

"But what of him, Master, what of him?"

"Be tranquil, my child. Your Hellas will be saved. But lie down. We're going to chat like good friends. Confide your heart to me. Have you loved him for a long time?"

"Who?"

"Hellas?"

"Who told you that I loved him?"

"Admirable child! Do you think I don't know it?"

"Oh, Master, since you know everything, what point is there in hiding anything from you? Well, yes, I love Hellas. If you only knew how I love him! But know that you have nothing to fear for Orea. To see him from afar, to know that he exists, that he is radiant, that he is filling the world with his name, that's my joy. He was so handsome when he came to my distant city for the first time. He appeared, and his gesture alone pacified the men, and his smile attached all the women to his footsteps. And to me, very small, he made a sign, and he put into my hands one of the white carrier-pigeons, which was palpitating less than my heart..."

Suddenly fearful, Glania interrupts herself and, alarmed, hides her face in her moist hands. Oreus listens, immobile, and looks at her with so much tenderness that the little Ligurian feels reassured. She goes on:

"Now that I've brought the news, like the traveling dove, I'll go. You'll never see me again, nor anyone..." Then taking the handsome old man's hands: "Yes, Master, I know that Orea is going to marry Hellas. For pity's sake, don't tell your daughter what my emotional heart has confided to you. I'd die of shame!"

But Glania feels her strength diminishing. And as if her breast were exhausted by that heated confidence, she lets her head fall back and closes her eyes.

Gently, Oreus stands up and places a cloak over the young barbarian. Then, withdrawing with muffled footsteps, he lifts a curtain and calls Orea.

"Here, my daughter, is a soul of light. With the ignorance of a wild bird, she's worth a thousand times more than me, or Hellas, or even you. The virgin breath of the gods palpitates within her. Better than us, better than anyone, she has found the secret of joy, which is to love for love's sake, to love recklessly, to love as one breathes, without desiring, without hoping, without comprehending..."

In a low voice, at the back of the room, in order not to disturb the Ligurian's sleep, Oreus repeats to Orea the young woman's amorous confidences, but without mentioning the danger to Hellas.

Orea remains pensive for a moment, and her anxious eyes interrogate the calm eyes of the old man.

"Father, will you grant me what I'm about to ask?"

"I grant all your wishes in advance...."

"Well, I want to keep that little Barbarian with me..."

"Oh, my child," Oreus exclaims, agitated by an ill-dissimulated emotion, "here you are, by that spontaneous gesture, almost as sublime as Glania herself."

So saying, Oreus withdraws, after having embraced his daughter tenderly, while Orea, advancing as far as the bed where the child is lying, kneels down and murmurs prayers.

"What's the matter?" asks Glania, waking up from her light sleep and seeing Orea in tears beside her. "You, so noble and so strong, weep like me?"

Surprised, Orea stands up. Pressing the hand of the little Barbarian, she says: "Little Barbarian, would you like to become my sister and live here, far from the city where your wild soul is beset by turbulence?"

"Me? But can I? If you knew...!"

"Yes, I know. You love him too.!

"Hellas! Your father told you? Oh, that's bad!"

"Don't hide your face, Glania, and don't feel any regret or shame. Your love springs forth fresher than the dawn, and doubtless, by your disinterested tenderness, you'll teach me the secret of happiness, which is to give without hope of return."

"But Hellas—do you think that your father can save him?"

"Save him from what?"

And Glania, speaking rapidly, reports to Orea the plot revealed on the Crimson Isle."

76

"Yes, I told your father everything, but to you, I didn't dare."

"You told my father everything? And he didn't show any emotion?"

"You father simply told me to sleep tranquilly, and that he would answer for it."

"My father never lies. And he loves Hellas like a son. But then, I believe that I divine...I divine... That noise overheard, those rumors in the night...the secrets that my father is hiding... Glania, tell me, the man who rescued you this morning, are you quite sure that you believed that you saw Hellas?"

"Doubtless I was dreaming, but I saw him."

"Well, Glania, it was him," exclaims Orea, transfigured. "Come, my child, come, my little sister, come and salute the Prince of the Empire..."

Suddenly, however, Orea stops, and murmurs: "No, let's be quiet. My father's will must remain sacred."

At the same moment, one of Orea's servants asks to speak to her mistress.

"Two men have just disembarked on the island. One looks like a giant, the other is a very young man. The giant affirms that he knows our lord Oreus well. The guard refuses to allow them to come any further. Your father is resting."

"A giant, you say? A giant has just landed on the island? Knephao, no doubt?"

"Yes, Mistress, Knephao, that's his name."

"Quickly, quickly, let him in!"

"Your father, Mistress—is it necessary to wake him?"

"No, I'll do that. In any case, I'll go see the two visitors."

And, raising the red curtain hastily, Orea advances toward the road, where the sun, already shining with its full force, is gilding the leaves of the palm-trees.

Scene VI
The Messengers

The Green Isle forms a kind of inaccessible cliff above the waves, and anyone who sees it surge forth, black and grim in the night or ruddy by day in the reflection of the sunlight on the porphyry, could easily mistake it for a desert of rock abandoned by the gods and humans. Those who have never penetrated into the island could not divine the vegetation blossoming on the vast plateau that extends on its summit. One might think that all the luxuriant and liberated flora expelled from the Atlantean isles by the work of machinery has taken refuge in this corner of land guarded by unapproachable rocks.

Amonou, who has never left the Queen of Waters and whose entire childhood has passed in the monotonous, regular and artificial landscapes of Atlantean civilization, is amazed by the verdant riches that unshackled nature displays. Very emotional, still, at having been able to disembark on the famous island, where no one can land without the consent of the master who resides there, the young neophyte forgets his tragic preoccupations momentarily and allows his enchanted eyes to wander from clumps of laurels to forests of oaks, silvery orange-trees and violet yams.

Knephao's rough voice recalls him to reality.

"Look, out there on the waves! Wouldn't one think that the debris of a broken boat?"

"A boat, indeed," Amonou replies. "I recognize the broad red and green stripes of the hull. It's come from the Crimson Isle. Poor little Ligurian! Why did I let her go?"

"Fatal destiny. Apart from the inhabitants and a few privileged individuals, no one can land on the Green Isle!"

"Could I know the dangers of the island?" groans Amonou. "I'd heard vague mention of the inaccessible circle in which the great Oreus was enclosed, but I didn't know that Nature could create a shelter so unapproachable. Dear little wild seamew! She must have perished trying to imitate the carrier-pigeons. My heart is as stricken with remorse as if her death were my doing. Oh, who can tell whether we ourselves..."

"Let's never talk about what might happen to us. And let's never regret what we've accomplished in all nobility."

At the same moment, under the grove of palm-trees, the servant who had gone to alert the master gives the two men a signal to approach.

But Knephao stops and Amonou, who is following him, sees a radiant apparition surge forth from a bend in the path.

"You, Orea? In person?"

And, bending his knee, Knephao devotedly kisses the fingers of the beautiful young woman. Amonou, to one side, struck by admiration before the irresistible prestige of the new arrival, and salutes her with a bow.

But Orea, smiling, says in her softest voice: "You're Amonou, no doubt?"

"Indeed—but how do you know…?"

"Yes, I know about our generous adventure. You went to warn Hermos and fetch Knephao. When I was told that a giant had landed on the island, I guessed that it was Knephao, and when I heard that the giant was accompanied by a young man, I thought of you. And you've come, no doubt, to speak to us about the dangers that Hellas is running?"

"Certainly," replies Knephao, stupefied. "But may I know by what magic you've divined what we've run to tell you?"

"No magic, my dear Knephao. Glania has told me everything."

"Glania!" cries Amonou, exultant with joy. "She's alive, then?"

"Yes, by a miracle she was able to escape the whirlpools in which her boat sank."

"But first, Orea, is your father on the island?"

"Yes, Knephao."

"Has he seen Glania?"

"Of course."

"The Ligurian girl talked to him about Hellas?"

"Glania has told him everything."

"What has he decided, then?"

"He's gone tranquilly to sleep."

"To sleep?" says Amonou, stupefied. "To sleep, when Hellas might perhaps be going..."

"If my father is asleep," Orea observes, softly, "it's because he judges any action vain. He always acts when necessary. In any case, here he is. In spite of my orders, he must have been alerted to your coming..."

"I guessed that it was you, my good Knephao," Oreus exclaims, as soon as he is within earshot of the group. "Your voice still vibrates as sonorously. But by the Sphinx, how you're clad, for a warrior! You resemble a stevedore from the docks. And what! You don't embrace me anymore? Must I too be metamorphosed into a valet of the sea to merit your accolade?"

And Knephao, simultaneously delighted and confused by the great man's bonhomie, throws himself into his arms. "Master, excuse me for arriving without warning you, and don't mock my disguise. If you knew how urgent it was to come to you..."

"I know! Do you believe that I can't guess your entire adventure? This handsome young man rushed this morning to inform you of the danger that Hellas was risking. He told you that a little Ligurian had departed in my direction in order to inform me personally. And, prompt in your actions, you immediately disguised yourself as an Ethiopian porter in order to embark with Amonou."

"Amazingly exact!" says Knephao, astonished.

"As for you, Amonou," Oreus continues, "I welcome in you a cherished guest of the island. I know the bounty of your soul, and you may ask me for hospitality any time."

Master," the young man asks, emotionally, "While Knephao talks to you, will you permit me to go and see the poor girl who nearly died in order to save Hellas?"

"Go, my friend; let Orea accompany you."

And while the two young people draw away toward the house, Oreus murmurs: "The delightful and eternal illusion of amour! There's Amonou, smitten with Glania, and the little Ligurian with Hellas, and Hellas with a dream; thus the desires of souls always go, pursuing without attaining...and it's doubtless the supreme happiness to launch oneself toward the inaccessible!"

"I believed, Master," Knephao observes, in a hesitant voice, "that Hellas loved Orea?"

"Him? Orea, or anyone else? May it please the gods that his heart might be touched by amour...! But we're alone now, Knephao, and you doubtless have very grave things to tell me."

Scene VII
The Head and the Arm

"So grave, Master, that I haven't hesitated to disturb your solitude in order to appeal to you for help. But before anything else, do you know about the peril that threatens Hellas?"

"Glania has told me everything."

"Is it too late?"

"Friend," says Oreus, softly, "would you see me as calm if I thought Hellas had been defeated? My greatest weakness consists of loving that adorable and naughty child too much..."

"Oh, Master!"

"Well, yes, you love him to, as much and more than me. By what charm has he cajoled us? We all love him, and he loves no one."

"Don't say that, Master. He loves everyone around him."

"Everyone or no one—it's the same thing. If he even loved himself we'd know that he was an egotist—but no, not even himself. And that's one of the mysteries that I can't penetrate. What is he pursuing in his avid activity? Glory, like Hermos? No, he scorns it. Fortune, like the majority of men? He doesn't care about it. Science and wisdom? Certainly, he's studied all our secrets for a long time, but the slowness of our research exasperates him, and he would like, as one takes a city, to take by storm the enigma of the universe. What does he desire, then? Empire? Perhaps—but not the minuscule empire that seems so great to Atlantean vanity. He would need the uncontested empire of all peoples, all hearts, all souls; and of those peoples, hearts and souls, he would like to fashion one immense being as noble and handsome as him. Oh, that mad dream of unity, that's doubtless his ideal. And I wonder whether Hellas, in the meantime, might not be the most dangerous of Atlanteans, more culpable than any other of the sin of pride."

82

"May it please the gods that there might be no other crime or pride in Atlantis!"

"Well, yes, I know. In any case, if he didn't possess a noble soul, he wouldn't have enchained us with his prestige. And will the people, without knowing why, demand his return? There is in Hellas a kind of superior fatality. Has he come to magnify or to doom the world? What does it matter? He has come; let destiny be accomplished. But reassure yourself, Knephao, he's alive, and will soon return to the heart of the Empire."

"Master, if he's alive, tell me the secret of his retreat, for it's necessary that I go to join him in order to hasten his return to Atlantis. Great angers menace the Holy Terrace, and the Empire itself might crumble if Hellas and you don't come to our aid."

Knephao then recounts to Oreus the events of the previous day.

"You can take it for granted," added the Egyptian, "that the enemies of Hellas who have become those of Hermos—they were his already—have not accepted the decision of destiny without anger or revolt. During the night the bitter genius of Mellena has revived the hopes of our enemies. That implacable woman convened the dispersed partisans of Guitche in her home, and has rendered them the ardor of the struggle. She has affirmed the death of Hellas; she has demonstrated that Hermos can be accused of lying and sacrilege, and that Guitche's party can easily reconquer power.

"These are the projects that she has formed for today. At five o'clock in the afternoon, the Festival of the Waters commences. All the fleets of Atlantis, in accordance with custom, are due to parade slowly around the seven peninsulas, decked with flags and decorated with flowers. The sacred vessel of the Empire will emerge from the Palace of the Waters and, manned by the Prince of Apostles, will receive the homage of the entire fleet. Now, as you know, Hellas having taken with him all the Ligurian, Iberian and Gaelic sailors, the only fleet that remain in Atlantis is composed of Aztecs and Guatchos.

All of them are devoted to Mellena and Guitche, who have distributed gold and silver in profusion to them this morning.

"As soon as the festival opens, therefore, a carrier-pigeon, cleverly launched, will bring the announcement of the defeat and death of Hellas. And, profiting from the disturbance sown among the people, the friends of Guitche will proclaim the fall of Hermos. They will have him arrested in mid-harbor by the Aztec sailors. Now, I've persuaded Hermos not to quit the city and to take refuge on the Holy Terrace, but you know what price the Atlanteans attach to the Festival of the Waters, and never, after his election, has a Prince of Apostles disdained to appear on the imperial galley. So, this evening, Hermos will be the first to fail in that tradition, and I leave you to imagine the surprise of the people. Oh, Oreus out of pity for Atlantis, out of affection for your disciples, save us, and save the City."

"Friend," says Oreus, mastering his emotion, "ten men like you could save a crumbling empire, if anything could still save what destiny has marked. It has come sooner than I thought, the time when the passions of Atlantis are bound to collide in an inevitable conflict."

"What, Oreus! You're despairing?"

"Let's not argue, let's act. It's necessary that today, everything returns to order, or the genius of Mellena will prevail over ours. Terrible and fatal woman! She incarnates all the old spirit of the red race, and perhaps she believes she's right. Return immediately to Atlantis, therefore, Knephao. I'll indicate to you, to the south of the city, on the flank of the mountain, an inlet where your boat can land without danger. From there, you'll go to Hermos. Let him not move! When the time comes to bring out the sacred vessel of the Empire, someone will be found to man it…me or another."

"Hellas, Master? Will it be Hellas?"

"Don't ask me anymore, Knephao. Have confidence, and go. Go and rejoin Amonou, and both of you, depart quickly! The hours, today, are worth future centuries for the destiny of the Empire."

"Thank you, Master."

And, hastening to Oreus' dwelling, Knephao looks for Amonou in order to return with him to the city.

"Poor Atlantis," murmurs Oreus, left alone, "already dying of her own vices. Permit, O Unknown God, that we will not arrive too late to cure her!"

Scene VIII
Hellas

On the threshold of the house, pale and frail, the young Ligurian appears, on Orea's arm, followed by Amonou. She advances into the warm sunlight and breathes deeply of the air embalmed with strong perfumes. At the corner of a path, however, they meet Knephao, still greatly agitated after his conversation with the Master.

"What's the matter, Knephao?" demands Amonou. "You seem preoccupied."

"Friend," the Egyptian replies, "forgive me for taking you away in haste; we must return to Atlantis."

"Already!" modulates Glania, with a moue full of an irresistible charm. "You want to leave already, Knephao, after hardly having seen me?"

Knephao too would far rather remain in the warm and restful atmosphere, but Oreus' last words are ringing in his ears.

"Come on, Amonou, it's necessary that we go make sure of the salvation of Hellas."

"It's for Hellas that you're quitting us!" exclaims Glania. "Then go, go quickly! Why can I not go with you in your fortunate boat?"

"Yes, go," adds Orea, in a calm voice. "It's necessary to save the destiny of Atlantis."

"How she loves him!" sighs Amonou.

"Yes, how they both love him," Knephao concludes.

And, as they pass Oreus again, the two men stop to salute him once more. But the sage, in spite of his habitual serenity, seems so eager to see them draw away that the giant hastens toward the shore.

Fortunately, thinks Oreus, following them with his eyes, *they have not seen him.*

And slipping sideways into a shady path, Oreus marches at a rapid pace toward a rock overlooking the sea, where a man is standing with his arms folded and his back turned to the island, contemplating immense Atlantis in the distance.

"Hellas! Hellas! What are you doing?" demands the old man.

The man turns round abruptly, recognizes Oreus and exclaims: "You, Master! What joy! But also, what a surprise! I thought you had gone far away and I was searching in the air for the wings of your…"

"Speak quietly! Don't stay on the cliff. I don't want anyone to see you or hear you. And above all don't pronounce aloud the word that might doom us or prevent us from saving Atlantis.

"What vain dread is agitating you, Master? Who, then, could suspect my presence in this place?"

"Who? Look."

And Oreus indicates to Hellas, on the meager waves, a boat that two men are directing, by the force of oars, toward the south of Atlantic.

"That boat and those two men? They've just been here?"

"Here, indeed."

"And you've sent them to Atlantis?"

"No, they're returning there."

"You receive strangers, then? What about your secrets, Master?"

"The strangers I received didn't come for me or for my secrets, my dear Hellas. Their hearts are too pure to seek to comprehend the enigmas of the world. They have no other desire than to save someone."

"Heroes, then? There are still some left?"

"Yes, my son, there still are, and that's why I preserved you, yesterday, from the most frightful of crimes. Do you know for whom those two men out there landed on the Green Isle?"

"I don't know."

"For you."

"For me! They know of my return to the isle, then?"

"No, they don't know that. And that's exactly why they came to beg me to save you. They believe you're in danger, on the waves of Gades."

"Who are they, then?"

"Knephao..."

"Knephao! He hasn't forgotten me then! And the other?"

"Amonou, your young relative, still an adolescent, unknown to all a few days ago, and who, by his present virile manifestation was able yesterday to reveal himself noble and handsome."

"Recount, Master, the recent events in the City. There are at least two generous hearts there, then?"

"More than you believe, Hellas, and perhaps even more than I believe myself. Hermos for example, the handsome young man with the harmonious songs, whom you supposed to be indifferent and vain, smitten only with appearances, and whom the envious called your rival, well, do you know what he has done? He has thrown himself into the most perilous action for you. He has risked death to keep the Empire for you."

"In truth? Are you not deluded?"

"Hellas!" snaps Oreus, gazing at the young man severely. And in rapid and precise words, he repeats Knephao's story to Hellas.

As he speaks, the face of Hellas, ordinarily handsome, is transfigured to become radiant, and the young man looks at the old man with an emotion that gradually rises from the heart to the eyes, making ill-contained tears tremble on his eyelids.

"Oh, Master, let me beg your pardon for the impulse of anger that made you doubt me. What! So many individuals who remain capable of bravery and devotion, whom I wanted to annihilate yesterday? How I must have made you suffer, Oreus, for a few moments! My Master! My Father!"

"Weep, my son, weep; your tears will wash away all the evil pride that remained in your soul. Oh, yes, you frightened me yesterday; I thought I saw overflowing from you all the tumultuous passions of men, and I confess that I was afraid that my love had engendered a monster. Now, the monster is becoming tender; he is becoming humanized, and, purified by regrets, magnified by voluntary humiliation, he will become a hero and a genius again. Now, my son, come; there are two beings here that your presence will fill with joy. Let's go join them."

"Isn't it appropriate that no one, until his evening, learns about my return?"

"No one? Who, then, this morning at dawn, was prowling around my dwelling?"

"Me, I confess. Knowing that the entire island was asleep, I took a walk along the cliff his morning."

"I'm not complaining at all, since, thanks to that fortunate fault, you saved from death the most charming creature to which the white race ever gave birth. But let's be quiet. I can hear footfalls. Someone's coming over there on the path. Go back into your isolated pavilion for a while. I'll go warn Orea and the little Barbarian of your coming."

Scene IX
Father and Daughter

"What are you doing, Father?" asks Orea, as soon as she sees Oreus. "What glad news has transfigured you? Your eyes are radiant!"

"Good news, indeed. Someone has just arrived on the island."

"Hellas, no doubt?"

"Truly, you divine marvelously. What, no more emotion?"

"Why be emotional? I know that Hellas slept on the island. It was him, this morning, who saved Glania. Dare to say that I'm mistaken."

Oreus remains silent.

"Oh, father, my good father, why hide something from me? You wanted to save Hellas and you brought him here in your *Alerion*, didn't you? And you did it out of love for me. Except that, once the act was accomplished, you regretted it."

"Terrible little seer!"

"Listen Father, you regretted it, last night, and I divined, this morning, by your sadness, that an anxiety must have alarmed you."

"Dear heart! Forgive me for having hidden something from you."

"It seemed, this morning, didn't it, that Hellas didn't merit our devotion, the devotion of both of us?"

"Yes, I thought so. But now I've recovered all my confidence. We can love him."

"I never doubted that, Father. And for my part, I've never ceased to have an ardent tenderness for him. But is he capable of being moved by the love of a woman? Until today, I still had, I confess, very excusable feminine weaknesses. I suffered in silence for having given all my soul to that vertiginous soul, incessantly in flight toward a new horizon. Now, today, wisdom has returned to me. That naïve child that the gods have brought, has taught me more in a few minutes than all your most inspired science in my entire life. Glania, truly, is the most inspired of us all. Dear child, who has given herself entirely without even suspecting that anything might be rendered to her in exchange. How she has understood the secret of happiness!"

"Mistrust yourself, my Orea, mistrust the intoxication of the sublime. One sometimes falls therefrom, permanently injured.

"What does suffering mater, at those heights? But let's not talk any more about love and dolor. The sun is radiant. The isle is all embalmed by its roses, the sea is resplendent with the reflected sky; in the distance, Atlantis in fête will give itself body and soul, this evening, to its returned hero. Come, Father, let's both chase away our old cares, to blossom in today's joy."

"All would be well, my daughter, if I were sure of three things: your happiness, Hellas' patience and the security of Atlantis. But tomorrow, I fear, you'll recommence suffering in silence; tomorrow, Hellas will depart again for some distant Colchis; tomorrow, in Atlantis, passions risen again will once again allow the threat of an imminent fall to hang over the Empire. And to think that one thing alone might suffice to prevent all three dangers!"

"What, Father?"

"Quite simply that you are able to make Hellas love you, that he marries you, that he settles his errant nature here, and that, under the soothing influence of your love, he is able to raise himself up, without dangerous leaps, toward the serenity of creators. To wait for Hellas to come to you is to demand the impossible. It's up to you to go to him. There are necessary sacrifices."

"What sacrifices, since I love him? But will he love me enough to understand me?"

"Yes, he will love you, or at least he will allow himself to be loved and will submit to your charm. It's necessary that the daughter of Oreus is able to keep Hellas in Atlantis and tame the force that is presently the only one capable of saving the Empire. I'm too old, Hermos is still without authority, Knephao an admirable instrument. It needs Hellas. Now, Hellas, without our fortunate influence, remains a worse danger than all the others. Have not his mad and heroic conquests intoxicated the pride of Atlantis to the point of vertigo? Have not his reckless exploits stimulated the passions of the crowd? And only yesterday, did I not fear the most terrible peril that the Queen of the Waters has ever run?"

"Yesterday, Father?"

"Yes, yesterday, at the very hour when we were returning through the air, and the *Alerion*, with her wings fully deployed, was traversing the broad arm of the sea that separates Atlantis from Iberia, I know not what vertigo gripped Hellas. Suddenly, he cried: 'Accursed city! Sewer of the world! To think that it would require such a little thing to destroy you!'

"And before I had time to recover from my surprise, he had already taken over the direction of the aerial vessel, and we were heading at top speed for the Mountain of Manou, as if our bird were about to swoop down upon the City. 'Are you mad, Hellas?' I said to him.

"'No, Master,' he replied, 'let me be, I'm saving the world.'

"'Save it how?'

"'By suppressing the old City of crime, the obstacle or corruption of civilizations that ought to grow!'

"And, so saying, he took in his hands the terrible cylinders of solid air, one alone of which, thrown into the waves from the height of the sky, would suffice to raise the sea up in a cyclone; and he was getting ready to carry out his insensate threat when I had time to leap upon him, to embrace him feverishly and hold his impotent body in my arms; then, taking the tiller in my turn I set a course abruptly southwards, directing our course away from Atlantis."

"Oh, Father, how you must have suffered!"

"Yes, especially to see the Hellas that I had before me: lips pale, eyes malevolent, brow furrowed, he was no longer the radiant hero whose gaze subjugated stormy crowds. One sensed that for a minute, he had had the vertiginous intoxication of believing himself a god, and he looked at me with rancor, cursing me for having stopped his arm. And I wondered whether my new invention might not bring about the doom rather than the salvation of the City.

"This morning, finally, repentance has shaken Hellas' heart, and I saw revealed in him a tenderness that I had not suspected, I confess. That is why, my daughter, it is necessary that Hellas remains with you. The two of you might continue my work, maintain my secret discoveries and save Atlantis from herself and others. Look, here he is coming toward us. Courage."

Scene X
Two Souls

"Orea!"

"Hellas!"

And the two young people, surprised by their sudden encounter, too sudden for either one of them to contain their spontaneous joy, embrace tenderly.

"Where are you going, Father?" asks Orea, anxiously, seeing the old man withdrawing.

"What need have you of my presence" says the old man, darting a tender and joyful glance toward Hellas. "Have you not a thousand things to tell one another after such a long absence? I'll go look for the young Ligurian."

"Oh, wicked father," said Orea, frightened to find herself alone with Hellas.

But Hellas does not divine the obscure drama that is playing in the young woman's heart.

"How changed you are, my dear Orea! You weren't yet the tall and strong young woman that I salute today when I left the Queen City. I would then have asked your father to take you away to the new world. While now...but what's the point of talking about my plans?"

Orea, upset, no longer has the strength to hide her emotion. She takes the young man's hand and, pressing it in her own burning hands: "Hellas, what's the point of hiding it from you any longer, since my entire life is attached to you? Yes, since your departure, day by day, night by night, I've counted your absence and waited...for now, since forever and for forever, Hellas..."

Then, in a low voice, she concludes: "I love you."

And, as if confused by the word she has pronounced, she adds: "Come closer, here, sit on this bench, and let me put my head on your shoulder. What futility there is in talking about my love, when your thoughts are shadowed by sadness. For my love is a vain and personal thing, whereas your dolor, Hellas, must have for a cause the very fate of the world...."

And, raising her face, moistened by tears, with a abrupt movement, Orea looks at Hellas fixedly, full in the eyes. "See, my big brother, I've become the daughter of Oreus again, and the companion of your youth. Talk to me, Hellas, as one soul to another...

"Yes, as one soul to another, if my soul in torment were worth as much as your serene soul. Oh, let me look at you Orea. How beautiful you are! What a divine genius I contemplate in your eyes! Insensate! You've loved me, you say, for a long time, and I've passed over such an amour like those black Barbarians of Libya who march over fields full of gold and die in poverty! How many years lost for my happiness, and also for my glory, and perhaps, O gods, for the splendor of the universe!"

"What do you mean, friend?"

"I mean, Orea, that from my enterprise in the land of the Pelasges, I've come back broken..."

At that word, Hellas stops, looks in all directions to see whether anyone is coming, pricks up his ears, and then, in a stifled voice, says: "...and defeated."

"You!"

"Speak quietly! It's something that I didn't want to say to anyone, even Oreus. Yes, defeated...since I have not accomplished my veritable project. You know that, Orea, for, while still a child, you heard me already dreaming aloud, before your father, the desires of my life. No, my goal was not to conquer for the sake of conquest, but to unify the world, in order to expel evil therefrom and to make the entire world, illuminated by the light of the Sphinx, an immense garden of concord and harmony. That is why, when young, I departed for the mysterious forests of Gaelia, the gilded shores of the Ligurians and the Tyrrhenians; that is why I wanted to become Prince of Apostles; and that is why, too confined in the heart of the Empire, I attempted recently to submit to our laws the turbulent tribes of the Pelasges and the Scythians..."

"Dear Hellas, soul too ardent, my friend! Have you truly so much of which to complain? Have you not brought the light of the Sphinx into the midst of nations unknown yesterday? Do you not have the right to the admiration of the world and the gratitude of Atlantis?"

"Admiration? Gratitude? What does it matter? If I do not esteem myself, all my victories are follies, crimes! For what good is there in winning battles if no one profits from them, either in the fatherland or in the world? Do you want to know the result of my conquests? When I submitted to the Queen of the Waters the rich lands of the Siculi, the masters of Gold wrote to me: 'Send us the product of the mines quickly.' To which the Assembly of the Literate added: 'It's said that there are beautiful white slaves there; we await them.' And the popular orators informed me that with the wheat of the fertile plains the host of idlers for whom labor seems a torture could be nourished more easily.

"If, on the other hand, I consider the destiny of the conquered Barbarians, I sense a future even more redoubtable. We have awakened in them the desire and the taste for vaster wars. I can already see them ready to arm themselves, Pelasges against Ligurians, Tyrrhenians against Siculi, Armoricans against Gaels. Is that, then, the evil end to which centuries of heroism, science and genius have led? Orea, my sister, the only person in the world capable of comprehending and sharing my pain, am I not defeated?"

"My beloved, dolor ennobles you more than all your victories. But be careful not to irritate against you the superior Spirits that, since your cradle, have inspired you and prepared you for a high destiny. To make the world a garden of harmony, only to form a single people down here, happy, singing and laughing in a land of delight, with joy, peace and love everywhere—oh, what a beautiful dream! But such a dream is developed against the divine will, and the suffering of the earth must doubtless serve for a higher purpose of the Unknown God."

"Oh, what does an earth condemned to evil matter to me? What does an Empire corrupted by passions mean to me? What does a victory whose intoxication perpetuates human vices mean to me? What is the point of a presentiment of perfect beauty, if we can only accomplish ugliness?"

"Oh, unhappy friend, conclude, then: 'What is the point of being a man, since gods exist?'"

"Have I said that?" stammers Hellas, troubled.

"You haven't said it, but you think it, Hellas, and that's why I'm stopping you. For a pride in good exists that is as dangerous as a pride in evil. To want to dominate the world in order to impose an impossible happiness on it; to believe that one can snatch the human race from the sentence of dolor and death, is sublime folly and magnificent disobedience! Remember the words written under the claws of the Sphinx:

You will no longer be human
You will not be divine....

"And know, my beloved, that you have almost ceased to be human, but a god you will never be!"

"If you wanted, however, my dream would become a reality."

"Insatiable dreamer!"

"Yes, if you wanted to go with me to the still-new countries where the white race is increasing, the two of us could transform the young world. Oh, if you knew what generous peoples are forming out there for the future of the world! It's necessary, Orea, to conquer that new empire without hatred; it requires a solar apostolate, an apostolate of mildness and bounty, and I am no longer pure enough to accomplish it. No man in Atlantis, moreover, except your father, could attempt such an endeavor. But a woman might—and that woman is you."

"Me, Hellas? And leave my father? And cease, with you, to watch over the destiny of Atlantis?"

"What does that red Empire matter, from which there is nothing more to expect than ingratitude? It's out there, toward the Orient, that the world is rising. Come, Orea, let's depart for the young world that wants to live."

"Myself, I'm staying with those who are going to die."

"Oh, why always that word *die*?"

"Because I always think it."

"Be reassured, Orea. Atlantis won't die. It will descend slowly in the crimson of its glory. It will take centuries to lapse into dotage. A great people can only die..."

"By its own hand.

"And by its own hand, it won't kill itself. And no one in the world will kill it."

"Really?" says Orea, with a dolorous irony. "Who, then, from the heights of the air, in a marvelous machine invented by my father, only yesterday, in mid-festival, wanted to annihilate it forever?"

"Your father told you, Orea?"

"My father? Am I not his living conscience? Nothing that he thinks, nothing that he creates, nothing that he plans..."

"You know about our adventure, then?"

"I know."

"And that he saved me at the entrance to the channel of Gades at the moment when the Barbarians of Armor were about to attack my fleet?"

"I know."

"And that he lifted me into the air?"

"I know that too."

"And that we landed on the island last night, silently, while Atlantis was resounding with its mad fête?"

"I know that too..."

"Then, Orea, you know about the *Alerion* and its power?"

So saying, Hellas, his eyes gleaming with curiosity, looks deeply into Orea's eyes, as if he wanted to read a secret there reflected in the mirror of her pupils.

Calmly, the young woman sustains the hero's gaze, and says, tranquilly: "I know it. I also know what you're thinking and dare not express."

"Really?"

"You're thinking, Hellas, about the *Alerion* devouring space and bearing you with its wings, over mountains and seas, toward these new lands that your dream transforms into gardens of light."

"Well, yes, I'm thinking about that, and you've just, in precise words, formulated the desire born in my heart. Oh, dear beloved, there it is, the divine instrument of our future work! No more war, no more slow conquest through decimate peoples and crumbling ramparts; no more blood, no more death, but radiant victory, with great wing-beats and in floods of harmony. Come, Orea, we'll depart together, on the *Alerion* completed by Oreus, and the surprised peoples will see falling upon them, from the height of the heavens, as if by a miracle, wisdom, order, concord and joy."

"And Atlantis, my handsome poet—what becomes of her in our grandiose project?"

"Atlantis?" says Hellas, suddenly recalled to terrestrial realities. "Atlantis? Have you not predicted to me her imminent decline?"

"And you're abandoning it to that, you, her son?"

"Ought I, then, to immobilize my young vigor to help a weakening force, when so many new forces are surging forth out there?"

"The millenarian city is like those old men who are being slowly extinguished because all their inner sources of energy are exhausted. What would you say to me, my beloved, if, seeing my glorious father weakened by age, I separated myself from him, under the pretext that he was going to die? To desert the beside of a dying man that one can save is a crime as great as taking away his life."

"It's not the same thing, Orea."

"It's exactly the same thing, Hellas. Atlantis is the mother of us all, and, although weakened, perhaps dying, we owe her all our breath."

And as Hellas shakes his head slowly and silently, Orea falls to her knees and takes him by the hands.

"See, my hero, I'm imploring you. If you quit Atlantis, if you renounce defending her, if you abandon her to her dolorous convulsions, no other living man can cure her and, near or distant, her end will come. You go away to conquer a new empire, then. But I'll stay with my saddened father, near agonizing Atlantis. With the last heroes, I'll attempt the supreme salvation and beg the gods to accomplish a miracle."

"Orea, I beg you!"

"But if you want to remain among us; if you want to re-animate the people who admire you and are appealing to you; if you want to reestablish the laws and dissipate he conspiracies of the rich; if you want, in sum, to devote to the revival of Atlantis all of your brain and all of our heart, than I retain the hope that our city will regain its prestige, and you will see me by your side, the most submissive of wives and the most affectionate of lovers."

"But in sum, Orea, what is it necessary to do?"

"This very evening, return to Atlantis; take back the power that Hermos is keeping for you and that is being contested; assemble around you the indecisive youth who lack a powerful leader; reaffirm with regard to the Barbarians the authority of the Queen City; become the true Prince of the Empire again."

"Is it not too late?"

"No, no," exults Orea. "It is never too late for a genius like yours. The people, with a single surge, will render you all their confidence, and Knephao his devoted soldiers. Your enemies, surprised, will only have time to prepare a shameful retreat. Tomorrow, perhaps this evening, your victorious Ligurians will bring you the support of their faithful fleet. And the Mother, the great Mother, will be saved."

"Adieu, then," said Hellas, pensively. "Adieu, beautiful new lands, blond valleys of the Pelasgian terrains, flowery isles of the archipelago, forests in which dense-crowned oaks render mysterious oracles to the sound of the wind, shores where fishermen recount marvels, nascent cities where everything is strength and youth: lands of the Orient, lands of the aurora where I wanted to leave my name, adieu! I am attached to the old world." Then, turning to Orea: "Well, so be it. Like you, I'll stay with those who are going to die."

But Orea is transfigured. "No, beloved, they're no longer going to die, now; they're going to revive! In a short time, the Queen City will have reconquered all its antique glory, and when your work here is consolidated, then, if you wish, we'll fly toward the new world on the *Alerion*, with wings outspread."

"Oh, adored one!" cries Hellas, in a movement of overflowing joy. And, taking Orea in his arms: "Oh, my love!"

Letting her head fall on to the hero's breast, however, Orea is weeping copiously.

"Forgive me, my love, forgive my weakness if sobs afflict me. But for a long time my heart has been beating against itself, and I have suffered so much from resisting you, my beloved!"

"What!" objects Hellas, smiling. "The daughter of Oreus might have lost all heroism?"

"The daughter of Oreus loves Hellas, and she is a woman."

Scene XI
The Vessel of the Empire

The Palace of the Waters rises up facing the occident, at the extremity of the broad channel that penetrates the Queen City and serves as the central port of the commerce of Atlantis.

At low tide, the excursion boats remain moored against the monumental steps of a basalt stairway that descends in a gentle slope toward the sea. But at high tide the waves sometimes come to lick the flagstones of the square. Broadening out all the way to the bay, the great channel extends like the mouth of a river, and on its two banks, sumptuous palaces and prosperous houses mirror their superimposed columns in the tremulous waters.

Once, the channel formed the estuary of the Gadire River, which flowed into the Atlantic Ocean at the very place where the distant ancestors established the first port of Atlantis, but the course of the river was diverted a long time ago; and the waters of the Gadire now aliment the immense lake that dominates the city. Ordinarily, the two banks of the channel are noisy with busy merchants and vessels bringing products from all over the world, but today, the closed warehouses are decked with flowers, garlands and banners. For at the foot of the Palace of the Waters, on the broad esplanade, the Prince of Apostles is due to appear, clad in a white cloak with metallic embroideries, escorted by the watchmen of Atlantis, in order to receive the investiture of the sea. And the Vessel of the Empire, with inflated crimson sails and guided by a thousand gilded oars, will go forth in all its glory to collect the master of the world.

People are calling to one another loudly in all directions. The news, in fact, has spread from peninsula to peninsula that the disgrace of Hermos is going to be publicly proclaimed.

"Will he come?" everyone is asking, curiously.

"He has to come," affirm people fond of tumult. "After all, he's the Prince of the Empire."

"No, he won't come," reply the pacific, "since it's planned to have him seized by the Aztec fleet."

"Well, too bad—he'll fight. One isn't Prince in order to remain tranquil."

"Yes, but who'll pay the expenses of that fight? Us, always us, poor merchants, eternal victims of civic troubles."

"Our affairs are already going badly."

"And there's talk of inflicting new taxes on us."

"Taxes on us, the masters of the world?"

"It's said that the Toltecs and the Aztecs no longer want to pay their tributes."

"And Mellena is supporting them."

"That Mellena, what an evil genius!"

"If only Hellas could return."

"Hellas? May the gods protect him! His death is being announced everywhere..."

"We no longer have anyone but Hermos: great courage but feeble prestige."

"He's right to remain on the Holy Terrace. But look out! Here comes the Vessel of the Empire, all decked out in crimson and gold."

"What audacity! Mellena has dared to mount the imperial galley herself!"

"And Guitche has taken the place of the Master of the Waters!"

"Look at that little boat dancing in the midst of the great ships," observes the bourgeois Azaes.

"Beggars, one might think. They're going to be crushed between two ships."

"Bah! Think about it! Those people slither like serpents Isn't that the little Ligurian, the one who plays the cithara in the squares? She's even holding the oars. And who's that at the tiller? Some other beggar, doubtless. His face is covered by a big cloak."

The moment is approaching, however, when the Prince of the Empire ought to advance to the edge of the channel and climb into the vessel for the betrothal to the sea, Queen of the World. What will happen? Will Hermos come down in response to Guitche's summons? Will he dare to brave the Aztec fleet? On the Square of the Empire, which overlooks the city, Knephao's soldiers can be seen lined up, and the chief of the cohorts can be seen, impassive on a large horse.

The hour sounds, however, and Guitche advances. He gives the floor to Belkis, the orator of the sailors.

"Atlanteans!" cried Belkis, in a loud voice. "In the name of the City, in the name of the people, I invite the Prince of the Empire to take his place on the Imperial Vessel..."

Only a long murmur of the crowd responds to Belkis' invitation.

"You see, Atlanteans, that those who call themselves your protectors disdain to appear at your popular festivals. Or rather, no veritable Prince of the Empire exists. The one who was named yesterday is nothing but an impostor, whose disgrace I proclaim in your name, since he refuses to come into our midst.

Cries rise up from the crowd.

"Long live Hermos!" clamor some. "Down with Mellena!"

"Long live Guitche!" responds the entire fleet.

"Look over there," observes Azaes to his neighbor, the merchant. "What is the beggar in the little boat doing? He's taking advantage of the general inattention to cling on to the flank of the Vessel of the Empire and scale it."

"Shut up!" replies the other. "What does it matter to us? Can he throw Guitche into the sea?"

Again for the sake of formality, Belkis advances to the prow of the Imperial Vessel.

"Atlanteans, one last time I summon the Prince of the Empire. Let him show himself, and we will acclaim him!"

"Yes," affirms the entire fleet. "We will acclaim him!"

"Acclaim me, then," says a man, bounding suddenly in front of Belkis.

"The beggar!" cries Azaes. "He's a madman!"

But the beggar removes his black cloak, throws back the hood covering his face, and appears in an embroidered tunic, his head circled by a crown of laurels, and from the crowd, a sudden cry springs forth toward the heavens, covering any other tumult in the city.

"Hellas!"

Scene XII
The Master of the Waters

From the central port the cry rises up to the seven Terraces, and is reverberated over the waters from boat to boat by the millions of voices of an entire people, causing a clamor of surprise and delight to roll through the air.

"Hellas has returned!"

"Hellas is in the port!"

"Long live Hellas!"

The crowd summons the crowd, and from all points of the City, disorderly mobs run through the streets or the squares in the vicinity of the port. Similarly, the indolent boats wandering in the vast bay hasten toward the great channel, where an innumerable flotilla is soon swarming, with sails of all colors. Those boats, pressing against one another, obstruct the great harbor to such an extent that the heavy vessels of the Aztec fleet, surrounded on all sides, are now immobilized, in the impossibility of joining the imperial galley.

Guitche's friends, surprised and disconcerted, cannot attempt to resist the sudden and triumphant Hellas without danger to themselves.

He, meanwhile, standing in the prow of the ship, his arms folded and his head high, gazes at the thousands upon thousands of heads accumulated around him, and he recalls the sad day on which, before those same Atlanteans, he went away, haughty and disgusted with power, in order to conquer a younger and more robust empire far away.

Sick people, Hellas thinks, *sometimes acclaiming the good and sometimes the wicked, ready to expel tomorrow those they exalted yesterday, people of drunken slaves, are you really my people?*

And while the rumble of voices fills the air, the hero feels the muted desire within him to crush that crowd beneath a few words of reproach and scorn; but so spontaneous, so

106

overflowing and so sincere does the enthusiasm seem that Hellas gradually feels himself carried away by the wind that is filling the metropolis.

And Orea's words repeat in his memory. Then he thinks about the good, courageous and just individuals who remain in Atlantis, those whose assembled energies might suffice to save the city.

Now, an enthusiastic clamor bursts forth in the middle of the Square of the Waters, covering all the other surrounding noises. The name of Knephao sings from a thousand throats, and with a tumultuous undulation, the giant Egyptian appears, on horseback, coming to meet his prince and friend.

At that sight, Hellas, completely calmed, feels reborn within himself all the love that he once nourished for the glorious City and with a broad gesture, his eyes radiant with joy, he makes a sign to the people to observe silence.

"Citizens of Atlantis, here I am before you, Hellas, your elected Prince; the man whose place no one could occupy, so long as he has not been unworthy of you. Do you find me still worthy to govern you?"

"Yes! Yes!" rumbles a human storm, which swells as it spreads from square to square.

"You were not expecting me, no doubt? You believed that I was still fighting in the brushwood of unknown peoples? Well, no. Here I am among you, victorious; and tomorrow, perhaps this evening, my great fleet will arrive in sight of the bay, bringing you the tributes of new nations and the oaths of our young colonies."

"Glory! Glory!" howl the citizens standing in boats, or hoisting themselves into the rigging, at those words.

"Glory and wealth for Atlantis!"

"I desire," Hellas continues, "that no memory of evil hours comes to trouble your joy. May Atlantis live eternally…"

"Eternally!" the crowd continues.

"…and may all hatred cease in the heart of her sons!" He addresses the giant, who has already dismounted in the Square of the Waters. "You, Knephao, I thank for having watched over the City that loves you, and which you love. Tell Hermos, our great poet, my beloved brother, that I praise him for having, before my return, sacrificed his repose to the protection of the Holy Terrace. And all of you, known and unknown friends, all of you who, during my absence, have not forgotten that I was fighting for you, I salute you."

"Salutations to you, Hellas," replies Knephao.

"To you!" echo the crowds.

Then, turning to the anxious group of his enemies. Hellas, in a loud and clear voice, lets fall the words:

"If, in the torments of my public life, I have been able to stir up a few hatreds around me, I beg pardon for that of those who, perhaps not without reason, have attempted to keep me away."

Then, addressing the people assembled on the shore again: "Who among you, Atlanteans, judges me unworthy of the Empire?"

"No one! No one!" vociferates a unanimous clamor.

"In that case, Atlanteans, allow me to leave you to your rejoicing, and, having proclaimed the immortal union of the Queen City and the Sovereign Sea, let me return to my lodgings in peace."

So saying, Hellas ordered Belkis, the orator of the sailors, to bring the vessel to shore, and, greeted by the jubilation of the people, he finally sets foot on the soil of the flag-decked city. Stupefied, Guitche's friends obey all his orders; Belkis, first and foremost, more submissive than a slave, seems to be attempting to anticipate the slightest desire of the hero.

"How does he come to be here?" murmurs Barkas to Guitche.

"I'm utterly at a loss," replies the Master of Gold. "Where did he come from? How? Did he fall from the sky?"

"Perhaps," says Moussor, the orator of the merchants. And, assuming an expression both knowing and mysterious, he puts a finger over his lips and whispers: "Silence. I'll tell you that later."

"In any case," mutters Barkas, "how did our guards let him enter the harbor?"

"Doubtless disguised as a simple sailor. Wasn't he in the boat where the Ligurian was singing?"

"Perhaps, but silence. People are coming aboard the ship."

"Where is Mellena hiding?" asks Guitche. "She can no longer be seen among us. Is she afraid of the terrible Hellas?"

"Mellena?" Barkas replies. "While the great actor was throwing his futile words to the winds, she took advantage of the general inattention to descend into a boat and quit the harbor."

"Admirable woman!" says Moussor. "While we hesitate and jabber, she acts!"

"Fortunately," said Barkas, "We have her with us. She will save us."

"Let's hope so!"

Scene XIII
In the Palace of the Waters

Meanwhile, Hellas, as he passes from the ship to the shore, is lifted up by a hundred enthusiastic arms and borne away on the shoulders of the people toward the Palace of the Waters.

"Hellas! Here you are at last!" cries Knephao, who is waiting on the threshold. "Thank the gods! Atlantis no longer has anything to fear."

"Thanks to you, Knephao. And Hermos?"

"He's guarding the Holy Terrace with a few young Apostles and the entire College of Hierophants."

"Dear Hermos! I bless the delay that has permitted me to know his valor. But you, Knephao, what do we not owe to you?"

"My métier, Hellas, is to risk death—but it is not that of Hermos, and he did so without hesitation."

"The blood of a hero!"

"Heroism itself. I already experienced that in Egypt. But here's Amonou, his faithful friend, who contributed yesterday to the thwarting of our enemies."

"Salutations to you, Hellas," says Amonou, approaching the Prince of the Empire. "Although you don't know me…"

"I know you, Amonou, and I know your deeds…Oreus has told me everything," Hellas murmurs into the ear of the young man as he shakes his hand with warmth.

"Oreus?" said Amonou, stupefied. "You've come from the Green Isle?"

"The Green Isle, indeed."

"Then it was you, this morning, who saved..."

"The little Ligurian? How do you know that?"

"She told us—Orea and me. She seemed certain that she had recognized you. She murmured your name in her delirium."

"What delirium?"

"Don't you know that she's slightly wounded and was suffering from a fever this morning?"

"Her? Impossible. She's just accompanied me in a boat as far as the harbor. If you knew with what vigor she plied the oars!"

"How did Oreus permit…?"

"That's why Oreus and Orea tried so hard to prevent her from leaving with me! But if you had seen, my friends, how she insisted! 'No, no,' she said, 'no one but me will be able to take him! I'm the daughter of a Ligurian sailor and I can row for an entire day without tiring. Alone, Hellas can't escape his enemies' spies. With me, he'll be taken for a vagabond, a cithara player…' And she seemed so lively, so alert, so happy to serve as my accomplice, that I gave in. And in truth, I declare that without her, I'd never have reached the Vessel of the Empire."

"Dear Glania!" says Knephao.

"Poor little Ligurian!" murmurs Amonou. And, without even taking the trouble to salute Hellas or Knephao, he leaves the Palace and heads in haste toward the sea.

"Brave young man!" says Hellas. "He forgets everything—the fête, the feasts, his legitimate glory, in order to go to the aid of a blue-eyes Barbarian. Do you think, Knephao, that he'll find the courageous young woman?"

"I believe so, Hellas. Firstly because he has the valor and perseverance of a generous soul, and secondly because he's in love…"

"He loves her?"

"Perhaps without knowing it.

"Well, Knephao, let's find a recompense for both of them. Let's unite them."

"I fear that might be impossible."

"Why?"

"She loves someone else."

"Really? She seems so pure!"

"Very pure, certainly, for she loves with a virginal candor someone who doesn't love her, and will never love her."

"In truth, Knephao, can one love eternally someone who does not love in return?"

"Yes," murmurs the giant, with a sigh that he dissimulates. "Yes, one can, Hellas."

But Hellas does not see the strange thoughtfulness into which the giant has just fallen. In fact, the Apostle, drawn away himself by a distant reverie, can hear the voice of Orea warm in his ear, ardent with a noble amour and vibrant with sublime promises. Then, the oath that he has made to save Atlantis from menacing disorders returns to his mind, and his intelligence, with rapid wings, chases away personal preoccupations and passes in a single surge to the interests of the City.

"Let's go, Knephao, time is pressing. Can you send word to Hermos to join us in the Palace of the Waters? It's urgent that we hold a council, concerning the affairs of the Empire."

"I'll have him summoned. It will seem natural that he should come to meet you. And then, the crowd will be swarming in the port all night. No one will be astonished to see our soldiers remain around the Palace. Thus, a good guard will watch over us."

"Why a good guard? Are you afraid, then?"

"We have everything to fear from a party exasperated by its recent disappointment. If your generosity pardons them, their hatred will not pardon you."

"Friend," says Hellas, smiling, "I bear no grudge against my adversaries. A people that abandons itself to absolute power, arrives at a brutalizing despotism, and agitators always make themselves useful to Princes, for they oblige them to watch over themselves and persevere in the good."

"In that case," exclaims Knephao, with a broad smile, "you can thank Mellena and her friends, for they'll oblige you to a rude perseverance!"

And the Egyptian summons one of his officers, in order to tell him to send someone to fetch Hermos.

Scene XIV
In a Boat

While Hellas harangues the crowd, Mellena, seeing the game irrevocably lost for that day, does not linger in vain on the imperial galley. So the entire crowd is acclaiming Hellas. What to do? Arrest him? Pure folly. Besides which, Hellas is still officially the Prince of the Empire and no action taken against him can have any appearance of legality. He has escaped the Armorican fleet—but how? None of the agents in Mellena's service has signaled Hellas' ships at sea. If the Ligurian fleet has disappeared in some distant disaster, an account will be demanded of its master. If he has preceded his fleet by a few days, then the triumph of Hellas will become definitive, and it will be necessary to resign oneself to it.

Oh, how the idea of defeat irritates the active woman! No, no, she will not resign herself. And while the entire city is shouting to acclaim its Prince, Mellena, without losing any time, quits the deck of the Imperial vessel and goes to a ladder at the stern, applied to the hull of the ship, by means of which she can descend to the sea and find a convenient boat.

At the foot of the ladder, there is a boat moored in which a young oarswoman, apparently of the Barbarian race, is drowsing.

Some beggar-woman, thinks Mellena. That's what I need. *She'll take me wherever I wish.* "Hey, pretty girl, will you take me in your boat?"

"Mellena!" murmurs the other. "What does she want with me?"

Suddenly, with the prompt intuition of amour, she says to herself: *If I refuse, another will be able to take her. At least I'll know where she's going. And if he's threatened, I'll go to warn him.*

So, she responds to Guitche's wife: "A woman as beautiful as you wouldn't disdain to climb into the boat of a poor Ligurian?"

"Little beggar, I have a desire to hear the songs of your savage land. Will you take me away from the harbor?"

"Wherever you like. I'll sing you a Ligurian song."

"So you know where the Golden Isle is?"

"Beyond the Crimson Isle—a long way."

"Well, it's necessary that I get there this evening. Do you feel strong enough to take me there? There'll be a rich recompense for you."

"Yes, yes," Glania replies. "I feel strong enough."

And she experiences such a desire to follow Mellena to the end, divining that this escapade conceals some menacing plan against Hellas, that she forgets the exhaustion of her strength.

And now she is rowing, rowing, gaining the open sea; already her head is spinning and she thinks she can see the sea slipping way under the boat. By means of a supreme effort, she stiffens herself, stiffens her arms, and lifts the heavy oars again—but soon it seems to her that the setting sun is dancing on the waves in vertiginous gleams, and then her dazzled gaze no longer sees anything.

Finally, she falls backward, crying: "Hellas! Hellas! Help me!"

At that name, Mellena leaps toward the young woman, and stares at her, trying in vain to recognize her.

"What are you saying? Why are you appealing to Hellas?"

But Glania cannot hear, cannot hear anything; her wide-open eyes seem to be following a spinning vision in the distance, and she murmurs between her lips: "Hellas! Hellas! I love you, and Mellena hates you!"

Then she loses consciousness.

Who, then, have I taken for a guide? Mellena wonders, throwing herself upon the young woman. *She knows Hellas,*

*and she knows me. Let's not hesitate. I'll go to the Golden Isle
alone. That way, no one will be able to betray me.*

And, lifting the frail, unconscious young woman in her
arms, she drops her silently into the water, and then, taking the
oars, draws away northwards.

Poor little Ligurian! Scarcely has she felt the water wet-
ting her face than her senses reawaken, and she finds herself
alone, lost, in the vast sea. She continues to resist for a few
strokes; then, resigned, her ears buzzing and her eyes blinded,
hearing nothing and seeing nothing, she finally abandons herself to the whirlpool of death.

But suddenly, she feels her hair grabbed by a robust
hand; then she has the impression of her body falling on to the
rough wood of a fishing-boat...

Soon afterwards, Glania comes round.

Night has already fallen. Above her head, the stars are
shining. Songs are audible, coming from the city in fête.

"I'm not dead!" she murmurs.

"No, you're alive. I've saved you. But don't move. Remain lying down in the bottom of the boat."

Glania looks around. A large fisherman's cloak is extended over her, to warm her up. Even so, she is trembling in
her wet clothes.

"Where did you come from, then, you who plucked me
from the sea?" she says.

"Don't talk," says the man. "You'll recognize me soon.
Rest. We're about to reach the harbor."

"I recognize your voice, Amonou! Always ready to save
those the other wants to destroy!"

"What other?"

"Mellena."

"It was Mellena who threw you into the sea?"

"In person."

"The evil woman!"

"And Hellas? How is he?"

"We're going to join him. He's waiting for us in the Palace of the Waters. You can tell him your adventure. We'll avenge you!"

"How did you find me?"

"I was following you."

"Why were you following me?"

"Because," says Amonou, hesitantly, "because…you love Hellas."

"Oh, thank you, thank you! I love you too, my dear savior!"

Gradually, the noise increases around the boat. The reflection of the gleams coming from the City is resplendent, forming a nimbus above the eyes of the supine young woman.

The boat stops. They touch land. And gently, like a mother, Amonou takes Glania in his arms and traverses the Square of the Waters at a run.

"Open up, open up quickly," he shouts, as he arrives at the main door of the Palace.

"No one goes in," says one of Knephao's soldiers, severely.

"I'm a friend of Hellas, and here's a woman that I've pulled out of the water. For her, if not for me, open up quickly."

"Yes, open up," replies Knephao, hearing Amonou's voice and running to met him. "What's happened? What are you carrying in your arms? A dead woman? By the Sphinx! Glania!"

"No, not dead, merely exhausted by fatigue. Quickly, fire, a soft couch and dry clothing."

And while maidservants hasten to prepare a bed for the Ligurian, and Hellas and Hermos come to join young Amonou, he reports to them in a low voice, very emotionally, the rescue he has just accomplished.

"Drowned by Mellena? But for what reason? What were they doing at sea, the two of them together?"

"I don't know yet. She could scarcely speak."

Soon, Glania, reanimated, recovers her senses and, in a faint voice, recounts to Hellas the drama in which she nearly died. Then, weary, exhausted by the day, in which she nearly sank into the Atlantic Ocean twice, the young Ligurian closes her eyes and, with one of her hands in Hellas' hands and the other in Amonou's, comforted and mournful, happy and worn out, she goes to sleep, smiling.

Around her, the people draw away quietly. Only Amonou remains and watches over her slumber.

It is dark. Outside, all Atlantis is singing. The sounds of flutes, citharas and sistrums rise from the sea.

Hellas, Hermos and Knephao converse in low voices.

"To the Golden Isle," said Hellas, pensively. "What is Mellena going to attempt there?"

"We'll know tomorrow," says Hermos.

"Let's watch and be on our guard," observes Knephao. "The others aren't disarmed."

"Yes, let's be on our guard. And may the Sphinx protect Atlantis!"

THE THIRD DAY:
THE FEAST OF GOLD

You turn yourself
The wheel of destiny...

Scene I
The Treasures of Atlantis

In spite of the fatigues of the previous day, Hellas and Hermos work together until dawn, in a high-ceilinged room in the Palace of the Waters. They examine the reports and accounts that the Hierophants of the Holy Terrace, the watchmen of Atlantis and the guardians of the treasure handed to Hermos the previous day.

"What disorder in a few months," says Hellas, scanning the sheets of papyrus.

"Who could believe, Hellas, that an empire so rich could arrive at ruination in such a short time?"

"That which it took centuries to prepare."

"And yet, when you left for the land of the Pelasges, everything seemed indestructible."

"Gilded façade, worm-eaten framework. As the prestige of Atlantis increased, the great city was rotting within. A city, this city of vertigo in which races and contrary interests collide? No, something formless and immeasurable, a frightening and turbulent society in which millions and millions of frenetic chatterers accumulate and stifle in a few square leagues of land hollowed out beneath. Oh, if people had only listened to Oreus and me; if this immense metropolis had been disengaged and new productive centers of civilization created in the

118

Occident and Orient, our power would have remained immortal..."

With those words Hellas stops, as if he were following a dream with his staring eyes, and then, suddenly, he shakes his head.

"So, Hermos, for the present, you believe that our coffers are empty."

"Not entirely empty, but almost."

"In three years!"

"Stunning constructions have been undertaken."

"The vanity of Barkas!"

"A circus has been constructed containing five hundred thousand places, in which hundreds of lions could battle; it cost more than your expeditions in the land of the Pelasges."

"Is it at least beautiful?"

"Enormous, but not beautiful. All the women of the merchant class have been heaped with gifts and favors."

"The pride of Mellena!"

"The pay of the Aztec sailors has been doubled."

"That schemer Belkis!"

"And the ransoms of the tributary peoples bring in hardly anything any longer."

"Why not?"

"They don't want to be treated as vanquished but as equals, especially the Aztecs and the Toltecs, who have become masters of the fleet."

"And in fact, they're right," sniggers Hellas, in a fit of cutting sarcasm. "What am I saying, our equals? They're the masters of Atlantis, since they control the sea."

Then, turning to Hermos, who is continuing imperturbably to examine the sheets of papyrus: "No more tributes, then? And do the rich Atlanteans, at least, consent to pay the feeble tax that I proposed?

"Them, a tax? Them, the masters of the world, pay to live? On the contrary; they're demanding the gold of new vanquished lands."

"Better and better. And the Inca cultivators, to whom all the workable land of the island has been delivered while the Atlanteans accumulated in the metropolis; they make, it appears, large incomes with the sale of the products of the soil. Do they continue to contribute a part to the treasures of Atlantis?"

"They no longer want to be called Incas; they've become Atlanteans. Guitche granted them the rights of citizenship at the last assembly of notables."

"Marvelous! And naturally, they no longer pay for anything?"

"Naturally," replies Hermos, affecting an ironic tranquility.

"So, suppression of revenues and multiplication of expenses: what admirable politics. Such as I know our people to be, they must be delighted; a dance on a bridge of flowers; too bad if it collapses.

"But there remain to us, Hellas, your beautiful peoples of the Orient, the Iberians, the Cantabrians, the Gaels, the Ligurians, and now even the Pelasgians."

"Oh, those are our future; laborious and rich and with a fine loyalty."

"Those Barbarians might become our masters tomorrow."

"In the meantime, they're our friends."

"But in the meantime, too, it's necessary to live; now, the organization of those new peoples requires long labor, and perhaps many years; do we have enough reserves?" says Hermos, not dissimulating his anxiety.

"Do you believe that the sacred treasure of the Holy Terrace still exists?" Hellas asks, a trifle anxious.

"So it seems; I don't know. Thebao, who has the secret of it, talked to me about it yesterday, after my election as Prince, and promised to reveal its existence to me."

"Then you think that our enemies haven't touched it," says Hellas, becoming animated.

"I think they don't know where it is, as I don't know myself."

At those words from Hermos, Hellas cannot retain his great joy. He stands up and begins marching from one end of the hall to the other in a fit of radiant excitement.

"Then we're saved, Hermos, for the moment. Later, the difficulties will recommence, but it's up to us to prepare for that in advance. The sacred treasure of the Terrace, amassed over the centuries by the successive princes, forms a reserve that has been incessantly augmented, in case of revolt by the submissive peoples. It contains millions and millions of gold coins. But are you sure that our enemies don't know about it? Doesn't their determination to take possession of the Holy Terrace have that treasure for its objective?"

"No, Hellas; their veritable objective worries me even more: it's the secret inventions and the terrible engines hidden in the temple of which they want to take possession."

His expression suddenly darkening, Hellas remains silent momentarily, reflects, and asks in a low voice: "Tell me, Hermos, do you have confidence in Thebao?"

"I can answer for him, Hellas. When Guitche's partly howled ferocious threats against me, Thebao manifestly supported me, and, taking advantage of the general disorder, he placed the crown on my head."

"So, in your opinion, we can trust him with our dearest secrets?"

"I knew him before, on the banks of the Nile, when he followed my father Hermes and was educated alongside him in the science of divine things."

"Very well, Hermos, let's not hesitate any longer. Let's go to him. Is Knephao asleep?"

"Knephao? He's been watching over us all night, and he's now arranging a new cohort of soldiers around the Palace."

"Will you go and warn him?"

And Hermos, calling one of the guards, orders him to fetch the chief of the cohorts.

Scene II
Festival Morning

"Let's see, Knephao," asks Hellas, when the giant appears, "You no longer want to sleep, then?"

"Later! I have plenty of time."

"How do you know? Get some now, while you can. I'll have need of all your vigor this evening."

"And this morning?"

"This morning, everything seems calm, and will stay calm. The city is asleep, harassed by two nights of celebration. Guitche's friends are still raging over their surprise. In any case, today is the Festival of Gold. Mellena is giving a great banquet in her gardens."

"And you're going to allow the feast to take place?" asks the Egyptian.

"Of course! I'll attend it myself, as I should."

"Hellas! You'll do that?"

"Why not? On this festival day, when Atlantis is celebrating its immense riches, do I have the right to stand aside?"

"So, that woman whom you know is meditating your death and who, only yesterday, as you're not unaware, tried to drown Glania..."

"By the way, Knephao, how is the dear invalid?"

"She's slept calmly. Amonou has stayed beside her all night. She'll be able to get up this morning. She'll want to return to the Green Isle, to Orea."

"No, I want her to stay in Atlantis. She'll being us luck."

"But Oreus is waiting for her, to know what has happened."

"One of your faithful soldiers can go to the island disguised as a fisherman and recount yesterday's events to Oreus. Now, Knephao, I beg you, go and get some rest. At the tenth hour, the Assembly of Notables and the College of Apostles are meeting in the Palace of the Empire. If you want, you can come with us."

"Certainly; but in the meantime, what are you going to do?"

"Hermos and I are going to take a chariot up to the Palace of the Empire."

"Alone?"

"No, some of your men will accompany us. It's appropriate that we don't seem to be hiding. As soon as we go into the Palace, your soldiers will mount a good guard at our door, and we'll go in secret, by the route that you know, to the Holy Terrace. We'll confer with Thebao. At the tenth hour we'll come back down for the Assembly of the Apostles. Farewell, Knephao."

So saying, and having saluted the giant cordially, Hellas goes out with Hermos into the Square of the Waters, from where a chariot drawn by four zebras departs at a rapid trot through the streets, followed by an escort of Egyptians.

The streets, still strewn with dead flowers, seem empty. Garlands are hanging from the palm trees bordering the broad avenues. Partly opened shutters allow the fresh morning air into the houses. The bright sunlight shines on the cupolas of the palaces, and in every street the water of small cascades is singing. But the immense city, in its ensemble, is slumbering heavily between the fête of the evening before and the fête to come.

The sound of a chariot followed by cavaliers with noisy weapons attracts all the chattering maidservants to the doors and a few awakened citizens to the windows.

"What cortege, at this hour, is troubling the sleep of the city?"

"By the Sphinx! Hellas himself!"

"And Hermos with him."

"Who said, then, that they were hiding in the Palace of the Waters?"

"Long live Hellas!"

"Long live Hermos!"

The cortege goes up at top speed; the two seated heroes, clearly in view, salute in passing all the early-rising citizens. And from house to house the commentaries fly.

"Already up at dawn! That Hellas is still indefatigable."

"He must have had difficulty, though, getting into Atlantis."

"And his fleet hasn't yet returned."

"There'll be a fuss at the Assembly of Notables. They'll ask Hellas what he's done with his sailors."

"It's said that if Hellas hadn't arrived, the Aztec fleet would have taken possession of the city to crown Mellena."

"May the Sphinx protect us and enable the Notables to give us plenty of gold!"

"Today is the distribution to the people."

Meanwhile, the chariot, in a clatter of hooves and harness, goes past the Palace of Gold where Guitche reigns, and where all Mellena's friends have been up all night.

Belkis is the first to shout from the window: "It's Hellas! Come and see. Where is he going?"

"Doubtless to the Palace of the Empire."

"Someone ought to follow him."

"What's the point? He thinks himself out of danger. He seems convinced that we'll accept his power without protest. I believe he's even saluting us!"

Indeed, Hellas, in passing the Palace of Gold, makes a courteous sign with is hand to Guitche's guests.

"Those poor people," he says to Hermos, "doubtless imagine that we're going to run head first into all their traps. What a pity for men like us to have to oppose cunning to cunning!"

"Do you believe, then, Hellas, that I didn't suffer, the day before yesterday, from entering the Terrace of the Sphinx by a secret stairway?"

"And I thank you for it, Hermos. In any case, we're going to make use of it again, so let's hurry. It's best to arrive at the Temple before Thebao arrives there to pray alone."

The chariot having finally come to a halt in front of the Palace of the Empire, Hellas and Hermos get down noisily, saluted by the soldiers, and affect not to give any order to the sentinels. However, the Egyptians of the escort, dismounting, follow them at a distance.

Hellas and Hermos penetrate into the great vestibule and make haste to go to the secret stairway, while Knephao's cavaliers nonchalantly place themselves in front of the doors that guard the entrance.

Scene III
On the Holy Terrace

"It's here," Hermos explains, "that I overheard the plot of Guitche, Barkas, Belkis and their band."

"Did they see where you emerged from?"

"No, I appeared suddenly on the perron."

"Marvelous. So they don't have any particular reference-point with which to find the secret door?"

"None."

"Excellent. And in the Palace, no one has been able to search for the entrance to the crypt?"

"No one. Since my election, Knephao's soldiers have been watching all the doors, and no one has penetrated into the Palace of the Empire except my surest friends."

"Good. Before our enemies find the secret entrance, we have time before us. Let's hope that we can put the arcana of the Temple in a safe place. Shhh! I can hear something. The door's opening. As long as Thebao comes alone!"

"Here he comes. He's quite alone."

And they emerge from hiding. The Temple is plunged in a silent gloom. Slowly, Thebao, in a trailing robe, goes to the altar. He hears footsteps, shivers, stops, and his about to utter a cry, but Hellas stops him.

"Friends! Hellas and Hermos. Don't say a word."

"Hellas? Hermos? Where did you spring from? What grave event can have brought you here in secret?"

"Let's pray first."

And, kneeling before the altar where the sacred triangle is resplendent, Hellas bows his head.

"Increase light, Hearth of all Splendor, Aliment of all Life, Source of all Movement, Reason of all Science, O Unknown God, O Eternal Soul, You of whom the Sphinx is the carnal image and the Triangle the celestial symbol, O supreme Master, if anything reaches you of the noise that humans make down here, may my prayer be heard, for it has for an object the earth itself and its destiny.

"And you, intermediate Spirits, souls of heroes and terrestrial gods who climb in an infinite ladder from our humanity toward the first cause, you whose souls palpitate around us and form, above our heads, an invisible rampart against the legitimate anger of the One who created the world, O pure spirits, unworthy as Atlantis is, have pity on her weakness and pardon the sins of her children.

"You have given us, O Lord, the empire of the world. And what have we done with that signal favor? Over the vast world, where we ought to have spread your enlightenment, we have excited hatred, war and evil everywhere. And now, in order to punish us, all the passions are rising up.

"Foreign peoples are grumbling around us, while the Atlanteans, once your elect, are intoxicating themselves in blinding sensuality. O Lord, do not take your vengeance yet! Those who are praying to you are feeble mortals capable of evil like all the rest, but their souls rose up toward you pure and disengaged from terrestrial passion. If there still remain in Atlantis a few heroic hearts and a few enlightened minds, by their grace, O my God, let all the rest be redeemed. And we three here, humble successors of the millennial glory of our ancestors, want to obtain by our prayer the pardon of all."

Thebao and Hermos repeat, in unison: "By the radiant Sphinx, we think as you do!"

The three men trace in the air above their forehead the sign of the Sacred Triangle, and remain united in silent meditation.

"My friends," says Hellas. "If our souls are pure, let us act."

"What do you want of me, Hellas?" asks Thebao. "You haven't come in secret to the Holy Terrace uniquely to elevate your soul toward the Unknown God."

"Hidden here, you hold the secrets of Atlantean science, and it's for them that I've come."

"You know them Hellas, since Oreus initiated you himself."

"Friend," says Hellas, "we have full confidence in you. Do you have confidence in us?"

"Fully."

"Then this is it: it's necessary to save the secrets of the Holy Hill."

"Save them how?"

"By transporting them out of Atlantis."

"Out of Atlantis? Out of the Temple? Never. You know how I love you and admire you, Hellas. Hermos can tell you what I've done to favor your maintenance of the throne during your absence, and Oreus, since he deigns not to forget his disciple, will tell you in his turn what care I bring to guarding the treasures that are confided to me. But for love of Atlantis, by obedience to the gods, don't touch the sacred arcana. I shall die on the threshold of the hidden place in which the eternal fluid is conserved, rather than allow a single spark to be removed from the Holy Hill."

And as Hellas and Hermos seem deflated to hear such a response, Thebao continues, softly: "Friends, what grave danger can have driven you, you who are so good, to desire that sacrilege?"

"Danger for Atlantis, danger for you, danger for your treasures themselves. Be certain of this, Thebao; if Barbarians ever take possession of Atlantis, or if the enemies of the gods raise a mob in the city, the first attempted assault will be launched against the Holy Terrace."

"Hellas, I swear to you, if Barbarians or seditious Atlanteans try to take possession of them, my hierophants and I will fight to the last breath for the treasures confided to our care."

"Is it not better to place them in surety immediately? We can take them to the Green Isle and hide them under the surveillance of Oreus."

"No, they shall not leave the Temple. A distant oracle assures that on the day when the secrets of Atlantis are removed, great misfortunes will strike the city."

At those words, Hellas passes his right hand over his forehead, falls silent for a few minutes, and then gazes at Thebao sadly.

"May the gods will that you're not mistaken. In any case, listen. There is in the depths of the temple the entrance to a hidden stairway that leads to the Palace of the Empire. It's by means of that stairway that Hermos was able to climb up to the Temple in spite of all the obstacles that had been accumulated before him. If ever the Holy Hill is attacked by the Barbarians or by a popular uprising, transport the secret arcana into the crypt of the Palace of the Empire."

"Depart without anxiety. All my hierophants are devoted to me until death. In any case, what is it that you fear?"

"Mellena, her partisans and her Aztec sailors. That terrible woman of genius dreams of rendering power to the antique nation of the Occident. She would like to suppress all the white colonies and make the white peoples slaves of Atlantis. The Aztec fleet obeys her blindly. For myself, I've been waiting in vain for my Ligurian fleet for two days,"

"Don't despair, Hellas, the gods will protect you. Listen—a tumult of marine conches is audible down below."

The three men hasten toward the stairway of the Sphinx.

"Oh, thank you, protective gods!" cries Hellas. "It's the Ligurians!"

Down below, in fact, in the open sea, a numerous fleet can be seen advancing majestically, all sails deployed. By the great crimson flags fluttering at the summit of the masts Hellas recognizes his ships. Already, in the city, a rumor is rising. The crowd, in floods, is moving toward the harbor. Hermos draws Hellas into the Temple, and they go back down by way of the secret stairway to the Palace of the Empire, before which the people are calling for them with loud cries.

"This time," said Hermos, "this really is our salvation."

"I regret Thebao's stubbornness, however," murmurs Hellas. "May we not have to deplore his overly strict fidelity."

"Let's make haste, Hellas. I can hear Knephao calming the crowd. They're waiting for us."

Scene IV
In the Palace of Gold

In a sumptuous hall in the Palace of Gold, Guitche's friends, gathered around him, are ardently discussing the Assembly of Notables that will open in an hour.

Outside, above them, on the Esplanade of the Empire, increasing rumors resound, but the rich and the guardians of gold pay no attention to them, absorbed by their immediate projects.

"It's the mob of people who've come to acclaim their hero Hellas," yaps Barkas. "Shout, shout, my worthies! We'll soon see who you'll be acclaiming last."

"However," Guitche observes, "if he has the crowd with him..."

"The crowd? It cried three years ago for Mellena; it cried yesterday for Hermos; it's crying today for Hellas. It howls for whoever passes by and shines; Give it gold and fêtes and it will exalt us."

"Gold and fêtes," grumbled Moussor, the merchants' orator, "that's exactly where we've been too stingy, and for that, the crowd has turned against us. It's necessary not to be intoxicated by illusions. We have to struggle against redoubtable forces. Hellas displays eloquence, prestige, even genius. He dominates the crowd, which submits to his splendor. And furthermore, he shows himself to be generous and disinterested."

"Go acclaim him, then," riposted Belkis, in a mocking tone.

"Shut up, Belkis. I leave to you the care of flattering Hellas or Hermos basely to their faces and insulting them at a distance. Me, I tell the truth, far from them, precisely because, although an enemy of their dangerous dreams, I don't hate them. I fight them. And none of you, I hope, suspects my fidelity to our party."

131

"No, no—speak, Moussor."

"Well, I repeat, Hellas remains powerful because he appears great. Sometimes, he frightens people by the fulgurations of his dominating genius, but in spite of everything, everyone admires him. Hermos, less powerful, draws the youth. Knephao commands, as terrible and powerful as an element. And above them, in a sort of mystery, is enthroned their master, Oreus, possessor of fabulous secrets. It's in a spirit of conservation that I combat those disquieting innovators, those eloquent fools who want to civilize the rest of the world and have new cities built out there, which will become rivals of our Atlantis one day. Insensate! Don't they see that the day when the white peoples, young, active and ardent, more numerous than the sands of the sea, rise up like us to the knowledge of things, they'll begin by taking possession of Atlantis and end up substituting themselves for our race in the direction of the future world. That's why, my friends, we have to struggle against them, and glory to the great Mellena, who was the first to be able to bring us together to attempt to render to the red race the exclusive science, the exclusive force, and the exclusive enjoyment of divine treasures."

"You're right, Moussor."

"Glory to Mellena!"

"So, since we want to fight, let's not ignore our own weaknesses. We know what Hellas has in his favor: his prestige, his bravery, the admiration of the people. And what do we oppose to it? A force that we haven't been able to employ. We possess gold. You, Guitche, govern the mines. You, Barkas, direct the enterprises of public monuments. You, Belkis, control the recruitment of sailors. You dominate maritime commerce, and all of you reign over some part of public wealth. Well, with all those treasures, we haven't been able to conquer the affection of a people so fond of pleasure that it dreams on nothing but celebrations and sensuality. What's the only thing we've given to the Atlanteans? A simple circus, in which ferocious animals are made to fight."

"A simple circus! How you go on! Five hundred thousand places!" says Guitche.

"And Barkas has built it!"

"I've let you talk, Moussor," Barkas remarks, "because everyone here respects your character and your merit. But I'm going to dissipate your anxieties in a few words. This evening, Hellas will no longer be calling himself Prince of the Empire."

"How do you know?"

"We have an infallible means of bringing him down. We'll accuse him of treason before the Assembly of Notables."

"How?"

"The simplest thing in the world. We'll ask the conqueror what he's done with his soldiers. How does he come to be here on his own, without the Ligurian fleet? He was doubtless able to escape secretly, in disguise, while his mariners were massacred."

"And what if you're mistaken?"

"Let him prove the contrary. And let him tell us how he arrived."

"Moussor, who knows everything, is going to tell us," mocked Belkis.

"Perhaps," said Moussor.

But at that moment, they hear such a popular tumult resounding outside that the members of the party of the rich shiver, even in their secret deliberations.

Scene V
Mellena

"Listen!" demands Guitche. "One would think that the crowd were acclaiming someone, or something."

"Oh, by the gods," brays Belkis. "Hellas must have appeared on the balcony of his Palace, and that's sufficient to make the fanatics howl."

"No, listen! The noise seems to be flowing from the top of the hill to the bottom, heading toward the sea."

And they all get up and are about to hasten out of the room when the door opens and, furious, terrible and disheveled, her garments in disorder, a woman appears.

"Mellena!"

"In what a state!"

"What have you to tell us?"

But having tossed back her hair, soaked with sea-water, she stops, looks them up and down, and says, in a disdainful tone: "Ah! You're deliberating!"

"Yes, beautiful queen, we're preparing for the Assembly of Notables," replies Belkis, ever eager.

"Fine work, truly! And you don't know what's happening outside?"

"We were holding our discussion, as is convenient, far from the noise of the crowd."

"Always the same! They deliberate! They'll deliberate eternally! And do you know what they're shouting, the crowd? Come and listen."

And she opens he window wide, though which the noise of the city in movement arrives in gusts. Some cries dominate all the others:

"Glory, glory! The fleet! Long live the fleet!"

"The Ligurian fleet!"

"Hellas' fleet!"

And, turning toward the men thunderstruck with surprise: "You hear? It's his fleet."

"Fatality!" moans Guitche.

"There you go, men that you are! Bewildered, immediately, at the first check! Since you love to deliberate, let's deliberate."

So saying, Mellena sits down and adjusts her disordered garments as best she can.

"Those rags?" Guitche queries.

"Fortunately for me...and for us, for without them, I'd never have been able to traverse the crowd cluttering the squares and the crossroads."

"They didn't recognize you, those brayhards?"

"No, for they're singing infamous songs against me. But don't worry! My day will come. So, my friends, it's no longer necessary to argue over an incontestable fact. We shan't overturn Hellas this morning. His fleet exists. I passed through the middle of his ships in a boat."

"In a boat!" moans Guitche. "Where have you come from, then?"

"Where have I come from? Well, while you were deliberating, I was acting. I've come from the Golden Isle, and I slept last night on the Crimson Isle. In spite of the solemn Xanthes, who retains I know not what generous scruple toward Hellas and Hermos, all the artists are ready to acclaim us when we declare ourselves the masters, and all of them have promised to attend our feast. As for the Blacks of the Golden Isle, all of them are firmly determined to revolt. This very night, they'll take possession of the Palace of the Empire, under cover of the popular fête."

"And the Ligurian fleet?"

"Let's not discuss, let's decide. This is the project it's necessary to execute. The fleet will disembark in the midst of popular jubilation. We'll give it the most triumphal welcome. Instead of accusing Hellas, on the contrary, we'll acclaim him, and we'll give him the place of honor at our feast. In the meantime, our popular agents will take care to draw his sailors

135

from pleasure to pleasure, and roll them in such a vertigo of deleterious intoxications that they'll fall down, overwhelmed by fatigue, in the absolute impossibility of resistance. Then, the Aztec mariners will take possession of Hellas' ships and assure us empire over the sea.

"It will remain to vanquish Knephao and the Egyptians: an affair of the Nubian miners, their most implacable enemies. Those will come in large numbers this evening, as is customary, for the Feast of Gold. At an agreed signal, at the very moment when the Aztec mariners are taking possession of the Ligurian vessels, the black miners will enter the Palace of the Empire and expel the Egyptians, taken by surprise. As for you, friends, be ready to scale the Terrace of the Sphinx. The sleeping Hierophants won't resist your audacity. And the secrets will belong to us, tomorrow, with the glory, the empire, and the domination of the world."

"Admirable!"

"Splendid!"

"Ah! Mellena, your genius surpasses all of ours combined."

Arrogant, her eyes ardent, her lips taut, Mellena looks by turns at each of the men present; then, emphasizing her words:

"Indubitable victory! The chief of the Blacks, Timou, the only one initiated into the entire ensemble of the plot, won't betray us. Hellas, certainly, can have no suspicion of my excursion to the Golden Isle. No one saw me leave yesterday evening. No one recognized me this morning. Even Knephao, in spite of his vigilance, rode past me a little while ago without suspecting Mellena under these pauper's rags. Which of you, I ask in all frankness, still opposes my project?"

"Pardon me," interrupts Moussor, who has remained silent since Mellena's entrance. "Pardon me! I don't say that I oppose it, but one simple question: it's a *coup d'état* that we're going to carry out?"

"Exactly: a *coup d'état*."

"We're going to overturn a legitimately constituted power without any plausible reason?"

"Since we can't do otherwise."

"I regret it. Such an action appears to me to be both unjust and scabrous."

At those words a menacing rumor circulates in the atmosphere of the room.

"Let's see," says Barkas, "were you not, a little while ago, the first to excite our energy to overturn the power of Hellas and display the danger of his genius and his work? Now you're stopping us?"

"Come on, Moussor," says Mellena, in an insinuating and caressant tone, "Moussor, the best of us, are you going to betray us, then?"

"Me, betray you?"

"Wouldn't quitting us, at this moment, be a treason? But don't you know, Moussor, that the triumph of Hellas represents the vertiginous rise of the white race? And you've just talked to us about the necessary precautions to take when the very fate of the red race is at stake?"

"Yes, Mellena," the merchant replies, shaken by that appeal. "Your plan seems superb. And the result? What will we do tomorrow?"

"We'll be the masters."

"What about Hellas? And the Egyptians? And the Ligurians? And all the partisans of the Prince of the Empire? Are we going, this evening, to order a massacre of those thousands of men?"

"Why not?" hisses Belkis.

But Mellena, divining Moussor's scruples and wanting to avoid a rupture, bounds toward Belkis.

"Shut up! You know full well that we don't want to kill anyone. Don't listen to Belkis, Moussor, he's making a game of exciting your just objections. No, we won't kill, because blood summons blood. And we'll be content, tomorrow, to send the Ligurians to Liguria, the Egyptians to Egypt, and Hellas and his friends to exile in the islands."

"Do you really believe that sending those brutal black miners against a Palace full of riches won't awake in them the most sanguinary instincts"

"We'll watch over them."

"Go watch over the tempest when it roars unleashed. I'll put my entire fortune at your disposal, since it's a matter of saving Atlantis, but let me retire to my home and abandon to you a glory that I don't have enough audacity to share with you. Let me, above all, recommend you to watch over your Aztec fleet very carefully, and even over our great Atlantis. Beware of all the dangers, and more than that, of unknown dangers!"

And Moussor, at a weary pace, his face sad, makes a move to head for the door. But Belkis and a few others come to stand in front of him and, in a menacing tone:

"Halt there, friend! You aren't leaving. The man who leaves a plot seems very close to going and spreading the rumor of it."

"Wretch!" roars the indignant merchant. "To accuse me of perfidy!"

"No, no," Mellena intervenes, running forward. "Moussor is loyal and just. I have full confidence in him. And you, Moussor, forgive our overexcited passions. But please, one last word. These dangers of which you speak, of what do they consist, then?"

"You alone I can tell."

"As you wish. Come with me to one side."

Scene VI
Moussor's Secret

Mellena and Moussor retire to a vestibule, separated by a long corridor from the large hall where their friends remain assembled.

"You can speak here without fear, Moussor. Oreus himself, with his pretended secret science, couldn't discover us and overhear us.

"Don't mock the secrets of Oreus, today less than ever. Tell me, Mellena, what were you doing, the other day, when the Apostles were acclaiming their Prince on the Holy Terrace?"

"I was awaiting our success at the Palace of the Empire, far from suspecting the unexpected elevation of Hermos."

"Good. Did you see, perchance, what was happening in the sky?"

"I saw nothing but the sun and the azure."

"Did you not remark a fantastic bird, whose wings open as broadly as those of the Sphinx?"

"Ah—the famous airborne monster that frightened you all? Truly, Moussor, your fear was not heroic. Doubtless some phantasmagoria invented by Oreus. He had, from the depths of his isle, produced some magical reflection in order to frighten us, in accord with Hermos."

"It wasn't a reflection, Mellena, it was a reality."

"An attempt by Oreus, then, to steer through the air the implausible machine on which scholars have been working in vain for centuries. You know full well that the secret will never be found. Barkas declares it impossible."

"Barkas is a false scholar or a scholar who is mistaken. The road of the air is open to humans, or at least to a few humans, for Oreus and Hellas are the only ones who have profited from it thus far."

"You're speaking seriously, Moussor?"

139

"Very seriously, Do you know who was flying in that monstrous bird?"

"Oreus, doubtless, if anyone has attempted such a trial."

"Yes, Oreus, but Hellas was flying with him."

"Hellas? In truth, Moussor, you're beginning to interest me."

"Yes, Hellas, I'm sure of it. Hazard revealed his arrival to me. One of my vessels was returning in haste, with its lights out, the night before last, in order to attend the Feast of the Waters. My sailors heard a strange noise in the sky. They looked up, and it seemed to them that an immense phantom was floating under the stars. Vast wings were beating the air. They were sailing close to the Green Isle. The phantom, the contours of which became more precise with every movement, appeared to be tacking above the island and descending slowly. The sound ceased and our men saw a rope thrown from the airborne monster to earth, by means of which two human shadows descended to the ground. Then the monster seemed to furl its wings and it disappeared into a forest of eucalyptus.

"Knowing the fantastic legends with which Oreus' island is still surrounded, our sailors were not overly astonished, but, gripped by a natural fear, they rowed in haste toward the city. Their captain narrated the nocturnal adventure to me. Then I connected my sailors' story with the vision we had all had on the Holy Terrace. And, giving me men orders not to say anything, I kept the secret carefully in order to reveal it when the time came."

"Very good, Moussor. It might, indeed, be the case that the airborne monster and the object glimpsed by the sailors are the same thing. But I don't see Hellas in the affair."

"Two men, I told you, descended from the aerial ship to the Green Isle. Now, do you know where Hellas came from, yesterday evening? From the Green Isle..."

"How?"

"Disguised as a sailor and guided by a little singer of the crossroads."

"The Ligurian singer?" exclaims Mellena, in an alarmed voice. "I understand many things now."

"Merchants recognized the girl. Now, she came from the Green Isle. The previous evening she was on the Crimson Isle, from which she escaped at dawn in the direction of Oreus. What is the significance of the young woman with regard to Hellas and Oreus? I don't know. We should interrogate her, if possible."

"I believe," says Mellena, in an enigmatic tone, "that you'll have difficulty finding her."

"What interests us, in any case, is Hellas. Now, Hellas had slept on the Green Isle. What had brought him there? The giant bird. Where had that giant bird come from? From very far away, from the land of the Pelasges, or at least from the Strait of Gades. The road of the air is therefore found, and our enemies possess it."

"So what?"

"What? You, so lucid, don't see our definitive ruin, the nullification of our Aztec fleet, the indisputable triumph of Hellas?"

"Not yet. In what way does this secret render Hellas the master of the world?"

"How can we fight against him? With the red fleet? Well, Mellena, from the height of the sky, Oreus and Hellas can, in a single day, annihilate the vessels prowling around our port. In the City, Knephao is invincible. The people, incapable of the last struggle, hate us fundamentally. And now you're talking about attempting a illegitimate *coup d'état* against the victorious Hellas."

Silent and meditative, her head bowed, Mellena sits down on a marble bench. Then shaking her head: "Very well, Moussor. I thank you. Go away, then. There's danger, you're retiring. Perfect. For myself, I'm returning to my friends, and we're going to act."

"I've warned you affectionately, and you persist in an insensate action? And you accuse me of cowardice—me! I repeat, if Hellas had failed Atlantis, I would oppose his tyranny.

But his power seems without reproach. He has returned from the land of the Pelasges victorious. His fleet has returned entire. What right do we have to overthrow him?"

"You ask what right we have, Moussor? But have you not just said it yourself. They've discovered a secret that might overturn the world, and instead of delivering it to our Atlantis, their fatherland, instead of communicating it to the Apostles, their brothers, they're keeping it for themselves alone? Flagrant treason!"

Shaken and hesitant, Moussor does not know what to reply.

Then, seeing that her first attack has struck home, becoming caressant and taking his hands, Mellena adds: "Stay with us, Moussor, my friend, fight with us. We're fighting to save our Atlantis from his power and his wealth. Help us—you should."

"Well, so be it. What do you want to do?"

"Break Oreus and Hellas this very evening. Take advantage of our last chance. Today, the entire city will be resounding with the noise of celebrations. We'll deceive our enemies with the appearance of our security. And this evening, at the height of the feast, we'll have Hellas arrested. In the meantime, a few Aztecs and a few intrepid Blacks will be sent to the Green Isle, and try to surprise Oreus while he sleeps. We'll tell the people tomorrow the superior reasons that forced us to act thus. And our power will be legitimated. Do you feel reassured now?"

"Almost..."

"Finally. And furthermore, who knows? Perhaps we can take possession of the giant bird and discover its mechanism. Then we'll become the masters—the true masters—of the world. Oh, what a perpetual fête in Atlantis, dominating the world and, like a living sphinx, opening its wings over the terrified peoples!"

"Come on, then, Mellena. Let's rejoin our friends. But let's not tell them the secret that I've confided to you. They'd lose courage."

Scene VII
The Other Secret

As they are heading toward the room where Guitche and his friends were deliberating a little while before, Mellena and Moussor hear an unaccustomed rumor. A large number of people are speaking at the same time. Women's voices burst forth in strident appeals. Just as they arrive at the door, Belkis comes out, very agitated.

"Do you know the news that has just reached us, Mellena? Well, Moussor, are you coming back to us?"

"Yes, he's still one of ours. I've converted him to our projects."

"What projects? Do you know how Hellas traveled from the Tyrrhenian Sea to the Green Isle?"

"No, Swimming, or on a cloud?"

"Mock, mock, Mellena. Not on a cloud, but through the air. Come and hear our friends the artists, who have arrived from the Crimson Isle, and who saw the Barbarians of the Ligurian fleet this morning."

And, opening the door wide, Belkis introduces Mellena and Moussor into the room, now full, where people are talking loudly and ardently.

"Greetings, Mellena!"

"Mellena, listen to the news..."

"Unexpected, unheard of, fantastic."

"Yes, I know. Belkis has just told me. It's a dream of a delirious mind."

"A dream? But the entire city is resounding with the rumor. The Barbarians told us themselves that near the strait of Gades, Hellas, attacked by an immense fleet, would surely have succumbed if a great bird that appeared in the sky had not spread terror among the enemy fleet and lifted Hellas into the air."

"Armorican cowards!" murmurs Mellena. Then, aloud: "You can't see that someone is making up an implausible story for you?"

"For what motive?"

"To frighten you, tremblers, by letting people believe that Hellas, if he wishes, can rise up into the air and dominate the city and the world, who would then remain to oppose his ambition?"

"But in truth, Mellena," Guitche intervenes, "how can we doubt the Barbarians' story? We've seen, really seen, ourselves..."

"You've seen nothing but a reflection! No one is unaware that Oreus can produce apparent phantasmagorias in the air. Isn't that true, Moussor?"

The latter, nonplussed, makes a vague gesture of acquiescence. And Mellena, fearing that he is hesitating in his response, hastens to add: "In any case, we can't waste time on these stupidities. The time for the Assembly of Notables is approaching. Go. We'll stay here, we women—or rather, we'll go to my gardens in order to prepare today's feast."

"What?" says Barkas. "The feast will take place anyway?"

"Certainly, and I intend that you will all come. Don't forget that your attitude at the Assembly of Notables must be respectful and submissive. Hellas will occupy the seat of honor. You can even, if you wish, celebrate his aerial prowess."

"They you persist in not believing it?"

"Absolutely." Then, turning to Barkas: "Come on, Barkas, you're not ignorant of any of the secrets of science, do you believe it possible to steer airborne vessels? If it could be one, would you not have found it yourself?"

Flattered, Barkas nods his head and recognizes that Mellena is, in fact, correct.

"In truth," explains Palmoussos, who was the first to bring the news, "it might be that we've been deceived."

"More than probable," Mellena affirms.

They all leave, somewhat confused, already recovering from their first impression, and spreading doubt around them regarding the white Barbarians' story.

Olbios the rhetor, however, stays behind the others and takes Mellena aside. "You believe, then, in the infallible science of Barkas?"

"The opinion gives him so much pleasure."

"But between us, I don't believe it. Whether or not Oreus has discovered the secret of aerial navigation, I deem it interesting, at any rate, to reveal someone to you who, at a given moment, could fight against the mage of the Green Isle and, if necessary, manipulate obscure forces, like him."

"Certainly. And do you know that someone?"

"Do you promise me secrecy?"

"My interest answers for my silence."

"Well then, it's a Black."

"His name?"

"Timou."

"Timou? I know him. I..." She is about to add, *I saw him this morning*, but she stops, alarmed by her own imprudence. She resumes: "I'll doubtless see him this evening. He might well come to Atlantis for the Festival of Gold, the only day when the Queen City is open to Nubian slaves."

"He's said to be a terrible sorcerer, the master of secrets kept by the priests of Saba. He was taken as a slave in Egypt, and brought from Egypt to Atlantis. By means that I don't know, he has the power to set an entire city ablaze. He could even launch his flames toward the sky and nip Oreus' invention in the bud, if it exists."

"Thank you, Olbios, but how do you know such things?"

"I've lived in Egypt, when Om-du-sud was built, where I taught eloquence in the Temple. I knew Timou as a slave, and I've often seen him since, on the Golden Isle."

"Tell me, then, why, having mastery of such a force, he consents to remain in the mines."

"Because he lacks a precious element guarded by the hierophants in the Temple of the Sphinx, If he were simply able to procure that substance, Atlantis would fall into his possession..."

"Many thanks, Olbius. I don't intend to give myself a Black for a master. But tell me, what reasons do you have for mingling thus in our quarrels?"

"You hate Oreus, Hellas and Hermos; so do I..."

"I don't hate them. I fight them because I believe them to be harmful."

"You hate them by virtue of ambition, and so do I. I resent them for shining while I'm obscure, as you resent them for being masters of the Empire, while you dream of becoming its ruler."

And Olbios, sniggering, leaves the room in the Palace, leaving Mellena surprised and full of disgust.

The people insult me, she thinks, *and cowards believe my soul to be as vile as theirs. Oh, how dear my ambition costs me!*

But she quickly shakes off the flood of bitterness that rises within her, and, smiling and lively, goes to rejoin the group of women that is growing by the minute.

"Well, my friends, it's our celebration today! What's the point of moaning about the city's vicissitudes? Believe me, we'll have our turn at empire. Let's show ourselves beautiful and smiling today. We'll reign and govern tomorrow."

"Glory to you, Mellena the valiant!"

"Follow me into my gardens while the men are exchanging empty words."

"Will Hellas be coming to the banquet?" enquire several young women.

"Certainly. We're not enemies, merely rivals."

And Mellena murmurs, very quietly: "Are they all dreaming of Hellas, then? Stupid sex? But the men are becoming cowards too! Oh, if only I could have the power of a god!"

Scene VIII
In the Palace of the Waters

"By all the crocodiles in the Nile, why didn't you wake me sooner?" grumbles Knephao, stretching his arms.

"You were sleeping so soundly, and Hellas had given me such firm instructions not to allow your slumber to be troubled that we would have thought it a crime to disturb you."

"Amonou, my friend do you take me for a little girl, to whom sleep is indispensable?"

"Not indispensable, doubtless, but very profound, for all the Barbarians' trumpets vibrated on the Square of the Waters without you deigning to emerge from your dreams."

"Barbarians? What Barbarians?"

"The Ligurian fleet."

"Hellas' fleet!" thunders Knephao, so joyful that the bound he makes shakes the walls of the room. "But by the Sphinx, what time is it, then?"

"Don't worry. The banquet won't begin for several hours. You can continue resting."

"And the Assembly of Notables?"

"A mere formality, now the fleet has come. Hellas is fully triumphant."

"Now, yes, but this evening…we must be relentlessly watchful. The more Mellena seems vanquished, the more I fear her. Yesterday's escapade causes me to fear anything. But now I think about it, what's become of Glania?"

A joyful song, like the twittering of a bird, arrives from a nearby room.

"Can you hear her? One might think that she wanted to reply to you herself."

"Cured?"

"Completely. Joy has resuscitated her."

"Yes—the arrival of the fleet! Very happy to see her brothers again!"

147

"Her brothers? She has scarcely given them a thought. Her joy has another cause. You can't guess?"

"Hellas?"

"Naturally. Oh, if you had seen her little hands clapping when the expected trumpet sounded."

"You've watched over her?"

"So sweet and so tender! She thanked me with such effusion. One might think that she loves me fraternally, not for having saved her, but for cherishing and serving Hellas, And I feel that I could spend my life listening to the song of her voice and gazing at the flame of her eyes."

"Worthy Amonou!" says Knephao, hiding his emotion, and thinking of another love similar to the young man's.

While speaking, however, he has finished dressing. He covers his head with the helmet with the rutilant plume, and, approaching the wall, adopting his least harsh tone of voice, he asks: "Glania, would you like to come to say farewell to your old friend the soldier? He's going to find Hellas."

Bounding lightly, clad in a short robe, her fair hair curling over her neck, the Ligurian appears and greets Knephao with a burst of laughter.

"Well, giant? I'm the invalid, and you're the one sleeping?" Then, pertly, she continues: "An Egyptian officer has been waiting for an hour for Your Greatness to wake up. He's come from the Palace of the Empire."

"Send him in right away."

Glania summons the Egyptian.

"You've come on behalf of Hellas?"

"Yes, great chief."

"What did he say to you?"

"To await your awakening, and to tell you to go to the Palace as soon as you can."

"I'll be there in a few moments. You don't have any other messages?"

"For Amonou," the officer adds. "The Prince desires that he only go to join him at the moment of the banquet. The Assembly of Notables will pass without incident. Until the time

148

when it's necessary to go to Mellena's gardens, he asks Amonou to stay with the Ligurian singer and, if she is cured, to accompany her through the streets in fête. The chariots, horses and mules of the Palace of the Waters are entirely at the disposal of the two young people. At the third hour after noon, before Mellena's feast, they will go to join Hellas, unless it pleases them to go back sooner."

"Oh, what joy, Amonou!" exclaims Glania. "We'll go up to the Palace of the Empire!"

"Farewell, my dear children," says Knephao. "May the Sphinx favor you!"

As brisk as a adolescent, the colossus heads for the sunlit door and is about to leap on to his horse, which is pawing the ground, when he stops suddenly, goes back precipitately into the vestibule of the Palace, lets the crimson curtains fall back over the doorway, and turns to Amonou and Glania, who have followed him as far as the threshold.

"Which of you knows Timou, the chief of the Blacks, the master if the miners who dig in the ground beneath the Golden Isle?"

"I do," says Amonou. "I saw him during a visit I made to the mines."

"Look, then. Take this telescope."

Amonou opens a gap in the crimson curtain. In the distance, at the entrance to the harbor, several boats are moored to the quay, laden with black men, simply dressed in large loincloths, their torsos bare. Standing in the stern of one of the boats, a tall man appears to be ordering the maneuver.

"That's certainly him—I recognize his broad shoulders and his imperious face."

"I'm not mistaken, then. What is he doing?"

"All the Blacks have just descended on to the quays. He's talking to them. Now they're marching toward the city."

"And him?"

"He's staying in the boat with two oarsmen. The boat's pulling away from the quay. It's heading southwards. It's out of sight. I can't see say more."

"Good. It's time for me to go up to the Palace of the Empire."

"What is it about the Nubian that can trouble you, Knephao? Isn't this the day when the Blacks attend the Festival of Gold, which is their fête?"

"Timou, never. He hates Atlantis. He's sworn that he would only come here on the day when he could avenge himself on the Atlanteans."

"You know him, then?"

"He comes from the region of Nubia nearest to Egypt. My father took him prisoner. He's born, it's said, of the royal and priestly family. His ancestors once governed the kingdom of Saba. He's vowed an eternal hatred against the Reds, which he's dissimulated for many years. I always told Hellas not to let him have the direction of the mines."

"Bah! I have confidence!" Amonou exclaims. "With you, Atlantis has nothing to fear."

But the Egyptian is already leaping on to his horse, and the reflection of his helmet disappears at the corner of the square.

The sun is blazing in the heart of the azure. The smooth sea reflects the light in silvery sheets, from which fiery arrows sometimes spring. The boats, in cleaving through the surface of the water, seem to be raising translucent metal, and one might think that the foam in their wake were molten gold. A mild frisson rises from the entire city, full of happy idleness, and something eternal and divine floats and expands over the Queen of the Waters.

"A beautiful day!" Glania sings. "Let's go mingle with the fête. Hellas wishes it."

"But not in a chariot, without horses or mules. Would you like to go on foot, like strangers visiting the City?"

"Yes, yes, on foot. We'll stop in the flower gardens."

And, their youth overflowing, immediately forgetting Knephao's fears, they set forth, light and curious, through the sunlit streets.

Scene IX
In the Palace of the Empire

The fourth hour after midday has just chimed, and Hellas, his shoulders covered by a white mantle, his head circled with a golden crown, interrogates with his eyes, several times over, the noisy square in which the people, guarded by Egyptian soldiers, are awaiting the departure of the Prince of the Empire.

"Master," says one of the officers of the Palace, respectfully, "I think I ought to remind you that the hour will soon sound to go to Mellena's gardens.

"Thank you, my friend. Is Knephao with us?"

"Yes, Master, ready to mount his horse at the threshold of the Palace."

"Ask him to join me in the vestibule."

And, one last time, from the height of the balcony, Hellas scans the entire square. Then, having made a gesture of resignation, he descends to the vestibule of the Palace."

"Well, Knephao, still nothing?"

"Nothing."

"None of your soldiers has seen them?"

"None."

"Did Glania seem fully recovered when you left them at the Palace of the Waters?"

"She was singling like a bird, and he was laughing. They were about to go for a walk while waiting for the time to come and join you. Amonou promised me to arrive here by the third hour."

"It's now the fourth, and we've seen nothing. I'm anxious."

"Bah! They'll be strolling in the streets. At twenty years of age, one forgets serious rendezvous."

"Neither Glania nor Amonou has forgotten that I'm waiting for them," said Hellas, shaking his head. "They're two bright and noble souls whom rumors of feasting couldn't have distracted from their devotion."

"By why does their lateness sadden you, Hellas?"

"Because it's surely caused by an accident or a crime."

"A crime?"

"Don't protest. You think the same. You're affecting doubt to reassure me. Both of us, however, have to envisage any occurrence. And since it's necessary to speak clearly, here it is: we're approaching a decisive and perhaps tragic hour of our destiny. The tempest of evil passions, accumulated over a long period, is already rumbling. When the storm threatens, the slightest shock is sufficient to precipitate it. The instinct of enjoyment that had driven the Atlanteans to flee the country-side in order to crowd together in a monstrous city, was bound to engender monstrous follies. But let's not groan; for the moment, it's necessary to save the Empire; it's necessary to keep watch on our enemies, who have excited the rancor of the Aztecs, the Incas and all the Occidental peoples. The reports I've just received allow me to comprehend that our adversaries have even stirred up the covetousness of the black slaves."

"You know that, then?"

"Would you like to know the reason for my anxiety on the subject of Glania and Amonou? I fear that, carried away by their imprudent enthusiasm, they might have caused the inevitable thunderbolt to burst forth sooner. My entire plan consisted of delaying until nightfall the shock that will be produced, if it has to be produced. I'm going to the Feast of Gold in order to lull our enemies' suspicions. For this evening, our Ligurian chiefs have orders to take their sailors back to their ships at the time when they are believed to be dispersed through the fête. This evening, too, the Egyptians will mount a good guard over the City. If a surprise attack comes, we'll be ready for it. Now, the inadvertence of those two generous children might ruin everything, and that's what I'm thinking at this moment. May I be mistaken! But it's far better to anticipate the unforeseen!"

152

"If only we'd though of these possible dangers this morning. I would have brought Glania and Amonou with me."

"Of course! But I was still poorly informed as to our adversaries' projects. And since our dear children haven't arrived, I'm going to leave for Mellena's gardens. You, Knephao, having assured a solid and entirely trustworthy guard around the gardens, will come back here to organize a search of the City by your most faithful and active agents."

"My agents are already going through the city streets."

"Ah! You recognize the peril yourself? Then I have confidence. Let's not wait any longer. Let's go. Let's not allow our anxiety to show. Let our cortege, joyous in appearance, depart for the Master of Gold's feast!"

Scene X
Mellena's Gardens

Everything that can be assembled in one corner of the world of the splendors of nature's gifts and human endeavors is on brilliant display in Mellena's gardens. The woman whom the people call the Queen of Gold, and whose friends sometimes call her, in order to please her, the Queen of Atlantis, has had a palace of porphyry built at the extremity of the Green Point, the extreme southern peninsula of Atlantis. The palace stands on a plateau above the sea. The broad and high colonnade made of fluted pillars extends across the entire breadth of the peninsula, and before the palace seven superimposed terraces descend, linked to one another by pink marble stairways. On each terrace, a jasper fountain with murmuring jets sends forth an abundant and limpid water that bronze monsters with open mouths project in cascades toward the sea. The last terrace, narrower than the others, terminates in a creek protected from the waves by a granite jetty, in the shelter of which elegant pleasure-boats lie dormant.

But today, to the ordinary sumptuousness of the garden, arches of verdure garlands in festoons and multicolored tents have been added. The guests' table is set up on the highest terrace, which is also the broadest, the one situated level with the palace, and from which the view overlooks the immense sea. On the other terraces are grouped the musicians invited for their art: the harpists of Armor, lyre-players from Libya, trumpeters from the Gaelic lands, Inca singers consecrated to the sun, and dancers with supple bodies from the kingdom of Saba. Thus far, however, only the lyres and flutes have made their sweet and languid melodies heard, and the guests, excited by the generous wines, are exchanging joyful words.

"Truly, Mellena," says Xanthes, "how many thanks we owe you for practicing with so much sagacity the supreme art of beauty! What is poor and disordered nature worth by comparison with the harmony of our palaces and gardens?"

"What is the stupid song of birds worth," Asmonia puts in, "compared with the science of lyres?"

"What are sterile cliffs worth," pontificates Barkas, "compared with terraces with marble flanks?"

"What are imbecile peoples wandering in natural forests worth," adds Guitche, "compared with the elect race by whom the holy city of Atlantis was built?"

"Yes, yes, we are becoming gods!" proclaim adolescents.

"And the rest of the word remains a herd," concludes Guitche.

"Please!" objects Barkas, with a ironic condescension. "Don't calumniate the Barbarians; there are powerful lords here who love them, and who perhaps even believe them to be our equals."

The dart is clearly directed at Hellas. An oppressed silence follows Barkas' perfidious observation. But Hermos cannot contain his impatience before the manifestation of Atlantean pride, and, turning to Guitche, he observes, in a tone of great politeness: "I have the regret of contradicting you, my host. I've seen the races that you call a vile herd, and I assure you that, save for the color of their skin, they greatly resemble the red races, and their intelligence, like ours, will awaken sooner or later."

A burst of laughter circulates through the feast.

"Ha ha!" says Xanthes. "To suppose that the moonfaces will one day have the intelligence of the red peoples is truly taking generosity toward the vanquished too far."

"Come on," says Psalmoussos, the musician, "if the Whites were equal to us in intelligence, Hermos, would they not already have manifested that virtue in some way?"

"Oh, my dear Palmoussos, is it not in music that they already affirm themselves your fortunate rivals?"

This time, a burst of laughter louder than the first shakes the entire table, but those laughing are taking the side of Hermos, and Palmoussos mutters in confusion. His great chagrin, in fact, is seeing that the bards of Armor and the Ligurian singers are obtaining more success with the people than him, with his savant harmony.

"In truth," Xanthes says, "the music of the Whites offers nothing comparable to ours. They remain similar, when they sing, to the birds of the woods or the waves of the sea, which repeat and always will repeat the same murmurs or the same moans. They don't invent, they repeat; and when they play savant chords on lyres and flutes, it's from us that they've borrowed that supreme art."

"Invention is, in fact, the key word," affirms Moussor. "We always invent, and the Whites recommence."

"They build houses that are always the same, like beavers' lodges," says Barkas.

"They retain the same virtues and the same vices as their ancestors." pronounces Guitche.

"And truly," Xanthes continues, "if they were capable of becoming our equals, they would construct marble palaces like us, and would have created arts that enchant life, like us. If they have inferior lives, it's because the gods have determined it. The world grew for the red race!"

"And the red race for the delights of Atlantis," confirms Asmonia.

Hermos is about to respond, but a scarcely perceptible glance from Hellas implores him to remain silent. And Guitche's friends continue their symphony of glory toward the Queen City.

"Long live the red race!"

"Empire to the reds!"

The voices rise from one minute to the next; minds are intoxicated by their own pride; the gaiety of the wines shines in the cups. Mellena, delighted to see her ideas triumph, allows the joy of her success to be divined. Standing up, cup in hand, she declares:

"Salutations to you, Atlanteans, salutations to our guests and salutations, most of all, to the Prince of the Empire. If there are sometimes struggles of ambition and competition for glory between people of the same race, let those noble rivalries not prevent us from communing today in the exaltation of our immortal city. Let us all celebrate Atlantis together!"

A triumphant clamor responds to those final words.

"Immortal Atlantis!"

"Eternal and unique!"

"My dear friends," Mellena concludes, whose voice has the ring of victory, "now that we have rendered the City the absolute homage that her children owe to her, let us not forget that its slaves and tributaries are to collaborate in our divine joys."

So saying, she makes a sign to one of the stewards in the garden, and immediately, buccinas and harps resonate; the Atlanteans, ecstatic, forget everything, even their pride, in order to lull themselves in the supple and enveloping waves of the melody.

But now, from the palace decked with flags, a tumult grows, soon drowning out the sound of the harps, and the guests, disturbed, irritated and furious, turn toward the place from which the rumor is coming. Mellena, visibly anxious, interrogates Guitche with her eyes, while Hellas, very calmly, makes a rapid sign to Hermos and his friends. One of the special guards attached to Mellena's palace hurtles in, his faced streaming with sweat.

"Mistress, Egyptians are trying, in spite of everything, to enter the garden. They say they have orders to speak to Hellas at all costs."

"Let them in," says Mellena, dryly. Then, turning to Hellas: "In truth, handsome Prince of the Empire, your men could have refrained from troubling my guests while they're savoring the joys of life."

But Hellas replies in a tranquil voice: "If my men have come this far to find me, at the peril of their lives, it's because the salvation of the Empire is perhaps at stake."

And, with a firm tread, he advances to meet the Egyptian soldiers.

Already, beside him, Hermos and the Apostles of the Sun still faithful to the Prince have formed up silently. The soldiers, on joining Hellas, say to him simply, in a low voice: "Knephao sent us. What was bound to happen has happened."

"And where is Knephao?"

"Departed on horseback, with proven men. It was necessary to go to save the two adolescents."

"Nothing more?"

"Yes. In the port, the Aztecs and the Ligurians are fighting."

"Let's go see!" Then, turning to the guests milling excitedly: "Adieu, Atlanteans; I'll leave you to your feasting and your songs. Excuse me, Mellena, for quitting your dwelling before the end of the banquet, but some of you perhaps know why."

"What do you mean?" demands Guitche.

"It's because," Hellas pronounces, in a curt and clear one, "your friends are attacking mine. My duty consists of reestablishing order. Adieu!"

And without leaving the stunned guests time to respond, Hellas, followed by Hermos and a few faithful followers, disappears under the colonnades of the white house.

"What's happening?" Mellena asks Barkas in a low voice. "Who has set forth before the agreed signal?"

"I don't understand it," says Barkas. "Someone has sinned by excessive zeal—Belkis, no doubt."

"Always that man with the shady allure. Where have you put him?"

In front of the Palace of the Empire. At the first signal of the revolt he was to scale the Holy Terrace above the Golden Gate."

"Plan failed! Hellas is escaping!" sighs Guitche.

"Courage," says Mellena. "Hellas doesn't suspect us yet. Otherwise, he'd have had us seized by his men. Are the three ships that are to take us away moored in the small port, ready to take to sea?"

"See for yourself. Their sails are swelling."

"Then let the feast continue. Start the music again. Excite the dances, and we'll slip quietly down to the port."

"As long as Belkis doesn't get caught!"

"If he fails, we'll put the entire adventure on his head."

Then, turning toward the terraces where the musicians have scattered in disorder, Mellena says: "Come on, my friends, here you are, agitated like children caught at fault. What does this terror signify? Simple police matters, which Hellas believes, in order to show his zeal, that he ought to regulate in person. Let us laugh and sing!"

Now the harps begin to vibrate again. Meanwhile, slowly, the sun descends into the blazing sea. Mellena and her friends insinuate themselves, through the palm-trees, by a path invaded by shadows, all the way to the final terrace, while some of the guests withdraw in chattering groups.

"Fire! Fire!" said Xanthes, coming back precipitately.

"Yes, fire!" exclaim other guests.

"Where is it?" enquire those who cannot see anything.

"Over there, can you see? In the direction of the harbor where the Ligurian fleet is anchored.

"Mellena? Guitche? Where are the masters of the house?"

But Mellena and Guitche are already far way. Outside the dyke that shelters the little port of the Green Point, three pleasure-boats are visible, under full sail, reaching the open sea. The music has fallen silent. The guests, frightened, run toward the gates of the garden or the doors of the Palace, and they hear, resounding from the direction of the Square of the Empire, a loud noise of trumpets, and an entire tempest of clamors.

Scene XI
Toward the Melee

While the anxious crowd runs through the broad avenues or circles, in bewilderment, the public squares, Hermos and Hellas, followed by the Egyptian guards, head for the center of the City, clearing a passage through the human tide. Soon, toward the military port, they perceive the light of the conflagration. They stop, and listen silently to the clamors coming from the sea.

At first, there is a confused noise, immense and increasing, like advancing thunder. Soon, through that noise, more violent cries burst forth, uttered by thousands of vices. Hellas recognizes the guttural accents of Aztecs, very different from the soft and musical timbre of Atlanteans.

"Death to the masters!"

"Death to Hellas!"

"Knephao! Stop Knephao!"

Then other cries respond, in the Ligurian language, cries as inarticulate as threats or appeals.

Impassive, Hellas turns to his men.

"How many are we?"

"Only a few thousand," replies an officer.

"Very few, but what does it matter. You, Hermos, take one party and go up to the Square of the Empire. I'll keep the others and go down there."

"No, Hellas, it's necessary that you don't expose yourself. The entire destiny of the City rests on you. I'll go myself in the direction in which Knephao seems to be in peril."

At the same instant, however, from the Palace of the Empire, a rumor as violent as that in the port reaches the impatient cavaliers.

"You see," says Hellas. "There's fighting up there as well as down below, and your valor, Hermos, won't be useless there. Adieu."

So saying, making a sign to the cavaliers placed immediately behind him, Hellas launches himself toward the blazing port, while Hermos goes up toward the Palace, as rapidly as the steep road will permit.

As Hermos' cohort advances, the sound of voices becomes more precise, and the poet distinctly hears vociferation:

"Open the gates!"

"Break down the gates!"

"They're going to violate the sanctuary of the Sphinx!"

"It's Belkis!"

"After him!"

"I saw him!"

"Long live Hellas!"

"Long live Hermos!"

"Where's Hellas!"

"Someone go fetch Hellas and Hermos!"

Then Hermos turns to the soldiers following him.

"You can hear, my friends, the crowd up there siding with us. Let five hundred of you, only, follow me. The rest go to join Hellas and Knephao. With your companions on the Esplanade, I'll make sure of the security of the Palace."

Meanwhile, Hellas, at a mad gallop, has just reached the vicinity of the large square that extends in front of the harbor where the vessels of the Ligurian fleet are ordinarily sheltered. That square, of grandiose dimensions, is known as the Square of Trophies because of the monuments erected a century before to celebrate the conquests accomplished over the peoples of the white race. It is surrounded by vast taverns where the mariners of the Empire go to mingle with the sailors of merchant vessels among the lower orders of the City. All day long, in the sunlight, poorly-dressed and idle men sleep extended on the paving stones of the square, and by night, brawls break out at the doors of the taverns.

This evening, it is no longer simple conflicts between drunken mariners or fallen women, but a true battle. In the gloom of the imminent nightfall, the melee seems even more sinister.

161

"Let's stop," Hells orders, "and look to see where Knephao is fighting, in order that we can liberate our friend by means of a vigorous attack."

The cavaliers gather in the shelter of a clump of palm trees.

"What's happening?" an Egyptian officer asks a woman carrying a crying child.

"Oh, handsome soldier," replies the tearful woman, "if you knew! The Aztecs have burned the Ligurian ships; they've penned them in the taverns, to which they're trying to set fire, and all that for a little white singer accompanied by a young man. It seems that the moonface picked a quarrel with the Aztecs because they were insulting Hellas. The young man killed an Aztec with a blow of a staff, and took refuge with the girl in a tavern where the Ligurians were drinking, and the battle started."

"But who's fighting, at the present moment?"

"A kind of giant, who's just come running with Egyptians, and with great sweeps of his sword he struck into the crowd. But he's surrounded, and won't take long to succumb."

Hellas does not wait to hear any more. Abruptly emerging from the clump of trees, he makes a sign to his men, and the cavaliers launch themselves into the square.

Scene XII
The Melee

"Hellas!" the crowd appeals.

Immediately, from the heart of the melee, a formidable voice makes itself heard:

"Hellas! Hellas! To me! To me! To us!"

"Courage, Knephao!" Hellas cries.

And blades fall upon the surprised Aztecs.

"Here comes Hellas! Here comes Egypt! Every man for himself!" howl the red sailors.

The square, in fact, empties almost instantaneously, and Knephao stops fighting. He lets his blade fall, and collapses, exhausted, into the arms of two Egyptians behind him, who have been supporting him in the battle.

"Knephao, my friend, what's wrong?" The Prince interrogates, leaping down from his horse.

"Nothing, nothing! My arm has been going up and down without a break for nearly an hour."

"And that blood on your head?"

"Almost nothing. A club that staved in my helmet."

And the giant, bounding to his feet, shakes his head, picks up his sword, wipes his forehead, and says, smiling: "It's very imprudent of you, Hellas, to come to the party. But up above, is someone looking out for you?"

"Hermos."

"Ah! I can breathe. Hermos knows the secret stairway."

"What do you mean?"

"That an immense plot has been woven, Master. Belkis, up there, surrounded by audacious bandits, is trying to scale the Holy Terrace in order to go and steal the secrets of the Sphinx. In order to accomplish such work, they strove to draw me here."

"And succeeded only too well, imprudent!"

"Fortunately. If I hadn't come, Amonou and Glania would be roasting at present, and numerous Ligurians with them. Let's go rescue them!"

From the nearest tavern, cries ring out,

"Save us, Hellas! We can hear you!"

The Egyptians following Hellas descend from their horses and strive to remove the beams and masses of iron that the Aztecs have piled up in front of the door. With a vigorous shove, one of the battens is disengaged, and the Ligurian sailors emerge, pell-mell.

"Hellas! Hellas!" calls a woman's voice. "It's you who came to save us. I expected you. You see, Amonou, that I was right!"

And Glania, in tears, falls at the feet of the Prince, kissing the hem of his tunic.

"Will you please keep out of the way and let the men fight?" grumbles Knephao, in a surly tone.

Scarcely has he pronounced those words than lights suddenly illuminate the city—for every evening, at the same time, from the height of the Terrace of the Sphinx, one of the hierophants, dedicated to that employment, touches a secret apparatus from which expands, in countless sparks, the luminous fluid by means of which Atlantis causes the stars in the sky to pale.

Immediately, the Square of Trophies appears in all its disorder, and the Aztecs who have taken refuge near the vessels see how small the number of cavaliers accompanying Hellas is.

"Look out!" says Knephao, emerging from the tavern, whose doors he closes. "The assault is about to recommence!"

Then, while Hellas and his cavaliers deploy in a single line, Knephao orders the Ligurians to be ready to offer a grim resistance,

Time is short, in fact. The Aztecs, well-armed and strong in numbers, sure of victory, advance in a compact mass, while Hellas, terrible, his sword raised, is the first to plunge into their ranks. But the Prince appears to be on the point of being tipped from his horse when trumpets suddenly burst forth and cavaliers emerge into the square, crying: "Courage Hellas! Here's reinforcements!"

They are the cavaliers that Hermos has sent, Taking advantage of the panic they have provoked, they penetrate into the heart of the melee, while Knephao and Amonou, on the other hand, reach the Prince's horse, which an Aztec is already holding by the bridle.

With a massive blow, the giant fells the Aztec and the young Amonou, for his first feat of arms, uses his sword to slash the arm of a sailor whose pike is directed against Hellas.

At the same moment, in the square and in the city, the lights are abruptly extinguished, and the immense night expands everywhere.

Scene XIII
In the Night

The Aztecs, comprehending nothing of that unexpected phenomenon, flee in fear in the sudden obscurity.

"Don't budge!" Hellas orders the Ligurians, who are trembling, while the impassive Egyptians retain their whinnying horses.

The sea, however, is illuminated in the distance by the flames of Ligurian ships, and in the indecisive glow projected by the reflections of the blaze, Hellas sees the Aztecs running for their boats in such disorder that a considerable number fall into the water, and the plaints of the dying are heard resounding in the lugubrious night.

Hellas and Knephao, rejoined by Amonou, grope their way toward the door of the tavern, where women are moaning

"Do you understand, Hellas?" asks Knephao.

"I can guess..."

"It's Belkis, no doubt?"

"Yes, Belkis. The wretch must have had time to reach the Holy Terrace, and, informed by Barkas, who knows the secrets of the Temple, he's succeeded in drying up at its source the immense reservoir of light that aliments the splendor of Atlantis."

"The Sanctuary must have been violated! And here we are at the other extremity of the city, impotent to find our way in the dark, incapable of going to the defense of the Sphinx"

"Which of us would be able to advance through the tangle of those thousands of streets? Who would be capable of venturing there without getting lost?"

"Me!" shouts a woman's clear voice.

And Hellas feels a frail little hand place itself upon him.

"Glania!" exclaims Amonou.

"You're always shining in my path, like a lucky star," Hellas says to her.

"Yes, very lucky, if you'll permit me to guide you. Have you not run to save me?"

"Enough talk!" growls Knephao, whose gruff voice fails to dissimulate his emotion. "Take the head of the cortege and let's go!"

A few Ligurians equipped with torches march in front of Glania then, and the young woman, bounding with delight, holding the bridle of Hellas' horse in her hand, goes up through the streets deserted by a populace crazed with fear.

And from corner to corner the cortege of cavaliers reaches the foot of the Holy Terrace on the occidental flank of the hill.

"We've arrived," says Glania. "Dismount and leave your horses in the guard of a few Egyptians. We'll go up a little-known stairway that leads up to the Square of the Empire."

Hellas, Amonou and Knephao set foot on the ground, and the Egyptians receive the order not to budge.

"Extinguish the torches!" Glania orders. "I know the way."

In a few rapid strides the three men, guided by the young woman, emerge at the level of the Square of the Empire, not far from the Golden Gate. As they draw nearer to the square, however, the rumor they can hear in the shadows swells to such an extent that Knephao halts, and recommends his companions to hold still.

""What strange accents the voices have!" he growls.

But Glania, trembling with fear, comes to huddle against Hellas. "Master! I recognize them! It's the Blacks!"

"The Blacks!" says Hellas. "They're going to invade the Terrace!"

"They're laying siege to the Palace."

"Hermos will hold firm, but he can't do much in the dark," mutters the Egyptian. "If one door of the Palace cedes, the entire band will enter, pell-mell."

"Let's slip silently among those howling demons under cover of the dark," says Hellas, "and let's try, by slipping along the railings, to reach the Palace without awakening the attention of the Barbarians. You, Glania, my child, go back down to the Egyptian cavaliers and guide them to the Palace of the Waters. Adieu!"

And, taking the frail child in his arms, Hellas kisses her on the forehead like a father.

"Adieu, Glania!" repeats Knephao.

"Adieu, Glania," murmurs Amonou, in a scarcely perceptible voice.

"Well, no," protests the Ligurian. "I won't quit you three, my saviors, my friends, my masters. It's me who'll guide you across the square, as I've guided you this far."

Scarcely has she spoken than an immense light, like a flash of lightning, springs forth from the direction of the occident, toward the Green Isle.

"You see," says Glania. "Some god is speaking; I ought to stay with you!"

"That's not a god," Hellas explains, "it's Oreus. Oh, if he could render us light! He alone can do it!"

At the same moment, another flash envelops the entire city. On the square, the bewildered black barbarians run around in disorder.

For the third time, a great jet of light inundates the city. It does not go out. It continues to shine, like an artificial sun that, instead of coming from the sky, is springing from the sea.

In Atlantis, cries of joy resound. In the square, the Blacks flee in disorder, disturbed by the miraculous light. Knephao, Hellas and Amonou, with loud cries, race through the frightened mob and, without turning their eyes toward the newly-appeared light, run toward the Palace, illuminated throughout its breadth.

Scene XIV
In the Palace of the Empire

"Open up! Open up!" calls Knephao, in a voice that dominates the tumult, and which the Egyptians recognize through the great portal.

"Knephao? You!"

And the high battens of bonze, freed from their iron bars, are opened to the three men and Glania, who plunge into the interior.

"Quickly!" says the warrior, addressing the Egyptians. "All the available men, sword or spear in hand, into the square, and sweep way the black barbarians!"

And, opening the door wide with a thrust of the shoulder, he throws himself on to the Esplanade himself, followed by his running soldiers.

A vain sortie! Unnecessary courage! Only a few of the negroes' backs can be seen in the distance, running away in panic.

"Strange rebels!" growls the giant, scornfully. "They've fled before being attacked. Is it before them that you ceded the square?"

"Oh, great chief," replies an officer, "if you had seen it! Nothing was as terrible as that Esplanade plunged into darkness. And as if the Nubians were waiting for the signal, they poured out of all the avenues. Then, groping our way, we retreated in order to defend the imperial dwelling."

"That's good!" said the chief, softening, "You did your duty. But it's necessary that some of you go in pursuit of the fugitives."

"There's no need, chief! The appearance of that supernatural sun—which, I confess, astonished us all—constitutes for them the sign of a certain disaster. They surely believe it to be a celestial intervention. Look at the square, cluttered with their weapons, thrown to the ground. Listen, up above, they're fleeing."

"What, up above?" says the astonished Knephao, hearing, in fact, cries of terror on the Holy Terrace.

"Yes, great chief. As soon as the darkness was precipitated upon us, a few of the black demons leapt over the Golden Gate."

"And where's Hermos?"

"Oh, Master..." The embarrassed officer hesitates.

"Well, speak! What's stopping you?"

"So be it. As soon as the Palace lost all light, Hermos had a torch lighted, quickly, and launching himself toward the crypts, he went to go and hide in the depths of unknown corridors, closing every door behind him."

"The poor fellow!" murmurs Knephao, in a low voice. "He's fighting up there, perhaps alone, against Timou and his band!" Then, in a loud voice, to the commandant of the phalanx: "You stay here with your men and guard the square."

In a few strides, he finds himself back in the vestibule.

"Ah! Come quickly, Knephao! The entire Palace is in disorder!" It is Glania, tearful, who is running toward the giant. "Hurry! All the servants of the Empire are going mad. They're accusing Hellas of having fled!"

"And Amonou. Where is he?"

"He's trying to rally the confused men, but he doesn't understand Hellas' abrupt disappearance himself."

At the same moment, Amonou appears desolate.

"Knephao," he stammers. "You know..."

"Yes, I now," the Egyptian ripostes dryly, "And I'm going to join Hellas and Hermos."

Then, in his most imperious voce, he summons the dispersed guards.

"You soldiers watch over this door. Remain calm and strong, no matter what happens. I confide command of these men to you, Amonou. You, Glania, go take refuge in the women's apartments."

And without turning his head, he heads for the door that opens to the crypts of the Palace, and closes it behind him abruptly, while the men, astonished, unable to doubt their infallible chief, sensing that they are confronted with a mystery insoluble for them, renounce its comprehension, fall silent and wait, as they have been commanded to do.

Scene XV
In the Temple

Soon after the extinction of the light, in fact, Hermos had understood that the plotters were executing the plan to attack the Holy Terrace, and that the most determined were already about to reach the Sphinx.

Immediately, without warning the guards, not yet fully recovered from their surprise, he has precipitated himself toward the crypts and reached the hidden stairway by means of which he has already been able, once before, to reach the Temple.

Now, here he is again, hidden in the solitary corner where, the day before yesterday, he chanced to hear the plot woven against Hellas and against himself. A vacillating lamp, a kind of night-light, suspended from the ceiling, projects a pale light on the walls. In that uncertain gloom, the Temple is filled with a heavy silence.

It is really here that, scarcely two days ago, Hermos threw himself into the struggle—he, who, throughout his youth had traveled, singing, through cities and races, confident in the eternal glory of Atlantis.

Then, the sacred words that he read before in this sacred place come back to his memory.

You turn yourself
The wheel of destiny!

What! he thinks. *I'm abandoning myself to vain regrets before the inevitable action? Yes, yes! I've done well to defend the cause that appeared to me to be just. If misfortune had to come, nothing could have stopped its fatal march, and I'd experience, moreover, the remorse of my cowardice....*

But now the door opens, slowly, almost silently. A large sheet of blue night enters into the Temple. The door closes again, and muffled footsteps glide. One shadow? Two shadows? Three? Yes, three, Hermos has counted them in the tremulous obscurity. They are creeping rather than marching. What do they fear? Humans, the gods—the Sphinx, perhaps?

"Come on Belkis," murmurs one of the shadows, "move. Are you afraid? You alone know the way; if only I could guide myself!"

"Patience, Timou; we've reached the Tabernacle. But let's go gently. It seems to me that the gods are stirring."

Hermos waits, without budging. While the three shadows slither silently he is wondering whether he ought to fall upon them when abruptly, a jet of light enters through the high windows and causes the vaults of the Temple to flare up. Is it a flash of lightning? Hermes, stupefied, remains motionless in his hiding place. The three men stop. The flash passes.

Now comes another one, longer than the first. The light shines like that of the sun. Hermos sees the three men clearly. The third is a Black, a companion of Timou. The light goes out again.

Finally, a third flash appears, and this time, remains. Hermos, bewildered, no longer understanding anything, abandons himself to destiny and gets ready for any adventure.

The black slave tries to flee, crying: "The sun of the night! It's a god speaking! We're going to die!"

"Coward!" roars Timou. "You're afraid of what will save us?"

"Only flight will save us, Timou," replies the other Black. "You know that the sun of the night is the curse of our race. Remember our defeat on the banks of the Nile!"

And Timou's companion is already hurling himself toward the door, followed by Belkis, who is even more panic-stricken. In a few bounds, Timou catches up with them and retains them with his robust arms.

"Coward!" he shouts at the other Black, in a language incomprehensible to Belkis. "Coward, imbecile or fool! What does it matter what happened on the banks of the Nile? I don't believe in human miracles. I make them myself. This is another secret of that old Oreus, our most terrible enemy, nothing but a jet of light!"

"You promise me, Timou, that I won't die?"

"I promise you victory, trembler. Thanks to them, now we can see clearly. Let's go open the tabernacle, and tomorrow, I'll cast fire over their accursed city!"

Dragging his two accomplished, poorly reassured—Belkis especially—the king of the Blacks returns slowly toward the altar of the Sphinx. Hermos, watching all his movements from the depths of his hiding place, still hesitates to show himself, hoping until the last minute that the Atlantean Belkis will refuse to show the holy place in which the secrets of the tabernacle are hidden. But finally, Timou, step by step, goes all the way to the wall beneath the mystic triangle.

Belkis, overwhelmed by fear, makes the gesture of holding out a key. Hermos, believing that the moment has come to act, raises his sword, which glistens like a beam of strange light, and bounds toward the group.

But just at the moment when the Apostle brings the blade down, and is surely about strike Timou, he feels his arm caught in a vice; then, the three men, trying simultaneously to wrench the sword from his hand, throw him down on the steps of the altar,

"Don't kill him, Timou!" implores Belkis, anxiously, accessible to oracles in spite of himself. "Don't kill him! Blood must not be shed in the Temple, or we'll all be in danger.

"Imbecile!" retorts the Black. "What do the threats of your gods matter to me?"

"And those of humans—do you have more believe in them?" pronounces a sonorous voice.

"Knephao!" exclaims the poet, who was already making his supreme prayer to the Unknown God.

"Hellas!" yelps Belkis, seized by the nape of the neck by another hand.

"To us, sons of Egypt! All come!" howls the colossus, turning toward the depths of the Temple.

"The Egyptians! The Egyptians!" cry a troop of Blacks, already penetrating through the Temple door.

And a great tumult of fleeing men is heard on the terrace.

"To us!" shouts Knephao, holding on to Timou solidly. "You've chosen a strange hour to ask for the initiation of the Sphinx."

"Mock at your ease, Knephao. You have me. So much the worse for me. Kill me, then."

"Mercy! Mercy!" begs Belkis, for his part. "Don't kill me, Hellas!"

The Prince is gripped by a scornful pity for his prisoner.

"No one will kill you, don't worry—nor you, Timou. But we'll keep you captive. You, Timou, we'll send you to some distant isle, and you, Belkis, will commence by returning light to the city, and then you'll reveal your accomplices' plot to us."

"Great Prince! Why didn't you say so sooner? Anything you want to know."

"And then let's get out of here," Knephao enjoins. "The voices of the wicked importune the gods."

Meanwhile, Hermos, although still aching from the blows he has received, has knelt down before the sacred triangle and is begging the Unknown God to save Atlantis as he himself has been saved, by an unexpected miracle.

"Come with us, my great Hermos," adds Hellas, without letting go of Timou. "There are times when actions are dearer to the gods than prayers."

And the three friends, guiding their two prisoners, one silent and dignified, the other whining, emerge on to the perron of the Temple.

As for the second Black, Timou's companion, he has disappeared—but no one thinks about him. They assume that he has fled, like the others.

"Divine hero!" exclaims Thebao, who runs to meet Hellas, Knephao and Hermos, so it's you who have come to save us? But I don't see the soldiers of Egypt!"

"What soldiers?" interrogates the giant.

"The ones who have just terrified the black cohort."

"Oh, a fine stratagem," says Knephao, bursting into loud laughter. "It was sufficient to throw down the threat of my soldiers for all the Blacks to take flight."

"The light coming from the Green Isle had already frightened them."

"It is the Green Isle, isn't it?"

"Yes, but beware," the hierophant observes, "for in spite of his science and his determination, Oreus can't maintain his solar lamp for long, the prodigious glare of which is being projected as far as us. Let's go quickly to restore the fluid current by means of which all of Atlantis is illuminated every evening."

Belkis is confided to the hands of the most robust hierophants. Hermos and Hellas follow Thebao, who tells the two chiefs of the Apostles how the hierophants, surprised in their sleep, had been subjected to the irruption of the black slaves

"A man spoke to us first," he recounted, "clad he in the mantle of the Apostles. He was an obscure merchant of the City, who represented himself as your messenger, Hellas, and no one saw Belkis slip in behind him. The man told my priests that a revolt had broken out in the port and that it was necessary to keep watch over the secret room where the fluidic current is found. My priests, a trifle ingenuous, took him with them to the accumulator that gives the Queen City its nightly splendor spread by millions of lamps, when, perfidiously, Belkis ran toward his accomplice and, with an abrupt turn of the hand, interrupted the light. Then, from all the points of the terrace, one by one, black men fell upon us; a fight began, and we barricaded the doors in order to protect the books and the religious documents. See, the pavement is soiled with the blood of a few hierophants."

"Without wasting time Thebao, let's return light to the city. This time, the Temple is safe."

And Hellas hastens toward the powerful and delicate machine, whose secret workings he knows.

Before he has put his hand on the apparatus that expands or suppresses the daily light at will, suddenly, the light projected from the Green Isle goes out.

A great cry of terror rises up from Atlantis, drowned in darkness. But almost immediately, the clamors of fear change into fanfares of joy. Over the entire city, and the entire port, in all the lighthouses and all the way to the outlying districts, millions and millions of lamps burst forth in flamboyant jets; and, without understanding anything of the events that have just been accomplished, the Atlanteans quit their houses and launch themselves once again into the city in fête.

"Now," says Hellas, reappearing on the Terrace, "let's go back down to the Palace quickly, where our soldiers must be anxious about our absence."

"I'll stay here to ensure the security of the Holy Terrace in case of another attack," declares Knephao. "I'll join you shortly."

He allows the two chiefs of the Apostles to depart, who, after having closed the door of the Temple, disappear into the unknown before the surprised eyes of the priests and the two captives. He has Timou taken to a cell under the surveillance of two hierophants; he contents himself with throwing Belkis into a well-guarded locked room. Then he returns tranquilly to the Square of the Empire via the path that leads to the Golden Gate.

Scene XVI
Gold

Meanwhile, Hellas and Hermos, having hastily descended the hidden stairway, have just emerged abruptly into the vestibule of the Grand Palace, resplendent with all its reilluminated lights.

No one has budged since Knephao's departure. The Egyptians, impassive, are standing guard at the doors; Amonou, calm and silent, is still at his command post—to the extent that it appears to the two Apostles of the Sun that their disappearance must have passed unperceived. So, they are quite surprised, as soon as they appear, to hear the soldiers of the Palace cry out, resoundingly:

"Hellas! Hermos! They've come back! They're not dead!"

"Nor fled!"

Haughtily, Hellas demands: "Dead? Fled? What do those words mean?" And, addressing the oldest among them, Knephao's favorite lieutenant: "You doubted Hermos and me, then?"

The other is so troubled that ill-suppressed tears trickle from his eyes over his wrinkled cheeks. "Master," he stammers. "Forgive us. Something mysterious frightened our souls."

"Even so, is that any reason to treat us as cowards?"

Lashed by that word, the soldiers bow their heads, no longer daring to ask for pardon.

"Forgive them," says Hermos. "There are moments in popular torments when the most valiant lose their reason."

"Very well," Hellas acquiesces. "Let everything be forgotten. But remember that the storms of Atlantis have barely begun, and prepare your souls for all surprises."

178

"Long live Hellas! Long live Hermos!" acclaim the men, relieved. But to that cry a frail voice trembling with emotion immediately replies:

"Hellas! You? You, Hermos? Run quickly to the square. Here comes a large crowd of Atlanteans who seem to be proffering threats." It is Glania, who, left alone, instead of going to rest, has been watching from the height of the balconies, still thinking about possible dangers that might menace the Prince.

"The Atlanteans? Them? Threats? Them, whom I've just saved? You're dreaming, Glania!"

However, increasingly, a din is rising, reminiscent of the sound of heavy carts advancing in disorder, and thousands and thousands of voices are resounding with staccato cries:

"Gold! Gold!"

"The people haven't had their distribution of gold!"

"The people want gold!"

"Gold! Gold!"

In fact, in the trouble that has turned the city upside down, Hellas, Hermos and the masters of the Palace have neglected to distribute to the crowd the gold coins and medallions that it is customary to distribute on the evenings of Festivals. And the people, who, for centuries, have refused to bear arms; the people, who have left to vanquished reds and white barbarians the care of their defense; the people, indifferent to the destiny of the City; the people are rising up now for the sake of a few gold coins, of which each individual share is insignificant.

"Gold! Gold!" repeats the mob.

Hellas remains crushed. The revolt of the Blacks, the plots of his enemies, the uprising of Barbarians against Atlantis: none of that has been able to trouble his firm soul. But this definitive baseness, this ignominy of the people, his people, is the supreme blow that he did not expect, and against which he feels impotent.

"Cowards! Cowards! Slaves, Souls of swine!" shouts Hermos, in the same sonorous voice that once sang the song of triumph. "People unworthy of glory, that is all you can find to say at the moment when death is perhaps hovering over you?"

But on the square, another voice, harsher and even more furious than that of Hermos, resounds:

"Soldiers of Egypt, charge! Clear away this rabble!"

It is Knephao, who, taking the horse of one of his soldiers, exerts a vigorous pressure on the crowd himself.

An immediate stampede follows that decisive action, and the square is emptied in a very short time. But scattered groups can be heard in the distance, throughout the town, who are turning round in order to continue crying out:

"Gold! Gold! Gold!"

Hellas can stand it no longer. That soul, which nothing has yet been able to depress, is weeping now over the abasement of the crowd.

"Let it die, then, that people! Let all the peoples die! Let stinking humankind perish!"

"Hellas, my friend," says Hermos, "don't despair. Perhaps there are noble souls among those crowds that your dolor is cursing."

And Glania, taking the hand of the Prince gently, murmurs softly: "Hellas, see how everyone here loves you? What is it necessary to do for you?"

And, at the same moment, Knephao and Amonou reappear, the one bleeding again from his reopened wound, the other with his garments in tatters. Hellas stands up then; his gaze becomes firm again; he smiles at the barbarian girl who has tried to save him several times, at the three men who have risked death; he remembers old Oreus spreading his light; he sees Orea again, the resuscitator of his nobility, and, in a determined voice, he proclaims:

"Well, so be it! Live, even so, our Atlantis! And let us die, if necessary, for the cruel, ignorant, cowardly peoples, since there might, in spite of everything, within their putrid rabble, be holy souls, radiant spirits and heroic hearts."

THE FOURTH DAY:
THE FESTIVAL OF THE OCCIDENT

A great dusk will come
Without a further dawn.

Scene I
Adieux to the Green Isle

Black and confused in the night that is about to end, the sleeping Green Isle is crouched beneath a sky heavy with stars, and the respiration of the foliage scarcely responds to the murmur of light waves. A breath of flowers floats above dormant things. Phosphorescent wings glisten over the sea. There is no sound in the houses, no bird in the branches. Only the murmurous chant of a cascade is alive; and that monotonous plaint fills the silence of the immensity.

"Listen, listen," says Oreus. "Let's stop for a moment. One last time, let the soul of the merciful night enter into my soul."

"My beloved father, why is your heart so sad? Why say 'one last time'? We'll come back this evening, to our palm trees..."

"No, no, I shall never return to these shores. Don't ask me anymore. My child, my flesh, my creation, my vibrant and beautiful soul, be strong enough for both of us, for now, having arrived on the threshold of my destiny, I'm beginning to tremble with fear before the future."

"My father, the friend of the gods, the confidant of the invisible spirits, tell me, do you sense the breath of death passing over us?"

"Death! For mercy's sake, may it take me as a hostage for all the prey that it has marked!"

A frisson agitates Oreus' handsome body, and his eyes become troubled.

"What do you mean, father? Have you not promised me never to hide anything from your child?"

"Shut up! Let's both shut up. The hour is pleasant. Let's breathe the extreme night.

And, letting himself fall to a sitting position on a stone bench facing the somber sea, the old man takes his daughter's head in his arms and kisses the golden hair from which a perfume of youth rises.

The quivering of the waves is so slow and so tender that one might think that the sea wanted to fall silent in order to allow the mute prayer of those two souls to rise toward the gods; the stars seem magnified, so radiant that they appear to be descending toward the earth.

But the old man can scarcely distinguish the twinkling of the stars. His eyes still retain the dazzle of the splendor that he projected over the city in disorder, and when he opens them slightly he sees nothing but a darkness in which troubling gleams are swirling. Then he closes his eyelids again, and words scarcely murmured spring from his heart toward mysterious beings. He prays.

"Unknown God, why is it necessary for that which you allowed to live and grow in beauty for such a long time must die? That you take us, whose task is measured and our hours brief, we know and we accept, but cities, Lord? Harmonious civilizations: things that we have edified stone by stone for thousands of years? O God, just but good, crush, if necessary, humans and races; ravage the fallen generations that have not been able to keep your law; bring new peoples into our ancient walls, but conserve, at least, the work of our forefathers, who were innocent of our sins, and let Atlantis subsist in its glorious form, in order that, already a reflection of your harmony, it might still give ephemeral humans the terrestrial appearance of your eternity!"

A profound and prolonged sigh rises from Orea's breast, and the old man feels his daughter's heart beating next to his own.

"However, Lord, let your will be accomplished!"

Having pronounced those words, the old man shakes his head, stands up abruptly, extends his hand to his daughter, and says, in an emotional voice:

"Let's go! Let the diviner disappear and the man carry out his single duty. So much the worse for the man who sees too far, for he suffers before the others, but shame upon him if he wraps himself up in his suffering. Have I said that Atlantis must die? But can I and should I know that? It is going to wake up prosperous still, perhaps it will remain so. Our action participates in destiny."

"Father, I've found you again! Yes, your genius can and ought to realize miracles. Have you not, yesterday evening, by means of the intervention of our solar lamp, prevented the satisfaction of a plot by which the Queen City was about to succumb, delivered to the Barbarians? And will not Hellas second your power? Have confidence in his nobility. Let's go, Father, let's go to Atlantis."

"Yes, let's go. But beforehand, as I might never come back to this Green Isle, let me give you, my daughter, the secret by which, whatever happens, you can carry away to a new world the treasures amassed by centuries of science and meditation."

And Oreus tries to draw Orea toward the isolated hangar where the *Alerion* is lodged, the supreme prodigy of Atlantean science.

But the old man's steps are uncertain, his eyes can distinguish nothing in the starlight, and he is groping his way along the path. A presentiment that is soon transformed into a certainty traverses his brain and upsets his heart: he is going to lose his sight! The prolonged effort that he made last night, in manipulating the fragments of condensed sunlight, the splendor of which expelled the shadows of Atlantis, has fatigued the strength of his eyes. Only a few vacillating glimmers of objects remain to him.

"My God," he murmurs, "grant me one more day, only one more day of material lucidity, in order that I can make the fire that saves move once more!"

And a great melancholy falls within his soul when he thinks that, at a very imminent time, he will no longer see the light of day.

"What's the matter, Father? You're hesitant. Your hands are seeking the support of the trees."

At that voice, Oreus trembles. Is it necessary to reveal to his daughter the malady by which he has been stricken? He has formed her so courageous and so patient. He has promised never to hide terrestrial dolors from her. But no! Not that. She would want to remain with him all day, in order to serve as his guide, and it is necessary that she comes back to the Green Isle in order to watch over the treasures. He therefore reassures his child.

"Often, after having touched the redoubtable eternal fire, I've felt a temporary weakness in my eyes. It's not in vain that one stirs the devouring and fecundating flame. It's sufficient to keep my eyes closed for a few hours, and my irritated nerves are soon soothed."

"Keep your eyes closed, Father; I'll guide you."

At a slow pace, however, they arrive at the clump of eucalyptus where the hangar is built under which the *Alerion* reposes, with its wings now furled.

"Can you see it better now, Father?"

"Yes, I can see it," says Oreus, whose hands recognize his work. "Listen to me, my child; this is the object of all my dreams, the most cherished of all my endeavors. I wanted to deliver it to my Atlantean people and thus open the doors to the azure to them, but human malevolence would have made that celestial gift an instrument of pride and conquest, and I've reserved it in order to watch over, sooner or later, threatened Atlantis. Already, I've saved Hellas. The time is perhaps coming when this giant bird might serve for an even vaster endeavor than the salvation of our city itself and the defense of its heroes.

"Beyond our City, beyond our race, beyond the limits of the Empire, there is the world, the vast world, and men everywhere who are our equals and our brothers. They are still living in ignorance of the divine sciences and in the servitude of their instincts, but one day they will rise like us toward he contemplation of eternal verities, and perhaps, in a few points of the earth still savage today, new Atlantises will one day be born. Well, that growth of civilizations to come we ought to hasten, with all our might, for if the gods have granted it to us to discover their secrets, it is in order to make a gift of them to the future world. That is why, my daughter, I have brought you to this aerial chariot, to which humankind will owe a new sense of life. If Atlantis must disappear..."

"Are you despairing, then, Father?"

"I still hope, since I'm acting. So, if Atlantis, under the blows of the Barbarians, the revolts of her own children or even by the excess of her vices, is carried away by a tempest of celestial fury, the world will not end for so little. Then, my child, you will climb into the *Alerion* whose mechanisms I have revealed to you today. You will go toward the Orient, to the extremity of the Interior Sea. It's there that the young humankind will grow that will direct the world again, until the day when, from stage to stage, it will carry the torch of life again over the shores of our Ocean. You will find out there, in a sea bluer and more even than ours, a bouquet of islands in flower, which, from the height of your winged chariot, will appear to you like roses in a field of azure. That is the land of the Pelasgians, the land dear to Hellas, the land that will bear his imprint. You will descend on one of those islands. You will deposit there all the treasures contained in the nacelle of the *Alerion*. Then you will reveal to the attentive peoples the splendors of our accumulated science, and, before long, a more vigorous Atlantis will surge forth."

So saying, Oreus plunges his arm into the nacelle and adds:

"Everything is in its place. Here are the books containing the clarity of just laws; here are the works to which are consigned the sublime verities of music and numbers; here are the thoughts of philosophers, here the smiles of poets; here is life. Now, take care; here in an isolated corner are the treasures of science and the redoubtable formulae of chemical combinations. In these cylinders of platinum and gold there is solid air, whose irresistible force can raise the earth and waters and displace mountains. Further away are fragments of condensed sunlight, carefully enclosed in cassettes of indestructible metal. At the back are the formidable powders of which a single handful thrown from the air is sufficient to burn entire cities.

"Now, all that, my daughter, you will bury before departing, five cubits underground, for it is death, the accursed work! Instead of making use of it to tame disordered nature, men would employ these presents of science to kill one another and to procure unknown enjoyments. I'm therefore counting on you, my child, to annihilate these testimonies to our pride."

But Orea does not reply. While her father has been speaking and invoking the coming civilizations toward which the *Alerion*, conqueror of the air, might sail with wings outstretched, the young woman has been remembering the words of Hellas, who also dreamed of conquering all the vast world by amour. She remembers the promises exchanged, and in her thoughts she murmurs:

If it's necessary to depart for new lands, why should I not depart with him?

Suddenly, however, the insidious amour that is speaking within her appears to her in all its egotism and, violently chasing away the overly dear image of Hellas, she looks at Oreus, who, in a tranquil voice, has been declaring his last will.

"Father," Orea remarks, softly, "you're talking to me as if I were never going to see you again."

"Yes, my child, we shall see one another again. I sense it; I divine it. But let's not stir our own future. Humans wound the gods when they dig into future things for themselves; they obey, on the other hand, their divine mission when they seek to foresee the destiny of peoples."

"No matter! If I have to do it to see you again, I'll accomplish miracles."

"For today, my daughter, let's go to the City. You'll take me to the Palace of the Empire, and then you'll come back in the same boat. And all day long, and all the days that follow—for I don't know how long the battle will last—you'll watch over Atlantis from afar. The rest regards your clear sight and your courage. Let's go. I seem to be able to glimpse daylight through my dolorous eyelids."

A slow dawn is, in fact, rising in the orient, and the sea is taking in reflections of white silk. The old man and his daughter head toward the tiny harbor of the Green Isle, where a boat is waiting for them, guarded by two sailors. But as they are about to quit the gardens of the isle in order to descend to the creek, a poignant emotion grips the old man. He bends down. He takes in his hand a clump of flowers and foliage and, raising them to his lips, he sniffs them, as if he wanted to extract in a final perfume the entire soul of the land where he has lived.

"Adieu, little isle, accomplice of my dearest dreams and my most patient labors; adieu, house gilded by the sun; adieu, fine gravel of the pathways where my feet beat time to the rhythm of my solitary thoughts; adieu, living flowers that spoke to me in the frisson of the dusk; adieu, mobile sea of the friendly murmur; adieu, City that I saw by night resplendent beneath the sky impregnated by crimson luminosity; adieu, finally, subtle air that bore the soul of my fatherland: you are all, house, land, flowers, blue gulfs, light atmosphere, only blind and inanimate things, but I sense that in losing you I shall lose the sweetness of life forever."

Then, throwing away the bouquet of foliage and taking his daughter's hand again: "Let's go, my child, let's go without fear. There will be new flowers out there!"

Scene II
The Palace of the Empire

The sun is about to rise. Egyptian soldiers have stood guard all night, but at this hour, as the city is in repose, they have tethered their horses to the rings of the Golden Gate, and, lying on their deployed cloaks, they are sleeping side by side of the pavement of the Esplanade. Only the chief of the group is on watch, indolently, sitting on the base of a pillar.

"Soldier," asks a young woman's voice, softly, "do you know Knephao?"

The Egyptian shakes his head abruptly. "To Hell with damned citizens who come to pester me at such an hour! A fine time, truly, to be asking for alms."

"It's not a matter of alms," replies the young woman, smiling. "I want to talk to Knephao."

"To Knephao, no less! And you think that I'm going to wake the great chief so early for two beggars? Why not Hellas, to do so much?"

"That will be for later," the old man interjects. "But for the moment, soldier, go fetch Knephao without any argument."

Those words are spoken in a voice so firm, no noble and so imperative that the soldier, without understanding anything, sensing confusedly that someone important is speaking to him, gets up and obeys.

A few moments later, the soldier comes back and takes the old man and the young woman into the vestibule of the Palace.

Scarcely awake, with neither armor nor sword, simply clad in dark cloth, with his bare head displaying a large scar, Knephao appears. "Oreus!" he cries. And, bowing deeply, in a scarcely perceptible voice: "Orea?"

"Is that you, Knephao?" asks the old man.

At that question, the giant looks at the young woman, who, divining the warrior's mute question, answers it herself:

"My father has to keep his eyelids lowered for a few hours. The light lavished last night on the city in disorder has fatigued his eyes. I've only come to confide him to your care, Knephao, to conduct him to the Sacred Terrace, where he wants to see the hierophants."

"To me, Orea? It's me that you thought of first?"

"Are you not the bravest of combatants, the surest of friends and the purest of heroes? But what do I see on your face? Blood has run over your cheek! You've been wounded!"

"Almost nothing," says Knephao, radiant with joy. "A blow I received yesterday, while defending Glania."

"Glania nearly perished, then?"

"And me too, and Amonou also. Hellas saved us." And the colossus gave a brief account of the previous day's adventures.

"Magnificent Hellas!" exclaimed Orea. "You hear, Father! You see how he merits your affection? But of all the exploits accomplished by the Prince of the Empire, the one dearest to my heart is to have saved Glania and Knephao."

"Oh, Orea," stammered the warrior, as emotional as a child, "you'll never know the extent to which I'm your slave!"

"My slave, no—my friend, for a long time. But let's not talk about our personal sentiments, Knephao. I'm counting on you."

"Command, Orea. After such words, what would I not do?"

"This morning, simply take my father to the Holy Terrace. Then tell Hellas to come to see me. The rest, I have no need to tell you. Your bravery will go before the actions to be carried out."

However, Oreus, having drawn the Egyptian to one side, murmurs a few words very quietly into his ear.

"Master," groans Knephao, overwhelmed by dolor, "is it possible?"

"Above all, don't let her overhear! I'm letting her believe that I'll be cured. I still have one day, one single day, to use my eyes. I'll make use of them for a gigantic endeavor, and their last vision will be grandiose."

"But who will look after you during that day, Master, when I will doubtless be obliged to guard the city?"

"Glania? What a subtle, devoted, joyous guide for a future blind man! Bring her to me right away."

Then, turning and groping his way toward Orea, he says: "Adieu, my daughter. You know your duty. I know mine. And let me say one comforting word: I sense that we'll see one another again soon, perhaps far away, in unknown lands, but both alive and strong."

"And Hellas, Father? Can you not see and reach an understanding with him?"

Oreus hesitated momentarily, and then, decisively: "No. Let's allow him to act in accordance with his own genius. He's one of those whom it's necessary to aid without their knowing it. It's up to you alone to fortify him, if he needs it. See him for a few moments before leaving the Palace, and recommend him to have full confidence. Kiss me, my daughter, and let's part without tears."

They exchange a long, tender kiss; then, separating, they depart without looking back.

"Knephao," says Orea, in a whisper, "send one of your men to fetch Hellas. I think I need to see him before either of us commences this rude day."

An Egyptian sets forth to the apartments of the Prince, while Oreus and Knephao disappear into the silent crypts and Orea, left alone, allows the tears to trickle from her eyes that she has been holding back since the night.

Scene III
Two Souls

Hellas, surrounded by his most faithful companions in arms, who returned with him from the land of the Pelasgians, is making the final arrangements for repairing, in the morning, the ravages of the day before, reassuring the people, consolidating the soldiers and halting the insurrection of the rebels. Hermos and he have fallen into accord regarding the plan to adopt in case of conflict, and already, in curt and precise words, the two leaders are distributing to every man the employment of his time, when an Egyptian guard comes to speak in a low voice to Hellas. Surprised, having difficulty dissimulating the emotion of his heart, the Prince gets up and goes down hastily to the vestibule, still deserted at this early hour.

And immediately, taking Orea's hands, he draws her into a solitary room.

Then he looks at her, sees her eyes reddened by tears and her lips still trembling, from which no words can emerge.

"Orea my beloved, you've been weeping? You're still weeping!"

But she, in spite of her determination, impotent to struggle any longer against her emotion, lets herself fall into the young man's arms, her head leaning on his robust shoulder.

"Hellas, my friend, my beloved, forgive me for weeping in front of you, who have so much need of all your energy today, but I'm exhausted, body and soul."

"Weep, my love; it requires very great ordeals to weary Orea's courage. Tell me your secret."

"My father is here."

"Where? Since when?"

"He's gone to the Terrace; we've just arrived from the island." Then, after a pause, speaking in a low voice into the young man's ear, as the marble sphinxes themselves ought not to overhear, she says: "He can no longer see me. He's blind."

"Blind? Him!"

"Last night he threw toward the city in distress, all the splendor of the sun, with which, by the same effort, he burned his own eyes forever."

"Blind!" repeats Hellas. "Blind!"

"Not yet, perhaps, but he will be by this evening."

"Why this evening?"

"Because he wants to lavish the supreme strength of his eyes in new exploits, today; if he's had himself taken to the Sacred Terrace, it's to manipulate there once again the hidden flames of the Sanctuary and preserve them from possible incursions by our enemies."

A silence.

"Orea, has your father said anything about the day to come?"

"Nothing," Orea replies, after a momentary hesitation, "except that Hermos, Knephao and you will accomplish great feats."

"But in such circumstances, why don't you stay with him? Why have I been told that you want to go back to the Green Isle?"

"Because it's necessary."

"No, no, Stay with us in Atlantis; stay with your father. If, by a decree of the gods, we have to die, at least let us die together."

"We won't die; my father has assured me of that. We'll see one another again soon. I have faith in him."

"Here, in Atlantis, delivered from evil?"

"Here or elsewhere. Perhaps elsewhere, in a new land, among younger peoples. But I'm speaking at hazard. My head is troubled by fatigue and dolor."

"Elsewhere? Why? Your father has said something? What has he said? What do you know?"

"Nothing, nothing. Hellas, for pity's sake, let me go. I've promised my father to return to the island."

"No matter! It's for your father that I'm keeping you, and for me too, since you have given me your life and your heart. I won't let you fall into enemy hands as a prisoner."

"You're forgetting, Hellas, that if have wings in order to escape them."

"The *Alerion*? Your father hasn't destroyed it? He's entrusted it to you?"

"Yes, entrusted, my love, and I now hold in a nacelle the destiny of the future world." And Orea tells Hellas how Oreus took her to the winged chariot.

Then Hellas, fully reanimated, takes Orea in his arms and seems to lift her into the air.

"Masters!" he cries. "We're the masters of destiny!"

"Friend, friend, will you love your eternal dream more than me?"

"No, no," replies Hellas, illuminated by joy, "I put nothing in the world above my amour. Henceforth, we hold an assured triumph, and I understand now the prediction that the clairvoyant mind of Oreus allowed to escape."

"I confess that it remains obscure to me."

"Yes, soon, thanks to you, thanks to the *Alerion*, all three of us—your father, you and me—will meet again in a distant land, in the cradle of new races, on the shore where I once glimpsed the future City of new Empires, in what will be called the land of Hellas."

"Explain yourself, friend: your enthusiasm carries me away, but vertigo follows."

"Listen, Orea. Here's the sun, already appearing, and the day will be terrible. The Aztecs repelled yesterday evening have reached the open sea in their vessels, and this morning will doubtless be joined by boats coming from the Occident for today's Festival. Mellena and her friends have joined them. Now, their fleet has not lost a single ship; that of the Ligurians, on the contrary, has been partly ravaged by the flames, and we're almost disarmed on the sea. Nevertheless, during the night, my companions in arms have recruited all the available ships scattered around the seven peninsulas and have

take control of all the merchant vessels. I can therefore recon-
stitute a fleet in haste. I'll advance my ships between the
Golden Isle and the Crimson Isle. I'll command the battle myself. In the meantime, Hermos and the most valiant young men
of the City will take up positions on the Crimson Isle, which
they'll defend, for it will be the advance citadel of the City.
And Knephao will stay in Atlantis with his soldiers.

"That's my plan. It might succeed. It might fail. We
have, unfortunately, many weak points. On the sea, our partly
improvised fleet is ill-prepared for the assaults of war. On the
Crimson Isle, the indolent artists will hamper Hermos' action.
And most of all I fear, in the City, the cowardice or the folly
of the people, capable of hurling themselves against their own
defenders. One mysterious resource remains, however: your
father. He will surely bring forth, as he did yesterday, some
powerful secret. But you're bringing me another hope: the
Alerion..."

"Hellas, be careful! I've sworn..."

"You haven't sworn to let me die, to deliver Atlantis to
the Barbarians. So listen, Orea: you're going to go back to
your blissful isle. You'll keep the *Alerion* ready to depart, its
wings open, the nacelle filled with all your father's treasures—all of them!"

"Impossible!"

"Yes, possible, if you do it. This, for my part, is what I'm
going to do. In a few hours, I'll depart in search of the Aztecs
and the Blacks. You will then go up in into the tower of the
Green Isle, and you'll watch all our maneuvers with the aid of
a telescope. I'll fight until my forces are exhausted. If I'm
victorious, then we'll return in triumph to the City, and you'll
fold up your unnecessary wings. But if the rebels triumph, the
Crimson Isle will be invaded in spite of Hermos' efforts, and
Atlantis threatened. Even Knephao will succumb, for the poor
fellow and his Egyptians cannot withstand the furious invasion
of the Barbarian hordes, let alone defend themselves against
the seditious terror of a people whom fear and cowardice will
render more dangerous than our enemies. That, Orea, is the

194

supreme peril, which it's necessary to avoid. And you alone can do it."

"How?"

"When you see my vanquished fleet retreating in disorder, when you see the ships running toward the Crimson Isle, and even your own isle, then you'll surge into the air with wings deployed, you'll come toward us, you'll recognize my ship by the crimson standard floating at the poop, and you'll descend toward it slowly. If I'm alive, I'll come to join you, and the two of us will deliver the City. But if I die..."

"Hellas!"

"On the morning of a battle it's necessary to anticipate everything. So, if I die, if you see my vessel disappear, then, you'll accomplish the destiny alone. You'll drop on to the Aztec fleet some of the cylinders of solid air, whose redoubtable effect will be sufficient to destroy their fleet and save the city..."

"No, no, Hellas, don't ask me to do such a thing. I can't, I don't want to..."

"Can't? Don't want to? Why?"

"Because I'd be breaking an oath that I swore to my father and committing a crime against the gods."

"Crime? Oath? Words that sound hollow at the moment of an action in which the entire Empire might perish."

"What a crime, Hellas, to kill men without danger, without struggle, from the height of the air!"

"Then go, Orea, go to your island. Go remain faithful to your oath. For myself, on the threshold of a decisive day, I only know my people to be saved, my duty to fulfill, death to await. Adieu. then."

And Hellas, throwing his cloak over his shoulder, gets ready to leave the room.

Orea, in distress, runs forward, grabs the young man by the arm, and turns him round with a superhuman gesture; then putting her hands together in a gesture of emotional prayer: "My master, my beloved, by what suffering is my heart not torn at this moment when my will is resisting yours? Don't go,

Hellas. For pity's sake, listen to me. What do you want? To save Atlantis? We both want that. But what danger is the city in? Can a few thousand Aztec mariners and black slaves subjugate millions of Atlanteans?"

"Poor friend! Don't you know that those millions of Atlanteans couldn't resist the slightest assault?"

"And to conserve those degenerate populations, to save those cowards abandoned by the gods in spite of themselves, you're going to disobey the eternal laws? You'll only hold back destiny by a few days, and we'll have accomplished an unforgettable crime."

"So be it, then. You reason marvelously. Let's let Atlantis die. But me, I shall die with her, as you once ordered me to do."

"Hells, Hellas! My heart hesitates! Don't crush me. We love one another, though!"

And the two young people fall silent.

Scene IV
The Morning of a Battle

Now, a clear and young voice bursts forth in the vestibule. Glania's! It comes nearer. It calls: "Orea! Hellas!"

Then, lifting the crimson curtain, her face appears, illuminated by joy.

"Orea," she says, throwing herself into the arms of the beautiful Atlantean. You're here, then, Orea? Knephao has just told me that you'd come. It appears that I'm no longer to quit your father and to stay beside him always. So, if I'm not quitting Oreus, I'm not quitting you, either! And if I live close to him, I'll also live close to Hellas, since he loves you, and I shall see you both together in the joy of the sunlight!"

That hymn of delight, sung in a clear fanfare in the radiant morning, brings a vague smile back to the lips of Hellas and Orea.

"The dear child doesn't know anything," Orea explains to Hellas. "Let's leave her joy undisturbed."

But Glania remarks the profound dolor that the eyes of Hellas and Orea cannot dissimulate.

"You're sad? And I'm laughing! And I'm singing! What gives me the right to come to disturb you? Adieu, I'll leave you."

"Sad?" says Orea. "Preoccupied, at the most. Hellas is thinking about the city's troubles, and I was talking to him about them. But sing, Glania; it does one good, in the morning, to hear the hymn of the birds, friends of the gods."

"Oh, no! I don't know why, but I can no longer sing or laugh now."

Then Hellas, pensive, raises his head and asks: "Reply to me frankly, Glania. If you knew that I was in danger of death, would you try to save me, if you could?"

"Why ask me such a question? I would try even if I couldn't."

"And what if the gods had forbidden you to do it?"

"What gods?"

"The god Thot, for example, the terrible god of the Ligurian lands, whom your forefathers worshiped and feared?"

"I would say that the god was mistaken, and I would save you anyway."

"Thank you, Glania. Well spoken!"

And Hellas looks at Orea, with a tenderly ironic expression

"Glania," exclaims Orea, "embrace your master, and tell him that this evening, he will be saved."

Then the young Atlantean, transfigured and radiant, advances toward Hellas and takes his hands.

"I've understood. No oath or prayer will stop me. The orders of the gods? Words whose meaning our hearts alone can interpret—and my heart has now divined everything."

"Glory to the Sphinx!" proclaims Hellas, radiant with hope. "Finally, I'm victorious; finally, we'll be saved. Glania my child, go join Oreus and tell him that his daughter and his son are certain of the triumph."

At that moment, Knephao and Hermos are announced and come in.

"Let's make haste," says Hermos, very gravely, after having bowed to Orea. The sun's climbing toward the zenith. We only just have time to carry out our plan."

"And you, little Ligurian," adds Knephao, "Come, so that I can take you to Oreus."

But Hellas says, in a sonorous voice: "Hermos, Knephao, and you too, Glania, rejoice and sing; this is the day from which a new Atlantis will emerge."

Hellas' two companions, infected by his ardor, celebrate the imminent victory then. Glania jumps for joy and Orea, happy and calm, her eyes filled with serene ecstasy, embraces Hellas silently and gets ready to go down to the port.

"What about me?" asks Glania. "You're leaving without permitting me to embrace you too?"

And she throws her arms around Orea's neck.

"You too, Hermos," says the daughter of Oreus, "you who are a poet, by nobility of soul, and have become so naturally a hero, come to my arms. On the morning of such a day, we're no longer anything but a united family."

Then, silently, turning to Knephao, she extends her beautiful arms with golden gleams toward the giant, who, tremulous and weak for the first time, feels his knees buckle, and approaches, his eyes troubled.

Then Hellas blesses them all.

"Radiant Sphinx! Mirror of light! Symbol of our eternal rebirth, O Sphinx, bearer of our destiny, be resplendent now and open your victorious wings wide to the sunlight; those who wanted to die, dragged down by your fall, will live, on the contrary, to exalt you even in new skies!"

Scene V
In the Sanctuary

"Master," Knephao pronounces, opening the little secret door of the Temple and penetrating quietly into the Sanctuary, "here's Glania."

But Oreus does not budge. Kneeling on the steps that lead to the altar of the Sphinx, his head hidden in his hands, his body inclined toward the ground, the old man in meditating and praying.

Surprised, Knephao falls silent and stops. Glania, utterly bewildered to find herself in this place of solitude and silence, tries to hide, fearfully, in the darkest corner of the Temple.

"How big it is!" she murmurs. "What men, superior to the rest of men, are those who constructed these pillars and sculpted these marble divinities; those who have made these resplendent Sphinx with golden wings and these triangles with dazzling gems! A city like this ought to last forever!"

But immediately, a grave voice rises in the Sanctuary, so profound and so enveloping, that Glania does not know at first whether the voice comes from the god or his great Apostle.

"My poor child," Oreus replies, "here you are, come to rescue me?"

"To rescue you, Master? From what danger?"

Then Oreus, raising his head, curbed over the steps of the Sanctuary, appears wearing a black bandage over his eyes. He extends imploring hands into empty space.

"Knephao, my friend, give me your hand. And you, Glania, come close to me. Forgive me for having left you in silence for a few moments, but I was trying to talk to the gods. Now, you, Glania, are going to take me out of the Temple, and you, Knephao, are going to bid me farewell, for other exploits than our humble prayers wait you."

But Glania, trembling and frightened, examines Oreus' black band and the old man's hesitant gestures; then, leaning toward Knephao, she murmurs: "Why can't the Master see any longer?"

Overwhelmed by dolor, Knephao does not know what to reply, but Oreus has heard.

"You don't know, then, my child, that I'm going blind?"

"Master! Master!" groans the young Barbarian, unable to say anything else. And she falls into Oreus' arms, sobbing.

"No one had told her yet," said Knephao. "When she found out that she was to follow you and live by your side all the time, she showed such surges of joy that Orea, always good, didn't want to interrupt that juvenile delight suddenly, and deferred the moment when Glania would learn the sad news."

Then Oreus shakes the rough hand of the warrior affectionately, and leans toward Glania.

"Don't weep, my child. Of what do I have to complain, since instead of my poor aged eyes I shall henceforth possess, in order to march through life, the beautiful and clear eyes of a young woman? They will describe to me the splendors of the sun and the fête of the stars."

Then the old man adds: "Tell me Knephao, what are Hellas and Hermos going to do today?"

Knephao explains the plan decided by the two Princes of Apostles.

"Very good. I see that Hellas still retains his marvelous lucidity. You believe, then, that he'll attack the Aztec fleet in daylight?"

"I'm sure of it, Master."

"And he's counting on a possible success?"

"He left us singing a veritable hymn of triumph."

"Admirable! Well, he'll doubtless be victorious, and the last rays that my eyes receive will bring me the reflection of his glory."

"You hope to see him again, then, Master?" asks Glania.

"While requesting the assistance of the Unknown God, I've just applied to my eyelids a powerful remedy kept by the initiate physicians. But tell me, Knephao, by your calculation, how long will Hellas require to take his fleet beyond the Crimson Isle."

"At least two hours."

"Very good. In two hours, the remedy will have taken effect. I'll take off the blindfold and watch the movements of the battle from the height of the Holy Hill. And perhaps I'll find an unexpected aid..."

"Oh, Master!" exclaimed the Egyptian, enthused. "You'll surely find it, the aid that we need."

"Farewell, then—go and join your brave cavaliers. Glania will take me to Thebao and stay with me until I remove the bandage covering my eyes." Then, collecting himself: "Count on victory, then! But a strong man must calculate everything and anticipate everything, including defeat. If, therefore, disorder invades the city, mount a good guard around the Holy Mountain. Finally, if tonight some catastrophe ravages the city, don't forget that the supreme citadel is the hill where we stand. Forbid access to it to any invader, and if, impossibly, you're overwhelmed by superior numbers, don't allow yourself to be killed in front of the Palace, and come up to join us. I'll need your arm here..."

"Master, your anticipations are making me shiver!"

"Who anticipates disaster, avoids it."

And, surrounding the giant with a paternal accolade, Oreus seems to communicate to him a fluid of superhuman force, by virtue of which the fearless warrior feels himself to be capable of lifting up the world.

Scene VI
The Guardians of the Fire

"Go gently, Glania. To our right and our left, can you see statues of heroes and gods?"

"Yes, Master."

"Good. In front of you, is there a massive door with heavy bonze battens?"

"I believe I can see one, in fact, above which a ventilation shaft allows an indecisive daylight to filter through."

"Perfect. Take me to it. Good. Look for a copper button above the lock. Press it hard. Now, pull the door toward you."

A great flood of light invades the Temple and inundates Glania's eyes, which have been plunged in the obscurity of the crypts and the Sanctuary for a long time.

"Oh, Master, what beautiful sunlight is illuminating the city. A sun of victory!"

"You see, child, that I've done well to put a black blindfold over my eyes. I'll remove it gradually, in order that the light can penetrate it progressively. Close the Temple door again. Go down the steps of the perron. Is there anyone on the terrace?"

"There are men dressed in long robes. They seemed surprised to see us—even frightened."

"Doubtless they don't recognize me, and are astonished that a white woman has been able to penetrate the Sanctuary. Take me to them."

"No need, Master; here they are before us."

Close by, in fact, a grave and severe voice, though still young, says: "Who are you, strangers, hidden by night in the Sanctuary of the Sphinx? Is it you who have stolen the liquid fire?"

"Malediction!" cries Oreus, in a suddenly-thunderous voice that terrifies Glania and resounds over the terrace all the way to the Palace of the Hierophants. "Malediction! The liquid fire has been stolen! Where is Thebao? Let him come quickly! There isn't a moment to lose!"

At that commanding voice, which reveals a superior individual, the young hierophant who has just interrogated the old man remains shocked by emotion, and his companions are struck by surprise. Obedient to instinct, they are already getting ready to go in search of Thebao when, pulling himself together, the first to speak replies: "It's perhaps inappropriate for you to give orders here, old man, nor to demand Thebao, the supreme pontiff."

"You're right, young man," replies Oreus, lowering his voice. "For, by the timbre of your voice I divine that you're young. Go, then, and tell Thebao that Oreus is waiting for him."

"Oreus? The great Oreus, the Master of Masters?"

"Oreus?" repeat all the young men, astonished.

And the word *Oreus*, pronounced, echoed and re-echoed, fills the Holy Terrace. Oreus! The quasi-fabulous individual of whom they have heard mention as a demigod, the master of terrestrial forces, here he stands before them, the great exile of the Green Isle! And the young men remain immobile, and neglect to go and inform Thebao.

But the chief of the hierophants has heard the name pronounced and repeated from mouth to mouth, and he comes running, followed by a few old hierophants.

"That bandage over your eyes, Master? What misfortune has struck you? The light, isn't it? The miraculous sun that you produced yesterday?"

"You've divined it, Thebao. I'll be blind tonight. Take me to a place less exposed to the sun, where we can talk at our ease."

"Come, Master, to my own laboratory. You, my children, and you, my companions, stay here to watch the terrace. And the young woman?"

"She accompanies me everywhere—my living eyes, henceforth. But she needs rest. Let a Temple physician ac-

204

company her to a cool and shadowed place, and leave her to sleep for an hour."

Then, when he and Thebao are alone, Oreus says: "What have I just learned, my friend? The liquid fire has been stolen?"

"Fatality! The Blacks took advantage of the darkness that weighed upon the City to invade the Temple and the Palace of Hierophants. Hermos defended it heroically, and the quasi-miraculous arrival of Hellas and Knephao put the Blacks and their leader Timou to flight..."

"And then?" questioned the old man, anxiously.

"Then, in the disorder of the fatal night, we did not immediately see the extent of the ravages committed by the Barbarians. We succeeded—or, rather, Hellas and Knephao succeeded—in saving the treasures of the Sanctuary, and you, by spreading light, completed the rout of the Blacks, but in the disturbance in which the sudden obscurity had plunged us, someone was able to remove parcels of liquid fire, and we've only just perceived it."

"An ironic jest of destiny! There, Thebao, is all the success of human wisdom. The fire that we have kept preciously in reserve for a long time in order to save Atlantis, will serve for our own doom!"

And the old man sinks into a silence that Thebao dares not trouble.

That liquid fire is, in fact, one of the redoubtable discoveries on the power of which Atlantis has repose in secular tranquility. The inhabitants, who have vaguely heard mention of it, regard it as a sacred gift of the gods, by which the city will conserve, they say, the eternal domination of the world. An ancestor of Oreus invented that savant compound, the effects of which, in criminal hands, would be sufficient to destroy entire cities.

Many times, when Atlantis went to war against the white Barbarians, many Apostles of the Sun, fanatical partisans of the red race and irreconcilable enemies of young peoples, proposed taking that terrible invention on the ships and thus spreading terror and ruination in all the vanquished countries, but the Princes of Apostles and the elite of the Initiates always refused those infernal conquests, and Oreus even wanted to destroy the secret of liquid fire forever, saying that, sooner or later, it would be disastrous for the City. The response was made to him that Atlantis, thanks to that formidable device, would remain unassailable by no matter what barbarian weapons. It would not have taken much in that epoch for Oreus to be reckoned an enemy of the people. He contented himself then with repeating, in a melancholy fashion, the mystical words of the Sphinx:

> *You turn yourself*
> *The wheel of destiny.*

And he repeats it again, mentally, today.

"Vanity of everything!" murmurs the old man, agitating his saddened dream. "Vanity of genius! Vanity of science! Vanity of wisdom! There is truly no salvation but in human courage itself. The secrets that we extract from the earth fall back upon us.

"But it's still necessary for our enemies to be able to know how to manipulate the redoubtable substance," Thebao objects, "and to employ it appropriately. Only Barkas knows how to do that, and I believe him to be incapable of delivering to barbarian soldiers the secret by which they might destroy Atlantis."

"I believe, in fact, Barkas to be noble enough not to bring ravages to his own city, even out of ambition to govern it. And yet…no one knows what perfidious counsels the insidious voice of passions in revolt might whisper to the heart of the prideful. But haven't you told me that among the invaders there were black slaves from the Golden Isle?"

"Yes, Master."

"And who was their leader?"

"Timou, whom Knephao and Hellas did not kill, by virtue of a generosity that was perhaps excessive. He took advantage of the emotion provoked by the crowd demanding gold—a rising provoked by Mellena's friends—and, seconded by his black accomplice who was hiding in the Temple, Timou broke his bonds and escaped during the night."

"Doom is upon us! This Timou knows the secrets transmitted by the chiefs of the black race. Have no doubt about it, Thebao, he knows how to spread the liquid fire."

"Master! What can we do, then? Timou hates our entire race mortally. He'll destroy Atlantis simply for pleasure."

"Poor Hellas!" murmurs Oreus, as if in a dream. "Poor hero departed for a naval battle! Already, no doubt, his fleet is advancing into the open sea, and there's no doubt that instead of the honest combat to which his courage is taking him, it's an ignominious and inglorious death that his sad destiny has in store for him."

"Master, is there not, in the Sanctuary or elsewhere, at your home on the Green Isle, some formidable resource by means of which we can forestall our enemies and destroy their fleet before they employ our own devices against us?"

At those words Oreus stands up and wanders around the room, groping his way, agitated by an emotion that shakes his breast and causes his limbs to tremble.

"Yes, there is a means, an irresistible means, and it's the assured destruction of the Aztec fleet..."

The old man stops. He is thinking about the *Alerion.*

But suddenly, he collects himself. "No! I cannot; I must not. Humans already have too many instruments of death. Atlantis must perish, rather than give the inhabitants of the earth the secret by means of which the entire planet would be ravaged."

At the idea of Atlantis destroyed, all the powerful instincts that attach a human being to customary things rise up in the old man's heart, and a combat begins within him. Why not send Glania to the Green Isle to beg Orea to go up in the *Alerion* and annihilate the barbarian fleet at a stroke?

But soon, another thought spring forth in Oreus' mind.

"Thebao, are the famous glass lenses that the great Orisis invented still kept in the Sanctuary?"

"Yes, Master, but why?"

"That's the weapon of our salvation!"

"Oh, Master, who among us would dare to make use of it? Who would dare to play with the fire of the sun?"

"Me."

"But…your eyes, Master?"

"Thanks to the savant remedy that I've just applied. My eyes will recover enough strength today to permit me to direct the solar fire again. Order your young hierophants, therefore, to go and fetch the lenses of Orisis, and to be careful to leave them in their black sheaths. The important thing is that Hellas provokes the Aztec fleet soon enough, and that it appears within sight of the city before dusk. Now, Thebao, let's not talk any more, let's not form projects: to action! Is Glania, my faithful guide, still asleep?"

A servant of the temple, summoned, reports that the young woman is profoundly asleep.

"That's good. Let her be left alone. I don't need her as yet. I feel that the remedy has had sufficient effect.

Carefully removing the bandage covering his eyes, the old man raises his eyelids slightly. He can see! Thebao, savant in the art of healing, carefully passes water impregnated with vegetable juices over his injured eyes, and in the radiant glare, all the splendor of the sun enters the delighted old man's senses.

"Salutations, immortal light!" he says. "Salutations, brightness of the fecundating and destructive star. For the last time, I implore you, be propitious for me, allow my gaze, in a supreme triumph, to see the monstrous bearers of shadow and souls charged with darkness perish by your agency. And afterwards, if necessary, let all light disappear from my eyes!

Scene VII
The Enemy Fleet

Behind the Isle of Iron, the most distant of all, hidden from the view of Atlantis by the high mountains of the island, the vessels of the Aztec fleet and the galleys manned by the black slaves are at rest, anchored in an inlet sheltered from the winds, and the unoccupied men, fatigued by the alerts of the night, are sleeping on the decks of the ships or lying on the sand of the shore. Among those who are still awake, however, the sailors of the red race affect scorn for the miners of the black race, and the ships of the two races have drawn apart from one another, some to the oriental side and the others to the occidental.

In the distance, in the open sea, there is another group of vessels: the large boats of the mariners of Armor. Some way inland on the isle, partly buried in the palm trees, is a white house around which a few soldiers are agitating. And as one gets closer to it, outbursts of voices are heard. Sometimes, those voices resound, hoarse and feverish; sometimes they calm down, and the silvery tones of a woman seem to reestablish order momentarily.

The Isle of Iron depends on Barkas, the architect, to whom the white house belongs, where the principal agitators are presently gathered.

The events of the previous night, the quarrel engaged too soon, the firing of the ships commenced without the signal, the departure of Hellas, the failure of Belkis, the quasi-miraculous intervention of Oreus; the expulsion of the Blacks from the Holy Terrace—all those memories, still sharp, of a recent defeat, have excited the indignation of some, the discouragement of some others, and reciprocal disputes among them all. Moussor, especially, never ceases reproaching Mellena for the imprudence of the adventure.

"We followed you," he says, "knowing the ardor of your zeal for the triumph of the red race, and knowing how, ordinarily, you bring to your actions clear sight and decision, and we designated you spontaneously to guide the faithful Atlanteans to the assault."

"Enough compliments, Moussor. What's your point? Was I wrong? Have I ceased to merit your admiration, or at least your confidence?"

"I'm not accusing you of anything, Mellena. But whether by misfortune or imprudence, our doom now seems certain, and in wanting to save Atlantis from future and dubious threats, you've now condemned it to an immediate and precise danger."

"What do you mean, Moussor?" Guitche interjected. "Are you accusing Mellena of putting us in danger?"

"Not Mellena herself, but her imprudence, or rather, the imprudence of us all. And that imprudence, you're the first to deplore."

"Certainly," Guitche continues, stammering hesitantly. "And I'm even not very sure about the future of our adventure."

"So," declares Mellena, haughtily, "all the men are abandoning me! It's necessary to attend to it myself! And you, Barkas?"

"As you know, Mellena, I'll follow you and our audacious enterprise to the death. But I can't see very clearly, at the moment, where we're going."

"How I regret the absence of Belkis! At least I'd have someone to defend me."

"Belkis?" riposted Moussor. "When the moment for the battle comes, he disappears."

"Don't calumniate him, Moussor. Belkis is a prisoner, perhaps dead. Did he not risk the greatest perils to go to the Holy Terrace in order to favor our friends' projects?"

"Oh, truly, a fine adventure," Moussor persists. "So that's the insensate action in which our communal work in favor of Atlantis ended up? Plunging an entire tumultuous city into darkness and whipping up disorder, pillage and devastation everywhere. To such an extent that if, by a miracle, Oreus hadn't sent toward the city the prodigious light of which he has the secret, this morning we'd find a city overturned from top to bottom."

"Always criticizing!" Barkas interrupted. "But what do you propose that's more practical and more effective?"

"I propose an honest battle in broad daylight, with all our ideas deployed. Are we right, yes or no? Yes, we're right. What do we want? To keep Atlantis jealously for the red race, and expel the innovators who want to bring our civilization to the white Barbarians. Well, what need is there to hide our projects?"

"And doubtless Moussor would have directed everything infallibly?" said Mellena, with a scornful smile.

"Infallibly, I don't know. But honesty, rapidly and without intrigues: that's what was necessary. If, this evening, as Mellena proposes, we invade the city, who can answer for the actions that Timou and his horde of unleashed slaves might commit? A singular fashion of delivering a city, to open it up to the ferocities of its vanquished in revolt."

"Shut up, Moussor," orders Mellena, imposing silence around her. "I've let you talk to your heart's content out of respect for your age and the dignity of your character. Now listen to me."

"We're listening to you, and admiring you. And know that, even if you're mistaken, we won't abandon you."

"I'm counting on it. That's why I'm deigning to defend myself before you. The true, the only danger, that threatens Atlantis is the increasing expansion of the white race. Out there in that vast and mysterious continent there are innumerable peoples who are growing by the day. They're ignorant of everything that makes the superiority of the Atlanteans. They possess neither our arts, or our sciences, nor our genius, nor out intelligence. And if, by hazard, they come to know the secrets of our civilization, they might take advantage of that to seek to become our equals, and steal our inventions and our discoveries.

"Has our entire race labored for thousands of years only for an inferior race, scarcely escaped from the forests, to enjoy the same pleasures as us? You know them, these vainglorious peoples, these Ligurians, Iberians, Gaels, Biscayans and Pelasgians! As soon as they're initiated into our sciences, they'll want to build cities like us; they'll found empires like us, they'll possess fleets, armies, treasures like us! They'll pullulate like herds of goats in the mountains, and a day will come when their cities will stand up against ours, and perhaps seek to destroy them. That's why, my brothers, we must overturn without mercy and without pity the party of those madmen who want to take the hearths of Atlantean civilization to the white Barbarians. Am I right or not?"

"You incarnate the genius of our race, Mellena!" cries Barkas.

"Then, what do a few pillaged shops and a few invaded palaces matter? Today, it's necessary for us to bring all our brothers together: Atlanteans, Aztecs, Incas, Toltecs and Guatchos; all the reds are no longer anything but relatives, reunited against the common enemy, the Whites."

"And the Blacks?" objects Moussor. "They hate us more than the Whites, because we destroyed their Empire."

"What do we have to fear from the Blacks? Their kingdom is relegated to the Orient and the south of Libya, beyond the Saharan Sea in the distant land of Saba; they remain the debris of a disappeared civilization, those fabulous Lemurians, of whom our people have even forgotten the name; whereas the Whites are surging close to us, on the coast of Iberia and in the tumultuous Gaelic forests; they're increasing and multiplying incessantly, and their innumerable rabble extends all the way to the glacial sea."

"You're counting without the unleashed instincts, Mellena. Those thousands of black men that you want to hurl upon the city in disorder will surrender to all the covetousness of their long-contained passions."

"Their passions? I know them better than you, Moussor, and I've reserved them a rich pasture. Wait a few minutes more, and you'll know that Mellena thinks of everything." Then, calling a servant she says: "Send someone to find the black Timou in the vicinity of his galleys, and ask him to me to join me."

"Ask him? Is that really the tone to employ for yesterday's slave?"

"And one of our most faithful soldiers tomorrow."

"One of our soldiers? What a strange project!"

"You'll find out."

Scene VIII
Timou

At that moment, Timou, clad in a short white tunic, superb in his tall bronzed torture, his cheek and shoulders marked by wounds sustained the day before, enters the room proudly, darting a suspicious glance at the assembly. He is carrying a thick canvas bag slung over his shoulder, which he is holding against his side preciously.

"Greetings Timou, come in. It's said that you're an enemy of Atlantis. Is that true?"

"Yes, the enemy of the City that reduced me to slavery and destroyed the kingdom of my forefathers."

"Is it Atlantis that defeated and humiliated you, or only a group of odious conquerors who gave themselves as representatives of the Queen City?"

"Too much subtlety, noble Mellena. I only know one thing: the soldiers of Atlantis defeated me, and for years I've been kept in slavery in the gold mines, in order to procure the Empire its wealth. So I hate Atlantis."

"And me, do you hate me?"

"No, I don't hate you. You sought me out to aid you in an enterprise, and I promised to follow you. But as soon as the adventure is concluded, don't ask me for pardon or forgetfulness. The slave always hates his master."

"And what if you ceased to be a slave forever? What if you became one of the masters of the City? What if you and your brothers were made the future guardians of the city?"

"Don't mock, Mellena. Explain yourself clearly."

"Do you know Knephao?"

"Yes, and I hate him."

"Very good. He'll doubtless perish tonight."

"I hope so. I'm counting on it, and have reserved his death for me."

"What would you say if you were given his position?"

At those words, Mellena's surprised friends make a movement, but the imperious woman imposes silence on them.

"Yes, his position? Won't the new Atlantis that we're going to govern ourselves need robust soldiers? Now, the Atlanteans don't want to fight. The Aztecs already form the imperial fleet. Assuredly, we'll get rid of the Egyptians loyal to Hellas. Given that, who could become our soldiers better than you and your brothers?"

"O Mellena!" says Timou, drunk with joy, his eyes shining, and his breast welling with an overflowing emotion. "I would be the chief of the warriors of Atlantis, then? I would have Knephao's prestige? I would live in the palaces like him? I would put on his gilded armor? My companions would march in the sunlight, covered in armor, armed with spears and mounted on those beautiful horses of the Inca lands?"

"As you say, Timou."

"O Mellena, don't deceive your former slave; he will avenge himself pitilessly."

"He won't have to avenge himself, Timou, but to serve us. From tomorrow, you'll become chief of the Atlantean cohorts."

Then the Black falls at Mellena's feet, kisses her robe, and, getting up full of enthusiasm, cries: "Long live Atlantis! It can count on our arms forever..."

"I'm counting absolutely on your bravery and your prudence," says Mellena, sending Timou away.

Turning toward her friends, mute with surprise:

"Well, you see how one attaches those one fears? There's someone who will serve us until death."

"But you're not seriously thinking of confiding Knephao's succession to him?"

"Why not? Won't we need soldiers tomorrow? Anyway, we're not going to argue about those we'll have. Let's first take possession of the city."

"Admirable!" exclaims Barkas. "When we think ourselves lost, you alone can reanimate us!"

"You give me confidence," even Moussor confesses, "but one fear remains to me." And, leaning toward her ear: "The airborne monster!"

"Yes, I'm still thinking about that, but I haven't said anything in order not to frighten our companions. That's why I'm putting off the attack to night."

"What if they come to attack us themselves during the day?"

"Who would dare? Only Hellas. But with what ships?"

"He'll gather the merchant vessels from all along the seven peninsulas."

"So be it. But if he comes at the head of a fleet he won't fly through the air, and we'll have nothing to fear."

"What about Oreus?"

"I don't fear Oreus. In a battle he'll be afraid of destroying the allied fleet at the same time as the other. Anyway, what does it matter? Who doesn't take the risk never knows success. But I hear noises. Who's coming toward us?"

In fact, the shouts are resounding from the harbor. An Atlantean escaped from the city is introduced, having come all the way to the Isle of Iron in a fishing-boat, sent by the friends of Belkis. The man comes in, distraught, spreading alarm.

"They're coming!" he cries.

"Who?"

"The Ligurian sailors."

"You see?" says Moussor to Mellena.

"Led by whom?"

"Hellas!"

"Marvelous!" says Mellena. "Timou will have a flamboyant welcome reserved for him."

"They've reached the Crimson Isle."

"Very good. Time to place ourselves in the battle-line. And Belkis?"

"A prisoner on the Holy Terrace. He can't escape, for Oreus has doubled the surveillance."

"Oreus in Atlantis!" cry Guitche and Moussor, frightened.

216

"On the Terrace?" adds Barkas, disconcerted by that news.

"Victory! Victory!" proclaims Mellena, not dissimulating her joy. "Hellas with the fleet! Oreus on the Terrace! No more doubt, no more dread! Go and inform Timou."

And while, in a hasty rumor, everyone launches themselves toward the vessels, already in movement. Mellena advances toward Timou, running in answer to her summons, and shouts to him in a triumphant tone: "The time has come to accomplish destiny! Depart, Timou, and destroy their fleet, before we even have to fight it."

"Follow us at a distance, Mistress. We'll enter Atlantis with no danger to you. And Knephao's days are counted!"

Scene IX
The Crimson Isle

In fact, Hellas' fleet, composed of merchant vessels of various dimension, is advancing slowly toward the Crimson Isle, and, in consequence of the difficulty that the Ligurians mariners are experiencing maneuvering ships new to them and not prepared for war, it will be several hours before they can attain the Isle of Iron.

In view of the Crimson Isle, the fleet stops. Two vessels are detached, and advance toward the island; one carries Hellas and the elite of the Ligurian mariners; the other bears Hermos, Amonou, Egyptian soldiers and a few Atlantean volunteers, who are to undertake the guard of the island and establish themselves there as a kind of advance citadel of Atlantis. Sitting among the flowers on the high terrace of their palace, the artists and poets, surprised by all the unexpected movement, simultaneously indignant and anxious, watch the noisy vessels coming toward them, which dare to trouble the peace of their retreat.

"What do they want with us, these men covered in armor?" enquires Palmoussos, the musician. "And by what right dare they present themselves in our flower garden?"

"Let them come," replies Xanthes, majestically. "I'll receive them as they deserve."

In one of the vessels, Xanthes and his friends recognize Hermos and Amonou, and in the other, Hellas himself.

"By the gods! Let's all rise up in protest against this violation of our sacred retreat!" says Thamoussi, indignantly.

"They envy us!" adds the rhetor Olbios "For a long time they've dreamed of annihilating our glory, which offends them. But patience! Their punishment will come."

Meanwhile, the two vessels draw closer to an inlet that serves as a harbor, and, putting boats to sea, warriors advance toward the beach, preceded by Hellas, Hermos, Amonou and a few young Apostles of the Sun.

"Profane individuals!" exclaims Xanthes, stopping in front of them a few stadia from the shore. "By what affront do you dare to bring the noise of weapons and the threat of fratricidal struggles here?"

"Calm down, Xanthes," says Hellas, mildly, while supervising the disembarkation of the men-at-arms "We haven't come to attack you, we've come to defend you."

"Defend us! From whom? No one has the right to trouble the Crimson Isle in its fecund idleness."

"Tomorrow, perhaps, the City will perish, and you talk about fecund idleness? What use will your lyres and your laurels be to you all, if the City is destroyed and the Barbarians take you into slavery?"

"Our genius will still remain, which nothing can tarnish."

"Your genius is only the supreme flower of the City. If the City dies, your genius dies with is, just as the rose perishes in the garden ravaged by the tempest. But the danger is imminent. It's necessary to act. Let those of you who are afraid go and hide, and await the end. And you, Hermos, arrange your soldiers quickly on the buttresses of the island."

"Shame on you, Hermos!" articulates Palmoussos. "Shame on a man who, having known the supreme honor of being called poet, soils his hands by touching weapons and will perhaps debase himself forever in bloodshed!"

"Yes," Asmonia puts in, intervening violently, "yes, you're behaving like brutes and scoundrels. And you want to oblige us to witness the unleashing of your sanguinary instincts?"

"In the name of art," roars Thamoussi, "I curse you, Hermos."

The latter, disdainfully impassive, looks at the wretches pityingly.

"Enough words," says Hellas. "You, Amonou, stay in the vicinity of the Palace with a few determined men, to prevent these fools from impeding the movement of the soldiers. And you, Hermos, mount a good guard around the island, and oppose, whatever happens, the disembarkation of the enemy fleet."

"A fleet would dare to disembark here?" asks Xanthes.

"And without consulting your opinion, Master," replies Hellas. "But adieu, all of you, poor manipulators of the wind! If you understand your true mission, you'll go to help Hermos. If you don't understand it, what do I care about your ruination?"

The artists utter menacing cries from a distance, and the women cries of fright, retiring into the Palace, summoning the malediction of the Sphinx upon their false brothers. Xanthes, silent and pensive, left alone facing Hermos, goes toward him.

Hermos extends his hand toward the poet, and in a mild voice, says: "Xanthes, you've hardly ever quit this isle of pleasure, and you don't know the forces of action. But I appeal to your heart. Will you remain inactive while the City might go up in flames?"

"Each to his role! It's for the soldiers to defend the city, the poets to sing its praises."

"That's betraying it, not defending it."

"What will my brothers says if I throw away the lyre to take up the sword?"

"They'll say what they said to me, and you'll despise them as I despise them—or rather, you'll feel your heart full of pity for them, for their souls are etiolating far from life."

As he pronounces those words, they hear in the distance a distant and confused clamor rising from the city, which increases and swells, and seems to be menacing the Palace of the Empire, The artists still on the terrace of the Crimson Isle go to hide then, frightened.

"What's that?" asks Xanthes.

"Nothing," says Hellas, retracing his steps. "The City's doubtless rising up, But Knephao is watching over it. Adieu! I'm rejoining the fleet. The battle is about to begin."

"And I," adds Hermos, "will go get ready to defend the Crimson Isle or to die."

"Don't go yet!" says Xanthes. "Hellas, have you other weapons on your ship. Do you have equipment to confide to me?"

"Yes."

"Give me weapons. And you, Hermos, let me fight beside you. My arm will doubtless lack skill, but the heart is eager to act."

"I knew," cries Hermos, "that you'd become noble and brave again. And I was counting on you!"

"Adieu," says Hellas. "I have more confidence now."

And Xanthes leans toward Hermos ear. "Forgive my brothers, forgive them if they hide and insult you. People have told them that they resemble gods!"

"Unfortunately," sighs Hermos, "they have said the same to the entire Atlantean race."

And as if in reply to Hermos' plaint, an immense and continuous tumult rises and grows on all the flanks of the agitated city."

Scene X
The Crowd

In fact, the city of Atlantis, in its entirety, is nothing more than a human tempest.

From the extreme capes of the peninsulas, from the distant outlying districts of fishermen between the Sandy Point, from the tumultuous quarters in which hybrid peoples formed from the mixture of the three races swarm, from all the shores of the vast sea to the flanks of the great mountain, Atlantis offers nothing anywhere but howls of terror, the fearful cries of women, threats of death, and the noise of marching crowds.

The rumor has spread since dawn to the effect that Atlantis is about to be subjected to an attack and a pitched battle.

Invaded! The eternal city invaded! The people of the Sphinx, the favorite people of the gods, condemned to struggle against rebels and Barbarians! The first people to learn the news refuse to believe it and, depending on their character, burst out laughing or become majestically indignant.

"Oh, what a joke!"

"The Sphinx wouldn't permit it!"

But other, frightened citizens, whose numbers are increasing by the hour, recount to one another in words charged with terror the dangers that are about to fall upon them.

The women now come to join the growing crowd, and their strident appeals, their hectic running, finish spreading the confusing on public disasters through the city.

Those who have husbands, fathers, children and brothers cling to the arms of the males, who resist, and violent scenes, suddenly engaged, cause obstacles to surge forth here and there in the cluttered streets around which the moving crowd circles and breaks into eddies.

Other women, alone, presently neglected, throw themselves vainly in front of running men. In the rich quarters of the Palace of Gold, where the white houses of courtesans shine under the flowers, semi-naked women are seen wandering, their hair in the wind, who have not even taken the time to put on morning clothes. And those women, whose mere presence caused all the men jealous of obtaining their smiles to swoon yesterday, women for whom floods of gold and precious stones were spread, are now offering themselves, tearfully, to anyone. Resplendent houses of marble, in the depths of which lie treasures guarded jealously and coveted by the envious crowd, now stand with their doors wide open, from which vigilance has withdrawn—and the mobs of people pass by repeatedly without even seeing them.

The beauty of women, the splendor of riches, the dignity of rank, sensuality, gold and pride—all the passions that animated the life of the Atlanteans yesterday—are all forgotten, denied, nullified. There is no longer any but one breath in all souls, one instinct in all hearts, one frisson in all flesh: fear! Fear, everywhere fear!

Matrons and courtesans, patrician women and maidservants, street-porters and merchants, Apostles of the Sun and street-sweepers, tavern waiters and Masters of Gold, all go forth in disorder through the vast avenues, now too small, as one sees gazelles, tigers, zebras, snakes and lions fleeing pell-mell from a forest fire. Where are they going? They are going forward, without knowing where, at hazard, away from the place where they spent the night—elsewhere! Wherever there will be no danger. Those from the hills run down toward the sea; those from the shore climb toward the hills. And the human streams intersect and mingle, repelling one another and dragging one another along, and in the millions of simultaneous clamors, no one can be heard, no one can be understood. Sometimes yesterday's friends, brothers or relatives encounter one another in the crowd and ask one another for news. Then, those questioned, who know nothing, talk while running about massacres and fires, invasions by the Occident if they come from the orient and by the Orient if they come from the occident.

Gradually, however, a more precise rumor circulates. Those who are climbing up toward the Terraces, fatigued by incessantly crossing paths with groups flowing toward the sea, cry to them: "What are you going to look for in the ports? You know full well that there are no more ships in the harbor."

"But what's happening, then?" reply the runaways who are descending. "It's said that the black slaves are going to invade us by land?"

And the eddies recommence, tumultuously and indecisively. A clamor soon goes up:

"To the Holy Terrace!"

"Yes, yes," affirm the reassured women, "let's go shelter under the wings of the Sphinx!"

"Glory to the Sphinx! Glory to the Sphinx!"

"Invincible Sphinx, have pity on your people!"

And, rediscovering vigor or their course, men and women, by the most rapid route, launch themselves toward the Esplanade situated in front of the Palace of the Empire.

In the beginning, the people flow through all the streets at an even pace, without collisions or trouble, like a stream with hurried but regular waves rolling between two majestic banks. As they advance toward the Square of the Empire, however, the broad avenues all join up in tumultuous confluences; space becomes tight, but the flood of the crowd is augmented without respite beneath a whirlwind of blinding dust.

Then the conflicts, collisions, cries and appeals began. At the intersections of the streets, the two streams dispute as to which will pass first, and so much the worse for the weak—the strong prevail by means of their fists. Children crushed by the crowd utter screams of mortal distress, only stifled by the trampling feet of the moving mob. Women caught between two currents of the populace rend the air with their screeches. Fathers and husbands launch forth to defend them, but the indifferent continue to advance, without wasting time in futile pity, and corpses gradually accumulate at the crossroads.

Then, as if death summons death, the human floods begin to pour upon one another; furious fists fall on bloody

224

faces, hand seize unknown throats, knives plunge into entrails, feet crush bruised flesh. And in the beautiful shady squares where jets of water murmur in the fountains, on the edges of avenues where the cascades of the hills steam, blood mingles with the soiled water, and the water, blocked in its course by the heaps of dead and wounded, spreads out through the causeways in pools of red and black mud.

"Move forward! Move forward, then!" howl the last to arrive, rendered furious by the resistance. "We'll never get to the Square of the Empire."

"Go back! Back, for pity's sake!" vociferate those who are stagnating in the middle. "The Square of the Empire is overflowing with people."

"Flee toward the sea, there might be a refuge in some island; all effort is vain here!"

"Vain or not, get out of the way! We want to fly under the wings of the Sphinx!"

And the latest groups to arrive throw themselves upon the first with a vigor that would break stones. But they only succeed in provoking a few further asphyxiations of women and old men here and there, the human mass becoming impenetrable. All of Atlantis is suspended in clusters packed against the flanks of the Hill of the Sphinx. And that enormous crowd, crammed together, immobilized by its own haste at the intersections of the avenues, seen from the height of the Holy Terrace, resembles a monstrous octopus expelled from the sea, extending its impotent tentacles toward the mute Sphinx, whose terror is resounded by millions of desperate voices.

225

Scene XI
The Square of the Empire

Knephao, meanwhile, has heard the clamors of the crowd and has seen that heavy mass rising toward him. In order not to repel the citizens or to submit to their invasion into the Palace, the chief of the warriors has had enormous superimposed chains of heavy iron extended from one side of the square to the other, especially in front of the Golden Gate, against which the most profound crowds can only hurl themselves in vain.

By virtue of that precaution, a fairly wide space will remain free before the Palace, where he and his soldiers can maneuver at their ease, without crushing men and women with the displacements of their horses.

Afterwards, Knephao lines up, some distance behind the chains, serried ranks of cavaliers armed with long lances, armored in bronze with steel helmets. Then, setting himself before them, his sword sheathed, his hands free and his visor raised, he awaits developments.

"My lads," he says, turning toward his soldiers and speaking to them in an emotional and fraternal tone that they have only heard on the morning of great battles, "Today will perhaps be grave and bloody. I'm counting on you, as I always have counted on you; but I expect your patience even more than your courage. Whatever these people say or do, don't strike them unless I give the order. This evening, doubtless, you will have manifested your valor before the rebels that will come."

The soldiers listen respectfully, and then murmur between them: "What's happened to our handsome chief, that he's become as eloquent as Hellas himself?"

"It's necessary to believe that the day will be hot!"

And the men instinctively sit tight in their saddles, lances at the ready.

"Keep calm! Keep calm!" orders Knephao.

And, having had the pikes raised, he advances into the middle of the square, in front of the people whose are flooding into it.

The first ranks of the people, hasty and noisy, come to press against the extended chains, and very rapidly, in successive layers, like suddenly-petrified waves that remain frozen against a cliff, the moving tide of the crowd stops in front of the soldiers.

The women, with their clothes in disorder and their faces covered in sweat, are even more agitated than the men, and the entire multitude hurls abuse and pleas, simultaneously and by turns, sometimes at Knephao and sometimes at the other Egyptian.

"Handsome chief, let us pass! We want to go pray to the Sphinx."

"Knephao, handsome warrior, we love you! Protect us!"

"Soldiers! Come and find our children. You'll be our saviors."

The Egyptians, silent and motionless, gripped simultaneously by disgust and pity, gaze at all the faces tumefied by fear extended toward them.

"You're good, Knephao! Save us! Deliver us!"

"From what?" growls the giant, tautly.

"From death!"

"Death! Poor folk, you're bearing it within you, like us. Everyone has to die."

"Wicked soldier, are you mocking us?" brays a merchant. "Sooner or later, so be it! But today, no! We don't want to die today!"

"And what tells you that you're going to die?"

"Don't you know that they're going to invade the City, Knephao?"

"They? Who?"

"I know, me! The Aztecs!"

"The Nubians!"

"The Ligurians!"

"The Armoricans!"

"All the wretches that our masters have brought into Atlantis."

"It was necessary to bring them, since you didn't want to row or labor yourselves," replies Knephao, scornfully.

Then, from all parts, the cries ring out:

"They're going to come!"

"They're going to invade us!"

"Let's take refuge in the Palace!"

"To the Palace! To the Palace!"

"Let's kill Knephao!"

Then, tranquilly, turning toward his men, he orders: "Lances at the ready!"

And before that second barrier, more redoubtable than the iron chains, the audacious recoil.

The colossus, advancing to within arm's reach of the foremost citizens, addresses the people: "Kill me, then—but once dead, I won't answer for my own furious soldiers, and I don't know who'll defend you."

"No, no!" clamors the maddened crowd. "Don't kill him! He's our only support!"

"So be it, then! But let me save you, or, better still, save yourselves."

"How do we do that?" enquires a fat merchant with thickset shoulders, who seems to be guiding the crowd.

"Quite simply by defending ourselves with your own hands."

"Us, fight?"

"Us, fight like soldiers?

"Us, the citizens of the City of the Sphinx?"

And the furious merchant continues: "It's well worth the trouble of having a College of Initiates, of maintaining scholars at great expense and respecting the hierophants of the Holy Terrace, if they can't find the means of annihilating all our enemies without our having to soil our hands with the blood of the impure!"

"And to accomplish that work of killing without danger, you've come to pray to the Unknown God?"

"Yes, yes—you've said it, Knephao!"

"You've understood us!"

"We want a miracle!"

"We've always been promised one!"

"Let the Sphinx open its wings fully!"

"And let it make our cowardly enemies perish!"

"Cowards yourselves!" roars Knephao, exasperated. "Well, let them come, then, the Barbarians, let them enter this mad City, and let them regenerate it, since one of them is worth a thousand of you!"

"Crude soldier! Brute!"

"Bastard of the red race!"

"The Atlanteans must live and the Egyptians must die for them!"

"Kill him! Kill him!" repeat voices coming from the middle of the crowd.

"Soldiers," Knephao articulates, "advance, lances extended!"

Scarcely has that movement commenced, however, than a gesture from the chief halts it. He has only wanted to frighten that Atlanteans; and, indeed, those who were threatening loudest recoil and are lost in the mass, leaving a new rank of Atlanteans placed against the chains.

An immense pity stirs the heart of the giant before the crowd, which, by virtue of its incurable weakness, seems to be sinking of its own accord into ignominy and imminent annihilation.

And very mildly, in an almost tremulous voice, he says: "Go away! Have no fear, my soldiers won't kill you. The others will suffice for that, and you yourselves. It isn't possible that among the thousands of healthy men rushing against us there aren't a few who are valiant. I will incorporate them with my brave Egyptians and, inexperienced as they are, those newcomers will be able to repel all the enemies."

Having said those words, he rides back and forth along the chains, addressing the crowd:

"Come on, who's with me? A few robust young men!"

A murmur of surprise runs through the ranks. No one comes forward. Here and there, however, young men are seen to hesitate. Then, spotting two handsome adolescents in the front rank, whom he recognizes by their tunics as rich citizens, Knephao insists: "You two, there, I can see in your eyes that you're burning to make your valiant souls manifest."

The two young men look at one another, evasively, and are doubtless about to scale the chains when, furiously, her complexion on fire, her hair plastered to her forehead by sweat, a woman hastens forward: their mother.

"Mercy!" she screeches. "Don't take my children, my flesh, my life! My children! My beautiful children! You want them to risk death like vile Egyptian pigs? Down with war! Down with battles! The women of Atlantis were promised that their sons would never run any risk. And it's mine that you want to steal to go and rot in filthy slaughterhouses? Oh, what do your quarrels and your stories of conquest matter to me? I'm a mother. I don't want my sons to die! Take two others! There are poor people who'll follow you for love of gold."

Seeing two young men of the lowest class not far away, of mixed red and white blood, she abuses them: "What about those? Can't they fight for ours?"

"Truly?" yells another woman who appears, sordid, her face dirty and her mouth toothless. "Truly, my sons are going to die for yours?"

"And by what right do they live, vile harpy, since they aren't of the pure red race?"

"By the right of my flesh, no more made for the slaughterhouse than yours."

"It already has the odor of it, at any rate."

"Filth! Thief! Eater of the poor! Here!"

And the old pauperess leaps upon the rich woman, grabs her by the throat, and a battle begins. The sons plunge toward their mothers in order to separate them. They collide with one another. The neighbors intervene. The melee is about to become general when, from the back of the square, someone cries: "Oreus! Oreus!"

Oreus has, indeed, just been seen to appear on the parapet of the Holy Terrace.

At those magic words, the combatants separate. All eyes turn toward the terrace.

"Oreus!" howls a merchant. "But then, if Oreus is showing himself, he's going to work a miracle."

"Saved! We're saved!" cries the crowd, delirious with joy. "Saved without a battle!"

Knephao is seized by scornful pity.

"Atlanteans, wait a moment. I'll go consult with Oreus, whose voice can communicate with mine from the Terrace of the Palace."

"Yes, yes! Let him tell us the future; let him reassure us."

Then Knephao, leaving his soldiers to defend the chains, goes to the Palace, and soon comes back, anxiously awaited by the multitude.

"Leave here, Atlanteans! Oreus assures you that you're running no risk, but it's necessary that you return to your dwellings immediately. My soldiers will watch over the security of your streets."

"And Oreus, what will he do?"

"He will burn all the Barbarian ships from above. But let no one remain outside their homes! They would run the risk of perishing."

"Glory! Glory! Long live the Sphinx!"

And the crowd, as madly as it arrived, withdraws in disorder, throwing itself into the avenues and cramming the crossroads.

Knephao, ashamed of having needed to resort to that trick to clear the square of an imbecilic people, far from rejoicing in his success, turns away and dissimulates his emotion from his soldiers. The latter, removing the chains, separate into two cohorts, one of which stays to guard the Palace with Knephao, while the other disperses through the city.

A profound sadness confuses the minds of those men, ordinarily so ardent in danger. Their stomachs rise with a heavy disgust for the people they are going to defend. And in the streets that they traverse, at the crossroads where they station themselves, from which the crowds are gradually retiring, an odor of putrescence and death troubles them with an ignoble nausea. For the entire city, especially around the Holy Mountain, is nothing but a wretched slaughterhouse.

And the soldiers of Egypt, silently, renounce counting beneath their feet the thousands upon thousands of Atlanteans with contracted features, open mouths and eyes bulging with fear who are asleep forever lying in the blood and the mud, and who, under the pressure of their formidable cowardice, have killed one another in obscure melees, for fear of dying.

XII
The Ardent Mirror

In his disdainful and merciful deception, Knephao was not, however, mistaken in announcing to the Atlantean mob that Oreus was going to burn the Barbarian vessels from the height of the Holy Terrace. And the Atlanteans believed him without effort because, in fact, a popular legend exists, widespread in the City of the Waters, to the effect that the most numerous fleets can be set ablaze before they have even been able to approach the distant circle of the islands. It is said that Orisis once annihilated a collation of Aztecs and Guatchos; so, since that time, no invaders have dared to risk themselves in the surrounding sea.

Only Oreus, the custodian of ancient secrets, still knows the art of manipulating the redoubtable mirrors and the powerful convergent lenses.

And at this supreme moment, sensing the danger that menaces the city, knowing what terrible weapons the enemies of Hellas carry in their vessels, he is not hesitating to attempt Orisis' experiment again.

Against the parapet that overlooks the city and the sea, and from which the slow vessels of Hellas can be seen in the distance, undulating on the waves, Oreus has had the young hierophants erect a solid scaffolding of wood and iron.

At the summit of that scaffolding and entire system of mobile hinges has been installed, and on those hinges, which springs can rotate at will, concave mirrors of exceedingly thick glass are placed. Thanks to an array of lens placed on pendant axes, a nucleus of heat can be projected over a vast distance, with a surprising precision, provoking abrupt blazes from afar. Such is the famous invention of Orisis, which only Oreus, knowledgeable in the science of lines and numbers, understands today. In order to manipulate such a delicate and redoubtable apparatus without danger, in fact, requires a great manual dexterity and an absolute infallibility of calculation. A simple error in an angle, and the fire that is being projected into the distance, might cause ravages in the places that one wants to protect.

Almost all the hierophants, pressing their eyes to telescopes, have their gazes turned toward the high seas.

"What can you see out there?" demands Oreus of a young hierophant, who is zealously following all the movements. "Is Hellas' fleet approaching the Isle of Iron?"

"It has scarcely quit the Crimson Isle, Master."

"Good. And has the enemy fleet appeared yet?"

"No, Master. It's still hidden behind the Isle of Iron."

"Then we have a little time before us. Let's pray." He turns to Thebao. "Is the young Ligurian who came with me still asleep? Send someone to wake her and bring her to me."

Glania soon arrives, delighted and amazed.

"Oh, great Master, how good the gods are! They've returned your sight. Let us bless the Sphinx."

"Yes, my daughter, let us bless it; and although it is not the god of your forefathers, kneel down with us to invoke it."

And, making a sign to the hierophants to curb their foreheads in the dust, Oreus lets himself fall to his knees on the first of the steps that rise up to the bronze Sphinx, with Thebao to his right and Glania to his left, and all the priests assembled silently behind them. A single hierophant remains at the parapet of the Terrace, keeping watch on the vast sea.

Then Oreus says:

"Increate fire, once you protected Orisis, please protect his unworthy disciple; you know, better than I do, with what a humble heart, submissive to your orders, I dare to employ the weapons of the gods."

"Unknown God, come to us!" cry the hierophants, in unison.

And there is a brief silence, during which mental prayers rise up.

Oreus raises his head slowly, and suddenly shivers. Like an ironic response on the part of the Sphinx, the inscription on the pedestal appears before his eyes:

You will no longer be human
You will not be gods.

And the old man, bending over toward the ground resumes his interrupted prayer in a loud voice:

"Have pity on us, ardent Light of the Ether! Which of us, in fact, thinks of becoming more than human? If, as we have been informed by our forefathers, humankind was the dearest of your creations, grant, O God, that humankind shall not die in its entirety, and will survive eternally in the supreme beauty that spreads out in the form of harmonious Cities; permit Atlantis to defend the noblest of her works against the basest passions of her lost children."

And the old man kisses the steps of the sacred stairway.

And the hierophants make their rhythmic prayers heard.

Then Oreus looks at the pedestal of the Sphinx, and this time, another inscription bursts forth:

You turn yourself
The wheel of destiny.

A profound anguish grips the heart of the old man. Ordinarily so calm before the necessities of fate, he feels himself seized by terror. He hesitates to act. But now the hierophant left on watch shouts:

"The Barbarian fleet! The enemy fleet! How strong it seems!"

"The fleet?" cries Glania, "The fleet enemy to Hellas?" And she runs to the parapet.

Even the hierophants, in spite of their respect for Oreus in prayer, agitate dully around him. The old man, in his turn, rises abruptly to his feet, and says in a firm voice:

"So be it! Let destiny be accomplished!"

Then, turning to the hierophants, he gives brief orders in a decisive voice.

"My children, go and stand near the Temple, you on the marble steps, you down there, against the obelisks of red marble, and all of you be ready to obey the slightest signal. The others, you remain behind me, awaiting my orders. Let no one advance toward the ardent mirror—he would die, consumed like a wisp of straw. Glania, you take the most powerful of the telescopes and indicate the movements of Hellas' fleet to me; you know the sailors better than anyone. Are the two fleets in confrontation?"

"Not yet, Master," replies the young woman, placed on the steps of the Temple, while two robust hierophants help her to manipulate the heavy telescope with enormous lenses.

But Glania suddenly cries: "Oh, poor Hellas! What can he do with his slow and scattered vessels against the skill and the innumerable host of Aztec ships?"

In fact, even to the naked eye, it is evident that Hellas' fleet is far inferior to the Aztec fleet. Disposed in several ranks, the enemy ships, preceded by the boats of the black slaves, are moving between the Isle of Iron and the Crimson Isle, and their formation is advancing, regular and menacing, toward the disorderly and sparse cohort of vessels recruited by the Ligurians.

"And Hellas? There's his vessel, advancing alone, before the rest of the fleet. I recognize it by the large crimson drape trailing in the water at the poop. Hellas is standing, armed and impassive, in the prow."

"At the head! In advance of the others! The fool! The wretch! He's going to fight with iron when implacable fire is waiting for him! Let's save him! Let's save him!" Then, addressing Glania: "And in the Aztec fleet? Who is directing the combat?"

"They're still too far way, Master, and I don't know anyone, in any case, except Mellena."

And as no hierophant in capable of recognizing the chiefs of the Aztec fleet, Thebao proposes: "Master, we have a prisoner in a cell in the Temple who might be able to inform you. His name is Belkis."

"Have him brought!"

Belkis, who is fetched, throws himself at Oreus' feet, trembling and submissive, hissing his mantle.

"Great Oreus, Master of Masters! You, here?"

"Get up, Belkis. This is what you're going to do! And if you deceive me..."

"Me, deceive you? I swear..."

"No oaths. Obey, that's all, for your own salvation. Take a telescope. Follow the movements of the Aztec fleet, and tell me, as soon as you recognize someone, where the principal chiefs are.

"Whatever you wish, Master of Masters. I hate the men who induced me to error. And if I lie, I wish..."

"If you lie, you die with us. In any case, two robust hierophants will remain with you to guard you, and two others equipped with telescopes will follow the movements of the enemy with you. Who is guiding the Aztec fleet?"

"Wait, I can't see yet. They're scarcely beginning to move in front of the Iron Isle. It's not Mellena and Guitche's vessel, nor that of Moussor, not that of the Aztec chief. One might think it were a boat manned by the Blacks. Oh, I see! I see...Timou."

"Timou? Are you quite sure?"

"It's him!" interrupts a hierophant. "I recognize him at the prow, alone before the rest."

"Then let's not hesitate" declares Oreus. And, turning to the hierophants: "Whatever happens, don't move toward the parapet. And you, Glania, don't budge from your position. Put your hands over your eyes to avoid the initial dazzle."

He covers his own face with a black veil, in which two openings are fitted with dark lenses. Thus protected against the excessive glare of the light, Oreus carefully removes the sheath covering the ardent mirror, and suddenly, an intense, prodigious, blinding light fills the space in front of the Holy Hill. Skillfully, Oreus maneuvers the lenses, and soon, all the scattered beams are condensed into one alone, which, projected toward the sea, resembles a blade of flame of infinite length.

The projection of the ardent mirror, initially directed into the sky, descends toward the sea, and, as if Oreus wants to try the power of the fire on an inanimate body, he directs the focus toward the Isle of Iron, covered at its summit by dense forests. A sudden fire illuminates the horizon, and black smoke rises up into the azure.

"Father of humans, Lord of the earth, God protector of our life, forgive me for spreading death," murmurs Oreus, "and if I am wrong, may I be struck by lightning!"

And, slowly directing the focus of the mirror toward the sea, he sets fire to a few vessels in the rearmost ranks of the barbarian fleet, with the objective of frightening the enemy, and awaits the initial result of his attack.

Scene XIII
The Sea on Fire

An unexpected result, alas, and not in conformity with Oreus' desires. Firstly, around him, there is unbridled panic. When he turns round he sees nothing but bewildered groups running in all directions on the terrace. Only Thebao is trying to bring back the dazzled and terrified priests; only Glania, as if clinging to her telescope, has not quit the resplendent sea with her eyes. The heroic old man cannot contain the surge of his wrath. He abuses the frightened young men violently:

"Truly, servants of the Sphinx, pontiffs of the Sun, you're dying of fright before the glare of the light?"

"Forgive us, Master," one of the youngest hierophants, approaching. "It suddenly seemed to us that the sun was about to fall before our eyes."

"Where's Belkis?" asks Thebao.

"Belkis, in fact, remains undiscoverable, and they suppose that, in the general tumult, he has gone to ground in some hidden corner of the Holy Terrace.

"Bah! Leave him!" said Oreus, impatient. "Let two hierophants try to find him. We have more redoubtable enemies to watch.

Suddenly, Glania cries: "Master! Master! It's frightful! They're fleeing!"

"Who?"

"All of them! All of them!"

In fact, Hellas' mariners, Ligurians, Gaels, Iberians or men of mixed-race, all brave and devoted to their leader, but ignorant and superstitious, believe that they have seen the sun itself flamboyant beneath the wings of the Sphinx. Frightened and disconcerted, with a spontaneous action, they have turned their sails toward Atlantis and now, at a hectic pace, are fleeing over the waves whipped by oars.

For their part, the Aztec vessels and the boats of the Blacks are dispersing in disorder toward the open sea, and Oreus, who is now directing the solar ray toward the sky, rejoices to see, through the holes in his mask, the two separated fleets fleeing in various directions.

Is it possible, however, that Hellas has also fled? Oreus cannot believe it, and picking up one of the telescopes abandoned by the hierophants, with his still clear-sighted eyes, he searches the sea in the direction of the Crimson Isle. He sees two vessels, and two alone, which are racing toward one another with a similar impetuosity.

"Glania, my child, tell me quickly what those two vessels are that are heading toward one another under full sail."

"Oh, Master, what a superb combat! He will surely be victorious!"

"Who, my daughter?"

"Hellas, of course. Don't you recognize the crimson of his ship?"

"Hellas? I suspected as much. And the other, the chief of the enemy vessel?"

"The other is the black, Timou."

"Timou! Oh, woe! Hellas is about to perish!"

And without deliberation. Oreus gets ready to operate the ardent mirror and project the blade of fire against Timou's vessel.

"Master! Stop! What are you doing?" Glania implores. "Can't you see that the two ships are in the same line? In burning one you'll burn the other!"

"Ah! Poor Hellas," moans Oreus. "It's me who has killed you!" And, tilting the henceforth useless mirror toward the ground, he renounces maneuvering the ardent fire. Then, removing the black mask that he has placed over his face, he approaches the parapet, and anxiously follows from afar the combat that he cannot prevent.

"Wretch," he says, "wretch that I am. What good has it done me to play with celestial forces? I've hastened the wheel of destiny!"

"Courage, Mater, courage!" says Glania, approaching in her turn. "See how Hellas is winning; Timou's vessel is already fleeing."

"Oh, poor child, look..."

"Great gods, what's happening? Flames are flying over the water..."

"In truth," cry the hierophants, "one would things that the waves are burning..."

"The liquid fire," says Thebao. "Oh guardian Sphinx, save Hellas, save us! The liquid fire is setting the sea ablaze!"

"The liquid fire," Oreus repeats. "All my science is vain. Everything is vain. The wheel of destiny has turned."

A great silence hangs over the Holy Terrace, where no one budges, and all gazes seem riveted to the horizon.

Out there, a splendid and tragic drama is being enacted between the radiant sky and the even more luminous sea. One vessel remains, struggling alone in the middle of a red sheet. One might think that the sea has changed element, and is undulating in waves of fire. In the distance, Timou's great boat can be seen, fleeing as fast as its oars can carry it. And standing at the poop, the black chief, proud of having brought his project to a successful conclusion, is contemplating the futile efforts of Hellas, surrounded by a flamboyant swell.

The sailors on the ship manned by the Prince are throwing themselves into the sea in panic and going to perish, burned or drowned, in frightful torment. Soon, only Hellas remains on deck. Calm and upright, his arms leaning in the tiller, facing the city, he awaits the end.

The vessel is rapidly attained by the tongues of flame. The prow is beginning to burn. The poop continues floating for a little longer, but is threatening to sink. Hellas, standing up, seems immense in the splendid flames that surround him. On the Terrace, sobs can be heard shaking beasts.

Oreus, impotent and crushed by destiny, curbs his head and submits to the gods. Already, his vision is weakening and he senses that the light is dying for him. Glania is twisting her frail arms in a tearful gesture, when a hierophant mounted

241

above the head of the Sphinx, from where his gaze can embrace the entire horizon, cries in a voice rendered superhuman by surprise:

"A god! A god is coming to Hellas' rescue!"

"A god, indeed! One might think it a god," repeat the hurrying hierophants.

"Joy! Joy!" exults Glania. "Look, Master! A gigantic bird is surging from the depths of the sky. It's heading for the Prince's vessel. It's flying, devouring the azure. It's stopping. It's descending. Hellas will be saved!"

But Oreus looks in vain. He can no longer see anything. Floods of tears have sprung from his eyelids, and as if their sudden spring had extinguished the last reflections of all light, the old man feels the effects of the remedy that have rendered strength to his wounded eyes for one day, vanishing forever.

It is over. But by the cries uttered by the hierophants and the joyful ones that the young Ligurian causes to resound, he recognizes his work and knows that the *Alerion* has just raced toward Hellas' vessel.

As the great blind man with the sighted soul, raising his useless arms toward the sky, begs the gods to save his children, to pardon the obscure crowds, and to draw down upon his culpable head alone all the misfortunes that he senses prowling confusedly in the surrounding atmosphere, charged for him with an eternal night.

Scene XIV
The Wings of the Sphinx

Since her return to the Green Isle, Orea has kept watch on the immense sea over which Hellas' ships were advancing slowly. She waited anxiously for the encounter of the two fleets. The *Alerion*, its wings wide open, was hovering above the island. All Oreus' treasures were accumulated in the nacelle, and, doubtless divining that Hellas might have to defend himself against unknown enemies, Orea had not buried the mysterious devices identified by her father.

She has seen the two fleets rising to meet one another, and considering the overwhelming superiority of the enemies, she was preparing to bound in a few wing-beats toward Hellas, menaced, when the ardent mirror projected its rays.

"Hellas is saved! My father is alert!"

Almost immediately, however, she sees the rapid encounter of the two vessels and the liquid fire that has just spread over the waves. And without even darting a farewell glance at the Green Isle, Orea sets in motion the powerful springs that move the monster's wing, and now it is soaring between two azures.

It directs its flight toward Hellas, passes near Atlantis, scarcely casts a rapid shadow over the Crimson Isle and, before the entire city stunned by astonishment, comes to an abrupt halt above Hellas. The *Alerion* tilts; Orea throws down a rope. Hellas extends his arms...

It is just in time! The flames, already, are swirling around the hero, and the poop is sinking into the rutilant waters.

Hellas, exhausted by the effort, overwhelmed by the ordeal, cannot resist the emotion of the rescue. He, who remained motionless and calm before inevitable death, now collapses, devoid of strength and will, his head spinning, his heartbeat erratic, throwing his arms round Orea's knees, he cries: "My sister, my sister, all is not finished, then?"

And with those words, he releases his grip, his eyes close, and he falls back inert, into the bottom of the nacelle.

"Dead! Dead!" gasps Orea, terrified.

And, using all the strength of her arms to turn the inanimate body of the hero over, she perceives on the left cheek and arm the horrible wounds caused by the fire. Then, letting the giant bird fly on in the direction already given to it, without worrying about whether it is flying toward the Occident or the Orient, or whether it is circling the same place, she takes from the depths of the nacelle a sovereign remedy of which Oreus has often shown her the marvelous effects, and sprinkles it amorously over the beloved face, which is gradually reanimated.

Meanwhile, the Atlanteans, emerging from their dwellings in spite of the advice previously given to them by Knephao, are swarming in compact groups; some descend toward the shore, others climb up to high places from which the view overlooks the open sea,

When the *Alerion* appears, a cry springs forth that rises into the sky in a gust of delight.

"Saved! We knew that we'd be saved!"

Exultantly or anxiously, they follow the movements of the dramatic rescue.

But what is happening?

"Hellas is fleeing! He's abandoning us!"

"He's quitting Atlantis!"

"Hellas refuses to fight and die for us."

"Coward! Coward!"

And thousands of fists are extended toward the sky. In the distance, like an immense arrow launched by some invisible god, the *Alerion*, its wings open, plunges into the limitless azure. Anger rises in all the indignant hearts. Knephao, in the Square of the Empire, sees grave citizens coming toward him, who evaluate Hellas' conduct in severe terms.

"Do you understand it, Knephao? To flee before danger, him, our Prince?"

But Knephao makes no reply. He is not even thinking about driving away those men who, a little while ago, were panicked and in disorder, and who are now judging the actions of others haughtily. He too is gazing at the blue horizon, where a black moving dot is drawing way. And, his lips blanched, his eyes wide open, his head leaning forward, he can hear nothing but the tumult of his own heart, and remains mute before the impossible...

What! Hellas, snatched from death, is running away from the city? Hellas and Orea are flying away, toward new lands? No, Knephao cannot believe it. He is dreaming! And yet, here is the crowd, advancing, their fists extended toward the fugitives.

They are escaping, abandoning the struggle. Have they forgotten the City and its perils, then? They love one another, undoubtedly, and they have put their love above their duty. Yes, yes! That alone can explain their flight.

And an irresistible anger swells Knephao's heart. The crowd is crying out around him, their fists extended, but he remains immobile and silent, inaccessible to clamors, for all the furies of the people cannot equal those that are howling within him, and which he is striving not to hear...

But there is a dolor as profound, though much less grim: that of Glania, up above on the Holy Terrace.

"Master, my beloved Master," she groans, on seeing the *Alerion* drawing away. "Master's they're going away! Your children are going away!"

"My children, you say? Orea and Hellas? What are they doing? Where are they going?"

And the old man's hand presses the little hand of the young Ligurian feverishly.

"Master, they're going away! They're going out there, toward the Orient, in the direction of the verdant continents, toward the land of my brothers, where we were supposed to go

245

together, and where they're going alone, forgetting me forever."

"And me too, my daughter, they're forgetting me, as you see..."

And Oreus' words expire on his lips. He does not want to let his pain show. And then, he ought not to be in pain. Have the gods themselves not granted his prayer? Has he not asked them to save Atlantis? Now, the *Alerion* might be its gravest peril. Let it depart, then, toward new skies. Let Hellas and Orea, strong in youth, go to rich lands, to found new empires, and leave futile old age to end in dying Atlantis! That, assuredly, is what destiny wants.

But an ill-stifled sob interrupts Oreus in his silent meditation.

"Don't weep, my daughter, it's not Orea and Hellas who are going away; it's the gods who are taking them away."

"Oh, Master, forgive me if my grief offends you. But I loved them so much! My brother and my sister of election! The souls that my soul followed! They deceived me! They were to take me with them toward the enchantment of my Ligurian shores!"

And, letting her frail body fall on to its trembling knees, Glania plunges her face, inundated by tears, into the paternal hands of the old man, who, impotent to console the young woman, inclines toward her gently and murmurs empty and soothing words to her, as if to a sick child.

Meanwhile, in the city, a clamor bursts forth and grows. In the Square of the Empire, a tumult of trumpets calls the soldiers to arms. Around Oreus, on the Holy Terrace, the hierophants run to the parapet,

"The Barbarian fleet!"

"The fleet is coming back against us."

At those words Oreus stands up, and Glania too, in spite of her tears.

"The fleet, Master; here comes Mellena's fleet. It can come and conquer now. Hellas is no longer here to defend us, and his ships are dispersed."

From the depths of the city, the desperate appeal of the crowd is also heard to rise up.

"Oreus! Oreus! Cast our fire on the accursed!"

But the old man remains immobile, not one tear in his eyes, not a single movement in his entire body, not a tremor on his lips. The wheel of destiny is turning now in a vertiginous whirl, and, no longer seeing anything, he hears the inevitable approaching.

"Master! Master! Save us!" beg the hierophants.

"Impossible," Oreus replies. "If I've been able to measure the time elapsed, then sun must be marching toward its decline. The ardent mirrors would only send forth dead flames. There's no more salvation, except in the courage and the patience of the Atlanteans."

"What poverty!" murmurs Thebao.

"What poverty," repeats Oreus. And, leaning toward Glania, who is gazing at a black dot in the depths of the sky, the old man consoles her: "Don't weep any more, my child. Strengthen your heart. Perhaps tomorrow we'll depart, and we'll go out there toward your Ligurian lands."

In the meantime, under full sail, as tranquil as on a festival day, the Aztec ships seem to be occupying the entire breadth of the sea. At the head are Timou's galley and Mellena's ship. The exploits of the Black have earned him the privilege of sharing the direction of the enterprise with her. Swollen with the pride of his victory, he is standing in the prow of his light vessel.

"Well," he shouts to Mellena, whose ship is drawing closer to his, "was I not right to assure you that we would find no resistance? Look, the sea is empty and the sky too."

Mellena, in fact, had shivered on perceiving the *Alerion*, but on seeing the giant of the air gradually disappearing, she and her friends have become hopeful again.

In Atlantis, in the distance, the crowd is swarming and complaining outside the dwellings. The rush begins toward the Palace of the Empire. In spite of everything, Knephao, prepares to hold firm. Oreus, whom Glania has come to rejoin, is seeking information continually about the events taking place continually, when the young woman, whose daze is still searching the impassive sky, lets fall the words:

"There they are! They're coming back!"

"Who? The Barbarians?"

"They're coming back! I can see them! Your children! Orea and Hellas!"

"What are you saying?" says the old man, leaping to his feet.

"The child is deluded by her desire," murmurs Thebao, who has just approached. "The sky is empty, alas!"

"No, no," Glania affirms. "The sky isn't empty. Can't you see those wings beating in the azure, out there, in the distance?"

"I can scarcely perceive a black dot, like a lost swallow..."

"It's growing, it's coming, it's hastening: it's the *Alerion*!"

Glania's voice is so piercing that a few hierophants approach, equipped with telescopes.

"It's true!" cries a young priest. "The barbarian girl has the eyes of an eaglet. She's divined the invisible. With the aid of my telescope I can scarcely glimpse a giant bird, which is growing with every wing-beat."

"You hear, Master? I knew that I couldn't be mistaken."

Scene XV
The Anger of Hellas

In the *Alerion*, in fact, since the rescue of Hellas, Orea, overwhelmed by the danger of death that she sensed weighing upon the hero's pale forehead, has no longer been thinking either of the Empire, or even her father, and while the remedy she had applied gradually took effect, she has been flying at top speed toward the Orient, where, far from the troubles of the mad world, she will be able to care for her beloved, returned to life, freely.

In the meantime, Hellas slowly recovers consciousness. And he utters an initial cry of instinctive beatitude.

"Where are we, then, Orea? We're alive! And I can feel you close to me." Then, suddenly, as if involuntarily, the hero stands up, looks into space and cries: "What are we doing. What's become of Atlantis?"

"Atlantis is singing out there, my beloved, in the peace of the setting sun."

"Out there? But then, we're fleeing?"

And as Orea remains silent, Hellas repeats: "We're fleeing? The daughter of Oreus and the Prince of the Empire are fleeing!"

At those words, Orea, bewildered, suddenly falls out of the dream in which she was flying, and tears come to obscure her eyes.

"Oh, forgive me," she implores, bursting into sobs. "Forgive me, my beloved. I love you so much that I was on the point of becoming ingrate and cowardly. Let's go back to die with Atlantis."

"Die? Certainly, death doesn't frighten me—but let's leave ideas of the end to the weak. For us, it's life that we're going to bring back to the Queen City. We're going to deliver it from its enemies forever. On those who have dared to spread on the waters the fire that devours without a battle, we're going to drop the secret forces of which we dispose. I shall destroy the Aztec fleet in a matter of hours. Have you kept the cylinders of solid air?"

"I don't know," stammers Orea. "What do you want to do with those frightful objects? Even my father was afraid of them."

"Nothing can any longer inspire fear in a man who has just seen the sea itself enveloped by flames. Yes or no, have you brought those devices?"

"Yes, Hellas."

"Well, if you're truly my companion, we're going immediately to attack the enemy fleet. If not, by the Unknown God, I'll throw myself this instant into the sea in which you don't want the Barbarians to be engulfed."

"Oh, Hellas! Only promise me that if the enemy fleet renounces the struggle, you won't attempt to raise up the sea."

"So be it. But let's go quickly. I'm in haste for Atlantis to see us return and not to suppose that we've fled."

And the *Alerion* accomplishes a vast curve in the sky and resumes its vertiginous course toward the Occident.

There is only just time. Already the liquid fire is surrounding the Crimson Isle, The frightened artists have gone to ground in grottoes or are hiding in the depths of palaces. Even Hermos has been forced to retreat into the center of the island, and Xanthes, now intrepid, is threatening the Barbarians with his useless engines as they draw away in the open sea.

The menacing vessels of the Blacks, all together, are drawing ever closer to Atlantis. Timou can be seen, joyously ferocious, standing in the prow of his vessel, extending his menacing arms toward the City. The crowds of people are running at hazard; terror is provoking blasphemies, the gods are being denied, or even insulted, when the cry uttered by Glania is repeated from hill to hill:

"Hellas is coming back!"

This time, the joy of the crowd erupts in delirium.

"Glorious Hellas! The true hero of Atlantis! We knew that he would return to us!"

"Come! Come, Hellas! Come and crush the Barbarian fleet! Come and render us peace and joy!"

And from everywhere, words fly toward the *Alerion* that are lost in the azure. Even those who, shortly before, were hurling insulting cries toward the fleeing monster are now heaping their insults upon those who are not acclaiming the Prince of Apostles loudly enough.

Knephao, on the threshold of the Palace of the Empire, does not try to contain his happiness; and the chief of the Egyptian soldiers, ordinarily impassive and silent, causes his horse to prance and starts conversing with the strangers who are passing in front of the Palace.

The enemy fleet immediately disbands. Mellena and Guitche are heading for the open sea as fast as oars can carry them, where ships can be seen colliding in the haste that terror inspires. A few vessels, passing close to the Crimson Isle, throw themselves into the waters set alight by Timou's artifice and disappear in the moving flames....

On the Holy Terrace, the trumpets of the Sun give voice to a fanfare of delight, in order to salute the coming of Hellas and the rout of the rebels. From time to time the trumpets fall silent in order to allow Glania the joy of singing a hymn to the accompaniment of her cithara, and the hierophants mingle their deeper voices with the winged voice of the young Ligurian.

All is delight, all is song, all is light in Atlantis. In the distance, in the Occident, the sun that is sinking toward the sea seems to be enveloped in waves of crimson radiance. Not a single cloud dares to cast the augury of a tempest. The earth and the sky appear to unite to celebrate the now-certain deliverance of the City.

Alone, leaning against the flanks of the Sphinx, seeing nothing, divining everything, silent in the universal tumult, the great blind Oreus is praying quietly to the Unknown God, and weeping in his heart over the destiny of the Empire.

Meanwhile, Hellas has arrived above the fleet. From the height of the nacelle, from which his view embraces the entire horizon, the Prince of Apostles evaluates in a single glance the danger that the Empire is running.

"This is the moment!" says Hellas to Orea. "Let the *Alerion* float gently over the enemy fleet."

"One more minute, my love, wait one more minute. Think of the harm that the incommensurable force to our devices might leash."

"Wait! Always wait! Look at Timou and his blacks hastening toward the City. Once in the city they'll be sheltered from out blows, and in order to strike them, we'll have to strike the Atlanteans. Give me one of the cylinders in which your father has condensed the forces of the air."

And Hellas utters that order in a tone so energetic that Orea, without the will to resist, hands the young man one of the requested tubes.

"Forgive me, Father; may Hellas save the city today, and not doom it forever!"

But Hellas, standing up in the nacelle, holding in his hand the mysterious secret from which the death of the wicked and the salvation of the good will fall, gazes without trembling at the city where the Sphinx is resplendent in the reflections of the sunset, and then leans over the waves, and in a clear voice, says:

"For the Empire of the Sun! For threatened civilization! For the future of the world!"

And violently, he throws a first metallic tube, which falls into the sea, not far from Timou's vessel.

A grandiose silence seems to spread over the City. Thousands of breasts hold their breath at the same time. Nothing can any longer be heard but the sound of oars in the water and a few frightened clamors of sailors. What is about to happen?

Nothing.

The sea has swallowed the menacing device, and continues its placid swell.

Orea breathes out.

Hellas stands there, dazed by astonishment.

Timou, joyful, urges his vessels toward the land. Already a few other ships are coming around and returning to the assault. Is the secret of Oreus a delusion, then?

Furious then, Hellas picks up several more cylinders himself, and in a rage, he hurls them to the right and the left, sometimes toward the vessels that are advancing toward Atlantis, and sometimes toward those in the open ea.

Orea, frightened by Hellas' anger, takes the *Alerion* upwards, and gets ready to head out to sea again. But the young man, who is frightening, does not stop, and from a height, without measuring his blows, disperses against the fleet all the devices that his hand can seize.

"Ah! Accursed race in revolt, wicked or cowardly humans, sordid humankind! Die, then!"

Suddenly, in the direction of Timou, between the Crimson Isle and the peninsula of the Green Point, an immense column of water erupts from the bosom of the waves, like the expanding jet of an erupting volcano. It rises up slowly to a prodigious height, and falls back with a crash on a few vessels, which it engulfs.

"Glory! Glory!" clamor the wonderstruck Atlanteans, with one voice. "Glory to you, Hellas!"

"Glory to you, beloved of the gods! Demigod yourself!"

And on the Holy Terrace, fanfares burst forth.

"Silence! Silence!" cries Oreus, in a superhuman voice.

And the tall blind man, standing against the breast of the Sphinx, stops the manifestations of joy to which the hierophants are about to deliver themselves, abruptly.

"On your knees, all of you," he orders. "On your knees before the Invisible. The supreme hour is sounding! Let us pray for those who, in requesting a miraculous salvation, have attracted death to the entire Empire! Atlantis herself has just summoned her destiny with millions of voices."

And the face of the blind old man, illuminated by the setting sun, appears to the hierophants so terrible and so transfigured that all of them, without understanding, and without seeking to understand, fall to their knees and feel their hearts sink.

Scene XVI
The Anger of the Waters

And the night gathers, rapid and lugubrious, with no warning dusk.

At first, the Atlanteans utter cries of triumph. They know that their city has nothing to fear and that the unknown gods are protecting them, as they have just proved by the intervention of Hellas. By the lights gleaming in the confused gloom, they contemplate the vertiginous swirling of the waters, where the heavy Aztec ships are lifted up and borne away like sea-gull feathers in the foam of the waves.

"Enough, Hellas!" shouts a rich merchant. "Enough! You've punished them sufficiently now; leave the sea to repose and come and join in the festival of Atlantic."

"Look," says a neighbor. "The bird seems to be floating above the wind."

In fact, the waters have gradually fallen back into the Ocean, now agitated over its entire surface, where the debris of wrecked ships and boats is floating at hazard. The atmosphere has cleared slightly, and in the moving twilight of the extinguishing day, the *Alerion* is perceptible on the horizon, immobile high in the sky. But clouds are rising from below on all sides, and the giant bird soon disappears definitively from the eyes of the Atlanteans. Then, it seems to them that with the visible form of their miraculous protector, they see their own confidence disperse, and, without exchanging their sudden fears, without saying anything, without even moving, in the heavy calm that weighs upon the city, all the Atlanteans are frightened by an inexplicable terror.

Gradually, the wind rises over the sea, blowing over the land, shaking the trees in the avenues, causing the dust to whirl in spirals, and ululating through the doorways.

"Pity! Pity!" moan the women, extending their arms at hazard toward the sky.

"Let's take refuge in the temples!" propose some.

"In our houses!" reply others.

But now, in the depths of the houses, in the stables and animal-pens, plaintive barking and prolonged whinnying are heard. Animals, having broken their tethers, knocking over everything in front of them, race out along the streets where the hurricane is raging.

Around the great circus built by Barkas, the lions and bulls escape in disorder, filling the air with their frightened roars and their bellowing, multiplying the surrounding terror.

Up above, in the Square of the Empire, the Egyptians' mounts, all saddled and harnessed, extend supplicant muzzles toward their riders; then, as if they feel invisible whips passing over them, the beautiful beasts rear up and bolt, and the Egyptians, impotent, see a vertiginous cavalry fleeing in all directions, manes in the wind, heads free, eyes haggard.

"Disaster!" proclaims one of Knephao's lieutenants. "When the animals are afraid, it's not of men, it's of the elements."

As he finishes those words, a sudden shock makes the earth tremble slightly underfoot. He only just has time to cling on to one of the masts planted in the square, and a few soldiers fall over on the ground.

"Courage!" orders Knephao. "We haven't cried for mercy before men, let's not weaken before blind forces."

And the Egyptians, in silence, come to line up under the peristyle of the Palace.

"Look out for whirlwinds!" says one of them, who has been navigating distant seas for a long time.

"Here comes a cloud that's descending upon us," says another.

"Not a cloud," observes Knephao, "but a flock of seagulls and albatrosses."

In fact, above the Egyptians' heads, a confused flock containing birds of every wingspan passes with a loud clatter of agitated wings, and goes to settle in disorder on the Holy Terrace, around the Sphinx, and still further away, along the artificial lake, the waves of which, always limpid, are now swelling like the waves of a sea.

"Glania." Oreus comments, "you no longer have anything to do next to me. My hour is marked. I shall expiate the crimes of my science among the merciful groans of these animals, and, by means of their plaints and the sounds of their wings, I shall follow the phases of the catastrophe that I have unleashed. But you, go and rejoin Knephao, whose strength might perhaps preserve you. Let me die in the turbulence of vengeful things."

"Oh, my Master, my father, if we have to die I shall die upon your heart. But perhaps Orea and Hellas will be better able to save themselves than us?"

"If the *Alerion* has crossed the zone of uplifted clouds, there is nothing to fear. But them...oh, how sorry I feel for them! Inert, they will see from on high the destruction of the city, and along with their remorse, they will experience their impotence to save us henceforth. For I know only too well, gods of the earth, what secrets I have stolen from your jealous caverns, and what force Hellas has just raised up from the raging abyss of the sea in revolt."

Scarcely has he finished speaking than a great wind envelops the city again, in all parts, tearing the roofs from temples, uprooting trees, causing the giant wings of the Sphinx to tremble.

And from the depths of the sea, from the very place where Hellas threw, in his rage, all the remaining cylinders of solid air, a mountain of water rises up, so high and so broad that the horizon seems closed all the way to the sky. With a horrible sound, the liquid mountain advances, driven by the force of the displaced air; it marches with a single movement toward the city, and abruptly, from top to bottom, crumbles and collapses upon the cupolas of Atlantis, where the bewildered inhabitants, seeing nothing, hearing everything, feel themselves crushed by unknown forces, believing that the sky has just opened up.

Then, some flee into the most obscure depths of houses, and the houses collapse on top of them; others come to pray in temples already filled with groaning voices, and he temples shaken from top to bottom, split along their entire height and bury the supplicants under their fallen vaults; others wander through the streets and, hanging on to the asperities of the monuments, try to climb up on to the roofs, but are dragged down by the collapse of walls or carried away by the hurricane that unfurls through the ravaged streets where waves rush in torrents.

Another mountain of water invades the city; another; and then yet another. The water rises up in funnels, advances, retreats, rises, descends, rears up, turns and turns again, like an exasperated monster, which, having struck the enemy, is gathering its strength by folding back upon itself.

The subterranean workings of Atlantis, hollowed out below sea level, fill with moving waters, which, encountering the vaults of cellars and tunnels, spurt through crevasses from which sulfurous vapors suddenly spring forth. Everywhere, the earth trembles; the great city opens up in a thousand wounds; finally, in the supreme blow dealt by the furious sea, the once-filled bed of the river Gabire swells up with muddy water; the old river, reanimated, cleaves throughout its length through the layer of stone that grips it, and lifts up the palaces that have covered it.

This time, the city shivers all the way to the Holy Mountain. Oreus and Glania have taken refuge by the flanks of the Sphinx. Thebao, who tries to join them, only just has time to take evasive action between the two folded legs of the monster, from which foaming water gushes, borne by the wind all the way to the feet of the mute idol.

From the Square of the Empire a rumor as stormy as that of the waves in fury rises into the air. All that remains of able-bodied Atlanteans want to take refuge in the Palace, and they hurl themselves toward Knephao, whom they implore. The soldiers, courageous to the end, unshakable before the furious elements, have lit torches, which they are holding in their hands and, lined up under the peristyle of the Palace, surprised again by the shocks of the trembling earth, watch that human tide coming toward them, just as blind and unconscious as the waves in folly.

"Great chief," ask the men, "it is necessary to continue struggling against these fanatics?"

"What's the point?" says the giant, shrugging his shoulders. "Tempest of waves, tempest of men; everything is whirling henceforth, and everything is going to end."

But the colossus, in spite of his calmness, has been unable himself to measure the power of humankind stampeding in disorder; the human tide driven by a surge of terror, is animated with an irresistible force. The torches are extinguished and Knephao, rolled in the popular hurricane, soon finds himself lost in an obscurity so complete that he does not even know to which part of the Palace he has been carried.

Shaken by the shock, he leans against the walls and utters a cry of surprise. He has been dragged all the way to the secret crypts of the Palace. He recognizes, by touch, the statues of the dead Apostles. Alone now, separated from his soldiers, impotent to get back to the square, where everything has been ravaged, he has nothing left to do than die in this subterranean solitude.

"Die?" he says. "So be it. But let's try to die beside Glania and Oreus, at the feet of the Sphinx, with people I love."

And, groping his way, he slips through the crypts, which his hand explores and recognizes. He arrives at the secret entrance to the Holy Hill, and climbs up all the way to the Temple. He guides himself by following the statues of the heroes, and has already opened the great portal giving access to the terrace when his foot, encountering a human body lying on the ground, stumbles.

He bends down, and touches a man who is lying along the wall. The man stirs; he groans; he sighs. The giant shakes him, and is lifting him in his arms when a swirl of fire and smoke abruptly gushes through the air behind him, and, with the noise of an explosion, the Temple leaps toward the sky, where a splendid storm has just burst, traversed by thunder and lightning.

Scene XVII
The Anger of the Sky

Knephao only just has time to leap to the bottom of the stairway, where he falls to the ground with his human burden. On the Terrace, which the explosion has suddenly illuminated, and which the lightning flashes now fill with dazzling light, he sees the hierophants, devoid of strength and virtue, fleeing toward the Palace, which they enter in disorder, crying:

"The God is burning us! The God is devouring us!"

Then the giant stands up and thinks to look at the man he has saved from the Temple, where he would inevitably have perished.

"Belkis!" he exclaims.

"Belkis!" replies the voice of Oreus himself.

And in the returned gloom, between two lightning-flashes, Knephao, dragging Belkis, trembling with terror, gropes his way to the feet of the Sphinx, where a lightning-flash shows him the old man, the young Ligurian and the chief of the hierophants, sheltering under the idol's wing.

"Knephao! Here's Knephao, Master! He's come to die with us!"

"Glania, Thebao, Oreus, I salute you. Let our last hour be that of poor mortals who having nothing for which to reproach themselves in this life, await the judgment of the Invisible without fear."

"Admirable hero!" says Oreus. "Speak for yourself and for Thebao, and for this dear barbarian child. But I, my friend, will go before the Unknown and severe God accursed and repentant, responsible for the evil that has fallen upon Atlantis."

"You, the noblest of the red race?"

"And the most vainglorious, perhaps, since I did not want to break the infernal discoveries of my genius."

"Reassure yourself, Master; I have seen, in this fatal day, the frightful soul of Atlantis opening up before me, and I know now that she had to die."

"I should have saved the city, not finished it off. We have turned the wheel of destiny. In our turn, that wheel is crushing us.

A lightning-bolt flashes at that instant, another follows it, and a clap of thunder explodes in the sky like a crash of colliding stars. The sound of a collapse is heard behind the Sphinx.

"The obelisks," Thebao explains. The obelisks from with all the luminous fluids of the nocturnal city obtain their source. The Palace of the priests will not take long to blow up. Oh, my poor neophytes! My poor children!"

"They might still be saved," advises Oreus. "It would be sufficient to open the fluidic current. The luminous force, instead of exploding in a conflagration, will flow away to be lost in the City and the waters."

"But in truth, why have my priests closed the central hearth?"

"Why?" asks Knephao. "Ask this man."

"Belkis! We'd forgotten him," says Oreus.

But Belkis does not budge. Lying on a step of the stairway, he is trembling like a submissive dog.

Knephao grabs him by the nape of the neck, lifts him up, places him facing Thebao, and the light of the blaze, which is increasing, shows the Atlantean's frightful face clearly.

"Go on, talk," orders the giant. "It's your last hour. Ours too. At least you'll have the consolation of dying with us."

Belkis says nothing. He is content to open a filthy mouth. His eyes seem to be tearing themselves out of their orbits. A rictus of terror sweeps each of his cheeks.

"Tell us what you did with the key you stole."

"Ba...a..." Belkis bleats, trying to articulate a sound, although his voice remains stupid an inert.

"The poor fellow," says Oreus. "He's gone mad."

"The key! The key!" insists Thebao, authoritatively. "Make a gesture, at least, if you can't speak."

But the bewildered Atlantean agitates his arms, raises them toward the sky, gazes with bloodshot eyes at the men who are speaking to him, and then, letting himself fall to the ground, rolls away weeping and crying: "Ba…a…a…"

"Let's throw away this rag," said Knephao.

And he pushes the sobbing body away with his foot, which rolls to the foot of the stairway of the Sphinx.

"Poor man," Oreus concludes. "Poor symbol of his race! They believed themselves to be capable of directing the world, and they die of fear before their own accomplished actions."

A sheaf of lightning-bolts is then deployed in the sky; one of them falls on the red pyramid erected behind the Sphinx, and this time, the Palace of the Initiates, where all the marvels of Atlantean science are conserved, blows up, throwing out an immense spray of fire.

"Our turn now!" exclaims Knephao.

"Master, Master," sighs Glania, "give me your hand. And you, Knephao, come closer. And you, Thebao, huddle against us; I'm afraid of the sky, which is opening up."

"My poor friends," pronounces Oreus, "we're doubtless the last survivors now."

"Let us pray to the gods," enjoins Thebao.

And, drawing closer together, maintained against the trembling wing of the Sphinx by Knephao's vigor, all four of them murmur a hymn to the Unknown God.

"The flame!" cries Glania. "The flame is reaching the Holy Terrace.

"Let the flame burn and purify us," replies Oreus. "That death is better than being engulfed in the soiled waters.

The fire, in fact, is now enveloping everything that remains of the city. Every flesh of lightning that springs forth sets fire to a cupola still standing on a hill. The sky is hurling fire at the vomiting earth. For in the distance, far away, over the entire archipelago of the Red Empire, a few mountains have opened up, and under the assault of the sea, under the quaking of the earth, the old extinct volcanoes have reanimated their hearths and are spitting vapor through craters with rutilant mouths. All the forces of nature, all the fluids of the air, all the powers of fire, awakened and exited by the prideful provocation of humans, are uniting, so to speak, in a universal accord, to efface from the planet the very trace of detested Atlantis.

Already, the smoke rising up to the Terrace is stifling and blinding the four survivors; already Glania is hiding her head in Oreus' bosom; already Thebao is closing his eyes before the Invisible that is approaching, when, behind the Terrace, a dull and prolonged crack makes itself heard.

The Terrace shakes violently. It seems to the condemned that they are about to plunge into the opening earth; they press their knees together. Only Thebao, still standing, risks a glace over the disorder that surrounds him, and cries:

"The lake! The artificial lake! It's just broken its dykes!"

The beautiful lake that dominates the entire island, the immense and marvelous lake to which prodigious machines transport the waters of all the rivers; the lake enclosed by high walls, for which entire mountains have been moved; the lake to which the sons of Atlantis had promised an eternal duration, now dislocated by the agitation of the earth and shaken by the storm in the sky, has just broken its once-unbreakable bounds and is spreading out in all directions in the lain and over the City. Its urgent waves, rolling over one another, seem to be in haste to rejoin the paternal Ocean and they are carrying away in their passage everything that still remains above the flood.

"Let us resign ourselves," exhorts Oreus. We won't even have the beauty of dying in the flames. Let the water be our tomb, then, as for all our brethren. Adieu, Empire of the Sun! Adieu, unfortunate City! Adieu, Atlantis!"

At that moment, the Sphinx, surrounded by flames, is struck by a rapid waterfall, which extinguishes all trace of the fire.

The bronze idol does not even flinch. Glania hangs on to Oreus' arm. Thebao takes refuge against his master, and the giant, in a desperate effort, embracing his three companions with one arm, clings with a robust hand to the claws of the

263

idol in order that, until death, the violence of the waters will not separate those who have loved one another on earth.

"Adieu everything!" says Knephao.

"Courage!" murmurs Oreus, again.

But the word, incomplete, stops in his throat. A new wave, launched by the lake overflowing its bed, displayed and amplified in a broad curve, is projected beyond the Sphinx; and its last four worshipers, clinging to the flank of the mute God, blinded by the fire, deafened by the waters, weary of struggling against the insurmountable, finally abandon themselves to the vertiginous anxiety of feeling themselves borne away without defense into the supreme catastrophe of the Great Dusk.

THE FIFTH DAY:
THE FESTIVAL OF THE ORIENT

"It is necessary that every world dies..."
"Even the worlds..."
"A world dies; a world is born..."
"And everything begins again."

Scene I
On the Crimson Isle

A slow first light hesitates on the horizon. Around the nascent gleam a milky and gray sheet is extended in the sky, while clouds accumulate toward the south. The sea, still seething with its recent fury, sometimes rises in swollen waves, and then falls back, rumbling.

"Daylight! Daylight!" cried Xanthes, bounding with delight.

"Life is reborn! Nature is continuing!" adds Asmonia.

"Let's sing a hymn!" says Xanthes. Let's sing a hymn to the day we no longer hoped to see!"

"We very nearly didn't see it," says Thamoussi. "But for the energy of Hermos, we'd have been swallowed up in our Palace."

"Poor palace of marble and gold, whose terraces overlooked the most beautiful horizon created by humans. Oh, how quickly the sea has destroyed it!"

"Bah! Atlantis is rich enough," yaps Olbios, "to repair the damage of the capricious waves!"

"But where is Hermos?" asks Xanthes. "The man who, by force, at the moment when the sea was howling around the isle, brought us to the summit of the hill—the man who saved us, where is he? I don't want anyone before me to go and tell him how much we love him!"

And without paying any heed to the grumbling of Olbios, who protests, he searches in every direction for his friend Hermos.

The artists of the Crimson Isle, however, delighted to receive the light of day, gradually emerge from the cavern where they have spent the night, on the mountain that dominates the entire island. It is there that Hermos led them at the moment when the tempest was unleashed. And now, wearied by a night of anguish, still trembling in their wet garments, they come to await the rise of the star, separated from Atlantis by the hill of porphyry.

The joy of rebirth, the intoxication of sensing the evaporation of the terror of universal death with which they shuddered in the obscurity traversed by lighting-bolts and cyclones, the surprise of contemplating the sky again, even dull and covered in cloud, all the great resurgence of life makes them forget the torments of fear and the insults of the frantic elements; and, in spite of the fatigue, in spite of the ravages of their dear Palace, they sing the first strophes of a hymn to the sun.

But scarcely have they begun than an oppressed voice falls from the hill:

"Wretches!" says Hermos. "Don't sing! Silence! Silence! Rather pray, pray very quietly, pray for the millions of dead, our brothers"

The word death multiplied by an enormous figure passes over the heads of the artists as wildly as the wind of the recent night.

"What's the matter now?" asks Palmoussos.

And Olbios, having become tremulous again, begs Xanthes to go and find Hermos and Amonou.

Now, however, they appear before the cavern, their eyes widened by terror, their gestures jerky, their throats hoarse with rising sobs.

266

Hermos throws himself into Xanthes' arms, stammering: "Oh, my brother! My brother!"

And Amonou, in the general silence, lets fall the words: "Atlantis is no more."

"Come on, come," says Hermos, straightening up and suppressing his dolor. "Come and see our poor mother."

Then, some run behind Amonou along the paths; others, more impatient, scale the sheer rock; all of them launch themselves toward the southern flank of the hill, from which the view overlooks the dear City.

Alas! Immense City, City once eternal, City that, yesterday still, covered the horizon with its resplendent cupolas: what a downfall!

Mute and motionless, Xanthes and his companions gaze but dare not see. Their staring eyes refuse to reflect the spectacle that unfurls; only their hair quivers in disorder, abandoned to the sea breeze. Asmonia utters a scream and falls to her knees; the other women hide their heads in their hands and moan; and the same appeal, with nothing more, springs from all their breasts:

"Atlantis! Atlantis!"

"Come on, my brothers," says Hermes, "let's pray and weep, and then get up, and try to live."

But the others hear nothing, make no response. Xanthes is devastated. Even Amonou, his young courage deflated, no longer has the strength to second Hermos, and with the others, murmurs tearfully:

"Atlantis! Atlantis!"

Scene II
The Remains of Atlantis

In fact, Atlantis no longer appears to be anything but an immense floating necropolis. Over the entire width of the horizon, the eye sees nothing but debris, swayed by the waves, and everywhere, flocks of cadavers that the waves cause to collide, mingling them with sinister foam.

Alone, of all the City, the Holy Hill rises up, but so ravaged that it resembles some symbolic monument left by the furious elements to the chastisement of the vainglorious Empire. The columns of the temples are twisted, the Palace has been opened up by explosions, and the Sphinx, leaning over the left flank, seems to be flapping its wings in the blowing wind.

"You who once protected us, symbol of our strength and our glory," exclaims Hermos, "O radiant Sphinx, here you are, vanquished by the obscure forces of matter!"

"O Empire," says Amonou, "what has become of your glory?"

"O Atlantis, what has become of your body?"

And so saying, Asmonia, with a broad gesture of both hands, indicates, on the sea, the scattered debris of the city, intermingled and floating like the hair of a gigantic drowned woman.

But Thamoussi, having remained silent, stirs and, in a lamentable voice: "And our fathers? Our brothers?"

"And our mothers?" says Xanthes.

"And all those we loved?" adds Amonou.

"Unknown gods, have pity on their souls."

And, like a mortuary psalmody, the entire lamentable troop resumes repeating, in a tremor of sobs:

"Atlantis! Atlantis!"

Meanwhile, Hermos goes from group to group. He takes the hands of the men, comforts the women, and lifts up the dejected young women.

"Courage! If the gods have left us alive, it is in order to impose a higher dolor upon us. Fortunate are the dead who can no longer see the innumerable corpses of their brothers floating on the waters. But let us, since life has kept us, be ready to submit to all the proofs that remain to us, and bow our heads, once too superb, before the terrible majesty of Destiny."

"Let us pray! Let us pray!" responds Xanthes.

And, falling to their knees on the stony flanks of the hill, hanging on to granite fissures with their hands, the Atlantean artists search in their memories for the forgotten words of childish prayers, and extend their suppliant hands toward the sky, where, behind the clouds, the presence of the Sun can be divined.

"Come on, men," says Hermos, "let's leave our sisters, too sorely tried, to weep, and we'll go along the shore in search of some boat that can take us to the other shore."

Making a sign to the others to follow him, the poet gets ready to go down toward the sea.

"Mercy! Mercy! Pity!" say the women, agitating in their turn. "Don't leave us alone! Who knows what the angry sea till has in reserve for us? Take us with you."

So, recovering courage, the entire group, men and women, are descending slowly toward the sea, when Xanthes stops and says: "Look, Hermos! All of you, look! It seems to me that something is moving on the Holy Terrace."

"You're right, Xanthes; one might, indeed, think that the Sphinx is moving and that its wings are flapping."

"A miracle of the gods?"

"A supreme effort of humans?"

"Living beings," says Asmonia, "but what living beings?"

"Perhaps Oreus," whispers Hermos in Amonou's ear.

"Or Knephao," adds Xanthes.

And Amonou, emotionally, murmurs: "Poor little Glania, what has become of her in that torment?"

Each of them, then, in the depths of his soul, resigns himself to the destiny of the City if, at least, some hope remains of rediscovering a dear individual.

And in the once-extinct eyes, the gray daylight is now reflected, and gleams, and sometimes smiles. Assembled next to one another, on a plateau that is still broad, situated a few fathoms above the sea, whose view overlooks the southern horizon, the last Atlanteans follow the movements observed on the Holy Terrace, palpitating with emotion.

"No, it's not the Sphinx," Amonou declares, "but a great black bird that's flapping its wings."

"The *Alerion* itself!" adds Hermos, very agitated.

"The *Alerion* on the Holy Terrace? How does it come to be there?"

"I don't know. But it really is the *Alerion*. No other machine of that sort exists, so far as I know. Look—the wings are beating rhythmically. It's taking off. It's hovering. Now it's climbing slowly and seems to be circling over the empty lake. Where is it going?"

"Fatality! It's going away!"

"It hasn't seen us."

"Look! It's turning southwards!"

"Let's not despair," says Hermos. "One last effort. Courage! Let's make signals. Let's do as shipwreck victims in the open sea do who see a sail passing in the distance!"

He sets the example; he takes off his tunic, once red, and, at the end of a stick picked up from the ground, waves it in the air, shouting, at the top of his voice:

"Hellas! Hellas!"

"Hellas! Hellas!" repeat the others, brandishing branches and shreds of cloth in their turn.

Have the passengers on the *Alerion* seen or divined them? Or rather, after having taken to the air, are they returning northwards of their own accord? The survivors tremble with emotion, seeing the *Alerion* gradually complete a vast ellipse and direct its aerial prow toward the Crimson Isle.

"Here they come!" cries Asmonia, deliriously,

"Joy! Joy!" clamors Olbios, beside himself.

"I knew it!" sighs Amonou.

And all of them, dazed by hope, throw themselves into one another's arms.

"Run, quickly!" appeals Asmonia, who has already launched herself toward the west of the isle. "Quickly! They're certainly going to disembark on the great strand, the only place where the *Alerion* can land without danger."

In fact, at that moment, the artists are all on the high and rocky part of the isle, where the *Alerion* cannot alight. But down there, toward the east, they see the vast beach with golden sand, where the people of the Crimson Isle and the richest people from the City once went to take sea-baths. Last night, the beach was covered and swept by the waves.

The survivors, at the risk of wounding themselves on the rocks, run down in great haste, hoping to arrive in time to witness the descent of the *Alerion*. But the great bird, more rapid than them, goes straight to the shore, and, after a smooth flight along the arc of a circle, settles gently on the sand. The artists run and leap from rock to rock, but they only have time to see three passengers descend from the *Alerion*, at rest, who are advancing slowly toward them, while a fourth, as tall as Knephao, seems to remain with others invisible in the nacelle.

The garments of those who are approaching are so torn, their hair in such disorder, that at first, the survivors of the Crimson Isle cannot recognize anyone. It appears to them, however, that one of them, the one in the middle, of tall stature, is walking with great difficulty, sustained by the other two, one of whom is very small and thin. A child? A woman?

Scene III
The Savior Alerion

But a cry goes up.

"Glania!" calls Amonou.

The young woman thus addressed puts a finger over her lips to demand silence; then, with her hand, she makes a sign to the artists to stop.

"By the Sphinx," says Xanthes, "the man she's sustaining is blind. His eyes are covered by a black bandage."

"Oreus!" exclaims Asmonia, who, carried away by her enthusiasm, advances toward the group.

But Hermos pulls her back, and says, in a low voice: "Yes, my friends, it's Oreus. But let's not trouble him with our cries and plaints. The light he spread yesterday has extinguished his sight."

And, in a few whispered words, he recounts how Oreus went blind. They all stop and fall silent, full of pity, anguish and admiration.

"Oreus!"

Now, all of them recognize him by his tall stature, his silver hair and his long beard. All of them also recognize Thebao. And Thamoussi, his contemporary and childhood friend, sends him a fraternal salute from afar, to which Thebao responds with his free hand. But while almost all of those present remain alarmed and dazed before the misfortune of the man they regarded as a demigod, four of them move aside, and come back carrying, effortfully, a large stone, which they deposit at Oreus' feet.

"Thank you, Hermos," sighs Oreus, who has recognized one of them by his voice. "And thank you all, my poor children."

And those words, pronounced by him, say so many things, that only sobs respond, and even Oreus lets his head fall into his hands. But he raises his head again, shakes it, and in a voice that becomes firm again:

"Come on, my friends, my daughters, enough tears. What I could say to you, you have already said, and repeated, since last night, since yesterday, since the great dusk of our beloved city: the great dusk announced by the mysterious prophecy, which no dawn will dissipate!"

"The dawn will come," says Xanthes. "The sun can be sensed behind the clouds."

"For how many Atlanteans?" says Oreus. "A hundred? Two hundred? A thousand, even? And the others, the millions and millions of others? When shall they see it? Where shall they see it?"

"They're all dead, aren't they? All swallowed up?" asks Asmonia.

"Yes, all of them," replies Thebao, while Oreus, overwhelmed, leans his head on Glania's shoulder and all the others remain silent, anguished.

"It seemed to us, last night," adds the Pontiff, "while we were trembling with horror, clinging to the Sphinx, that millions of the dying were howling beneath us, calling for help— and how have we not joined them in the abyss? Miracle or hazard? I don't know."

"A miracle, indeed," Xanthes puts in, "To have escaped the lake that opened up above you."

"It opened up principally on the side of the plain and toward the low quarters of the city. After a threat of a few minutes, the terrace remained, spared. Sheltered under the wings of the Sphinx, expecting death at any instant, we prayed until the first frisson of light, listening hour after hour to the sea, which was calming down, and the dying, who were falling silent, Finally, a strange noise rolled over our heads. The end of everything? The supreme vengeance? The exterminating god? Surprise—the *Alerion* itself."

"It's me, me," says Glania, "who saw it first."

273

"This sublime child has the eyes of a savage," murmurs Oreus. "Before I had even recognized the sound of my own machine, she had cried: 'Hellas! Hellas!'"

"And Hellas was suffering so much, in body and soul," adds Glania, that he wanted to cast himself down from the nacelle over the dead city."

"But Knephao and I retained him," Thebao continued, "while Oreus ordered him to live, Orea begged him and Glania still had hope—and she had reason to hope. A few moments later, with Hellas guiding us himself, we took off, at random, toward the south, and we would have departed toward Iberia if Glania, with the eyes of a seagull, had not seen human beings agitating on the Crimson Isle."

"Glania! Glania!" cries Amonou, "so it's to you, then, that we owe life."

"Then," Thebao concludes, "the *Alerion* veered northwards and we passed over the poor city again. Frightful! Frightful! Not a house left standing, all the low quarters engulfed, all the peninsulas drowned; not a human being anywhere; not a cry, not a movement, and in the distance, toward the south, the volcanoes reigniting. Atlantis is dead! Atlantis is dead! Atlantis is dead!"

A silence punctuated by sobs follows the hierophant's words, but from the depths of the nacelle a voice rises, and a wounded head is seen to appear.

"No, no! Atlantis cannot die! Its walls are annihilated, its palace and temples engulfed, almost all of its inhabitants rolling under the waves, and the island will disappear, but its soul still lives; it's soul lives in you, Hermos; it lives in Xanthes, it lives in all of us; it lives, above all, in our great Oreus. It lives in the treasures accumulated in the depths of his nacelle, which will bear to new peoples the eternal breath of Atlantis. Here, in this aerial vessel, the clairvoyant Oreus had amassed the most beautiful works of his intelligence, the formulas of our science, the discoveries of our genius. It is that which represents Atlantis; all the rest was merely sterile stones. And of that, my friends, we shall soon make the spiritual nourishment of the new world. You want that, don't you?"

From all breasts, a single cry escapes: "Hellas! Hellas! We want it. Become our master again!"

"My friends, my brothers, my victims of yesterday, you have the right to hate me, and you're now forgiving me?"

"Us, hate you!" cries Xanthes. "Who could hate you, Hellas?"

"We don't see in you," insinuates Olbios, "the man who has killed Atlantis, but the man who will save us."

A few murmurs...

"Hellas didn't kill Atlantis," Amonou snaps. "Atlantis wanted to kill itself."

"We're all guilty," adds Hermos.

"And you still remain Prince of the Empire," interjects Asmonia, "so the Empire can't die entirely."

"Empire or not, Atlantis lives in us. And since you want me still to command, well, for the last time, I'll give you orders. It's necessary, isn't it, to leave here?"

"This evening, if possible."

"This evening, scarcely probable. Tomorrow, perhaps, or in two days at the latest. That depends on your labor. To find boats, impossible. All broken—but debris, perhaps, is prowling around the harbor. So you, Amonou, take the youngest and most alert under your direction; go along the edge of the sea, to the south, and try to pick up all the floating planks and all the wrecked hulls. You, Xanthes, and you, Hermos, take all the rest of the male artists with you, and go into the ruined Palace, from which you'll remove the beams that are still solid and the woodwork that's still smooth. And bring all of that back to the old Esplanade beside the sea, where we'll construct a raft for all of us. As for the women, they'll go to the rocky north-western promontory, guided by young Glania, and they'll look for shellfish, fruits of the sea and fish, so that we won't die entirely of hunger, for a few days."

"All that is well organized, Hellas," interrupts Olbios, "but afterwards? Where are we going on the raft?"

"Toward the Orient."

"Without a sail or rudder?"

"What about the *Alerion*?"

"What do you mean?"

And while they all listen, anxiously, Hellas, leaning against the nacelle, addresses Oreus.

Scene IV
Around the Alerion

"Oreus, our Master, do you think that your *Alerion* can, from the air, with its long cable, tow the raft that will transport us, on its own?"

"A trifle bold," says Oreus, "but not impossible. How many survivors are there, approximately?"

"Fewer than two hundred," declares Xanthes..

"Then you can attempt it

"More than two hundred," says Glania, in her soft voice. "We haven't counted the others."

"What others?" asks Olbios, anxiously. "The Egyptian soldiers who came to our defense yesterday?"

"All dead," replies Hermos. "Not one wanted to flee to the hills in spite of the fury of the sea. All of them died at the posts that Hellas had assigned to them."

"Knephao's soldiers never quit their posts," Hellas affirms.

"The poor fellows!"

"The brave men!"

"What others then?" persists Olbios.

"I saw them, from the height of the *Alerion*," says Glania, "So did Thebao, and Knephao."

"It's true," affirms Thebao

"Over there, in the direction on the northern hill. They seemed to be descending slowly through the rocks."

"How many?"

"We couldn't tell from a distance," says Thebao. "A rather compact group. Let's say a hundred, no more."

"A hundred!" groans Olbios. "That's frightful! Let's hurry, then. Let's leave before they arrive."

A unanimous cry of reprobation rises up.

"If the raft isn't large enough," Oreus interjects, "we can make two voyages. We can extract the two groups that way. I'll stay here with the second."

"For the second voyage, there'll be no need of the raft," says Hellas, "I have the intention of taking you to the mouth of the River Adour, among the peoples of Basconia and Biscay, whom I know well, and Knephao has treated so generously that they've become his friends. I'll go to find the famous Gaouran, the veritable king of those regions, a king by virtue of his influence and the love that people have for him. A trifle rough and sharp in his speech, but a heart devoid of treason. He didn't like Atlantis; he fought it honestly, but when peace was made, he embraced Knephao on the battlefield; he'll give us everything we need—I'll answer for him."

"I'll answer for that too," affirms Knephao.

"You know that the Biscayans and the Basconians are the greatest navigators in the world, and he is the best navigator in Basconia; he's already traveled the world.

"He was even due to come here for the Festival of the Orient," Hermos interjects. "Last night's torment must have prevented him, and forced him to turn back."

"As long as he hasn't been swallowed up!" murmurs Asmonia.

"No tempest can swallow Gaouran," affirms Knephao, tranquilly.

"In any case," complains Olbios, "We remain in uncertainty."

"Even if, by misfortune, Gaouran is no longer alive. I'll answer for the other Biscayans even so," Hermos puts in. "I know them better than Hellas. I lived for several months in the Gulf of Cibour; they're the most generous people in the world. I knew Xambo, Buxo, Markis and all Gaouran's lieutenants there, and Hossegor's mariners and the fishermen of Biarris, and the vine-growers of Nogaro, and I swear that none of them would refuse to rescue Atlanteans."

"Courage, then, Olbios" says Hellas. "Go on, my male friends, search for the materials for our savior raft, and you, my female friends, for our poor nourishment. But in the meantime, help me to descend, as well as Orea, and we'll stay with Oreus, for I still feel too weak to join you."

"What's the matter with Hellas?" Asmonia asks Glania, in a low voice.

"Oh, the poor fellow! He nearly died in his struggle against the flames. He has a large burn all down his left side and on his face, from which he's suffered atrociously. It's by a miracle of energy that he was able to struggle and act yesterday evening. This morning, Oreus has cauterized his wounds marvelously by means of a sovereign remedy hidden in the depths of the nacelle."

Meanwhile, without waiting any longer, Xanthes, Hermos and Amonou go toward the *Alerion*, toward which, with a movement of irresistible curiosity, all the others draw nearer, without daring to mingle with the groups of acquaintances. Knephao sees them coming, advances toward his friends Hermos and Amonou, whom he embraces, and takes Xanthes' hand, which he shakes ardently.

But what a Knephao! Where is the handsome captain armor in gold? A long scar on his cheek; his hair and beard full of clotted blood; his garments wet, torn, a wound on his hip; he limps when he walks. He would look like a vagabond or a beggar without the ever-fulgurant gleam of his eyes. And his voice, still sonorous and good, takes on the mildness of a muffled harp in order to murmur to the group that is approaching and acclaiming him:

"My dear friends that I don't yet know, my brothers henceforth, be silent, I beg you; don't disturb poor Orea, who is still asleep.

At the prestigious name of Orea, they all stop; the women interrogate the Egyptian in low voices:

"Orea is suffering?"

"Yesterday's events have fatigued her so much that she is now without resistance to dolor. So long as her father remained by her side, all her effort was extended to continuing to talk and to appear confident and tranquil, but she was fading before our sighted eyes."

However, a soft and faint voice rises up from the depths of the nacelle: "Hellas, my love, help me to get down. I want to replace Glania next to my father."

Such an emotion seizes the survivors that they all approach silently, as if each of them wants to assist the daughter of Oreus. But Knephao, extending his strong arms toward the nacelle, picks Orea up and deposits her gently on the ground, while Hellas, getting down himself, guides the young woman to the stone on which Oreus is sitting, through a double row of mute Atlanteans. Knephao, having become apparently impassive again, stays by himself to guard the *Alerion*, now empty, quivering in the sea breeze. Hermos and Amonou approach momentarily and interrogate him in low voices about Orea and Hellas.

Orea! Hellas! Those two individuals about whom there has been so much talk, who have been exalted and cursed, now they are exhausted by lassitude, and even weaker than all the rest. The men look at Orea's face, ravaged by so many tears. The women look at Hellas' wounded visage, in which his vigilant eyes are still shining. Oreus, alerted by Glania, stands up and goes toward his daughter, and the latter, half-suffocated by emotion, falls into her father's rms.

Knephao remains alone, to one side, sitting beside the *Alerion*.

"Come on, dear companions," says Hermos. "Forgive me if I trouble this minute of sublime anguish by a recall to life, but it's necessary to live, since death didn't want us. And to live, it's necessary to get away from here. I therefore invite you all to follow Hellas' orders."

"And you, my dear companions," cries Glania, addressing the women, "follow me to the nearby promontory. I'll show you how we fish for sea-urchins and fruits of the sea on my distant Ligurian coasts."

"And I," Orea interjects, "will go with Glania. I've often fished for shellfish in the little port of the Green Isle."

"No, no" says Xanthes, smiling. "You and Hellas remain with Oreus. You'll form the Council of the Empire."

"And you'll watch over Knephao, who appears to me to be very agitated," observes Thamoussi.

In fact, Knephao, until then so calm and so indifferent in appearance, suddenly seems to be gripped by a feverish preoccupation. He gets up. He goes from one end of the *Alerion* to the other. He climbs on to a stone, puts his hand above his eyes, and suddenly shouts: "Look out, everyone! Here come the others!"

Scene V
The Others

Everyone turns round. Even Hermos, Xanthes and Amonou stop what they are doing. Asmonia and Glania, who have already departed, come back at a run. In fact, toward the north, on the summit of the hill that descends in a promontory toward the sea, moving shadows stand out against the nebulous sky. People can be seen from afar people agitating scraps of cloth on dead branches; they seem to be asking for a sign of peace and welcome. They respond to them by opening their arms.

"Who are they?" asks Xanthes.

"People escaped from Atlantis, no doubt."

"But they would have landed to the south. Why are they coming from the north?"

"Perhaps they're the Toltec or Aztec travelers who arrived yesterday for the Feast of the Occident," explains Thamoussi. "Because of the encumbrance of the port, their vessels dropped anchor to the north of the Crimson Isle. They came yesterday morning to ask me about the best location."

"You're right, Thamoussi," says Xanthes. "I've traveled to Palanque and I recognize their rhythmic gait and their taller stature. For the most part, they're Toltecs from out there."

"They're not all Toltecs from the continent," adds Hermos. "I see before them individuals who, by their gait, their attitude and what remains of their garments bear more resemblance to people from Atlantis."

"By the Sun!" cries Knephao. "I recognize them. It's..."

He falls silent, as if the word sticks in his throat.

"Of course," Xanthes explains. "I recognize her too. That's Mellena."

"Mellena!"

"And Guitche...and Barkas...and Moussor...and all the rest..."

"Except Belkis, though," growls the Egyptian.

"Come on, Knephao, my lad," says Oreus, who has heard everything. "Nothing must remain of our old quarrels. There are no longer any but unfortunate brethren."

And, drawing himself up to his full height, handsome and radiant in spite of all his wounds, Hellas resumes his appearance of Prince of the Empire."

"Come with me, Orea," he says. "Let's go to meet them."

And without saying a word, Orea gets up and follows him.

The new arrivals, as if they have divined the scene, have halted some distance way, and are waiting. When they see Hellas himself coming to meet them, with Orea, their hands extended, they too advance, with Guitche and Mellena at the head.

Orea throws herself into Mellena's arms. Hellas takes Guitche's hands. On both sides, an acclamation rises. Thebao, meanwhile, reports what is happening to Oreus.

"Great souls! Fine children!" murmurs the old man, satisfied.

In the general emotion, only Knephao remains apart, sitting on the cable of the *Alerion*, thrown to the ground. He lets his head fall into his hands, as if he does not want to see any more.

Meanwhile, Hellas and Orea lead Mellena and Guitche by the hand to Oreus. The others follow.

"Salutations, Mellena and all of you, and be welcome. You know everything, don't you?"

"Yes, great Master, Orea has told me everything briefly. And we too only survived by a miracle."

And she recounts how she and her friends, having taken refuge on the Toltec fleet, saw all the vessels precipitated on to the sand of a funnel-shaped beach. They were able to escape before the vessel was carried away again by the offensive return of the waves. In the morning, from a distance, they perceived the other survivors but dared not approach.

283

"Why not dare?" remarks Oreus. "Did you take us for wolves?"

"Unfortunately," groans Mellena, "we have all been wolves to one another."

"Let us forget our hatreds," says Orea. "We'll all depart together."

And Hermos, in a few words, explains the plan of departure to the newcomers.

"And you believe, Hermos," Mellena asks, "that that fragile bird will suffice to draw a heavy barge capable of carrying us all? What does Barkas think?"

"I'm sure of it," says Oreus, authoritatively.

"If Oreus affirms it, Mellena, there's nothing to fear. We all bow down like schoolboys before him," Barkas replies, obsequiously."

"Oh, the admirable aerial machine!" cries the beautiful Aztec, becoming suddenly vibrant again. "Oh, sublime Atlantis, which could create such miracles. Oreus, Oreus, why have we not allied our forces. What an eternal Empire we might have deployed!"

Gradually, however, Mellena and her companions have drawn closer to the *Alerion*, and, either by hazard or by calculation, the woman who was called the Queen of Atlantis is standing on the side opposite to the one guarded by the motionless Knephao. Orea and Hellas, glad of the peace that seems to be reigning in souls, and delighted by the hymns of admiration to the genius of Oreus that are rising, accompany Mellena and her friends to the edge of the fatal and formidable instrument of death.

"Truly divine!" Barkas utters. "I did not believe that human genius could go so far."

"The genius of the red race," specifies Mellena,

"Look, Guitche," Barkas continues. "Almost nothing. A little iron, a little wood, a great deal of cloth, a few tubes of liquid air, and humans can fly in the sky."

Hellas, in his turn, cannot rest exalting his master.

"What is most gripping about this endeavor of Oreus' is the extreme simplicity of its working. A child could guide it."

And he indicates with his finger the various items of apparatus at rest, and operates the principal mechanisms. Mellena, her eyes flamboyant with curiosity, follows all the movements of Hellas' hand. One might think that she wants to leap into the nacelle, so much does she seem to be drawn to it with her entire body.

But on the other side of the great bird, Knephao is standing, attentively. He has seen everything. His old warrior instinct puts him on guard against his friend's imprudent excitement.

"Hellas, you're forgetting that the hours are passing. Do you think that the raft will make itself?"

"Very true!" the Prince of the Empire acquiesces, struck by the suggestive recall to reality. And he seeks the eyes of Hermos, who, a little further way, is already organizing the men into two groups. Then Hellas, turning to Guitche and the others, with the design of drawing them away from the *Alerion*, says: "And you'll help us too? You, Barkas, the best of constructors, can give us precious advice."

"Hellas and Knephao are right," responds Moussor. "Let's live first, and dream later." And he takes the arm of Barkas, flattered that Hellas has treated him as a master. Opposite, Knephao, his brow furrowed by anxiety, is following all the movements of the newcomers.

"And you, Mellena," suggests Hellas, "won't you help my companions to search for shellfish? aren't you hungry?"

But Mellena has not heard anything. She remains visibly absorbed. "And there, at the bottom, in the nacelle in that box—what's that?"

"All our treasures, Mellena. Books, scientific formulas, instruments, inventions, works..."

"All of Atlantis, in sum"

"Or at least, all that remains of it."

"And what are we going to do with all that?"

"What it's necessary to do: the education of the new world."

"The new world?" exclaims Mellena, straightening as if by a feline movement.

"Well, yes. It's necessary that civilization continues."

"And it's for those moonfaces that great Atlantis will have found so many things?"

There is a moment of silence and embarrassment. The renascent conflict fills the watches with surprise. The crews, already organized by Hermos, suspend their departure. Then, the masculine and imperative voice of Knephao rises: "There are not only those you call 'moonfaces,' in the Orient—who are, in any case, worth as much as us. There are also the brothers and sons of Atlantis, the Egyptians."

"And it's for scarcely-born Egypt that the red race will have labored for so many centuries?"

"The Egyptian race is the daughter of Atlantis."

"But the Toltec race is its mother!"

"Civilization goes toward the future, not toward the past," Hellas cuts in.

At those decisive words a silence falls on both sides. The conflict grows. Already, groups are forming and agitating. Barkas, Guitche, Moussor and their retinue surround Mellena. But blind Oreus divines everything.

"Silence! Are you going to fight again for dreams, when we don't know whether we'll be alive tomorrow?"

"The *Alerion* is not a dream," replies Mellena. "The sole reality that subsists of Atlantis: the supreme flower of its genius. We have every right to it."

"So be it. But who made the *Alerion*?"

"You!" cry almost all of the audience, in chorus.

"The objects that it contains, who possessed them, who collected them?"

"You!"

"I therefore have the primary right to dispose of them. Do you have confidence in my spirit of justice?"

"Yes!"

286

"Yes," repeats Mellena.

"Then I shall decide. What I order shall be done."

"It will be done," affirm the Atlanteans.

Mellena falls silent and draws nearer to the *Alerion*. Then, Oreus, in a slow and grave voice, says:

"I have therefore decided that the *Alerion*..."

Scene VI
A Ship

But at those words, the joyful and strident cries of women's voices are heard. It is Glania, Asmonia and all the others, who come running, waving their hands.

"Saved! Saved! A ship!"

"A ship!" proclaim the others, who, in an instant, launch themselves toward the sea uttering loud cries of delight.

"Saved! Saved!"

Even Hellas and Orea draw away from Oreus, and Guitche too, and Barkas and the others.

"A ship! A ship!"

And, indeed, sails appear on the horizon; not one ship, but three at least are outlined against the sky. No one remains around Oreus, immobile and emotional, but Thebao, who is serving as his guide, and Knephao, standing next to the *Alerion*. Even Thebao, drawn by curiosity, is shading his eyes with his hand, and gazing at the horizon. As for Mellena, she is no longer visible.

Suddenly, a cry of alarm departs from Thebao's throat. Knephao only just has time to throw himself upon the cable of the rising *Alerion*. Hellas and Orea also return, uttering cries for help. The *Alerion* has quit the ground. It hovers at first, and then it rises up slowly. Those who have gone toward the sea turn round, not understanding immediately, but the truth soon becomes manifest.

Mellena, agile and skilful, having retained the suppleness and rapidity of her former métier as a dancer, has taken advantage of the moment when all attention was turned toward the signaled vessels; then, climbing into the nacelle and maneuvering the tiller, she has launched herself into the air, and is now attempting to fly.

But someone is striving to resist; it is Knephao, clinging to the cable. For a moment, it seems that the giant might retain

288

the still-hesitant apparatus, but the terrible machine draws the Egyptian away, who does not want to let go. The bewildered watchers call out to him to give up; some race to help him, but too late. As for him, frightful in his determination, he is still resisting, hanging on with all his might to what remains of Atlantean glory, until, lifted some way above the ground, he falls like a mass on to a heap of stones, while a cry of horror escapes from all breasts and the *Alerion*, lightened, rises into the sky with a vertiginous leap.

Hellas, Hermos, Xanthes, Amonou, even Olbios, and all the men, without saying anything, their throats tight, run to the place where the immobile giant is lying.

Is he dead?

No, he can breathe, even speak, but he cannot move; his back is broken. Hellas, Hermos, Xanthes, Amkonou and Olbios pick him up gently in order to transport him on to the sand, away from the stones. At the slightest shock the poor fellow utters heart-rending cries.

"For Knephao to cry out, how much he must be suffering!" observes Oreus.

"He's going to die!" sobs Orea.

"Take me to him, my daughter."

Meanwhile, Hellas and Thebao on the one hand, Guitche, Barkas and their friends on the other, are following the *Alerion* with their gaze into the clouds, departing at top speed toward the Occident. It is already so far away that it has certainly passed the limits of the island and must be flying over the open sea.

"Is that Mellena going to take the treasures amassed by Oreus to the Occident," asks Thebao.

"What does it matter?" sighs Hellas, with a discouraged gesture. "Let that malevolent instrument go wherever she wishes!" And a sob escapes his breast, while he turns away to hide his tears. But two strident cries cause him to raise his head.

Guitche and Barkas are waving their arms wildly toward the sky. High, high above, the *Alerion* is seen spinning in place; it seems that smoke is escaping from its wings. It descends, rises up, descends again. Suddenly, it plunges vertically toward the sea and disappears behind the line of the horizon.

Amonou and a few alert young men run to the summit of a small hill nearby from which they can look out over the Ocean, and they perceive debris scattered on the distant waves, the last vestiges of what had been Atlantean science.

A few young men cry: "Poor secrets of Atlantis, lost forever!"

But Hermos, gripped by pity, replies to them: "Let us bow our heads, my friends. There are among us one individual who is suffering and another who is about to die..."

And the Atlanteans see on the one hand Guitche, who has placed his hand on Barkas' shoulder, and on the other hand, Knephao, racked by pain, whom Hermos and his friends have deposited on the sand.

"Poor Guitche," says Oreus, softly, to the former King of Gold, whom he can hear weeping nearby. "Our portion of grief is not yet complete. You have just lost the wife whom you loved, and I a friend like one of my children. They both died heroically and foolishly in pursuit of a dream of glory, one to carry to her own people what she believed to be the grandeur of Atlantis, the other to save and protect that false grandeur. You have the right, Guitche, to be proud of your wife. She had a soul of fire!"

Having comforted his former enemy with his warm voice, he addresses Orea, who is guiding him: "Take me silently, my daughter, to what remains of our admirable Knephao."

"There still remains enough of him," sighs the giant, "for him to rejoice in your presence and to ask you, before dying, for the benediction of your divine words."

Scene VII
The Death of Knephao

Knephao is, in fact, lying motionless on a bed of algae that Glania, Asmonia and Amonou have gone in haste to collect, and he has been deposited on that bed at the very feet of the father and the daughter. Hellas, one knee on the ground, is sustaining his friend's head in his hands. Hermos and Xanthes, with slow and gentle gestures, are gradually removing the wounded man's clothing in order that Thebao can examine his wound.

"My poor friends," murmurs the giant, "you're giving yourselves a great deal of needless trouble. I know death; it has often passed close to me. I've seen so many dying men on battlefields. I know my fate. There are only a few more moments..."

Thebao, who has just examined the back and breast, cannot dissimulate his anxiety.

"Come on, Thebao! Smile, then...why that sinister expression? Do you think that death frightens me?"

Meanwhile, Oreus has sat down on a stone on one side of the giant, and Orea on the other side.

"Thank you," says Knephao. "That's the only remedy I need." And he asks them each to take one of his hands. Every movement he makes wrings plaints from him, which he immediately stifles.

Glania, aided by Hellas amasses a heap of seaweed against his body.

"Glania, my girl, you saw the vessels arriving? Do you know where they're coming from? If they could only be those of my friend Gaouran...I could die reassured and happy. Go and see, Glania..."

And the Ligurian runs in haste toward the shore. Only a single vessel is now visible. The others are doubtless exploring the vicinity of the dead city. The one that can be seen has five large masts laden with sails. One of the sails, on the foremast, bears in the center a red star with seven branches.

"That's him!" exclaims the Egyptian. "That's Gaouran's insignia. He had promised to come. Oh, my friends, what joy! I can die tranquil now: you're saved, and not only saved, but in the hands of the most loyal man there is in the Orient. Thebao! Thebao! Give me enough life for me not to die before having confided you to that worthy man."

"Before anything else," Thebao interrupts, "don't get so excited. Oreus—calm Knephao's foolish joy."

But Oreus does not reply. Since he has been holding the hand of the dying Knephao in his, one might think, on seeing his breast so agitated, that an unknown soul is breathing in his. His dead eyes seem to be fixed on a mysterious point in space. The blind man appears to be contemplating the invisible. Only Orea soothes Knephao with her soft, musical voice.

"Our great brother Thebao is right; stay still. Your fried Gaouran is about to disembark. Our young friends will run to meet him and bring him to you."

"With him, Orea, you and Hellas can go to the land of the Pelasgians. Xanthes, if you wish, he will take you to the Etruscan lands. You, the Aztecs, he will enable to depart for the Occident. And you, Hermos, and you, Thebao, he will disembark in my beautiful Egypt, where the soul of Atlantis ought to be reborn. Is it not the case, Oreus, that my Egypt will be beautiful?"

Then, as if the completion of those words has suggested to the grand old man the vision of his blind eyes and his illuminated soul, he exclaims: "I see it, your Egypt! I see the future, Knephao; the Unknown is speaking to me!"

Everyone falls silent. Even Knephao stops sighing and clings hard with his hand to the blind man's hand.

"I see radiant on the banks of the Nile cities with a hundred gates and capitals with golden temples, where the splendor of Atlantis will be reborn. I see a strong people standing at the feet of the Sphinx, a chain of Holy Mountains, that will be the astonishment of the new world until the end of centuries. I see all our sciences, all our wisdom, all our poetry, jealously preserved in the depths of sacred crypts. I see a glorious nation becoming by means of its hierophants the educator of the new world. I see the Sphinx governing the earth..."

"Glory! Glory!" exalts Knephao.

"Oh! What do I see?" groans Oreus, whose oppressed breast heaves. "Hordes of herdsmen coming from savage lands falling upon the great Nile. Everything is ravaged. Everything is overturned. Everything is destroyed. Atlantis crumbles again. The Sphinx disappears beneath the shifting sand..."

"Pity! Pity!" sighs Knephao.

"But the centuries pass and everything is reborn. The Egyptians take back the land. Science and faith spring forth again from the depths of crypts. The Sphinx surges forth again from the sands. Egypt becomes the educator of the future world again."

"God of Oreus, protect us!" prays Knephao.

"...Now something entirely new appears on the horizon of the world: something of which we have been unaware... What do I see? The Sphinx! The Sphinx! A beautiful sky full of stars...in thousands and thousands of years... A vast solitude extends around the statue granite reddened by the sun and by the burning sands... A woman more beautiful and gentler than Orea... She is carrying in her arms a child that she is hiding. She is fleeing far from persecutors... She stops at the feet of the Sphinx. She places the sleeping child against the granite breast and the child wakes up...oh, what eyes! What a gazes! He is no longer a human being: it's Him, the one that we have summoned in vain for hundreds and hundreds of centuries—the Infant God—the God... Glory! Glory! Knephao, we can die!"

With those words the old man curbs his head, and Thebao takes him in his arms, his strength exhausted. A murmur of anguish runs through the assembly. Knephao, his eyes radiant, seems in his turn to be looking into the future.

Now, in the midst of the general emotion, a man who has not yet been perceived slowly approaches Knephao, guided by

Glania. Scarcely has he arrived before the body of the recumbent hero than he kneels down and touches the giant's arm. He is a white-skinned man of tall stature and broad shoulders. He has blue eyes and a bond beard and hair mingled with threads of silver. His gaze reveals a saddened affection.

"Gaouran!" sighs Knephao, whose voice is weakening. "Now I can depart in joy!"

"Not depart," says the newcomer, who speaks Atlantean with a strange accent. Not depart, but remain. Hope! I have elixirs on my ship that will resuscitate you."

"Gaouran, Gaouran, there are no elixirs for broken backs. But how happy I am to see you! My friends, my friends, this is Gaouran…adieu, everyone!"

And the body of the giant, agitated by a supreme spasm, falls inanimate on his bed of green algae. Gaouran places his ear over his heart.

"Finished! Knephao was..."

Hellas kisses the Egyptian on the forehead. Oreus, groping, places a hand on his breast. Orea is weeping. Glania is sobbing. But Gaouran, although trembling himself, wants to react against the general depression.

Scene VIII
The Funeral

"Great Oreus, whom I don't know, it is sufficient to see you, and especially to hear you, to divine in you the master of masters, in spite of your wounded eyes. I listened just now, transported into the sky, to the prophetic inspiration of the invisible. Yes, yes, incomparable master, a new future is open again for your children. They will come to our plains and our mountains, treated like my own brothers, and those who wish to disperse into the great world, I shall take them."

"Thank you, Gaouran; I know you too without knowing you. I shall never be able to see you, but I know that you are strong and good, and the father of all your people. Hellas and Knephao have told me a great deal about you. Don't call me master, though; there is henceforth but one master for us all, and that is you."

"So be it, then. Since it is necessary, Oreus, and you order it, I accept to be your master temporarily, or rather, your guide. And first of all, it's necessary that you change clothing; you have nothing about you but sordid rags, soaked by rain and soiled by mud.

And, quitting the group without further ado, he goes to find two of his lieutenants, with whom he converses in low voices.

"That's it!" groans Olbios. "He's just talks and then leaves us. How loquacious these Basconians are!"

"Don't worry, Olbios," Hellas affirms. "If Gaouran's leaving us, it's to occupy himself with us. He knows how to talk, but he knows even better how to act."

Indeed, Gaouran is returning, followed by his two lieutenants, Xambo and Buxo, who, in their turn, bring forward several sailors whose shoulders are laden with burdens that they throw to the ground.

The amazed Atlanteans see garments distributed of fine wool and pure linen.

Then Gaouran picks up a white tunic and a red cloak.

"Glania, my child, help me to dress Knephao. Let him enter the tomb ornamented like a king, for he was nobler than a king."

Meanwhile, the men and women, having changed to one side, group around Gaouran, transfigured by the soft sensation of new linen and delighted with the man who foresees everything, like a God.

"Buxo, Xambo, bring forward the pavis and the banners now."

And ten men bring on their shoulders a pavis of white wood covered with foliage and flowers, on which Knephao is piously deposited; and the ten men, with slow steps, preceded by Buxo and Xambo and a group of mariners, set forth toward the promontory. Behind the hero, Gaouran has Oreus placed, guided by Orea and Glania; then he follows himself with Hellas and Hermos; then come Thebao, Xanthes Thamoussi and the others, spontaneously arranged in threes. The cortege advances slowly.

Gaouran, in a voice that remains warm and profound, gives a signal, and immediately the men placed at the head intone a Basconian funeral song, of an amplitude and simplicity so moving that the Atlanteans, all musicians, without understanding the words, begin to hum the tune while marching with slow and measured strides.

But Buxo and Xambo halt, and the entire cortege is immobilized. Before them is an open grotto, at the back of which torches held by sailors are burning. Knephao's body, lifted off the pavis, is carried into the grotto. The Basconians who have remained outside kneel down, as do the Atlanteans. A lugubrious and monotonous psalmody accompanies the placement in the tomb, but even more lugubrious are the sobs of the women.

Oreus, his eyes burned by tears, cries out, in a voice that trembles: "Adieu, Knephao! Adieu the man who, alone, could have saved Atlantis!"

"Adieu the last of the heroes," adds Hellas.

"Not the last," says Gaouran. "There are others among you who will accomplish many promises."

And to put an end to that scene of dolor, by which everyone feels heart-broken, Gaouran gives the order to wall up the grotto with the aid of a large block of stone that ten of his men can hardly shift. And on the stone, someone has already engraved, in Atlantean and Basconian:

KNEPHAO, STAINLESS KNIGHT

"Thank you, Gaouran," says Hellas. "He could not have dreamed of a more beautiful funeral."

"He merited it," replies Gaouran. "He alone was able to defeat us!"

Then, addressing the Atlanteans who are standing, dejected, before the sealed tomb:

"Sons of Atlantis, come on, let us not weep any more. Knephao would have forbidden us to do so. A great soldier, dying was his métier. He followed his métier magnificently, and as he loved to repeat so many times in his tranquil amiability, it is necessary for everyone to die."

"Even worlds!" sighs Oreus.

"A world dies, a world is born," replies Gaouran, whose serenity has returned.

"And everything recommences," finishes Hellas, who, with an abrupt and resolute gesture extracts himself from melancholy contemplation of the eloquent stone behind which Knephao is asleep forever.

"Come on, my children," says Gaouran, who wants to react. "Our ship will be ready to sail this evening. In the meantime, shall we have something to eat? You must be dying of hunger."

Scene IX
The Meal

Then, setting the example, he marches with great strides toward a group of rocks, in a kind of shady and cool circle, where Atlanteans once went to lie on the sand after bathing. There, they find a number of dishes on blocks of stone, a few spoons, a few cups and a small meal already prepared; an odor of fresh bread and flavorsome fruits came to cress the nostrils of the poor survivors who have not eaten or drunk anything since the previous day.

Going from group to group, Gaouran and Xambo distribute to everyone white pancakes with gilded crusts, which have just been brought, very fresh, and small terrines containing meat preserves, while Buxo pours wine.

"Oh, this wine," says Hermos. "This, Xanthes, is infinitely better than all the Etruscan wines celebrated in your verses."

"It's our everyday wine," replies Gaouran, modestly. "We harvest it on the hills along the River Garo."

A miraculous return of human nature! These people who have just taken part, as witnesses and victims, in the most frightful of cataclysms, who were still weeping a little while ago over the tomb of their beloved hero, now abandon themselves gradually to the invasion of physical joy, allowing themselves to be drawn toward a new hope by the indefatigable animator, bringing them in his words and his gestures all the soul of his fortunate land.

"Gaouran, O tempter," says Xanthes. Why are you enchanting us with your magical beverages? Are you trying to force us to forget Atlantis?"

"And what courage I shall require," adds Hellas, to quit your land and go to live among the Pelasgians."

"Don't go then, and stay with us; where can you live more happily?"

"And my work?"

"What work?"

"The Empire to remake."

"Madman!" exclaims Gaouran. "Crazier than a man in love or a sistrum-player. What need to you have to found an Empire, only for it to collapse one day like Atlantis? Did you not hear the predictions of the great Oreus? Poor dreamers! Here you are, a few bewildered survivors, with neither arms not hearth, and you're already talking about going to conquer peoples? Always the same! Always the enemies of others! Always your own enemies!"

And, shrugging his broad shoulders, he returns, without saying anything more to the ship.

There is a sudden reversion in the souls of the poor Atlanteans. Their momentary joy has capsized. The intoxication of the open air, wine and hope has all turned to sadness or bitterness.

"So," growls Xanthes, "he thinks the end of Atlantis just?"

"He finds our pride unjust," said Orea, "and perhaps he is right."

"With all that, we've done well," groans Olbios, looking at Hellas furiously. "Now Gaouran is going to abandon us. No more *Alerion*, no more ship! Nothing remains but for us to die here. That's cheerful!"

But Hellas, who has been agitating on the spot nervously and impatiently for a few moments, suddenly leaps to his feet and heads in haste toward Gaouran, who is continuing his march toward the sea. An anguished curiosity weighs upon all the witnesses

"Hellas! Where are you going?" shouts Orea.

"Leave me alone, let me be...I'd rather die in Atlantis than live for a few days on the charity of Barbarians."

And he gets ready to resume his course, but an imperious voice stops him and silences all the surrounding murmurs.

"Hellas! Come back here. That's an order!"

Scene X
Three Men

It is the blind man, drawn up to his full height, and who, dressed by Gaouran in a magnificent gold-embroidered tunic, is more majestic than ever, in spite of his blind eyes. And as Hellas does not come immediately: "I'm giving you an order, Hellas, do you understand? And it's already too much that you hesitate for a single instant at my voice."

This time, subdued by an irresistible force, the former Prince of the Empire returns to the old man, his head bowed, murmuring the single phrase:

"I obey."

"Good, my child. You have mastered your pride."

Silence on all sides. Then Oreus continues, in a softer voice:

"Hellas, my son, do you remember your despair this morning, when you wanted to throw yourself from the height of the *Alerion* and Knephao prevented you from doing so? You felt so guilty that you wanted to die to expiate your sins—the sins of your pride, you said. And I replied to you that no one has the right to punish himself. If punishment is necessary, it will come from others, for it's always from others that it ought to come."

"I'm expecting it, Master."

"And here it is. I'm giving it to you, I who love you more than a son. For I divine that you're suffering in hearing me humiliate you before the others."

"Everyone was silent. Hellas, immobile, kept his eyes lowered.

"Hellas, my son, you have been and you are greatly culpable. Not for having cast death over Atlantis, for you did not know. You thought you were saving the city. Your arm became the arm of destiny."

A great sigh escaped the breast of the young man, and a murmur of approval ran through the assembly.

"But you were, you are, and perhaps you will remain greatly culpable, for you have dreamed of the empire of the world; you wanted to possess it, and believed that you possessed it."

"If you had read the foundations of my dream, you would have read their love for humankind."

"Ah! There, then, is the perfidious word, the criminal word, the word of the beast that thinks itself divine! To possess the world in order to ameliorate it! To subjugate humans in order to save them! O vanity! By what right, Hellas, do you believe yourself destined to guide the world? Your own genius? Divine genius, truly, which will last scarcely a few decades, and which a bad chill or a simple canker might hurl into oblivion from one day to the next."

"Oh, master!"

"When one loves human beings, Hellas, one does not conquer them, one gives oneself to them; one does not make them suffer, one suffers for them; one does not kill them, one dies to save them. It isn't humankind that you love, it's your dream of humankind, and that dream is summoned by the delirium of your pride."

"Pity, Master!"

"Pity, my son, is talking to you in accordance with injustice, in order that you do not recommence, in order that no one should ever recommence. Illusion, in any case! One always recommences! The filthy beast that breathes in the depths of our souls speaks more loudly than the divine spirit that appeals to us. But sooner or later, the divine spirit ends up prevailing. It prevailed today. All of you who can see, contemplate what remains of your Empire..."

A cry of protest and dolor rises from all breasts. Orea hides her tears. Hellas puts both hands over his convulsed face. Xanthes begs: "Spare us Master. Why are you angry with us as well?"

"With you all, and with myself! Hellas is doubtless the most culpable, by virtue of the very excess of his genius, because, more than any other, he incarnated the soul of Atlantis. It is Atlantis that was greatly culpable, and she has merited her punishment."

"No! No!"

"She merited it! I confess it!"

Silence.

"Don't worry; in any case, it will be the same with all Empires. Except that, instead of crumbling at a single stroke, into the open sea, like Atlantis, they will sink slowly in blood and putrescence."

Silence.

"Now, Hellas, it's necessary that your punishment be complete. Your punishment and ours. You will go to Gaouran immediately and beg his pardon, in the name of Atlantis."

"Pardon? Never."

"Never? Then I shall go myself. Guide me, Glania, the only truly pure individual in this vainglorious humankind."

"And may I not accompany you, Father?"

"Stay with Hellas, my daughter. Remain united forever. Come, Glania."

And Oreus, at a slow pace, his arm leaning on the Ligurian girl's shoulder, heads toward the ship, majestically.

Then Hellas, metamorphosed, emerging from his mutism, advances toward the old man, bows piously, kisses the hem of his tunic and says: "No, not you, but me. You're right."

Xanthes makes a movement, as if about to protest. But Hellas, without waiting, continues: "You're right, my father. I hear you. My eyes are open. I won't go to beg Gaouran's pardon; I'll do better."

"Be careful once again, of pride" groans Oreus, in a softer tone.

"Yes, I'll do better. I'll swear to him that in my beautiful Pelasgian Orient, I won't found a new Empire, but a harmonious union of free cities, in the fashion of the Biscayans, the Basconians and the Cantabrians."

And in one of the irresistible movements of his genius, he runs toward the strand, without anyone having the time to go after him, or even to say a word to him.

"What a brave man!" whispers Oreus, to whom Glania describes what is happening.

Now, a troop of men descends on to the shore from a boat, carrying bundles of wood, who come toward Hellas, preceded by Gaouran.

Hellas, who has run with a adolescent agility, stops a few paces from Gaouran. He extends a hand toward him. The Basconian takes it in both of his. They come together. Gaouran is seen to hug Hellas to his breast twice; then he taps him on the shoulder in a familiar fashion, and both of them, arm in arm, advance at the head of the sailors.

Gaouran, his face beaming, burst into mocking laugher.

"That's a good story," he says. "It appears that you thought that I was annoyed with you?"

"But there would have been reason to be," replies Oreus, smiling.

"What! Why? Because we're not entirely in accord regarding the manner of governing the world? Well, when you live with us, you'll hear many others. We squabble about it every evening when we sit up late in Basconia; it doesn't prevent us from liking one another."

Then, turning toward the vessel, he clapped his hands and shouts a signal: "Quickly, all toward the sea. The tide's going out! It's time to go. Everything is ready."

Scene XI
Toward the Orient

And the sailors come forward carrying large planks on their shoulders, in which the women and old men are taken to the boats, and from there to the fine vessel that excites Hellas' admiration.

"Now, my friends, you're in my home, or rather yours. Xambo has prepared everything to receive the survivors of Atlantis worthily.

And without another word, he goes away in tranquil haste toward the high poop-deck, while the ship, having raised anchor, is already taking to the sea.

"Genteel Atlanteans," says Buxo, to whom Gaouran has confided his guests, "if you need sleep, here are your dormitories; if you're hungry or thirsty, here is the larder where you'll find pâtés from Sos, fruits from Gaoure and Nogaro wine.

But a vague anxiety is manifest among the passengers. The Atlanteans, in fact, either in isolation or in groups, as if covertly, are heading toward the poop. Xanthes Hermos, Thebao, Amonou and even Hellas gradually abandon the old man, who feels solitude weighing around him.

"Where are they going, my daughter?"

"A sentiment stronger than hunger or somnolence is dominating them. They want to see Atlantis again, which ought to be visible in the west as soon as we've passed the archipelago of little islands."

"The poor creatures! How I understand them. Go join them, then, Orea. Leave me alone for the moment.

"Oh, Father, leave you?"

"And you, Glania."

"You permit it, Master?"

"Dear little storm-bird, fly toward them quickly."

And Glania runs to join the Atlanteans, grouped at the rear, their eyes fixed on the horizon, where dusk is already descending.

But Buxo intervenes with Oreus.

"Great Master, in the name of Gaouran, I have a favor to ask you. The region we're traversing isn't without danger because of all the debris floating at random. An excessively heavy grouping at the rear disturbs the service and the stability of the ship. Only you can bring them back gently."

"I understand, my friend. And where is Gaouran?"

"Up above on the poop-deck. He's observing the winds, the atmosphere and the horizon. He wants to know what the weather will be tomorrow."

"What a man!" Orea lets slip. "Always in action."

"A man!" says Oreus.

Orea, meanwhile, conducts her father to the poop, where cries, tears and appeals are already escaping from all breasts. In the distance, in the Occident all black with accumulated cloud, recumbent Atlantis seems to be asleep on the funereal Ocean. What remains of its collapsed roofs, open palaces and split cupolas stands out against the somber sky where the invisible sun is still casting a crimson fringe.

"Look," remarks Xanthes. "The sun still exists."

"For others, perhaps," weeps Asmonia, "but not for us any longer."

"Hope, Asmonia, hope for the future."

"Oh, what hope is here before such a disaster?" And she extends her arms toward the horrible Occident.

Immense, infinite, the dead city appears more imposing than the City they knew. The entire western horizon is traversed. Confused masses whose substance is unidentifiable in the distance undulate on the waves with phosphorescent reflections.

"Atlantis! Atlantis!" repeat the survivors in chorus, hanging on to the rigging.

"Wretches," said Hermos. "It's scarcely a day since all that has ended, and we've eaten, and we've drunk, and we've laughed, and we've almost sung!

"And we'll sing far more yet," observes Xanthes. "Humans don't have the strength to suffer forever."

"We're too favored!" exclaims Asmonia. "We haven't wept sufficiently, we haven't expiated sufficiently...oh, what pain does the future have in store for us?"

But the sun, which is shining through the clouds, extends a broad crimson curtain over the horizon, against which the jagged ruins of Atlantis still stand out. And over the somber violet sea, night falls, the slow night.

"Come on, my dear children," advises Oreus, appearing, "don't intoxicate yourselves with your suffering. There's danger in staying here."

And as the women do not move: "We, the men, let's set an example. Men, we have a duty to respond to the desire of our great friend who is saving us and who asks you to return to the deck.

And he draws away, sustained by Orea, followed by Hellas, Hermos and the silent artists.

"Look," interrupts Xanthes, the last to remain. "A light! A light! Over there! Behind the broken wings of the Sphinx. There's life there; there are living people!"

They all turn round, troubled and trembling, searching for the light at which Xanthes is pointing with his finger.

"He's right!" exclaims Asmonia. "Something's awakening; someone's appealing to us."

But Hermos says, gently: "It's a light, in fact, but the light of a star. Look: it's rising above Atlantis."

"Thanks be to the gods," said Xanthes. "Lights still remain in the sky!"

"The stars, at least, will always shine," murmurs Hellas, in a melancholy tone.

"Not even them," concludes Oreus.

And with those vertiginous words, the pensive Atlanteans, without even contemplating the rising moon, return toward the deck illuminated by vividly colored lanterns. Heavy with sadness, their paces drag. Above them, however, a powerful voice resounds whose warm tone comforts them like a joyous appeal coming from life.

"Ahoy! Ahoy, dear companions!"

Heads are raised, eyes search.

"Gaouran," Oreus explains. "He's watching over us."

The voice resumes, even more loudly: "My friends, my dear friends..."

Great silence. Everyone stops. Then, putting his hands to his mouth like a loudhailer, the Basconian announces to the reanimated Atlanteans:

"Rejoice and sleep in peace: we'll have a beautiful dawn tomorrow!"

And, driven by a following wind, the vessel sails on, boldly.